'A well-pace ... otional torture' *Tribune*

'Grippingly intriguing from start to finish' James Herbert

'Too many horror stories go over the top into fantasy land, but *Dreamer* is set in the recognisable world . . . I guarantee you more than a frisson of fear' *Daily Express*

'A thought-provoking menacer that's completely technological and genuinely frightening about the power of future communications' *Time Out*

'This compulsive story is a tale of the search for immortality . . . I cannot remember when I last read a novel I enjoyed so much' *Sunday Telegraph*

'Gripping . . . plotting is ingenious . . . in its evocation of how a glossy cocoon of worldly success can be unravelled by one bad decision it reminds me of Tom Wolfe's *Bonfire of the Vanities*' *The Times*

'Peter James, Britain's closest equivalent to Stephen King' *Sunday Times*

'The suspense holds on every page, right to the end . . .' *She*

*By Peter James*

Dead Letter Drop
Atom Bomb Angel
Billionaire
Possession
Dreamer
Sweet Heart
Twilight
Prophecy
Alchemist
Host
The Truth
Denial
Faith
Dead Simple
Looking Good Dead
Not Dead Enough
Dead Man's Footsteps

CHILDREN'S NOVEL
Getting Wired!

Peter James was educated at Charterhouse then at film school. He lived in North America for a number of years, working as a screenwriter and film producer before returning to England. His novels, including the number one bestseller *Possession*, have been translated into thirty languages and three have been filmed. All his novels reflect his deep interest in the world of the police, with whom he does in-depth research, as well as science, medicine and the paranormal. He has produced numerous films, including the *The Merchant Of Venice*, starring Al Pacino, Jeremy Irons and Joseph Fiennes. He also co-created the hit Channel 4 series, *Bedsitcom*, which was nominated for a Rose d'Or. He is currently, as co-producer, developing his Roy Grace novels for television with ITV Productions. Peter James won the Krimi-Blitz 2005 Crime Writer of the Year award in Germany, and *Dead Simple* won both the 2006 Prix Polar International award and the 2007 Prix Coeur Noir award in France. *Looking Good Dead* was shortlisted for the 2007 Richard and Judy Crime Thriller of the Year award, France's SNCF and Le Grand Prix de Littérature award. *Not Dead Enough* was shortlisted for the Theakstons Old Peculier Crime Thriller of the Year award and the ITV3 Crime Thriller Of The Year award. He divides his time between his homes in Notting Hill, London and near Brighton in Sussex. Visit his website at www.peterjames.com.

# TWILIGHT

*Peter James*

An Orion paperback

First published in Great Britain in 1991
by Victor Gollancz Ltd
This paperback edition published in 2005
by Orion Books Ltd,
Orion House, 5 Upper St Martin's Lane,
London WC2H 9EA

An Hachette UK company



A CIP catalogue record for this book is available from the British Library.

Printed and bound in Great Britain by
Clays Ltd, St Ives Plc



www.orionbooks.co.uk

*To Joe and Lilly*

# *Chapter One*

*Tuesday, 16 October 1990*

The first hint came less than an hour after the funeral cortège left the small cemetery behind the church. Three muffled thuds from the partially filled-in grave. It was the verger who heard them, although one of the pall-bearers would admit later that he thought something had moved inside the coffin, but had not wanted to make a fool of himself by saying so.

The verger was a widower, sixty-seven years old, a diligent and not impressionable man who carried his private grief in the slack of his face and sometimes envied the dead in their graves. On that particular afternoon he came through the rear gate, as he always did, and hurried down the brick path through the cemetery, anxious to prepare the church for the following morning's communion service and get home before the rain started.

He cast his eyes down respectfully as he passed the fresh grave, and the wreaths and sprays of flowers laid around it, and felt the prick of discomfort new graves always gave him, bringing back the pain of his wife's funeral seven years before. Since her death other people's tragedies seldom touched him. This one did, for some reason; perhaps because he had known the girl all her life; perhaps because of her age; or perhaps simply because she had been so pretty and so lively it was impossible to accept that she was dead.

He stopped suddenly, startled by a sound that seemed at first to have come from the ground, and listened, looking around, wondering if he had imagined it. A branch of a yew tree rattled noisily against the church wall. Above him the marble sky, darker than the tombstones, darkened further.

The wind, he thought, just the wind, and hurried on, his head bowed. As he reached the entrance to the porch he heard it again.

The first spots of rain were falling, but he ignored them and listened carefully, trying to hear above the sound of his own wheezing. He walked slowly back through the lines of headstones of the tiny cemetery, approaching the new grave warily, the way he might have approached the edge of a cliff, and stopped at a safe distance, staring at the dark rectangle and the neat mound of raw, chalky earth beside it that the gravedigger would finish shovelling in tomorrow.

Sally Mackenzie. Or Mrs Sally Donaldson as she had become. Twenty-three years old. Sparkling with life, always had time for everyone. Christened here; had been a Brownie, a Girl Guide, then had won a place at university where she met her husband, Kevin, a sharp, confident young man, in insurance, someone said. They had been married here barely a year ago and he could remember their wedding day, the husband beaming with the pride of a man who had won the greatest prize on earth. Yesterday that young man's face had been twisted into numb shock, everything that was good and happy wrung out of it by a tourniquet of grief.

It was the way it had happened, people said. Sudden, so sudden. That made it even worse, if that was possible, they murmured. The verger was not sure whether sudden death was any worse than long lingering death; whether it was any better for the person who was dying or the people left behind. Merciful release they had said when his wife died. For her, not for him.

A red sweet wrapper scudded along the path in front of him. He listened, motionless, ignoring the rain. The wind blew again; the cellophane around a spray of flowers rustled, and he was aware of the intensity of their colours: whites, reds, pinks, vividly alive against the raw earth and the dry grass and the autumnal shades of the beech hedge that bounded the cemetery. A tag fluttered and he bent to read it. 'To Sals, with all our love.' Another, on a huge bouquet of crimson roses, flipped itself over, tugging capriciously on its leash of green string. 'To Sals, for ever. Kevin.'

A lone pigeon raced above him and the branch of the yew rattled again on the church wall. The patter of rain increased. Tomorrow the verger would collect the flowers and take them to the hospice in Brighton at the suggestion of the girl's husband. He watched the dark rectangle; only a thin layer of soil covered the coffin so far. The earth was still hard and crumbly after the long dry summer, and a few chunks had fallen away from the sides of the grave. Bits of chalk rattling on to the coffin roof, that was all it had been.

He turned and hurried into the shelter of the porch, past the notice board with its thumb-tacked signs, JUMBLE SALE, COFFEE MORNING, CHURCH ROOF FUND, turned the iron ring of the oak door and went inside the small church, closing it with an echoing clunk behind him. It was silent in here, and still. His eyes glanced routinely at the stone font and the neat stacks of hymn books and the faded frescoes on the wall. Christ stared mournfully down from the stained glass above the altar. Tablets on the wall near the door contained a roll of the local war dead. A wooden rack beneath it held badly printed booklet histories of the church and parish; thirty pence each. There was a box for the money.

He walked down the aisle to the pulpit and pulled the yellowing bakelite numbers of the hymns sung at the funeral off the indicator on the wall – 'Abide With Me' and 'Jerusalem'. As he tidied away the kneelers, prayer books and service sheets left by the mourners, and listlessly mouthed 'And did those feet in ancient time,' he did not hear the frantic burst of muffled thuds that again came from the grave of the girl they had buried that afternoon.

# *Chapter Two*

*Tuesday, 9 May 1967*

Harvey Swire sat pensively on the bench in the locker room that smelled of stale sweat, latrines and boot polish, a short eighteen-year-old, with straight brown hair and small grey eyes set deep in his pudgy face. He was overweight and unfit, and sport bored him. He had a small, slightly high-pitched voice that had earned him the nickname Piggy which he had only succeeded in shedding in recent years.

He was always distant, aloof, wrapped in his own thoughts, in his own world inside his head. His mother had been his only close friend in life. She had nurtured him through his childhood sickliness, protected him from his father's scorn, believed in him and loved him and understood him. She had died five months ago, aged thirty-eight, from a heart attack.

She had been beautiful and he had been proud of her, had loved it when she came to school to collect him and he could see the heads of other boys and their parents turn. It was different when his father came. They had never got on with each other, and since his mother's death their relationship had deteriorated further.

One day he would understand that his father resented him because although he had not inherited her beauty, there was so much of his mother's looks in his face. And because he had lived and she had died. There were a lot of things Harvey Swire would one day understand.

He began to tie the laces on his cricket boots, oblivious to the clatter of studs on the stone floor and the banter of conversation going on around him, thinking about the letter that had arrived that morning and was in his jacket hanging on the hook above him. Angie. He hadn't expected to hear from her again, after what had happened. Part of him felt disgusted by what he had done. Embarrassed. He could still see clearly the expression on her face, feel her flinching, and his face reddened. He stared at the ground, at his boots. Part of him thought, 'You deserved it, you bitch.'

He wasn't sure why she angered him so much. She'd been good

when his mother had died, comforting, caring, genuinely upset. She had even managed to make his father smile back at the house, after it was over. But she had not let him go any further than snogging and made even that seem as if she was doing him a favour. Until ten days ago; the last night of his Easter holiday, before returning to boarding school, when he'd forced her to touch him, had grabbed her hand and pushed it down inside his trousers and held it there whilst she struggled, and she'd refused to speak all the way home.

And now, unexpectedly, the letter had arrived; like the ones she always wrote, on small, thick sheets of paper tightly folded and smelling of her perfume, chatty and affectionate in her large looped handwriting, in fountain pen with aquamarine ink.

'Love you lots, Angie.' A dozen kisses.

She hadn't even mentioned it.

He double-knotted each lace. There was the hiss of an aerosol and he smelled a sickly sweet whiff of Brut. Dacre was standing above him, pursing his face in the mirror, checking for spots; his study-mate shook his blond hair off his forehead, sprayed his other armpit, gave a quick squirt inside his jock strap, then tugged on his cricket shirt. Dacre had a thing about smell at the moment. He seemed convinced that the way to score was to smell right.

Rob Reckett came into the room, chewing gum, and farted loudly.

'God, Reckett, you're revolting,' Dacre said.

Reckett responded by pushing his bum further out behind his jacket and farting again.

'You're a yob, Reckett,' Worral said.

'He's not a yob, he's a slob,' Walls Minor corrected him.

Reckett blew a bubble which popped with a sharp crack and tugged off his tie. A hulking, arrogant boy with a fringe of brown hair that covered his forehead, Reckett claimed he was banging the assistant house cook, a hugely fat girl who, it was rumoured, was willing to 'do it' for the asking. 'Wild for it,' he'd announced. 'Put it everywhere; even in her ear. Older women are the best. They're crazy for it.'

Harvey Swire found Reckett's description of 'putting it in her ear' oddly arousing and he wasn't sure why. He'd thought about making advances to the girl himself, but she was too fat, too greasy. Her skin reminded him of an oven-ready turkey. He did not want it to be like that, not the first time, not any time. He tried to imagine Angie grabbing him and putting it in her ear. Some chance.

Her letter bothered him, suddenly. His relief at receiving it was turning to anger. Part of him wanted her to be furious with him. To be disgusted. He almost felt cheated that she wasn't.

'Jesus, you're a poof, Dacre,' Tom Hanson said.

'Screw off, will you, Hanson? At least I don't go around smelling like an arsehole.'

'No, just looking like one,' Hanson said, opening his locker and laughing with glee at his own wit.

'Poof in boots!' Jones Minor said, pulling on his trousers, his brow furrowing as he grinned, making the spots on his forehead break through their thin layer of Clearasyl.

'If you think I'm a queer what about that new pop group with the high voices? What are they called? You know, Harvey. You nearly puked over their photograph yesterday.'

'The Chimpanzees,' Harvey Swire said.

'Monkees, you wanker,' Horstead said. 'God, you're really thick, Swire, you don't know anything.'

Harvey tossed his hair off his face and finished the second knot.

'You're never going to get to medical school. You have to be intelligent to be a doctor.'

In eight weeks' time he would be sitting his A-level exams, physics, chemistry and biology for a place at Queen's Hospital, his father's old medical school; where his father had graduated top in his year in gynaecology with the Queen's medal of merit that hung on the wall of his Harley Street clinic. Quentin Swire, a strong, dapper man, who had made a fortune from providing an abortion service for overseas visitors, and had survived a major exposition by the *News of the World* whom he had successfully sued.

His father had also been to Wesley, where Harvey was now. Quentin Swire had been good at everything here; his name looked down from the honours boards in the halls and corridors. Cricket. Football. Hockey. Scholarships to university.

'There's a new Beatles LP coming out,' someone said.

A voice in mock falsetto screeched, 'Strawberry Fields Forever.'

'I think the Beatles are really infra-dig,' Worral said.

'Bugger off, Worral, they're groovy.'

'Pink Floyd are a million times groovier.'

'I'm going to get tickets for Bob Dylan when he's over in August. You coming, Harvey?'

'Dylan's cool,' Dacre said.

Harvey watched Reckett pull off his trousers and stained underpants in one go. Reckett had an enormous circumcised cock; he wondered suddenly what happened to people's penises when they died. Someone had told him that hanged men died with an erection. Reckett swirled his cock around several times like a bandolero before stuffing it inside his jock strap.

'Matlock went the whole way on Saturday,' Walls Minor announced.

The others looked at him, startled. 'All the way?' Dacre said.

Walls Minor nodded.

'Never,' Horstead said, his voice clogged with envy. 'He couldn't possibly have done – he never went out of the dance hall.'

'He said he did it when the girls were getting ready to go, before the coach came.'

'Where?'

'In here.'

'Crap!'

'He probably got a finger up. Wouldn't know the difference.'

'I think he's telling the truth,' Walls Minor said.

'How come?' Harvey said with interest.

'Coz he's been worried sick all week; said he used a thingummy, and it came off inside her – all the spunk sort of leaked.'

'What a prat,' Powell said.

Horstead nodded at Swire. 'Poked that bird you brought to Reckett's party at Easter yet? What was her name?'

Harvey reddened and said nothing.

'Why d'you never talk about it, Harvey?'

'Hey, come on, we're late.' Dacre tapped his watch and tucked his cricket bat under his arm.

Harvey lifted his sweater off the hook above his head. The name tag was coming off; it was now only held on by a single stitch. He stared at it for a moment, his name in small red letters on the white background, *H.Q.E. Swire*, and a wave of sadness swilled through him. His mother had stitched the tags on, in the small upstairs room where she did her ironing, listening, as she always seemed to be, to a play on the radio, her head tilted to one side so her blonde tresses of hair fell that way and her pretty face which always looked a little tired, a little sad.

He wondered how she was now. Sometimes he could feel her around. She had been in his room at home, recently, when he had been doing his experiments in the holidays; he could tell she approved. He had never let her see his experiments when she was alive, because he knew that she was squeamish. But now she was dead it was OK.

'Hey, Harve, coming?'

He grabbed his bat, and they clattered out across the stone floor and down the path to the corrugated iron bicycle shed.

'It's quicker to walk,' said Powell. 'We're playing on Horizon and can cut straight through.'

'Bollocks,' Dacre said. 'You carry our bats.' He swung his white Claude Butler racer out and jumped on to it in one manoeuvre, then pedalled at Harvey ringing his bell. 'Hey, Harve, what's up? You're half asleep today.'

'He's always half asleep,' Powell said.

There was a clacking sound as Dacre freewheeled in a loop over the rough grass, accelerating down the side of the house and out into the street without looking. He arced round and pedalled fast back. 'Come on, I'm meant to be doing the toss in two minutes.'

'Toss yourself off,' Powell said.

Harvey climbed on to his blue Raleigh, flipping the pedals over and sliding his spiked cricket boots awkwardly into the toe straps. Dacre charged at him and he swerved out of the way, irritated, and caught a strong whiff of the Brut.

'Race you, Harve, last one there's wet!' Dacre zoomed off ahead. Harvey dropped a few gears, heard the grating of the chain and pedalled hard after him, racing down the side of the house. Dacre swung out into the street and Harvey heard the blare of a car horn as he followed him, heeling the bike over hard.

Out of the corner of his eye he saw the car. It seemed to be motionless, like a still photograph. He could see detail so clearly it surprised him. It was a large Ford with dull green paint and a shiny chromium grille. A woman was driving, her hair neatly curled as if she had just been to the hairdresser, and there was a filter tip cigarette in her left hand wedged between two jewelled rings on her bony fingers. Her glossy red lips were forming a circle as if she had just blown a smoke ring, and there was too much white of her eyes showing, much too much, as if her eyes were about to pop out.

The photograph changed as if a projector had moved on to the next slide, and the car was a towering shadow over him. A voice somewhere screamed: 'Harve! Look out!'

Then he felt as if a brick wall had hit him, powering him into the air. He saw the woman's face even closer. The eyes bulging even more. He was looking down on her, through the windscreen; her hands were raised to her face. He could hear her scream.

The projector clicked and there was a close-up of the windscreen now. A split second before he heard the crack, he felt a crunch deep inside his body; the windscreen exploded around him into brilliant white sparks. Red hot, they seemed to burn his face and hands in a million places at once.

Then he was hurtling up in the air and the sparks were dropping away beneath him. Something else dropped away, a huge shadow. At first he thought it was his bike, or his cricket sweater; or his trousers. He watched it fall back into the sparks, strike the bonnet of the green Ford and bounce up, flopping like a rag doll; a huge dent appeared on the bonnet and paint flaked off it. The shadow flew up in the air beneath him, fell back down, thudding on to the roof of the Ford, slithered off the rear, on to the boot, then thumped to the tarmac of the road and rolled furiously, jerkily along, as if electricity were shorting through it, until it slammed to a halt against the kerb.

He watched the door of the Ford open and the woman stumble out, wailing. Dacre was getting off his bike. Reckett was sprinting across the road. Harvey saw his bike trapped under the front of the Ford; its front wheel was sticking up at an odd angle, buckled; several of the spokes were broken and splayed out and he was annoyed, and wondered if he could get it fixed without his father finding out.

'Harve? Harve? You OK?' Dacre was kneeling beside the thing in the gutter, the thing that had dropped away from him. Then he realised, with interest, that the thing Dacre was kneeling beside was himself.

He was watching his own body. Watching all of them from above. He could see blood trickling from his forehead.

'Don't move him!' someone shouted.

'Oh my God, I've killed him,' the woman screamed.

'Get an ambulance,' Dacre said. Harvey watched Dacre frantically feeling for his pulse; he wondered if Dacre had any idea what to look for. He saw Worral throw his own bike on to the pavement and run back into the house, shouting, 'Mr Matthey, Mr Matthey! Sir, Mr Matthey, sir! Sir! Sir!'

Harvey saw an Austin car coming the other way stop sharply and a man in a blue blazer jump out and sprint across. 'I'm a doctor!' he said.

'I didn't see him!' the woman screamed. 'Oh, God, I didn't see him!'

The front door of the house opened and a woman came running out. Mrs Matthey, the housemaster's wife. She tripped and sprawled. He watched the doctor kneel down beside him and feel his pulse. The doctor tensed and slipped his hand inside his chest on to his heart. Then he saw the doctor prise open his mouth, and thrust his hand in. 'He's swallowed his tongue,' he said, panicky. 'Has someone called an ambulance?'

'Yes, sir,' Dacre said.

The doctor prised his tongue out. Harvey could see his face was blue. 'How long has he been here?' the doctor asked, moving fast, methodically.

'Only a few seconds.'

He laid Harvey flat, clasped his hands together and pressed hard downwards on Harvey's chest. Then again, more urgently. He studied Harvey for a second, pressed down again, then again, getting increasingly frantic in his movement.

The housemaster's wife ran up, breathless. 'Is he all right? Is he all right?'

The doctor spoke without stopping his artificial respiration. 'No,' he said grimly. 'He's not breathing.'

'I'm fine,' Harvey said. 'I'm OK, really, I'm fine!' But his mouth did not move, no sound came out. He tried to speak again, but felt himself being sucked upwards suddenly. He was being pulled away from the scene and did not want to go. 'No!' he screamed. 'No!' But no words came out of the mouth of the motionless body between the doctor's knees. Darkness closed around him. It was getting cold, icy cold. He felt alone, helpless. Fear swept through him; walls of a tunnel encircled him, sucked him like an insect down a drain and he was hurtling, spinning through a vortex of blackness.

It seemed as if he would go on spinning in blackness for ever, getting colder and colder. Then he saw a tiny pinprick of light in the distance, and felt the first faint glimmer of warmth.

The light grew larger and with it he felt warmth coming down the tunnel to greet him, seeping through him, melting away his fears, becoming a part of him, giving him a strange new energy.

Then he was immersed in the light and the tunnel had gone. He was no longer moving. The light was brilliant but did not dazzle him; it seemed to flood through him the way the warmth had done, and he sensed someone was in the light with him whom he could not see.

For a brief moment he felt a deep sensation of ecstasy. He wanted to stay here in this spot in this light and never move.

Then a man's voice spoke, calmly, chiding. 'What do you think you are doing, Harvey? Do you think you are being clever?'

The voice chilled him. Chilled the light which faded, seemed to drain away and left him standing in an opening that was like a glade in a forest under a grey sky. He felt exposed, as if there were people around watching him. He turned. There was nothing but empty fields behind him, stretching away to the horizon.

Then he heard his mother's voice.

'Darling!'

A figure was coming towards him, indistinct, bleached out at first, but it grew darker, more distinct, as it came closer. A woman walking slowly, elegantly, effortlessly, as if she had all of time in which to reach him.

Then suddenly he could see her clearly, see the familiar blonde tresses of hair, the serene smile, the summer dress he had always liked her in so much. A feeling of immense joy swept through him as he reached out, tried to run towards her. 'Mummy!' he shouted. His voice was strangely flat, as if he were shouting underwater. He could not move, but stood, arms stretched out, trying to reach her, to hold her, to hug her.

She stopped, a few yards from him, and smiled a deep loving smile. 'You have to go back, darling,' she said.

Other figures were appearing out of the grey light behind her, dark, shadowy shapes, people with no faces.

'Mummy! How are you?' He tried to run to her, but he could not move forwards.

'Darling, God is very unhappy with you.'

'Why?' he mouthed.

The dark shapes were getting closer, were surrounding him, were crowding between him and his mother.

'Because you're – ' The words faded. She was shouting now, as if she was having to shout above a crowd to be heard, but the words were sucked into the dark shadowy shapes.

'Why?' Again he tried to run towards her, but icy hands were pulling him away. 'Why?' he yelled.

The shadows pulled at him.

'Let me talk to her! Let me!'

He struggled, thrashed.

'You have to go back,' a voice said.

'She doesn't want you,' another said.

'She doesn't ever want to see you again,' said a third.

'You're lying!' he screamed, trying to break free of the cold hands that were tearing at him. He felt their breath, like the air of a freezer. The light was fading.

He was falling.

# *Chapter Three*

*Monday, 22 October 1990*

Kate Hemingway was woken from a troubling dream at six thirty a.m. by the click of her radio. She listened to the headlines as she did every morning, then pressed the snooze button and savoured the silence and the snug warmth of her bedclothes for a few minutes more whilst she tried to stop the dream fading completely from her mind.

Another of the anxiety dreams she had most nights at the moment; worrying about her new job, she realised, or her sister, Dara, or her recently terminated disastrous affair.

Kate Hemingway was twenty-four years old, and five feet five inches tall. Born in Boston, she was strong and slender, with grey-blue eyes that sparkled with life behind high, deep cheek bones, a small, straight nose, and a smiling mouth with good teeth that she took care of. With her long flaxen hair, currently styled in a fashionable ragged look, and her fresh, healthy complexion, she had the kind of sensational all-American college girl looks to which few men failed to respond with interest, and some women with envy.

Kate was an intelligent girl who read widely and was as happy at times to be on her own as in company. The two things she lacked were self-confidence and a boyfriend. The sarcasm and scorn she had received throughout her childhood from her elder sister, Dara, and the way her parents had always seemed to favour Dara rather than her had left her flayed and uncertain about her abilities. She did not even believe that she was attractive, and worked hard at keeping herself in shape by eating sensibly – but not faddishly, because she enjoyed and was knowledgeable about food and wine – and by jogging at weekends.

Life was going well for her at the moment, for the first time in a long while. She was doing a job she loved, in a town to which she had come as a stranger and already liked a lot, and was living in an apartment which she had decorated herself and was proud of.

After three months in her new job as a reporter for a local newspaper, the *Sussex Evening News*, she still found her work fresh and challenging and looked forward to each day, happy to be on a paper from which she had a real prospect of moving to Fleet Street. It was a considerable change of pace and quality from the free weekly rag she had worked on in Birmingham previously.

Her confidence was growing and the wounds from her last relationship were healing. Getting the job on the *News* had been a real career break, although her elder sister, smug in her Washington duplex, would never understand that. Dara sneered at her for not being married, not having any children and not having achieved anything yet. Dara, an economist in Washington married to a rich lawyer who was a budding senator, and had three exquisite children, reminded Kate constantly, in her own subtle ways, that she had always told her she would be a failure in life and Kate got scared sometimes that she was being proven right.

Tony Arnold had been a disaster. A nowhere relationship. And yet she still thought about him, got reminded of him every time she smelled Paco Rabanne out on the street, still fancied him, dammit. Kate liked to pretend to herself that she wasn't sure how the affair had begun, but she knew she was deceiving herself. He had been the deputy editor of the *Birmingham Messenger*, a position that had seemed to her then, at twenty-two years old, of immense power, and she had been flattered initially by his interest.

She'd never had an affair with a married man before. At first it had been a game and she did not realise how deeply she was falling in love with him. For eighteen months she dutifully maintained the conspiracy with him to keep it secret, cooked meals for him which he'd never had time to eat, and spent whole weekends waiting in for him to get an hour away; all the time he told her his marriage was on the rocks, and they planned their future together.

Then she had bumped into him in a supermarket one Saturday, arm in arm with his wife and trailing three cute kids. In the brief glance they exchanged, Kate had realised suddenly how little she understood about life.

He got offered the editorship of a Scottish paper shortly afterwards and made no suggestion she should join him there. Instead he put in a good word when the vacancy on the *Sussex Evening News* came up. They had left the *Birmingham Messenger* within one week of each other and she had not heard from him since.

Kate had come to England when she was fourteen with her parents, and Dara. She had an elder brother, Howie, who drowned in a sailing accident, and it was his death that had brought about the move. Her father, a lecturer in English at Harvard University, thought it would be good therapy for them to have a change and accepted a two-year posting at the University of London that turned into five years.

They lived a bohemian existence in a draughty Victorian house in Highgate. Her mother was a small-town girl who had dropped out in the sixties along with half of America because it had been the thing to do. Whether it was the lousy heating and spartan furnishings of bare oak floors and hessian mats and Afghan rugs on the walls, or the dope-smoking student lodgers whom they needed to help with the rent and who always drank the milk and ate the bread and left dirty dishes lying around, or her father's continued practising of his 'free love' philosophy, Kate was not sure, but her mother finally had enough and ran off with a pleasant but dull civil engineer who had a cosy modern house in Cheam. Soon after, he had been sent to oversee a project in Hong Kong and her mother now lived there with him.

Kate had stayed on in England after her father had returned to Boston. Dara had got a scholarship to Berkeley and in part, Kate knew, she had remained as much to try to prove something to Dara as to get out of her shadow.

A gust of cold salty wind fresh off the English Channel blew down the dark street, rolling a clutch of dead leaves along the gutter and rattling the sash window panes of the Edwardian terraced houses. Kate could feel the cold air on her face and she heaved herself reluctantly up a few inches against the hard rails of the brass bedstead; the last unread sections of *The Sunday Times* slid off her duvet and joined the heap of other Sunday papers on the floor.

She tugged her feet free, swung them out of bed and on to the white shag carpet. The cold air cut through her. She shook her tangled blonde hair out of her face and hugged herself, trying to retain some heat inside her nightdress, padded across the carpet and pulled the sash window up, then struggled with the catches on the secondary glazing unit, as she always did, and finally got that closed too without losing any skin off her fingers.

Heat from the ribbed cast iron radiator rose as she rubbed condensation from the window with her fingers and stared through the smeared gap across the road at the uninspired nine-storey headquarters of the Friendly & Mutual Assurance Company. The lights were on, cleaners were moving through the building. Some employees were already at work.

When Kate had signed the one-year lease on the unfurnished apartment three months ago, she had taken into account that the rent was low for the area because of the lack of a view, and as she would be out, working long hours most of the time, and, anyway, had never had a view before, it would not matter.

It was the living room that she had fallen for, a fine, wide and airy room with a deep bay window and elegant open marble fireplace with its grate intact, and the original cornices, mouldings and picture rails. A great room for showing off the bric-a-brac she liked buying, for reading in, for watching the box and for entertaining. There was a tiny kitchenette that was clean and modern, a narrow entrance hall, a bedroom which was on the small side but had good, deep, built-in cupboards, and a cramped bathroom.

It was the first unfurnished apartment she had had, and she was pleased her choice of colours had worked so well. The previous occupant had been heavily into lurid green paint and jungle wallpaper. Over the past three months Kate had stripped the walls, relined and repainted them. The woodwork and mouldings she had restored to white; the walls of the living room she had painted terra-cotta, and the bedroom a light apricot. The bathroom, which already had avocado-coloured fixtures, was harder and she had settled for a white tinged with an appley green.

The soft geometric curtains had come from Laura Ashley, and the comfy sofa was a shop-soiled bargain from Habitat. The grungy beige wall-to-wall carpet she had inherited with the apartment looked better after she had spread a few rugs she had trawled from car boot sales over it. She had hung on the walls old framed advertising posters, theatrical billboards and some black and white photographs she had taken in her teens, when she once had a fancy she might become a photographer, and which were extremely good.

After breakfast of muesli, low-fat yoghourt, apple juice and tea, she scanned the *Independent* and checked the television page for anything she might want to record, then opened her post.

There was a letter from her mother, a subscription reminder for Greenpeace and a postcard from a girlfriend on the *Birmingham Messenger*, postmarked Turkey. Her mother wrote once a week and she wrote back about once a month – maybe not even that often, her mother occasionally reminded her, and they spoke on the phone once a week, normally on a Sunday afternoon when Kate, for some reason, always felt low.

Since her mother had moved their relationship with each other had closened, as if they had become the side of the family that was flawed and her father and Dara were Mr and Miss Perfect.

Her mother had rung last night. She was fine, happy, and seemed to have come to terms with her guilt over leaving Kate's father and her curious mid-life change of lifestyle. Kate was worried about her remaining in Hong Kong with the Gulf crisis deepening, in case she got cut off out there. She was nervous the whole world would erupt in war and travel would become impossible.

Her mother told Kate she was glad she had moved from Birmingham, that a smaller town like Brighton was a much safer place to be.

In a short while her mother would find out how mistaken she was.

# *Chapter Four*

Images came and went. Harvey Swire heard the clatter of his bicycle pedals, the screech of brakes, the scream of the woman through the windscreen. The scream burned into the darkness, ate it away until it was flat, dull light. Harvey was still screaming when he opened his eyes.

The shape of a face formed, like the first traces of an image on a Polaroid film. A girl, not much older than himself, quite pretty with a tiny snub nose like Angie's, but made too severe by her hair gripped tightly back against her scalp. 'It's OK,' she said. 'It's OK.' Her voice was soothing, gentle. Her face went into soft focus; her mouth changed shape several times in rapid succession and he heard someone talking nearby. Then he realised that the two were connected, like a movie running out of synch.

He tried to lift his hands to his ears, confused, as if there was something he could tune that would correct the situation, but his left arm would not move and his chest felt as if it was pinioned in iron. He saw his arm above him, a blur of white. The voice kept coming at him.

' . . . A long time. Now? Better . . . we? Sleep?'

She reminded him of Angie. Bossy Angie who pushed his hands away and gave him quick pecks on the cheek. Angie who had slapped his face in anger, real anger, not feigned this time. Then he had grabbed her, grabbed her hard.

His face stung. But Angie faded; the slap was somewhere else, another play, a long way off. He felt as though his cheeks were packed with wadding and he was peering out from a dark cave past them. The face went out of focus and came back in again. Someone shuffled by behind her, an elderly man with grey hair in a red paisley dressing gown, coughing.

'Shock . . . alive . . . to be . . . bicycle lucky . . .'

He smiled blankly through puffball lips. His mind was full of the image of the car, the woman's face through the windscreen. He raced down the side of the house, chasing Dacre, out in front of the car. He flew through the air. Stayed in the air.

Cold water eddied inside him, and he swallowed, feeling prickles of icy sweat. He could see in her eyes she had detected the change, the alarm.

'OK,' she said. 'Fine. Going to be.'

He was focussing better now; he could see her breasts pushing against the inside of her tunic and a sudden sensation of lust stirred then faded and was gone. He shivered, afraid suddenly. Afraid that he was dead. 'Where am I?' he said.

She wore a white tunic. A watch hung on a short chain from her lapel and her name was printed on a badge pinned to the opposite lapel. Anthea Barlow. 'Better; more sleep from.' Her voice was still out of synch; it disoriented him, worsened his fear. Dead. I'm dead. He began to shake.

She stooped towards him, her face melting, globules falling from it like wax. He cowered back, screamed again, but she was still coming, was going to fuse with him, melt him. There was a dull prick in his arm; it seemed to be swelling and for a moment his fingers felt fat; a wave of nausea swept through him.

'This'll stop the pain,' said a voice, any voice, he no longer knew whose. He slept.

When he awoke again everything was clearer. He was in a small ward and could see the sky through a large, grimy sash window that was closed in spite of the brilliant sunlight. There were four, maybe five beds opposite him; several visitors were crowded around the one directly across, obscuring it; someone was holding a bunch of flowers. His left arm hurt, and there was a sharp pain somewhere in his back, as if he were lying on something that was burning.

His right hand was grazed and there were several strips of plaster on it; some of his nails had jagged edges and he glanced around for something to file them on.

Then his heart sank as he saw his father strutting down the ward, walking upright, bullet head in the air, hands behind his back as if he owned the place. He was wearing a check suit, pink silk shirt with an op-art black and white tie and black loafers. His hair, bald on top, greying and too long, was brushed back, curling over the tops of his ears and the collar of his shirt. Harvey wished he did not always look so ostentatious.

His father stopped at the end of the bed. There was more warmth in his expression than usual. 'How are you feeling, old chap?'

'OK,' Harvey said, managing a smile.

'Gather you had a close shave.'

'I was silly; I didn't look.'

His father's voice became harsher. 'Damned fool bit of cycling, I understand.'

'How long have I got to be in here?'

'Couple of weeks. You've bust your arm and two ribs; the ribs have to have a chance to knit, and you've had a nasty bash on the head.'

'Where am I?'

'Guildford. In the Surrey County Hospital.'

'Is my bike all right?'

Something glinted; he heard a click, and watched his father take an untipped Player's cigarette from his silver case, snap the case shut and tap the end of the cigarette against it. 'I shouldn't think there's much left of it from the description.' He stuck the cigarette in his mouth and lit it with his gold Ronson.

Harvey watched him perform his usual ritual of allowing the smoke to begin coming out of his mouth before sucking it back in then slowly releasing it through his nostrils. Wisps of the sweet blue smoke curled around Harvey and he inhaled them gratefully, tantalised by the smell.

*What do you think you are doing, Harvey? Do you think you are being clever?*

The voice startled him, as if it had been spoken into his ear, and the memory returned to him, complete. The tunnel. The light. His mother.

*You have to go back, darling.*

Trying to run towards her. The shadowy shapes getting in the way.

'If your bike's had it, tough luck, I'm not buying you another one. You're just bloody lucky to be alive.' His father glanced around for an ashtray.

'I saw Mother.'

His father frowned. 'You what?'

'I saw Mother.'

His father's face reddened. 'Good God, boy, your mother's dead.'

'She's fine, I saw her. She told me I had to come back.'

'This is damn fool nonsense, chap. Damn fool.'

'It's not, Father. I did see her.'

'You've had a bad bash on the head and an operation; had all sorts of drugs in you. You've been hallucinating.'

'It wasn't hallucination.'

His father looked at his watch. 'I have to be off.' His mouth was quivering and his anger always frightened Harvey. 'I'll come and see you tomorrow. Anything you want?'

'Some books and things.'

'Better bring you some text books. If you're going to be in here for a week or two you can start swotting for your exams.'

Harvey felt tired again after his father had gone. Too much effort to talk, to say anything. He dozed. When he awoke, a man in a white coat was standing at the end of the bed. 'Awake now?'

Harvey nodded, and after a while drifted back into sleep.

When he woke again, he was surprised to see Angie sitting beside him; she was wearing a miniskirt that barely covered her pink knickers, and her legs were tanned golden brown. Her face was tanned too and had come out in freckles, and she tossed her long fine blonde hair away from her eyes and smiled at him. She was holding a paper bag and a battered rag doll that was wearing a cloth cap.

His first waking thought was how could she sit there the way she was doing, with her skirt hitched to her crotch, yet get mad when he tried to even fondle her tits.

Then the dim memory rose inside him, and disgust and embarrassment intermingled and he wondered why she had bothered to come here. Instead of smiling and greeting her, he thought, sullenly, *prickteaser*. Next time there would be no stopping however much she screamed and swore and bit him. Reckett, bully Reckett who boasted he had lost his virginity at twelve, said that women liked to be treated rough, it turned them on. Maybe that was the answer, maybe he had done it and it had worked; that was why she had come.

'Hi,' she said. Something had changed in her appearance. She was dolled-up and had tiger stripes of mascara under her eyes. It made her look older, years older than sixteen, but it wasn't just that. 'I brought Fred to look after you.' She laid the battered gonk on the bed, then held out a rustling bag. 'I wasn't sure what to get. There's a James Bond novel, and some Turkish delight. You like Turkish delight, don't you?'

He said nothing. The make-up disturbed him and he felt a prick of alarm that she had not put it on for him. Bitch, he thought.

'I wrote to you the other day.'

'I got it.'

She tossed her hair again. 'How are you feeling?'

He shrugged. 'Pretty stupid. How did you know – I – ?'

'I – I heard.'

He tried to get his bearings, tried to sit up a little but it hurt too much.

'Want some help?'

He shook his head. There was the sound of a curtain being pulled. A man was gasping somewhere near him and he heard a flurry of feet, the rattle of a trolley.

'How did it happen?' Angie said.

'I was careless.' The images replayed again. The windscreen. Floating. The horror on the woman's face. He closed his eyes then opened them and stared, unfocussed, on the mound of sheets in front of his chin.

She was about to say something when a self-assured man in a grey suit, with grizzled hair and a yacht club tie, stopped at the end of the bed. Behind him were a houseman in a white coat with a stethoscope curling out of one pocket and a nurse, both grinning, sharing some private joke.

'Mind popping into the day room for a few minutes?' the man said to Angie. 'I want to have a peep at this young man.'

Angie looked at Harvey uncertainly. 'Shall I wait?'

He nodded.

The nurse pulled a curtain around his bed and the houseman lifted away the bedclothes.

The man in the grey suit smiled down at Harvey. 'Thought you were a goner when they brought you in. I'm Mr Wynne, the surgeon who operated on you. Is your father the gynaecologist Quentin Swire?'

'Yes.'

'We were at Queen's together.' His expression became serious suddenly, his eyes boring into Harvey. 'A doctor happened to be driving past when you had your accident. He said you had swallowed your tongue and stopped breathing – that you were to all intents and purposes dead – when he got to you. You were bloody lucky he was passing or I don't think you'd be here now. We're going to run some tests to make sure everything's OK. We don't know how long you were starved of oxygen, but it sounds like it must have been a couple of minutes at least.' He held up a pin. 'I'll give you a tiny prick in your big toe. Tell me if you can feel it.'

Harvey felt a sharp pain. 'Ouch!'

'Good!' said Wynne. 'Now your left foot.'

Harvey called out again.

'Excellent,' Wynne murmured, cradling Harvey's leg in his arm and tapping his knee with a rubber hammer, then he shone a pencil torch into each eye in turn, studying them carefully.

'I saw what happened,' Harvey said quietly.

Mr Wynne raised his eyebrows a fraction and turned off the torch.

'I saw the doctor get out of his car and go over to my body. I was watching him.' Harvey saw puzzlement on the nurse's face.

The surgeon shook his head. 'I think you must have been dreaming, old boy.'

'I wasn't dreaming,' Harvey said insistently. 'I can describe him.'

The surgeon nodded for him to go on.

'He – ' Harvey saw the doctor clearly in his mind, jumping out of his car, running across. Then the image dissolved into fragments, like water disturbed by a stone. He saw the doctor's car, but that faded into the car that someone was sitting in, driving, a woman, screaming. He tried to pull the memory back but it slipped away.

The surgeon smiled sympathetically. 'I'm afraid you had a pretty good bashing from the anaesthetic, old chap.' He glanced down at the notes clipped to the end of the bed. 'You had a Ketamine anaesthetic because you were in a shocked condition. That can give you hallucinations which go on for a few days.'

'I'm not hallucinating.' Harvey stared at the nurse for reassurance, but her face had a numb frown set in like a mask. Through a gap in the curtains he saw a woman in a cloth hat pushing an urn on a metal trolley.

'How's your left arm feeling?' said the surgeon, his expression distant, as if his mind was already on something else.

'It's OK.'

'You right handed?'

'Yes.'

'You're lucky. You won't be able to use the left one for a couple of months.'

'I did see it,' Harvey said. 'I – I saw – '

The surgeon's quizzical gaze made him falter, uncertain now what he had seen. He wanted to tell him he had seen his mother, and he knew that would sound even more ridiculous.

'I'll keep an eye out for your father,' Mr Wynne said. 'I haven't met him for about ten years. Give him my regards. I'll pop by in a couple of days.' He stepped back, said something to the houseman and nurse in a lowered voice, and walked out.

The nurse unclipped the notes from the end of the bed, wrote something on them and clipped the sheet back. She opened the curtains, then whispered something to the houseman and he snickered as they followed the surgeon out of the ward like puppies on a leash.

# *Chapter Five*

*Monday, 22 October*

Kate Hemingway walked to the office, as she did most mornings, striding quickly, anxious once she had set off to get down to work. She had lost her gloves and her hands were dug into her raincoat pocket, a fifties Burberry she had bought in a second-hand shop in Covent Garden and was a size too big. Beneath it she wore a man's double-breasted suit jacket from the same shop, an unstructured black skirt and black leggings.

Putting on make-up bored Kate and her face needed little, although she did not believe that. It had strong bone structure and the natural colour of her healthy skin was enriched by a light dusting of freckles around her forehead and on either side of her pretty snub nose. She wasn't good at make-up and tended to put on too much, and messily, which, together with her tangled flaxen hair, added to her designer jumble-sale image, making her appear more like a college student on a project than a reporter searching for an angle.

The staff entrance was down a side street that housed on the opposite side an office block, a row of lock-up garages and a builder's yard. A dustcart was stationary behind Kate, the howl of its lifting gear grinding through the chilly overcast air as she nudged open the blue door with her shoulder and went into the dingy concrete-floored lobby; there was a fire extinguisher on the wall in front, a cork notice board with a yellowed and torn section of the Employment Act pinned to it, racks of punch cards beside a time clock for the print workers, and a wooden counter with a mesh grille and a large printed notice, VISITORS MUST BE SIGNED IN, behind which the two security men sat chatting to each other. They looked up as Kate came in and greeted her amiably.

'Hi!' She flapped a hurried wave and dashed up the flight of stairs, with chunks of plaster missing from the bare, blue-painted walls, down the long, narrow corridor past the accounts and sales offices. She checked her watch, a fake Cartier she had bought in Bangkok three years before. Eight fifty.

She quickened her pace, and came out on to the landing at the top of the corridor which had a faint smell of greasy food. There were stairs up to the canteen and down to despatch and the printing presses, and a row of staff notice boards. 'Reporting accidents – what you must do.' 'Ten per cent off domestic house removals.' 'Menu. Mon. Beef stew. Tue. Madras chicken curry.' The building was a labyrinth; she had been here three months and still hadn't fully sussed the geography. There were people who'd been here years who hadn't.

She pushed open the double doors in front of her and went into the newsroom, a vast open-plan area occupying the width of the building filled with rows and banks of cluttered desks, each with a VDU screen. Many were already occupied and the room had the sense of quiet urgency that was always there at the start of the morning, and slowly wound down during the course of the day as each of the six editions of the paper went to press.

The room's stanchions and girders and heating and air-conditioning pipes and ducts were exposed and accentuated in red paint to make them stand out against the cream walls and brown carpet and desks. Flat, grey daylight drifted in through the windows that looked out both sides on to taller buildings, and cold deadpan lighting shone from the neon strips strung on chains from the ceiling. There was a steady background hiss of the heating system and the soft putter of word processor keys.

She passed the features desks. Only two were occupied. A phone warbled, unanswered, on an empty one. There was a stack of hardback novels on the literary editor's desk and a jumble of videos on the film and TV reviewer's desk. Most news reporters were in and working; the sub editors were beavering hard, and there was a discussion going on around the picture desk. Two of the copy takers had phones wedged to their ears and were typing fast on their keyboards. The editor, deputy editor and overnight editor were sitting in line at their row of desks, square on to the room behind the news editor's team.

Kate hung her mac on the hook on the wall at the back of the room, then slipped behind her own desk, sat on her swivel chair, dumped her handbag on the floor, and smiled at Joanna Baines, another reporter, who sat opposite her, and noted that neither Darren White nor Sharon Lever who occupied the desks to the left of her was in yet. Joanna Baines was typing furiously on her keyboard, a thread of cigarette smoke rising beside her; she raised a hand in acknowledgement without looking up.

Kate began to tidy the chaotic jumble of paper that littered her desk, and had been made worse by being out of the office all day Saturday. She'd been on duty. There had been a sex attack on a student nurse and the mugging of an ex-mayoress, and paperwork she had hoped to catch up on had piled up further in her absence.

She pushed several things she had now dealt with on to the growing stack on the metal spike. The desk was like all the others, mahogany-grained plastic with metal legs and four drawers. It felt almost as much like home as her flat did, although there was nothing on it of a particularly personal nature, just a standard issue black diary, piles of paper, a jumble of pens and the VDU screen, already on, with the single command staring out: 'Press to restore display.' But it was hers, her place, her familiar mess.

She tapped the keyboard, calling up the overnight basket, and scanned news that had come through on the wires, concentrating on stories within the paper's catchment area in Sussex. When she wasn't specifically assigned a story to cover, it was up to her to create copy; she could choose anything she wanted.

She scanned *Scaffold Death Inquest*, *Gatwick Plane Near Miss*, *TV Blackout by Transmission Failure*, *Former Policeman in Drugs Bust*.

There were two follow-ups she had to do today – the nurse's story, and the ex-mayoress who was now in hospital. She took her pad out of her handbag and leafed through her shorthand notes. Out of the corner of her eye she saw the news editor walking towards her holding a sheet of computer print-out. He was a mild, quiet man in his mid-thirties, with thin, fair hair prematurely balding above his forehead, and was wearing one of the grey worsted suits he invariably wore that was quietly trendy but looked as if it had been slept in. He had the slight slouch that Kate had noticed most journalists seemed to have, probably from the hours bent over the word processors.

'Good weekend?' he said.

'Fine,' she said. 'What there was of it.'

'You're getting the splash,' he said.

'Hey!' She beamed.

'The old lady who was mugged, the ex-mayoress. Terry likes it a lot. Wants to lead the first edition with it.' Terry Brent was the editor.

'And a byline?' she asked.

He nodded.

'Great! That's terrific!'

'I've got something for you this morning. It's a bit ghoulish.'

'Oh, yes?'

'Rapping sounds from a graveyard.'

She raised her eyebrows and saw him grinning. 'Rapping sounds?'

He handed her the print-out he was carrying and their eyes met for a fleeting moment. She glanced away, down at the sheet, embarrassed. She found him attractive, but wanted to get that right out of her mind. He was married. She liked the way he was so even-tempered, never seemed to lose his rag. She wondered if he ever got mad, really mad. Somehow she didn't think so; he was like a stone on the beach that the sea washed over; the rougher it was, the smoother it rubbed him. Solid; nice. She read the print-out.

'Phone report from PC Tucker, Brighton Police. Rcd 8.10 a.m. 22 Oct. Exhumation request made to Coroner's office following rapping sounds reported from grave in St Anne's cemetery, Brighton. Expect exhumation order to be granted this a.m.'

Kate flicked a loose strand of hair away from her face. 'Do you know anything more?'

'No.' He paused. 'Exhumations are difficult. They'll be screened off and won't tell you very much. Just go and see what it's all about – a short piece. Pictures want something. They're sending a photographer with you.'

'Rapping from a grave? What are they going to dig up – some Victorian ghoul?'

'It's a twenty-three-year-old girl. She was buried last Tuesday.'

She blanched. 'They think she's alive?'

He smiled. 'I doubt it. These things happen from time to time. Graveyards make people jumpy; a twig snaps and they think the dead are coming back to life.'

'Do you know anything about her?'

'No, but perhaps you can hype it. Get some colour, make a bit of a story out of it.'

She unhooked her coat, walked across to the picture editor and asked which photographer had been allocated. Then she went down to security and signed out a mobile phone.

# Chapter Six

Harvey watched the cloud of blue smoke tumble out across the room towards him. The Reverend Bob Atkinson, the school chaplain, lay comfortably slouched in his battered horsehair-stuffed armchair, his feet clad in grey socks and black lace-ups sticking out of the bottom of his cassock and resting on a needlepoint footstool. He dropped the spent match into a tin ashtray on the carved wooden table beside him, tugged his pipe out of his mouth and held it thoughtfully in the air.

The room was small and cluttered; a faded Persian rug lay on the floor, a shelf sagged ominously under piles of books, a birthday card had fallen on to the coal in a pitted brass bucket; several framed prints of religious scenes broke up the faded flock paper on the walls.

Harvey could smell cooking and heard the chaplain's wife clattering about in the kitchen, with the radio on rather loudly. He sat on the edge of the tired leather sofa, crossed his grey flannelled legs then uncrossed them and glanced at his fingernails whilst waiting for the chaplain to reply; he noticed to his annoyance calcium flecks appearing at the edge of the cuticles of several. There was a trace of dirt under his index finger and he discreetly levered it out with his opposite thumbnail. Through the window, he saw a robin land on a sundial in the small overgrown garden.

'Very interesting,' the chaplain said. He had a broad, easy face and a fringe of fine black hair with a balding patch in the middle; he could have passed as a drummer in a pop group, Harvey thought. 'It's certainly what people in biblical days would have considered to be a mystical experience.'

Harvey said nothing.

The chaplain tapped his teeth with the stem of his pipe. 'What you've had is really a sort of vision, isn't it?'

'Vision?'

'Yes.' He closed his hand over the bowl of his pipe and sucked noisily; it had gone out. 'Were you very close to your mother?'

Harvey shrugged. 'Yes – quite, I suppose.'

'And you're convinced you really did meet her, that it wasn't a dream or hallucination?'

'I'm sure it wasn't.'

'Some dreams can seem very vivid, can make you think in the morning they were so real they must have really happened.'

'I could see everything when I had the accident.'

The chaplain scrabbled in the box and took out another red-tipped match. 'Extraordinary. You don't think perhaps you might have pieced it together from what your chums told you?' He struck the match and held it over the bowl of his pipe.

Harvey felt angry suddenly. 'Don't you believe in life after death?' His left arm itched inside the plaster.

The chaplain drew on his pipe and snorted the smoke out through his nostrils. He uncrossed his legs. 'Of course I do,' he said softly.

'Provided it doesn't happen to anyone you know?'

The chaplain frowned. 'I'm not with you.'

'I had stopped breathing, the doctor told me. So I was dead for a couple of minutes. I had tests, X-rays and things because they were so worried. What I saw happened whilst I was dead; surely you can't have a hallucination when you are dead?'

'We don't know, Harvey; none of us knows; we have to rely on the teachings of the scriptures.'

'Why? Why not on me?'

The chaplain sucked several times on his pipe. 'You were fond of your mother, quite rightly, and you took her passing on heavily. It was only a few months ago and you are bound to be in a deep emotional state about it. Something like that takes years to come to terms with. You're a strong chap and you will get over it. You've had a big set-back with this accident and I think it's made you very confused, if you want the honest truth.' He raised his eyes and stared directly at Harvey.

Harvey bit his lip to stifle his disappointment. Bob Atkinson was regarded by the boys as a good bloke, someone they could talk to, unlike most of the teachers here. Harvey had hoped he might understand, offer some better explanation.

'I saw it clearly,' Harvey said. 'I was floating up above. I watched the doctor trying to resuscitate me. Then I went down this tunnel and my mother was there.'

'Where do you think you were?'

Harvey hesitated. 'Sort of at the frontier to – heaven.'

'What makes you think that?'

Harvey blushed and pushed his mop of hair back from his forehead. 'It felt so good. For a moment I was really happy, incredibly happy. I – I'd never felt so happy in all my life.'

'And then you felt scared?'

'No, I don't think I was scared. I was more angry because they wouldn't let me – sort of – stay. Sort of come in. Wouldn't let me talk any more to my mother.'

The chaplain looked serious. 'You didn't meet God, or Jesus? Or St Peter?'

Harvey shook his head.

'Don't you think that's a little strange? Going to heaven and not seeing any of those?'

Harvey felt something sag inside him.

The chaplain smiled kindly. 'Harvey, I don't think God allows us to cross these frontiers. That's not part of His plan. Remember St Paul's letter to the Ephesians? "When I was a child I spake as a child, I understood as a child, I thought as a child: but when I became a man I put away childish things. For now we see through a glass darkly, but then face to face."' He leaned back and struck another match. 'Do you understand what Paul is saying, Harvey?'

'Not really.'

'He is saying we are not meant to understand, not meant to see beyond this world. We will see through that glass when our time to pass on comes; then we shall both see the other side and understand more about this life. But not until then.'

'Why not?'

'Because that is God's will.'

'And we have to accept God's will just like that?'

The chaplain seemed perturbed. 'Of course we do, Harvey. We are His servants. We disobey Him at our peril.'

Harvey shrugged. 'Don't you think we have a right to question His will?'

There was a silence. 'When you dabble, like you are doing, Harvey,' the chaplain replied quietly, 'you open yourself up to malevolent occult forces. You lose God's protection.'

'I'm not dabbling.'

'You are. Questioning God's will and talking about it like this is dabbling; you are providing the weaknesses that allow evil in.' He smiled. 'Shall we say some prayers together, for your mother and your father?'

# *Chapter Seven*

*Monday, 22 October*

Kate Hemingway sat in the passenger seat of the small Ford from the *Sussex Evening News* car pool, as Eddie Bix, the staff photographer assigned to go with her, drove up the hill towards the church. A gangly hulk in his early twenties, wearing his uniform of Timberland boots, jeans and bomber jacket, the photographer had a cheery baby face with crew-cut fair hair, and wore a single gold earring. Every time Kate went out on an assignment with him he was on a different craze. This week it was flotation chambers.

'Incredible in the dark, you just let it all drift away. I mean you really come out feeling – wow!'

She was only half-listening, distracted. Rappings from a grave. A twenty-three-year-old girl. One year younger than herself.

She remembered once as a child playing hide and seek, and getting stuck in an old trunk; she'd tried to get the lid up and it wouldn't move, and then she'd felt something crawling up her leg. She'd nearly gone crazy, screaming and pounding, and her sister had come into the room and instead of freeing her had hammered on the lid and made ghostly groans; and the thing had carried on crawling up her leg and she'd wriggled and tried to brush it away and it bit her sharply on the inside of her thigh. Later Dara had held it up to her face; a wriggling black beetle three inches long.

'It's the dark,' Eddie Bix enthused. 'Like an incredible experience, you're in your own private universe.'

The car was grubby and smelled of air freshener. A no-smoking roundel was stuck on the dash in front of her. The wipers squeaked across the screen, smearing a light film of drizzle.

'You ought to try group dynamics, self assertion. I didn't used to feel assertive enough. You get treated like shit so often in this job. Now it doesn't bother me. I know what I'm doing is the right thing.' He raised a hand and pointed. 'This is it. My cousin got married here a couple of years ago.'

The church sat well back from the road. It was small and old; the tower looked Norman, Kate thought, from her architecture studies at school; there were perpendicular windows in the chancel which seemed out of place, and some of the cement rendering on the walls was missing. It was run-down, like the graveyard in front of it; like a lot of churches.

To the right was a modern brick vicarage. Across the road was a row of flint cottages and beyond the churchyard was a small modern close, with several of the houses backed up to the church wall. They stopped behind a police car and a dark green van. Kate could see no other vehicles nearby, and no other reporters. A man in dungarees was on a ladder cleaning the chancel windows.

Her stomach knotted. Normally at the start of any assignment she wanted to be out of the car and there, amongst the action, finding some way in no one else had found, a witness or a victim or a passer-by no one else had interviewed, an angle no one else had spotted. Today she felt reluctant, hoped there was nothing, that it was a false lead they had been given.

A blast of cold air surged into the car as Eddie opened his door. He scooped his two Nikons and a long lens off the rear seat and slung them round his neck, then stared at the sky, did a mental calculation and muttered to himself dubiously, 'Two-eight.' He removed the lens cap on one of his cameras and adjusted the f-stop, then rubbed his nose with the back of a finger, and studied the flint cottages across the road carefully. 'Never done an exhumation,' he said. 'Done a few corpses, though. Good thing about them is they don't keep moving around.'

'Yech!' Kate said, her hair thrashing wildly in another strong gust.

There was a blue hoarding with the times of services and the vicar's name written underneath, the Reverend Neil Comfort.

'Great name for a vicar,' Eddie said.

They walked through into the graveyard. It was old and uneven and some of the stones had tilted. Quite a few were coated in moss and lichen, and on several others the inscriptions had weathered away. 'There's a modern cemetery round the back,' Eddie said.

Kate eyed the tombstones uneasily. Graveyards spooked her. She had toyed with becoming an organ donor but, for the same reason she had not made a will, she was nervous of taking any steps that would confirm her own mortality. She tried not to dwell on death too much, maybe because she came into contact with it most of the working days of her life: bodies being cut out of twisted cars; door-stepping grieving widows; trying to purloin snapshots from numb parents. Sometimes human tragedy meant as little to her as the names on the graves she was walking past now, and there were moments when she was scared that she was becoming too tough, too hard. Then she'd be sent to interview a four-year-old girl dying of leukemia, and she'd spend the rest of the day fighting back tears.

They went up the brick path through the graveyard, past a large yew tree with some of its branches rattling against the wall. A volley of leaves blew in front of them.

'They used to plant yews in churchyards to ward off evil spirits,' Eddie said.

'Is that what you make cricket bats out of?'

'That's willow. God, you're dumbos, you Yanks! How long have you lived here?'

'Ten years.'

'And you don't know what cricket bats are made of?'

She grinned, then felt more sombre as they walked round the side of the church and saw the uniformed policeman. He was standing in front of a white tape that cordoned off the cemetery behind him, a small neat cemetery bounded by an autumnally brown beech hedge. There was a gate at the rear with several strips of white tape pinned across; one had come loose and was trailing like a kite's tail.

Kate had already got to know several of the local police, but she hadn't seen this one before. He was young, and looked hostile and bored. She held out her press card; he glanced at the cameras around Eddie's neck with a faint sneer. 'No press,' he said. His cap lifted slightly in a gust and he tugged it on more firmly.

'Who is allowed in?' Kate said.

Behind him, towards the rear of the cemetery, two men were erecting a makeshift green screen on tent poles. It was flapping wildly and they were struggling. The policeman stared ahead as if Kate and Eddie did not exist.

'Come on, man,' Eddie said. 'Who is allowed in?'

'Authorised personnel.' He continued staring ahead, like a sentry, saying nothing further. Kate felt herself getting angry. 'Is there a police spokesman here?'

He shook his head.

'There's an exhumation taking place, right?'

Again he did not reply.

Eddie winked at her and walked back down the path. She followed. He stopped and jerked his head towards the modern houses. 'Be able to see everything from one of those.'

'I want to find the vicar,' Kate said.

'I'll come for a mug-shot. Clergy always lends a bit of tone.'

The vicar opened his front door and gazed at them edgily. He was a tall, sharp-looking man in his late forties, with short brown hair that was brushed straight back and surprisingly trendy tortoiseshell glasses. He wore a military jumper over his dog collar, and leather slippers.

'Mr Comfort?' Kate said.

'Yes,' he said with distinct reluctance.

'*Evening News*. I wondered if you could give us a bit of information about this exhumation.'

His expression hardened and he held the door stiffly against the wind. 'It's really a very private thing.' His voice was crisp and assertive. There were tiny quivers of nerves or anger at the corners of his mouth. His gaze moved from her to Eddie.

'You married my cousin, Dick Billington,' Eddie said. 'Couple of years ago.'

The vicar was thrown off balance. 'Oh yes?' he said, his expression mellowing a fraction. 'Came from Cornwall? Married a local girl, Jenny Vallance?'

'Devon,' Eddie said.

'Yes, I remember him.' His tone of voice and his expression proffered no opinion on Dick Billington or Jenny Vallance.

'We wouldn't want to intrude on anything private. It's not the *News*'s policy,' Kate said. 'But we hoped you could give us some background information.'

The Reverend Comfort hesitated. 'An exhumation licence has been requested but it has not yet been granted,' he said.

'But you expect it to be granted?' Kate took out her notepad and began scribbling shorthand.

He eyed the pad the way he might have eyed a foreign coin in the collection box. 'The coroner has given the order. It's up to when the Home Office grant the licence.'

'Is that likely to be today?'

'I'm afraid I'm not familiar with their bureaucratic processes.'

'Could you give us any details about the person – body – you want to exhume?'

'I'm afraid not. It's a private matter. The application has been made at the request of the deceased woman's husband.'

'What was her name?'

He hesitated. 'Sally Donaldson. Mackenzie was her maiden name.'

Kate wrote it down. 'Have you had any experience of exhumations before?'

'No. None.' He smiled wryly. 'You've probably had more experience than I have.'

Kate smiled back, trying to break through the block of ice. 'Is it true that people have been hearing rapping sounds from the grave?'

The vicar looked at Eddie who was changing a lens on a camera, his leather bomber jacket billowing. 'One or two of the locals think they might have heard something,' he said.

'Have you heard them?'

'No, I haven't,' he said emphatically.

'Is there a possibility she might still be alive?'

'Absolutely not. We've been in touch with the hospital, and the correct procedures for certification of death were carried out. There is no question she could possibly be alive.'

'So why are you exhuming her?'

He blinked several times in nervous anger. 'For her bereaved husband's peace of mind,' he said.

'Have you ever known of anyone being buried alive?'

'I think,' he said, 'that is something you are more likely to find in Edgar Allan Poe.'

'So you don't feel there is any urgency – that you should go ahead without waiting for the official licence?'

Anger increased in his eyes and his voice tightened. 'No, I don't.'

'Do you know what she died – passed away – of?'

'A respiratory problem, I understand.'

'At her age?' Kate carried on scribbling.

'There were complications due to her pregnancy.'

'She was pregnant?' Kate said, startled.

'Six months, I understand.'

Kate turned the page in her notebook. 'If this is a private matter, could you tell us why the police are here?'

He drew a breath before replying. 'We asked them if they would come to help us maintain privacy.'

'So you don't believe there are any suspicious circumstances?'

There was a gust of wind, and a sharp thudding as the rain began to fall. He looked at them defiantly, as if telling them he was damned if he was inviting them in. 'No.'

'Could I just ask you about the actual procedures?'

'I'm afraid I am very busy at the moment.'

'Of course. I'm sorry. You have been very helpful.'

Eddie took a couple of paces back. 'A quick picture for the files.'

'No, I really – ' the vicar began.

Kate heard the shutter click, then again.

The vicar turned and went inside. Kate thanked him but he made no acknowledgement, as if regretting what he had already said, and closed the door firmly behind him.

Eddie capped his camera. 'Try the houses?'

She nodded, and they walked up the road, heads ducked against the rain, and turned right into the close of small modern houses. 'The end one?' Eddie said.

It was becoming colder and Kate dug her hands deep into her mackintosh pockets. They walked down a crazy paved path, past a small lawn, so green and free of weeds it looked artificial, and rang the doorbell. It chimed mournfully. Inside a baby cried and a radio pounded out crackly music.

A woman of about Kate's age answered the door; she was wearing a Snoopy apron over her jeans and T-shirt and her hair was bunched sloppily above her head and tied with a strip of rag. She was chewing a toffee and looked harassed. The house smelled of nappies and baby powder. Toys were strewn around the hallway.

Eddie flashed his press card, and leaned forward with a cheery grin. 'Hi! *Evening News*. We're doing a story on the cemetery. Any chance of borrowing one of your upstairs rooms to shoot a few pictures from?'

She frowned at him as if he were mental. 'What's going on over there?' she said. A small boy appeared behind her on a tiny tricycle. He banged into a skirting board and she spun round and yelled at him, 'Tommy! Get off that at once or I'll thump you.' She looked back at Eddie and Kate.

'An exhumation,' Kate said.

'A what?'

'They're opening a grave of a girl who was buried last Tuesday.'

She stared at Kate and Eddie in turn, still chewing. 'Oh, yeah, someone said about some raps or something.' The baby bawled on.

'Have you heard anything unusual yourself?' Kate said, keeping her notebook tucked in her pocket.

Eddie pointed. 'I was wondering if you had a back room or something that overlooked – ?'

The woman's expression changed, subtly, into hardness. 'How long will you be?'

He produced his wallet, rummaged inside it and took out a fiver. 'Little something,' he said, handing it to her.

She stuck it in her apron without acknowledging it. 'I'm going out at eleven.'

'That's fine.'

They followed her upstairs. The house was sparsely decorated, as if they had only recently moved in. They went into a small carpeted room that contained nothing but a few cardboard boxes, a bag of golf clubs and a carton of nappies. It smelled of fresh paint and had a large window. 'This is the best view,' she said.

It looked directly down on to the cemetery with its neat rows of headstones in sharp contrast to the crumbling graveyard at the front. Twenty feet away, two workmen were finishing erecting the screen. Kate felt frustrated that she could still see nothing beyond it. There was a gate at the end of the cemetery guarded by another policeman.

A flap in the canvas parted, and a distraught-looking young man in a business suit came out and wandered around aimlessly, oblivious of the rain. Eddie pulled out the telescopic leg of his monopod and screwed the base-plate on to a Nikon.

'That might be the husband, in the suit,' Kate said.

'I'll shoot everyone I see.'

'I want to try to talk to him. Catch up with you later?'

He nodded abstractly, concentrating on his gear.

She let herself out, went to the next door house and rang the doorbell. There was no answer. She tried the next one and a woman with greying hair answered.

Kate smiled. 'Sorry to bother you. I'm from the *Sussex Evening News*.'

'No, not interested,' she said in a deep, faintly horsey voice and started to close the door.

'I'm not selling anything. I'm a reporter. I was wondering if you knew anything – '

'Sorry. Absolutely not interested.' The door shut with a firm click.

'Cow,' Kate muttered under her breath and moved on to the next house. A bouncy, cheerful woman with short brown hair and neat brown clothes opened the door.

'Oh yes, the raps!' she said in a voice that smacked of women's guilds and fetes and church roof fund-raising. 'Can't actually say I've heard them myself. Have you been to the cottages?'

'The flint ones opposite the church?'

'Yes. Number twelve, Mrs Herrige. She's absolutely certain she heard someone crying out a few days ago. Problem is she's a bit – you know?' She tapped the side of her head.

'Could I make a note of your name?'

'Pamela Weston. Mrs.'

'Do you think this woman might have been buried alive?'

She tilted her head to one side, then the other. 'It's an awful thought, isn't it? I hope not. Gosh, I can't think of anything more awful. I mean, how would she breathe? Do people think she might still be alive?'

'They seem to be going to a lot of trouble,' Kate replied.

'Let me know, would you, if you hear anything?'

Kate promised she would, then went down the road, to the flint cottages, to try to interview Mrs Herrige at number twelve.

Mrs Herrige had heard raps; an SOS in morse code, repeated regularly. She'd also heard moans and cries for help. And she'd seen visions of Jesus. He visited her regularly, giving her urgent advice for mankind. Once he'd even visited her when she was on the lavatory with a message that could not wait. Mrs Herrige pressed upon Kate the importance of printing these messages in her newspaper. Kate assured her she would mention it to the editor.

She covered the rest of the cottages, and the houses in the close. One other person, a retired dentist, thought he had heard something but could not be quite sure. Everyone *knew* of someone who had heard something.

At eleven fifteen she used the portable telephone she had signed out to dictate her first report to a copytaker at the office and spoke to Geoff Fox, the news editor, who told her to stay with the story.

She managed to get the policeman on guard to confirm that the man in the suit behind the screens was Sally Donaldson's husband, then waited by the entrance of the churchyard for him to come out.

During the next hour a couple of other local reporters turned up. Kate knew them and they traded the scant information they had. All except one bit she kept back: that Sally Donaldson's husband was here, behind the screens.

Her first piece appeared, considerably edited and condensed on page five of the midday edition. It was a single column of fourteen lines, headed: PLEA OVER BRIDE'S GRAVE

> The body of tragic bride Sally Donaldson is to be exhumed following stories of rapping sounds in St Anne's Church graveyard, Brighton.
>
> Sally, 23, died on 14 October at

Brighton's Prince Regent Hospital following complications caused by pregnancy.

The request for the exhumation was made by the vicar of St Anne's, the Rev Neil Comfort. The East Sussex coroner has given the go-ahead.

# *Chapter Eight*

Dusk seeped through the windows into the silent laboratory. The dull, pungent reek of formalin hung in the room. Bunsen burners with red rubber tubing sat neatly spaced down the long wooden work benches. Racks of test tubes stood on the shelves above, and rows of glass-stoppered bottles with typewritten labels. Hydrochloric acid. Potassium chloride. Zinc oxide. One shelf contained a row of jars in which several dead frogs lay pickled.

It was quiet outside, too, as if all time was waiting for him. He stared around at the shelves, the jars, the chemicals, the instruments. Science. Knowledge. Harvey Swire felt a tingling excitement, and breathed in the formalin as if it were a fine perfume.

The word PHOTOSYNTHESIS was chalked on a blackboard. The power of nature. Life within life. There was a point, a definitive point, at which you could see the life force vanish. But that did not mean death had started. Death was elusive.

The frog wriggled in his closed hand. He felt tremors pulsing through its body; fear and energy. Its mouth opened and shut, its glands secreted slime, it blinked, flexed its membranous legs. It wanted to escape, to be free; in a moment part of it would escape, would be free.

In the quad below a boy's voice pierced the silence with a single shout. Another voice replied. The frog wriggled again. The clock on the wall said eight forty-five. Harvey had to be back in the house by nine for evening roll call.

He dropped the frog into the perspex bowl of the Kenwood blender, pushed the lid on tightly and put the blender on the weigh scales. He placed the weights on the other end, carefully. Four pounds, three ounces, seven grammes. He had already weighed the blender and the frog separately. The frog jumped up against the glass, its feet kicking the sharp motionless blade at the base.

Harvey plugged the flex into a wall socket and the green warning light on the side of the blender came on. He stared at his weight measurements, barely looking at the frog, and gripped the on–off toggle switch on the side of the blender with his index finger and thumb.

A shadow moved, startling him. He turned. It was Mr Stipple, his biology master, in a paisley bow tie and linen jacket, an acid, rather arrogant man with slicked centre-parted hair and small, neat features. He walked forwards a few paces on crêpe-soled shoes. 'Good evening, Swire. Working rather late?'

'I'm doing an experiment, sir,' Harvey said.

'Ah.' He peered into the blender. 'Would you care to explain your experiment to me?'

Harvey glared defiantly at the master. The frog jumped; he took his fingers off the switch.

'This is a cookery experiment? You are making amphibian soup?'

'I'm conducting a weight-loss experiment, sir,' he said.

The master peered more closely at the frog. 'A weight-loss experiment?'

'I'm measuring change at the moment of death.'

'In a food mixer?'

'By killing the frog in this sealed container and without adding or removing anything from it, I should be able to detect whether there is a loss of weight or mass at the point of death.'

'And what would loss of weight or mass at the point of death prove, Swire?' He always spoke a decibel higher than was necessary, as if for the benefit of an unseen audience.

'It might prove that the frog has a soul.'

'A soul?' the master echoed, astounded. 'You believe it is possible a frog has a soul?'

'I think it's possible all living creatures have souls, sir.'

'Did you ever read Pope, Swire?'

'No, sir.'

'You should, boy. "Like following life through creatures you dissect, you lose it in the moment you detect." '

'You dissect animals all the time in here, sir.'

Mr Stipple raised a finger in the air. 'For a reason, Swire. Only for a reason.'

'I have a reason,' Harvey said.

'This laboratory is for the purpose of O- and A-level exam syllabus studies, Swire. It is not a place for sick games.'

'I'm not playing sick games.'

'I don't think liquidising a frog in a blender can be considered serious scientific research, Swire. Is this one of our frogs?'

'I collected it myself, sir.'

'I suggest you hurry back to your house, Swire. It's nearly nine. And let your frog free on the way. Where did the food mixer come from?'

'It's mine, sir. From home.'

'I think I'll hold on to it.'

Harvey left the laboratory tight-lipped, went down the stone steps and out into the quad. He released the frog reluctantly into some bushes and walked quickly towards his school house.

The biology master watched him from the mullioned window of the Victorian gothic building. The boy disturbed him; disturbed everyone. He was bright, could be quite brilliant at times when he concentrated, but usually he was lost in a world of his own. He'd always been a bit of an introvert, with a rather strange manner that several of the masters remarked on as being menacing. But since his accident he had definitely worsened, coming up with bizarre ideas, asking strange questions. He should have been concentrating on his A-level syllabus; instead he seemed to have become obsessed with death.

Perhaps, to be fair, he was still disturbed by the loss of his mother.

A huddle of boys stood furtively by the side door. Harvey saw a red glow, and smelled a wisp of cigarette smoke. Several of his colleagues glanced round as he walked up the path. One of them said, 'Here comes the zombie!'

There was a titter of laughter.

'Hey, Harvey, how's your friend God? Is He going to help you pass your exams?'

'Hey, Harve,' shouted another, Horstead. 'Anderson said that people who come back from the dead are zombies. He thinks you must be a zombie!'

Harvey said nothing.

Walls Minor wrinkled his nose and sniffed. 'He's dead smelly!'

'No he's not, he's a dead bore!'

Laughter followed him into the lobby. They were ignorant. Everyone in this school was ignorant.

The laughter stayed with him as he lay in his bed later, restless, unable to sleep. The plaster had been off for two weeks and his arm ached like hell. It hurt to lie on it, and he rolled on to his back, but his arm, unsupported now, hurt even more. He rolled on to his right side, but the pressure on his broken ribs was too much and he stifled a cry of pain.

In the darkness he could hear the breathing of his five dormitory mates. Dacre was snoring noisily and irregularly, sucking the warm night air through his clogged adenoids. Someone to his left, Powell or Walls Minor, shifted and the bedsprings clanked. It was a still, hot night, and through the curtainless windows he could see the chestnut tree glazed like porcelain under the glare of the moon.

He closed his eyes and tried to sleep again, but the intense moonlight seemed to burn through his skull into his brain. He saw Mr Stipple in his natty bow tie and imagined torturing him with acids and scalpels; in his mind he could hear his screams of pain, could feel him wriggling, the life sliding out of him, and he smiled and nearly drifted into sleep.

Then a fresh anger rose through him. His friends smirking, whispering to each other as he came along, sniggering behind his back as he walked past.

He was not sure when it had started – whether it was after he had told them about his experiences or after he had hit Reckett. Reckett with his enormous circumcised cock and his sexual conquests, who'd sniggered the loudest when he told them what had happened, what he had seen.

'Did you get to screw Angie when you were up there in heaven, Harve?' Horstead had jeered. 'Because Reckett's been shafting her rigid whilst you've been in hospital. Says she goes like a stoat.'

Reckett was taller and heavier, but Harvey had hurt him badly, blackened an eye, even though he'd been virtually one-handed. His friends had been startled. He had, too; he'd never hit anyone before. Never *really* hit someone the way he'd hit Reckett.

He should have kept quiet about what had happened to him. It had been dumb telling them, trying to imagine they would understand. They were stupid, would always be stupid. They had no interest in understanding life.

His mind drifted back to his accident again, the way it did all the time, endlessly replaying the details. The car with its dull green paintwork and the woman driver through the windscreen with her newly coiffed hair, smoking a cigarette. He felt the slam, saw the woman's face closer, the windscreen exploding into brilliant white sparks. His own body dropping away beneath him like a shadow. Mrs Matthey, his housemaster's wife, running out of the front door, tripping, sprawling. The doctor in his blue blazer kneeling over him, turning to Mrs Matthey.

Then his mother walking towards him, with her blonde tresses of hair, her smile. The dark shadowy shapes; the icy hands pulling him away.

Harvey had been summoned to his housemaster's study earlier that day. Mr Matthey was a tall man with a large nose, a furrowed forehead and a permanently bemused and slightly hostile expression. A few solitary strands of hair had been laid across his bald dome like fishermen's rope left out to dry. He dug both his large hands into the pockets of his Harris tweed jacket as he spoke, making the shoulders lopsided. He told Harvey he was sorry about his accident, but hoped he wasn't intending using that as an excuse when he failed to get the grades in his exams, as, in Mr Matthey's opinion, clearly shared by Mr Stipple and apparently the rest of his teachers, he most certainly would.

A levels started in just over one week's time. Harvey was taking physics, chemistry and biology. To get into Queen's medical school he needed a minimum of one A and two Bs.

The light in the dormitory darkened as if a cloud was passing in front of the moon. He felt pressure in his ears and a numb silence.

Then a sensation of floating.

The window slid by beneath him like a door in an elevator shaft. He could see shapes asleep below him. His dormitory mates.

Himself.

He stared at them, fascinated, then something pressed down on his back. It was the ceiling. For a moment he thought it had lowered, then he realised, puzzled, that he had drifted up against it.

His body lay motionless and he was afraid suddenly.

Dead.

Really died this time.

He thought of Angie. Horstead's goading. 'Reckett's been shafting her rigid . . .'

Dead.

He saw his bedclothes rise and fall. His mouth moved slightly, quivered. The liquid ceiling held him suspended. He wanted to be back in his body; panic rippled through him. He tried to wake, but nothing happened. He looked around the dormitory for help. Walls Minor. Dacre. Powell. Horstead. Smith. All asleep.

Dreaming, he thought.

Just a weird dream. He tried to sink back down towards his body. Instead he drifted forwards across the dormitory. He passed above Walls Minor who was sleeping on his back, his mouth open, hands neatly above the sheets like a dormouse.

The wall was getting closer, coming up fast; he stretched out his hands, could see them clearly, trying to fend himself away.

His hands disappeared into the wall.

Then his face was going into the wall, being sucked in as if it were a magnet. The wall was no longer solid. He could see millions of particles which parted in front of him; they looked silky soft but he could not feel them.

In spirit, he thought. I'm in spirit. Astral.

He went through the layer of plaster, then the bricks, then more plaster and was out in the next dormitory. Reckett was beneath him, mouth open, eye bruised. Harvey drifted over more beds, through another wall, into the washrooms. He drifted towards a mirror which shone like water in the moonlight, looked in it for his reflection.

Nothing.

He moved closer. Still nothing. He was travelling into the clear glass, then the reflector, then the wall behind and out into the landing beyond. It was dark, but he could see clearly. It was unfamiliar, doors were closed, there was patterned wallpaper; a pot stand; pictures of flowers on the walls. He was in the private quarters of Mr and Mrs Matthey, he realised.

He stopped outside a panelled door, then drifted towards it. Going through it was like staring into a microscope; he could see the layers of paint, five of white and one of green, then the grains of the raw wood beneath; strands moved out of the way as if they were tendrils of seaweed parting for a snorkler and he drifted silently through them into a large dark bedroom, with the curtains closed.

He felt the ceiling above him, and it stabilised him, gave him a bearing. Below him two figures were in bed. He grinned, nearly sniggered out loud. Mr Matthey, his housemaster, lay sleeping on his back, snoring hoarsely, the sound echoing around in the quietness of the room. Mrs Matthey, her hair in a net, lay with her head on her hands as if she had fallen asleep saying her prayers. On the table beside her was a copy of *Sons and Lovers*.

Mr Matthey's snoring stopped abruptly, and he stirred, opening his eyes. Harvey squirmed, embarrassed, frightened he might be spotted, or wake up and find he had sleep-walked here. His housemaster's eyes closed again.

Harvey drifted back through the wall into the landing and stopped, rested against the ceiling, except he realised he did not need to rest. He seemed able to stay suspended at any height he liked, with no effort.

He turned and drifted into another wall, paint, plaster, brick parting effortlessly for him and he was outside, above a rhododendron bush close to the front door. He could see Mr Matthey's Dormobile parked below; light and shadow from the street lamps on the pavement. Two cats were fighting somewhere.

He felt afraid.

Then he told himself to relax again, enjoy the dream.

Just a dream.

He drifted down the street towards the main school buildings. The teachers' common room was ahead. It was an imposing building, like a large gatehouse with an arch for carriages in the middle. The common room was directly above the arch. Boys were not allowed in the building; there were rumours of what it was like inside but no one was sure, and masters, when asked, would smile politely, keeping their little secret.

Light was shining through the upstairs window. Harvey drifted towards it and went in through the glass and the stone mullions. The room was disappointingly dull. There was a long table in the middle with old, leather-covered chairs arranged around it, and several smaller groups of armchairs and coffee tables, a mix of styles, periods, jumble sale stuff mostly. He could see only two people in the room, Mr Stipple and Mr Duncton, the physics master, seated in armchairs next to each other.

Mr Stipple sat forward in his chair, sipping a cup of coffee and smoking a cigarette. Mr Duncton, a portly widower in his sixties, was cradling a beer tumbler, his head lowered, his three chins concertinaed into each other. His voice was deep and ponderous. 'Are you the master in charge of exams again this year?'

'Yes,' said Mr Stipple.

'Have the physics O and A levels arrived yet?'

'Yes.'

'Ah.' He shook his beer glass, swilling the last drops around, then drained them and stood up. 'Well, that's me done for the night.' He walked on unsteady legs across the room and put the glass down on a bar top cluttered with empty glasses and full ashtrays. 'I don't suppose you saw the instructions for the practical examinations? Would they have arrived with the papers or separately?'

'I didn't look, I'm afraid.'

Mr Duncton hesitated by the door. 'Ah, no hurry. I just never seem to have enough time to get prepared. If you could let me have them a few days before . . .'

'I'll dig them out for you now and let you have them in the morning.'

'Jolly decent of you, thanks. Leave you to lock up then?' He wandered out and closed the door behind him.

Mr Stipple finished his cigarette and coffee and walked across the room. Harvey followed him into a small lobby, then down a short dark passageway. At the end was a heavy oak door which the biology master opened to reveal a tall, old-fashioned metal safe. He unlocked it and removed several large, fat, brown envelopes and laid them on the floor. The typed address on the top one said: 'The Headmaster, Wesley School', and in neat handwriting on the front someone had added the words *CHEMISTRY 1*.

Mr Stipple glanced furtively over his shoulder, slipped his hand in and pulled out a printed sheet of folded paper. Harvey could read it clearly over his shoulder. He felt a thrill of excitement, afraid Mr Stipple might look up and spot him.

OXFORD AND CAMBRIDGE SCHOOLS EXAMINATION BOARD
General Certificate Examination
Advanced Level
CHEMISTRY I
Monday, 3 July 1967. $2\frac{3}{4}$ hours
Answer *six* questions
Write on only one side of the paper

Harvey began reading the questions.

1. *What is meant by the terms 'atomic number, atomic weight and isotopes'?*

2. *Describe briefly the preparation of methyl cyanide (acetonitrile) starting from (a) methanol, and (b) ethanol.*

The biology master was reading them too, nodding to himself, and knew he shouldn't be doing that because he kept glancing around. He reached the end of the first side, where the words in heavy black type said *turn over*. He opened it out and Harvey could see pages two and three. Crazy hallucination; he allowed himself a smile.

Mr Stipple folded the sheet and put it back into the envelope. Then he took out in turn the other exam papers for chemistry, physics and biology and read through them. Harvey memorised the questions as best he could. To his surprise he could repeat the questions straight back, as if he had photographed them with his mind.

Waste of time, he thought. Memorising exam questions that did not exist.

He read the last paper. It was getting darker, harder to read and he was suddenly afraid. Something was behind him, something dark, menacing, blocking his path.

He tried to move out of its way, but it was closing in on him. He slid sideways, but instead of drifting through the wall, he was being absorbed into it as if it were blotting him up. He went through the paint and plaster into thick stone. It was getting darker. The menacing thing was still behind him.

Then hands clutched him. Icy hands. He could feel them. Feeling had returned. Cold air blew around him. Hands gripped him tightly and he had to struggle to break free of them, struggle to get away. He heard his mother's voice as if she were whispering in his ear.

'Darling, God is very unhappy with you.'

Dark shapes were pulling him, jostling him.

'She doesn't want you,' said a harsh voice.

'She doesn't ever want to see you again,' said another.

He turned in terror. The molecules around him were becoming heavier, more cloying, as if they were trying to hold him, to prevent him from getting out. Wanting to keep him encased in this stone wall for ever.

He screamed.

Cold, so cold.

He screamed again. Then again.

'Harve, shut up!'

'For God's sake, Harve.'

Someone grunted. A light snapped on. A figure was standing above him. Dacre in striped pyjamas. Cold sweat was pouring down Harvey's face, down his body. He was drenched.

'All right, Harve?' Dacre said.

'A dream,' Harvey whispered. 'Nightmare.' More bedsprings clanked.

'Who put the fucking light on?' someone said.

'OK?' Dacre asked Harvey.

Harvey made no reply. He was thinking, trying to go back to the dream. The exam pages ran through his brain. Clear, vividly clear.

*State Snell's Law of refraction and define refractive index.*

*Tabulate two differences and two similarities in the chemistry of carbon and silicon.*

*What do you understand by the term 'adaptive radiation'?*

*Discuss adaptations in mouth parts and legs in those insects with which you are familiar.*

'OK, Harve?' Dacre said again, more insistently. 'You were really screaming, you know. What were you dreaming about?'

'Yeah, OK,' Harvey said, trying to concentrate on the replay that was going on in his mind; scrolling through the examination questions. Physics; chemistry; biology. He waited until his dormitory mates were sleeping again then climbed out of bed, pushed his feet into his slippers, padded out of the dormitory and along the dark corridor to the tiny study he shared with Dacre.

He pushed open the door, went in and closed it behind him, laid a towel carefully along the bottom to blot out the light, then switched on his Anglepoise, sat at his desk and began to write the questions down.

# *Chapter Nine*

*Monday, 22 October*

By two thirty p.m. the knot of reporters gathered outside the churchyard were inventing rumour for lack of fact. Someone said his contact at the police had told him the dead woman, Sally Donaldson, had been murdered by her husband; poisoned. It was a life assurance job, he announced with certainty.

Kate dug her hands deeper into her raincoat pocket and hugged herself tightly, envying Eddie Bix his warm, dry perch in the house overlooking the cemetery. Sally Donaldson's husband had not yet emerged from behind the screens. Word had leaked out that he was in there and the pack was now waiting for him.

The morning's rain had stopped; the wind had moved round to the north-east and turned colder, and dark autumnal clouds were shovelling the daylight out of the sky. Kate had snatched a twenty-minute lunch break in a pub down the road and had wolfed down some mulligatawny soup, which was still burning the roof of her mouth, and a limp ham salad which had failed to stop her feeling hungry.

Cars lined the road, belonging to the press mostly, and a van, bristling with aerials, from Radio Sussex. There was a faint whiff of beer in the air and snatches of cigarette smoke. It was a quiet news day, and the reporters were hanging around until a better story came along.

'I had an aunt who was declared dead when she wasn't,' announced Rodney Sparrow of the *Mid-Sussex Times*. Kate never knew whether to take him seriously. 'She was laid out in the morgue for a post mortem. When the pathologist made his first incision into her, she sat up, grabbed him by the throat and asked him what the 'eck he thought he was doin'. Honest!'

'Hypothermia,' said another journalist, one Kate did not recognise, a hulking night-club bouncer of a man with a scarred face, and a thick Geordie accent. 'A doctor told me hypothermia can slow the pulse down to one beat an hour, and they can miss that when they're certifying death, y'know.'

'Often happens in wartime, people getting buried alive,' wheezed Harry Oakes, a tubby reporter for the *Eastbourne Gazette*. 'Wounded soldiers. Their comrades have to deal with them in a hurry and they don't always notice someone's still breathing. If you haven't had medical training it's not always easy. I was in Arnhem when they opened up some war graves in fifty-two. It was horrible. At least half a dozen of the skeletons were in crouched positions and there were scratch marks on the inside of the coffins. Poor buggers.'

'It happens in hot countries too, someone told me,' said Shane Hewitt from the *Evening Argus*. 'Where they have to bury them within two days by law. They reckon quite a few come round in their coffins.'

'How long could you survive, buried alive?' Kate said, frowning in horror.

'Not more'n a couple of hours,' said Rodney Sparrow. 'Not much air in a coffin.'

'Bollocks,' said the bouncer. 'You could survive for days.'

'It's bloody small in a coffin,' Sparrow said. 'Work out the displacement volume. Compare it to a couple of aqualung cylinders.'

'Yeah, but if you was pushin', you'd probably get the lid up a bit, wouldn't you, and that would let air in.'

'They nail 'em on pretty tight,' said Shane Hewitt. 'You'd have that and the weight of earth.'

'They don't nail them, they screw them on.'

'Anyhow, you'd die of dehydration even if you got air,' said Sparrow. He nodded towards the graveyard. 'How long's she been down?'

'Since last Tuesday afternoon. About seven days.'

'Well, there's no chance now, is there? Even if she had been alive.'

'Someone heard rappings this morning.'

'Yeah? Who was that?'

Shane Hewitt pointed to the cottages across the road. 'The woman in number twelve.'

'She's a fucking fruitcake,' said Jim Barnhope from the *West Sussex Gazette*. 'Kate's already spoke to her.'

'I have, too,' said Gail Cohen from Radio Sussex. 'She's out of her tree.'

'Tell you something,' said Harry Oakes in his hoarse voice, cigarette bobbing in his mouth as he spoke. 'I'm going to be cremated after what I've seen. I don't want to be down there like those boys from Arnhem, scratching their fingers raw.' He winked at Kate. She grinned back bravely.

'I dunno 'bout cremation,' Jim Barnhope said. 'Fancy waking up in the coffin knowing you're going into the oven. Feelin' the heat. The flames coming through the coffin walls at you. Best to be embalmed; that's all right, being embalmed; if you aren't dead by the time they start, you are when they've finished.'

'Same if you have a post mortem.'

Harry Oakes looked at Kate. 'You guys going to stay here the whole time?'

She shrugged. 'I don't know.'

'I have to get over to Eastbourne. A council meeting. Got your mobile?'

'Yes.'

'Mind if I call you later and see if anything's doing?'

'Sure,' she said through gritted teeth, knowing he'd probably spend the evening with his feet up in front of the telly and cash in on her story – or what she let him have of it. On the other hand he was knowledgeable and had given her good advice before. And his paper paid her when he used anything.

'I interviewed this spiritualist geezer,' said Shane Hewitt. 'He reckons the spirit hangs round until the funeral.'

'What number did you say was the woman who'd heard the raps?' Jim Barnhope asked Kate.

'Twelve,' Kate said.

'Thanks.' His voice dropped almost to a whisper. 'I've heard Princess Di might be in Worthing on Saturday; some old school friend getting married. Trying to keep it quiet . . .' He tapped the side of his nose.

'Thanks,' she said.

Barnhope winked and sauntered across the road. Kate watched him and smiled to herself, wondering if he'd have any better luck with the batty woman.

'Well, if it's not the lovely Kate!'

She felt a friendly hand on her shoulder and turned round. It was a reporter she had worked with for her first week on the *News*, who had then moved to the *Daily Mail*. Patrick Donoghue.

'Patrick! What are you doing here?'

'I was in the area and heard there was a story. Is there?'

'Not yet, but there might be.'

At five foot ten, he was five inches taller than Kate. His short brown hair, parted slightly off centre, had been dishevelled by the wind and rain, and strands hung forward in damp flick-curls either side of his parting, framing his forehead.

Thirty years old, sturdy and wiry, pitted with a few pockmarks from childhood acne, he had beat-up, weathered good looks, a no-nonsense but kind expression and a twinkle of humour in his alert green eyes that betrayed his Irish ancestry. He wore a battered greatcoat over an equally battered tweed jacket and ribbed blue jumper, corduroy trousers and scuffed brogues. He clutched a mobile phone in his fist. He could as easily have passed for an off-duty soldier as a newspaper reporter.

He had been kind to Kate in that first week, gone out of his way to help her, and she had bumped into him briefly a couple of times since, once covering a court hearing and once door-stepping the prime minister at a party conference. There was a rebellious streak and a trace of mischievous immaturity in him that touched a nerve of recognition inside herself, and attracted her to him. He seemed to have got better looking than ever since she had last seen him.

There was a sharp warble and he raised his mobile phone to his ear. 'Donoghue,' he said, capped his hand over his other ear and pivoted round, trying to improve the signal. 'Take me about an hour,' he said into the phone, 'if I went now . . . No, nothing so far.' He stared at Kate. 'Yup, could probably sort something out. Right. Is John Passmore back from lunch yet? No, it's all right, I'll talk to him later.' He pressed the *end* button then lowered the phone. 'Marching orders.'

Kate raised her eyebrows, teasingly and a little disappointed. 'A better story?'

He tilted his head back a fraction. 'There are more things in heaven and earth, Horatio, than hanging around in wet graveyards.'

'As long as someone else hangs around for you?'

'Actually, I was coming to that. Any chance you could string this one for me if it turns into something?'

'I'd have to be discreet,' she said. 'There have been some ructions at the paper about other reporters.'

'You don't want to worry about that. Usual rates. It's good money.'

She smiled. 'Sure.'

'It helps get you known in London. You don't want to be chasing fire engines in Sussex all your life.'

'When I could be chasing them in London?'

'Bigger fires.' He grinned. 'Bell me if there's anything doing.'

'What about this better story you're going to?'

'Off your patch. South London.'

'Hey!' she said indignantly. 'We're not hill-billies. I am allowed to cover South London if it's newsworthy enough.'

'It's a cat stuck on a roof.' He winked and was gone.

Kate went into the church to get some relief from the weather and found the verger polishing the communion chalice, a wispy-haired man in his late sixties who looked as if he once might have been plump but now was almost emaciated. He was happy to talk. He thought he might have heard some thuds on the Tuesday evening after Sally Donaldson's funeral, but had said nothing for a few days until he'd discovered that there were others who had also heard something. He had known Sally Donaldson all her life, gave Kate a potted biography, the names of several of her relatives and some of their addresses.

As Kate walked back towards the pack there was a sudden murmur of interest as a blue Vauxhall pulled up and Dennis Falk, the police spokesman, climbed out. The reporters clustered around him like moths at a lamp before he had even closed the door of his car. He was rather sly-looking, with slick, thinning hair and a new blue mackintosh. He held up a placatory hand. 'OK,' he said, and took a folded sheet of paper from his jacket. 'I have a statement.'

An ex-reporter himself, he knew most of the journalists. He read from the sheet. 'Following reports of unaccountable sounds from the deceased's grave, and a request from the deceased's husband, the East Sussex coroner, Dr Stanley Gibson, has issued an order for the exhumation of the remains of Mrs Sally Donaldson, buried on October the sixteenth of this year. The Home Office has granted a licence in accordance with section twenty-five of the Burial Act of eighteen fifty-seven for the exhumation to be carried out after dusk this evening, Monday October the twenty-second, and before daybreak tomorrow, Tuesday, October the twenty-third.' He folded the sheet of paper and tucked it back into his pocket.

There was a brief silence. A police car came down the hill and parked opposite.

'Can you tell us why the exhumation isn't going to be carried out until dusk, Mr Falk?' Kate said.

He gave a weaselly, patronising grin, which infuriated her. He seemed to revel in keeping information to himself. 'All exhumations in this country are carried out after dark for privacy and to minimise distress to the general public.'

'But Mr Falk, rappings have been heard coming from the grave. Isn't this an emergency? Shouldn't the digging start right away if there is any chance of her being alive?'

'I understand the coroner has studied the medical reports and evidence and has drawn his own conclusions. In his opinion there is no evidence to support a theory of premature burial, nor is there any possibility that Mrs Sally Donaldson could still be alive.'

'Will the press be allowed in?' Jim Barnhope asked.

Falk crossed his hands behind his back and stuck his small chest out. He leaned back slightly on his grey shoes. 'The churchyard will be closed to the public at dusk, and the press are requested not to attempt to photograph beyond the screens.'

'Er, Mr Falk,' said Rodney Sparrow in a respectful voice, 'we understand that Mr Kevin Donaldson, the deceased's husband, is in the cemetery at the moment. We would all like to have a comment from him.'

'Mr Donaldson is in a state of considerable emotional distress. He has made it known that he does not wish to speak to anyone at the present time.'

A white Volvo estate pulled up, followed by a green van. Two sombre men in black suits got out of the Volvo, their faces stiff, like setting plaster. Three men in overalls climbed out of the van, opened the rear doors and began unloading heavy plastic sacks on to the pavement.

Roy Pinner from the *Leader* leaned towards Kate. 'Ground lime. Full of germs, graves. If you get infected from a rotting body, you'd be dead within minutes. Most infectious thing in the world.'

'Mr Falk, why aren't the press being allowed in?' someone asked.

'Standard regulations, for privacy and hygiene reasons.'

'Can you tell us who will be allowed in?'

'Only gravediggers, the undertakers, immediate relatives, the coroner's officer and an environmental health officer.'

The men in overalls unloaded a large oblong chipboard box from the van and carried it into the graveyard. Kate watched with morbid fascination.

The photographic department of the *Evening News* had checked the records and found a wedding photograph of the couple on file. Kate had not yet seen it. She wondered what Sally Donaldson looked like, tried to imagine for a moment the girl alive in the tiny dark box under the earth behind the screen. Would she be aware of the activity going on up here? Kate stared again across the churchyard. She couldn't be alive. God, please not.

The men in overalls returned and carried the sacks of ground lime behind the green screens. The story was behind the screens, she realised. That's where the drama and the emotion – and the horror –

would take place. Behind the screens they would dig up the coffin and open the lid.

She slipped away from the other journalists, who continued to lob questions at Falk, walked around to the close and borrowed the keys to the staff Ford from Eddie Bix, who was still at his perch in the back room overlooking the cemetery. Then she went back down the road, climbed into the Ford, switched on her telephone and dialled directory enquiries.

A few minutes later, the number she wanted was ringing. A sharp voice answered: 'Environmental Health Office.'

'I'd like to speak to Barry Liverstock, please.'

There was a click, then a long silence. The reception on her portable was poor and the line fizzed, died, fizzed again. A secretary quizzed her, then she heard the Deputy Director of the Environmental Health Office's voice, leaden and pensive. 'Liverstock,' he said.

'Mr Liverstock, it's Kate Hemingway from the *Evening News*.'

'Oh, yes, how are you?' His voice lifted several notches on the enthusiasm scale.

She saw him clearly in her mind. A self-important swaggerer of a man, with lank blond curls and a lechy grin, and a wedding band that was thick and vulgar. He'd leaned across his oceanic desk and suggested a quiet lunch one day. Kate hadn't accepted but had not declined either; she believed in keeping doors open.

'I'm fine, thanks,' Kate said. 'Did you like the piece on the traffic pollution monitoring scheme? Your "Breath of fresh air in Brighton" campaign?'

'It was great. I had no idea you were going to give us so much space.'

'I persuaded my editor it was really important,' Kate lied. It was only due to a threatened libel writ that the planned page five feature had been pulled at the last moment and her piece, the first interview she had done for the *Sussex Evening News*, had gone in. 'Actually, that's why I'm calling. You said that if you could ever return the favour . . . ?'

'Yerss?' His voice slowed, dubious now.

'It's only a tiny little favour.'

There was an uncomfortable silence.

'I might be able to do another piece,' she said.

He wasn't biting. She could feel the sudden coldness down the other end, and cursed herself for trying to do it over the phone. She should have gone and seen him, she knew. 'Are you in your office all afternoon?'

'I have a meeting at four.'

'I could be with you in twenty minutes.'

'Yes, all right, I suppose,' he said reluctantly.

Barry Liverstock's office was out of character with the dingy institutional block that housed it. It was large and airy with a view out over the Palace Pier and the sea, and plushly carpeted in cornflower blue. The furniture was teak and his desk was swanky with a small conference table in front. The walls were lined with framed photographs of greyhounds, and there was a row of silver-plated cups and shields above a bookshelf. A pair of silver greyhound paperweights sat on his desk beside leather-framed photographs of a pleasant-looking woman and two small girls.

He stood up as his secretary showed Kate in. Kate had tidied herself up in the washroom downstairs, undone an extra button on her blouse, and as she sat in the soft chair in front of his desk she hitched her skirt as high up her black leggings as she dared.

He leaned back in his chair in a white shirt and loud tie. He was wearing rhinestone cufflinks and a gold bracelet hung from his wrist; he was even larger than she remembered, plumper and pastier faced. 'What can I do for you?' he asked, running his eyes over her as if she were a whore wheeled out for inspection. He stared at her cleavage and she felt cheap and embarrassed.

'I want a job.'

He frowned. 'Not happy with the paper?'

'I'm very happy with the paper.' She forced a smile. 'I just need something temporary. I – ' She paused. 'I want to work for you for the next twenty-four hours.'

He continued ripping her clothes off with his eyes. 'Work for me?'

'I want you to employ me, in your department – for twenty-four hours.' She looked away, out of the window, then back at him.

'You want to shadow someone?' He was staring at her legs.

'Just for twenty-four hours?'

'Why?'

'I need an ID card, or a letter, that says I work here.'

He cradled his chin in his hand. 'What are you up to?'

Kate moved so more of her cleavage was showing. 'There's an exhumation this evening. I want to be there.'

'Sally Donaldson?' He took a packet of Rothman's cigarettes and a disposable lighter from the breast pocket of his shirt. 'I can't do it that quickly. We have very stringent procedures. I'd have to go through the channels – it would take a few days.'

Kate tossed her head back in a deliberate careless gesture. 'Oh, I thought you had the power, that you ran this outfit.' She shrugged and his face turned a little pink.

'I do run it,' he said testily. His eyes were drawn back down to her legs. They flicked up to her face, down to her legs then up again. He smirked knowingly. 'What would be in it for me?'

'An interview with you, perhaps.'

'How about over lunch?'

Their eyes met. Kate felt a heel. 'I'm sure I could arrange something,' she said, giving him more of a come-on smile than she had intended.

He picked up his phone, punched a number and leaned back. 'Brenda, who's doing the exhumation tonight? Judith Pickford? Put her on, will you?' He lit a cigarette. 'Judith, I've got a – ' – he hesitated – 'writer who's doing a study on exhumation. Would you mind taking her along with you this evening?' He inhaled deeply then blew the smoke up at the ceiling. 'No, don't worry. I'll give her a letter saying she's shadowing you. I don't think anyone'll bother too much.'

He hung up, then pressed another button and Kate heard a sharp buzz through the door. His secretary's voice crackled through the intercom.

'Hallo?'

'Could you do a quick letter for me,' he said, and winked at Kate.

# *Chapter Ten*

Harvey Swire joined the line of boys filing into the school hall. They were dressed either in navy blazers or the standard school herringbone jacket and grey flannel trousers. They wore black ties with a single coloured stripe repeated down the blade, differing colours denoting the different houses. The morning sun beat down intently; it was going to be a scorcher of a day.

Harvey had polished his shoes and put a clean handkerchief in his pocket. Everyone seemed more neatly turned out than usual, as if tidy dressing might help keep a tidy mind.

He stood next to Dacre. His chum's pong of sickly sweet Brut did not help the collywobbles in his stomach. The atmosphere was subdued, in spite of the bright warmth of the summer morning. Even Reckett was quiet and his swagger less pronounced.

'I bet we get a question on gravitation,' someone said behind Harvey.

'Not in chemistry.'

'No – God you're thick – in physics. You're taking physics, aren't you?'

Harvey went up the final stone step, through the narrow entrance and into the large oak-panelled school hall. It was filled with rows of desks, each with two pencils, a fresh white sheet of blotting paper and the chemistry exam paper face downwards. Irritating rays of sunlight streaked through the stained-glass windows, but at least it was cool in the room at the moment. At the end of the hall was the podium used for school plays and for speeches, and today for the invigilator's desk, on which stood a lonely-looking glass beaker and an unstoppered decanter of water.

The invigilator was a maths master whom Harvey did not know well, a stern, heavily bearded man with gaunt, slavic features. He was staring around the room with the air of a bird of prey guarding its roost.

Harvey found the desk that was to be his workplace for the next fortnight. H. Swire was typed on a white card and sellotaped on the top right-hand corner beside the inkwell. It was a newish desk in a light-coloured wood and had a depressingly pristine smell. He lifted the pencils and put them back down in a slightly different position. Animals mark territory, he thought. Around him feet scuffled, chairs scraped. The hands on the large clock on the wall said nine fifty-five. The invigilator checked his watch.

One of Harvey's pencils clattered to the floor. He leaned down to pick it up and saw to his annoyance that the point had broken off. His hands were shaking, felt clammy; the minute hand of the clock jerked to nine fifty-six. The invigilator was staring at him.

Harvey looked away, saw Dacre leaning back in his chair sniffing his index finger. Dacre's girlfriend, Anastasia; he had told everyone he wasn't going to wash his finger until he saw her again; it was the only part of his body he had not anointed with Brut.

There was a sudden complete hush in the room. The minute hand hung poised on nine fifty-nine. Harvey stared down at the blank sheet of paper; he could see the faint shadow of the black print on the reverse; it was double-folded with another sheet inside; five pages of questions.

Unconsciously, he picked a pencil up and began to chew it. And if it had been just a dream? He would know; in a moment. The questions still burned bright inside his mind and he could recall them in detail, in their exact order; he had written them down and memorised them and swotted up on the answers. If it was these questions, if it really was, then two fingers to Mr Stipple and to Mr Matthey and to everyone else.

The invigilator's voice cut the silence. 'You may turn your examination papers over.'

A rustle swept through the room. Harvey turned his over and hunched, hardly daring to look.

OXFORD AND CAMBRIDGE SCHOOLS EXAMINATION BOARD
General Certificate Examination
Advanced Level
CHEMISTRY I
Monday, 3 July, 1967. $2\frac{3}{4}$ hours
Answer *six* questions
Write on only one side of the paper

*1. What is meant by the terms 'atomic number, atomic weight and isotopes'?*

2. *Describe briefly the preparation of methyl cyanide (acetonitrile) starting from (a) methanol, and (b) ethanol.*

Harvey tried to staunch the grin that spread like spilt ink across his face. The invigilator was looking at him again. Harvey read on through the rest of the questions, but by the time he had got halfway through the third sheet, he knew he need not bother to read on any more.

He knew all the questions and all the answers.

# *Chapter Eleven*

*Monday, 22 October*

It was shortly after five p.m. and almost dark when Kate Hemingway drove the *News*'s Ford back up the narrow road to St Anne's church, following the environmental health officer's blue Renault.

Vehicles were parked on both sides, and they had to go some distance past the church before finding parking spaces. Kate locked the door of the car, turned up her mackintosh collar and pulled down the rain hat she had bought earlier, hoping it would obscure her face enough to avoid being recognised by the other reporters in the falling darkness. The wind was blowing and the steady insistent rain made visibility even worse.

'All right?' the environmental health officer, Judith Pickford, said. She was a quiet, serious woman in her mid-thirties, with short brown hair, neatly and warmly dressed and carrying a small umbrella. Kate sensed she was not best pleased at having a shadow foisted on her.

As they walked down the pavement, Kate was tense and nervous. Clammy perspiration built up inside her clothing. A generator roared on the back of a massive truck, and the pavement was strewn with electricity cables running through into the churchyard. There were at least a dozen reporters hanging around; two local radio station vans were parked outside, and a larger TVS television van. It must be a quiet news evening elsewhere, she thought.

The harsh white glow from the floodlights behind the screens backlit the church into a dark and forbidding shadow. Several members of the public were hanging around, watching the general activity, adding to the air of unreality about the whole thing. It felt like a movie set.

Kate hesitated. It had seemed a great idea an hour ago. Now she wasn't so sure. Did she really want to see what was in the coffin?

A short distance ahead the reporters she had been with earlier looked cold and wet, mostly huddled underneath umbrellas. A couple were sharing a mug of coffee from a Thermos. She ducked her head, trying to hide like a tortoise inside her collar. Three men wearing protective PVC suits, rubber boots and gloves appeared around the side of a van parked in front of the church, and walked in through the gate.

Kate and the environmental health officer followed them. She passed without being noticed Shane Hewitt from the *Argus*, and Rodney Sparrow from the *Mid-Sussex Times*, miserably biting a Mars bar, and felt a sudden pleasing sense of smugness and a surge of adrenalin.

She slipped her hand into her inside pocket and checked she still had Barry Liverstock's letter. 'Funeral directors,' she heard one of the men say to the same sour police constable from earlier. He nodded them through, barely glanced at Judith Pickford's pass and let Kate in without giving her a second glance.

As they crossed the cemetery, one badly positioned floodlight shone straight at them; in its beam the rain looked like metal spikes. The screens were tall close up, much taller than she had realised, made from green canvas, and they flapped precariously, tugging on their guy-ropes. The entrance was a simple overlap, and they followed the undertakers through it.

The area inside was large, a good thirty feet across, and it was even more like a movie or a stage set with the wet grass and the brilliant lighting from the overhead floods, and two rows of gravestones. Sally Donaldson's was obvious, the only recent grave, a rectangular mound of heaped newly turned earth with a wreath of roses on the top. There were several ropes laid out down one side, two spades and a pile of plastic sacks of ground lime. Out of one end of the earth stuck a metal pole with a wire running from it. She followed the wire across the sodden, boggy ground to a glum and solitary figure who was sitting on top of the large chipboard box she had seen carried in earlier, wearing headphones, his face buried in his hands. She thought he must be Sally Donaldson's husband.

The undertakers walked past him and joined a small group of people huddled together in the corner, having some sort of briefing. They were all in protective clothing except for a woman of about thirty in a dark coat and thick scarf, holding an umbrella.

The environmental health officer walked across and introduced herself to the group. Kate stood watching the solitary figure for a moment, the screens flapping and cracking around her in the wind, the generator roaring in the distance. He suddenly shouted hysterically at the huddled group: 'For God's sake! Why can't you hurry? All day it's taken. Surely to God it's dark enough now!' He dropped to his knees and began scrabbling at the earth with his bare hands, the wire trailing from his headphones. 'I'm not waiting any more. She's down there, damn you!' He raised his voice and shouted at the earth. 'Darling! Darling! It's OK, we're getting you out!'

The woman in the dark coat knelt beside him and put a steadying arm around him. She spoke, addressing the group, and Kate recognised her as the coroner's officer. She had seen her before at an inquest. 'I think it's dark enough.' The officer looked at the man beside her. 'Mr Donaldson, they're going to start now.'

Kevin Donaldson turned his face and Kate saw the twisted anguish in the white glare. He was crying hysterically. 'Please hurry. Oh God, please hurry. She's been down there since last Tuesday. Can you imagine how she feels?'

The woman eased him gently away. Two men removed the probe, picked up spades and began to dig sombrely and slowly, with no apparent urgency, as if they were digging a garden; sharp raw scrapes of the blades and the dull rattle of loose earth were joined by sobbing from the husband.

The environmental health officer came and stood beside her. Kate glanced at her impassive face. 'How many of these have you been to?'

'Four,' the woman said.

'Were they all like this?'

'No. They were old graves being moved.'

Kate looked uncomfortably at the husband, wishing there was something she could say, then up to see if she could spot Eddie Bix at his window, but the screens were too high. She watched the scene around her carefully, trying to memorise it for atmosphere.

A tall man trudged towards them. He took his rain-smeared glasses off and focussed with difficulty first on Kate then on Judith Pickford; the skin around his eyes was white and soft from years of wearing glasses. His voice was low and courteous. 'I'm Reg Burton, general manager of Dalby and Son, Funeral Directors. Are you relatives of the – er – deceased?'

'I'm from the Environmental Health Office,' Judith Pickford said. 'This lady's with me.'

'Are you with the EHO as well?' he asked Kate.

Kate hoped he would not be able to see her blushing. 'Yes, temporarily.'

'You're American?'

'Yes. Well, born there.'

'Whereabouts?'

'Boston.'

'I was there once. Nice city. Gas lights on a hill.'

'And a harbour full of tea.'

The man smiled. 'I don't think I caught your name.'

She felt increasingly clammy. 'Kate,' she said, proffering no surname and hoping he would not ask any further.

'Have you been monitoring the grave for sound long?' Judith Pickford said.

'It's a mining probe that unfortunately only arrived this morning. We had been promised a laser scanner, but that hasn't turned up.' He lowered his voice so Kevin Donaldson could not hear. 'Frankly I don't think we're going to find anything at all; this whole thing has got out of hand. If you ask me the vicar has got a lot to answer for.'

'Where is he?'

'I said we'd call him when the coffin is exposed.'

Reg Burton wandered back over to the group and said something to them. Kate saw a couple of heads turn towards them. The spikes of rain seemed to be lengthening, thickening; the wind had penetrated all her layers of clothing and was chilling her perspiration. She wrapped her arms around her body, wondering how much longer it would be, and kept a watchful eye on Kevin Donaldson, waiting for an excuse or an opportunity to talk to him, to get a good quote she could use later, and at the same time fighting the emotion within herself that made her want to be as respectful as possible and stay quietly in the background.

Kate asked Judith Pickford various questions, but the woman was noncommittal about her work and previous experience and Kate wondered if she had been warned not to say too much to her as she was press. After the men had been digging for three quarters of an hour, someone produced a Thermos and polystyrene cups of hot coffee were passed round. Kate took one. Its sweet warmth cheered her a little and she drank it quickly, then held on to the cup, not knowing where to put it.

Another man in a protective suit came into the area. He looked around then walked purposefully across to Sally Donaldson's husband, shook his hand and spoke to him. The husband stared dully at the ground, his eyes still streaming, his face mangled with grief. The man then walked over to the coroner's officer. 'Miss Willow?' he said, raising his voice above the wind and rain and distant roar of the generator.

'Yes.'

'I'm Dr Sells. Mrs Donaldson's general practitioner. Mr Donaldson asked me to be here.'

'It wasn't you who issued the death certificate?'

'No. I didn't see her after I had her admitted to hospital. Ghastly business, this.'

The coroner's officer nodded her head. Kate made a mental note of the doctor's name and moved a fraction closer to them, trying not to look obvious; they walked over to the furthest corner from Kevin Donaldson. Kate followed them, straining to hear their voices.

'She was pregnant, I understand,' the coroner's officer said.

'Six months. Healthy girl.' Dr Sells sounded bewildered. 'The obstetrician was concerned about her blood pressure, but he didn't think it was anything serious. A touch of pre-eclamptic toxaemia. Popped her into obstetrics just so they could keep an eye on her for a day or two.'

'She died of an epileptic seizure, didn't she?'

Dr Sells stared at the ground before replying. 'It's an effect of toxaemia. She wasn't an epileptic – at least she never showed any symptoms.'

'It can develop at any time, can't it?'

The doctor was hesitant. 'Well – it can.' He was about to say something further when a thud rang out. Kate felt the stiffening of tension among the people in the enclosure. All eyes focussed on the grave. The two diggers climbed out. The burly one with the shaggy hair nodded at Judith Pickford. 'Coffin's uncovered.'

Everyone surged forward a couple of paces, then slowed as if not wanting to step any closer to the edge. Everyone except Kevin Donaldson who pushed through to the front. 'Sally!' he shouted. 'Darling!' He was whimpering in short gulps, fell on to his knees and tried to lower himself into the grave. One of the undertakers and a grave digger gently restrained him. 'Let me!' he screamed. 'Let me!'

There was a lump in Kate's throat as she watched him, then she too stared into the dark trench. She could see the lid of the coffin through patches of earth and lumps of chalk.

'Mr Donaldson,' the coroner's officer said, 'please be patient for a few minutes more.'

The tall undertaker who had introduced himself to Kate earlier climbed down into the hole, knelt on top of the coffin and knocked loudly. 'Hallo?' he called, knocked again and put his ear to the lid. It was absurd, Kate thought.

He climbed back out. 'Can't hear anything.' He looked at two men. 'If you could sprinkle the lime, I'll fetch Reverend Comfort.'

The men cut open two of the sacks and began to shovel the off-white powder into the grave over the lid of the coffin. It filled the air around with an acrid smell. Whatever small dignity there had been in the proceedings so far vanished in the chalky powder and the smell.

Kevin Donaldson watched in stunned silence. Kate had to fight a desire to reach out and hold his hand, to say something to him, give him some reassurance.

Then the gravediggers lowered two lengths of rope, clambered down and stood on the lid of the coffin. They looped each rope through the coffin handles and climbed back out. They picked up the ends, took up the slack, nodded at each other, then heaved. Nothing happened.

'Shit,' the burly one said. 'She's sticking, Ron. Get one end free first.' He moved around, stood behind the other digger like two men in a tug of war team and heaved again. Still nothing happened.

'Have to dig her out some more,' said the pony-tailed one.

They dropped back down and dug for about ten minutes, then tried again. One of the undertakers joined them. There was a loud sucking sound from inside the grave. They pulled harder, the coffin moved very slightly. The three men released their grip and took another breather.

'Right, try again.'

They heaved again, more steadily. The end of the coffin rose. The two grave diggers held the strain and two undertakers took the other end. Slowly the mahogany coffin came up, trails of powder falling off. They swung it clear of the hole and lowered it on to the wet grass.

The sides were coated in wet mud and leaves. Rivulets of white lime ran down the sides. A worm wriggled, dying in the burning acid. The three brass handles glinted dully under the lights. Kate sensed everyone staring at the coffin. Kevin Donaldson kept his distance, scared now the moment of truth had arrived.

Judith Pickford stepped forwards, unfolding a printed document. She looked down at the brass plaque on the coffin lid, already washed clean of lime by the rain, and checked the name against her document. Then she nodded to the undertakers to proceed.

One of the undertakers moved forward with a screwdriver. He methodically undid each of the six screws that held the lid down, then inserted the blade under the lid, banged it in with his hand, then levered it. There was a scream that made Kate jump.

Then the lights went out.

Kate held her breath and her heart thumped. She heard the wind. Then a shout. A torch beam flashed on to the coffin. The lights flickered, came back on again.

There was another scream; another. Kate breathed out. Just wood rubbing against wood, she realised as the undertaker prised the corner up a fraction. Another undertaker helped him and as they began to raise the lid away from the coffin the lights flickered once more.

The stench hit her faintly at first. It smelled like the guts of a long-dead fish. For a moment Kate thought there must be a drain blocked somewhere. Then as they lifted the lid further the stench grew immediately stronger. Kate gagged, swallowed, struggling not to throw up. Others around her were reacting the same way.

The undertakers raised the lid further.

'Oh, Christ,' one of them said, staring into the coffin.

They paused, then lifted the lid clear and took a step back with it, shock widening their eyes. They seemed to freeze for a moment and Kate stared at the lid, which was blocking her view of the coffin. She stared in mounting horror, wandering whether it was just a trick of the light or whether there really were scratch marks running across the grain.

Then the lid moved away, out of her line of vision, and she could see straight down into the coffin. There were highlights and patches of darkness from the stark glare. Her legs weakened. Her stomach heaved. Her scalp shrank around her head; a shiver of revulsion and horror exploded through her. She tried to back away, bumped into someone, trod on their foot, backed further into the screen, felt it give, scrabbled with her hands, trying to push it away.

She could still see inside the coffin.

Sally Donaldson filled it, packed in between the white quilting and lace frill lining like a doll in a gift box. Her eyes were wide open, staring in despair and coated with a matt glaze. Her skin white, like wax, shone translucently in the glare of the lights. Her blonde hair was tousled and lay either side of her cheeks and her neck, like stuffing from a cushion that had split.

Her mouth was open, as if it had frozen in mid-scream. White, immaculate teeth protruded from her blue lips which had contracted into a hideous rictus grin. Her hands lay at her sides, the nails blackened. Stumpy, ugly nails as if she had bitten them, except for her thumbnails, which were long and elegant.

Her blue nightdress was hitched up over her crotch and had coppery stains, her knees were raised and her legs were as much apart as they could be. Lying between her thighs was a foetus, still attached to the umbilical cord, shrivelled and shiny like a skinned rat.

# *Chapter Twelve*

During the summer holidays Harvey Swire went to Spain with Dacre. They spent five weeks camping on the Costa Brava, travelling in the old Volkswagen Dacre's father had bought him.

Everyone said Harvey had changed since his accident. Dacre had not given it much thought at school because he had been busy swotting for his exams. But on holiday he had noticed his friend was quiet, moody, seemed to have no interest in getting drunk or stoned, or trying to pick up women.

He wondered whether it was because Harvey was missing Angie, or was worried about his exams. His old man was a hard bastard, and maybe Harvey was frightened of failing; he had not talked about them.

He remembered the first few weeks Harvey had been back at school after the accident, the strange remarks he had made about visions of God and of his dead mother; his vicious attack on Reckett. Then this wall of isolation he seemed to have put around himself.

It was a hot, listless late-August afternoon when Dacre dropped Harvey back home outside the large, swish, mock-Tudor house in Wimbledon. He sprang the bonnet catch on the VW, hauled Harvey's duffel bag, camping gear and plastic bag of duty free Scotch and cigarettes out of the dusty, untidy cavity, and shut the bonnet with a dull clang.

They were both tired and greasy and unkempt after a night sleeping rough on the Southampton ferry, and for once Dacre did not reek of Brut. They made vague plans to call each other; Dacre revved the engine and let the clutch out feeling as if he had dropped off a stranger to whom he had given a lift for a couple of miles rather than his best friend of the past five years.

Harvey walked up the short gravel drive in his grubby T-shirt, bell-bottom jeans and desert boots, past his mother's blue Mini which stood under a coating of dust, untouched since her death. His father would not allow the gardener to clean it nor Harvey to drive it; it sat there as if giving the illusion all was well, that his mother was in the house, preparing tea.

He rummaged in his duffel bag for his key and unlocked the heavy oak door. Without closing it, he hurried across to the hall table and stared down at the pewter tray where the post was always laid out by the housekeeper.

On the top was the morning paper, the *Telegraph*. He stared at the headline: 'BEATLES' MANAGER, EPSTEIN, IS FOUND DEAD.'

Harvey scanned the story, interested to discover how he had died, then moved the paper aside. Beneath was a pile of post, on the top of which was a postcard of a bullfight. It was the one he had dutifully sent his father three weeks ago, which must have arrived only this morning. He wondered if Angie had got her cards. He'd sent her three.

Tonight he intended to screw her.

He sifted through the post, but it was all for his father. Nothing for him. He dropped the bundle back into the tray with a loud slap, disappointed. The house was dark and empty and smelled of polish. His father was away in France and would not be back for another week and he was glad about that.

He checked through the letters again, in case he had missed it. Then he checked the postmarks, in case they had written to his father instead of himself. Nothing. Restlessly he tugged open the drawer in the centre of the table and saw a small, neat stack of mail addressed to him.

His heart thumped with nervous excitement as he flipped through it. There wasn't much: a couple of envelopes that looked like party invites; a bank statement; the September issue of *Paris Match* magazine. Then he saw it.

A small buff envelope, with his name and address typed and the postmark showing it had come from his school. It had already been opened.

Trembling, he tugged the white printed form out, and for a moment did not dare look at it. Then he turned it over. It said:

OXFORD AND CAMBRIDGE BOARD
*A Level Examination Results Certificate*
*Harvey Quentin Edward Swire*
*Biology: A*
*Chemistry: A*
*Physics: A*

He read the results again, then again.

Christ.

A twitchy grin of disbelief broke out on his face. The grin faded. He caught sight of his face in the mirror above the table, grimy and tanned, his hair a mess, too long, a wispy stubble around his chin and upper lip. His eyes flickered like candles in a draught. He looked back down at the typed sheet. Something cold was sluicing through him.

He was afraid.

Through in the kitchen he could hear the dull hum of the fridge; the grandfather clock ticked on the landing above.

Three As.

They wouldn't believe it.

Then he got angry. Bugger them. They didn't believe he had seen his mother. Well, they were right. Hallucination. Just a hallucination that he had seen his mother. Just a hallucination that he had seen the exam papers. The truth was that he was a brilliant pupil. No one else had had the intelligence to appreciate that.

He stared at his reflection for confirmation. His reflection looked away. He thumped the table angrily and the pewter tray echoed like a gong. He picked up his bags and his kit and started to climb the stairs.

Several times on holiday he had nearly told Dacre. Then each time he remembered the ribbing he had had from his friends when he told them how he had seen his accident. Once he had even started to tell him, but Dacre had spotted a girl he fancied and had swaggered across the disco floor to try to pick her up.

Angie had listened to what he had told her about his mother and had not laughed. She might understand. Except now it had happened, was real, he realised he could not tell her; could not tell anyone.

Three As. He had tried to think back to that night, lying in the dormitory, floating above his body the way he had floated when he had been hit on his bike. Once, after the exams were finished, he had retraced his steps, trying to see if he could have gone through his housemaster's private apartment unnoticed and out into the street. The doors had been locked and bolted, but it was easy to unlock them. The door to the masters' common room was locked, too; he had not been able to unlock it. Except, he knew, it might have been left unlocked on that one night. Might.

Must have been.

Must have sleepwalked there, seen the exam papers lying on a table. Reading them over Mr Stipple's shoulder had been a dream.

Must have been.

He worried that his answers in the exams had been too pat, too flawless, that he should have made some mistakes deliberately so he would not be suspected of having cheated. But they would have to prove he had cheated. He remembered the invigilator noticing him, walking up and down past his desk several times during those days, the creak of his shoes on the bare wooden floorboards. But he had not spoken to him, had not queried anything he was doing.

Because he had done nothing wrong.

He smirked, when he thought of their faces, the arrogant masters who told him he would have no chance of passing, Stipple the Nipple. Mr Matthey.

He wondered why his father had not tried to contact him when he'd opened the envelope, then realised his father did not have an address for him in Spain. He might have left a note, the bastard. Might have said something nice, congratulated him. Maybe he didn't believe the results. Too bad, he was going to have to believe them. They were all going to have to believe them.

His bedroom still had the 'DANGER – KEEP OUT' sign fixed to the door that he'd put there maybe ten years before. He went in, pleased to see it was the way he had left it, though a little tidier which was a good thing. He liked rooms to be tidy, liked everything to be dusted, even the places he could not see. Mrs Mannings, the housekeeper, understood; he had once threatened her with the sack when he was seven for not dusting on top of the wardrobe. If he was in a room that had not been properly cleaned he could feel the dirt attaching itself to him.

The room was his domain. It was a good size, with a worn red carpet that had once been in his parents' dining room, a washbasin and a window looking on to the rear garden and the neighbours behind. The walls were decorated with a cold, brown regency stripe paper his mother had had put up when he'd gone to Wesley, because she thought it looked grown-up. There was a damp stain on the ceiling the shape of a bat that had been there for as long as he could remember. Above his bed was a large black and white still of Janet Leigh in *Psycho*, her face frozen in shock, blood running down the tiles of the shower. The top left-hand corner of the poster had come unstuck and hung downwards.

By the window was a wooden table on which was a small microscope, several instruments, and the skeleton of a mouse with a tiny strip of fur still attached to its rib cage. One foot was in the air, as if the poison his father had put down years before had stopped it in its tracks. A row of shelves contained laboratory specimen jars of newts, frogs, mice, rats and beetles preserved in formalin. Another row contained his medical books, some he had bought in second-hand shops, others had been cast-outs from his father. *Gray's Anatomy. N. Kirkham's Pathology Today. Chambers Medical Dictionary. Cunningham's Manual for Dissection.*

In pride of place in the room, on top of his chest of drawers, was a rectangular block of glass containing five aborted human foetuses, curled as if they were still in the womb and stained with red dye to make them more visible. The smallest was an inch high and the largest four inches. It had been presented to his father some years before, and his father had eventually thrown it out. Harvey had retrieved it from the dustbin.

Death had always fascinated him. The drawers of his desk were full of newspaper and magazine pictures of death, many of them clipped from *Paris Match* which had the best pictures of death he had ever seen. His father thought he took it because he was trying to improve his French. Often they showed car crash victims lying as twisted and broken as the vehicles that entombed them. Sometimes a good murder victim.

One he liked to look at was a fat, elderly gangster in a suit with a waistcoat and watch chain, slumped over an uneaten meal in a ritzy restaurant. Blood trickled from the hole in his temple down into his wine glass, as if his head was a macabre decanter.

He wondered if Angie would be at home. Before going to Spain he had been making progress. Outside in the garden at a party she'd let him feel both her breasts. And pressed her crotch against him, rubbed herself against his hardness. He had never managed to find out the truth about Reckett. Whether Reckett had really screwed her whilst he'd been in hospital. He did not believe it, did not believe she could have made it with an ugly slob like Reckett and still been prim with himself.

He went through into his parents' bedroom, a large pastel-pink room with walnut furniture and a view on to the garden and the swimming pool. It was stifling with the windows shut. A colour photograph of his mother sat on the dressing table; she was laughing and the light had caught her eyes and he stared at it sadly and wondered.

*Darling, God is very unhappy with you.*

Like a slap.

*She doesn't ever want to see you again.*

Slap.

He could smell her perfume in the room rising from the bedclothes, from the glass jars on her dressing table. He went across to the walnut wardrobe, opened the door, pulled out a drawer and pressed his face down into a pile of her jumpers. He felt the soft warmth of the cashmere and smelled the deep, rich scents of her body.

If he could have talked to her more.

If he had struggled harder, fought harder.

*You have to go back!*

He buried his face further in the drawer, closed his eyes tightly, felt the wool grow damp with his tears, and rocked backwards and forwards, a long slow whine escaping between his clenched teeth like steam from a kettle.

Then he shut the drawer, sat down on the deep, soft bed and composed himself. He picked up the phone and dialled Angie's number. Angie's mother answered, sounding pleased to hear him as she always did, and went to fetch Angie.

'Harvey?' Angie's voice sounded frosty, as if he had interrupted her from something important and it knocked the steam out of him because he had been expecting her to sound pleased.

'I'm back,' he said.

'Oh, right.' She hesitated. 'Great.'

There was a silence. 'This afternoon,' he said.

Another silence. 'I thought you weren't coming back until next week.'

'We ran short of dough.' Another silence. 'And I really wanted to see you.' He bit his lip and wished he hadn't said that.

'Did you have a nice time?' She sounded as if she was in a hurry.

'Yes. Cool. Really groovy.'

'Great,' she said.

'I got my exam results.'

'Oh, right.'

Something was very strange in her voice. The harder he tried to get her to reciprocate some enthusiasm, the more distant she became. 'I – I did better than I'd thought.'

Silence.

'I thought we could maybe – you know – celebrate?'

There was no response. He heard the click of a cigarette lighter and the sound of Angie inhaling. He thought of her wavy blonde hair and her soft skin and her snub nose and her freckles and her long, tanned legs sticking out of her miniskirt or hot pants, and large, cool breasts which he had now touched, caressed. 'How about tonight?' he said.

'No, I can't,' she said. 'I have to wash my hair.'

'Oh. My father's away,' he said lamely. 'I have the house, you know. I – ' His voice tailed away. 'How about tomorrow?'

'It's Mummy's birthday tomorrow. We're having a family dinner.'

He hesitated. 'How about Thursday or Friday?'

'I think I might be going away for the weekend, sailing.'

'I see.' He stared at his reflection in the dressing table mirror. 'I thought . . . while I had the house – '

'I'll give you a call when I get back, some time,' she said.

'What's the matter? Before I went you said you were going to really miss me.'

'I don't know.' There was a coldness in her voice he had never heard before. 'I think you've become really weird lately.'

'Weird?'

'Uh huh. Freaky.'

'What you mean?'

'This stuff about your mother. You really freaked me with it.'

'I – I thought you were interested.'

'For five or ten minutes. Not all the time.'

'Can't I see you and talk about it?'

'About what?'

He tried to think clearly. 'Us.'

'I'll call you next week, OK?'

She was gone.

He glared at the dead receiver. At his reflection again; then he hung up. 'Bitch,' he mouthed. 'Cow.' He felt the anger rising, stinging, and stood up, kicked the side of the bed, kicked the seat in front of him, sending it banging into the dressing table. His mother's photograph fell off on to the carpet. A silver hairbrush fell on top of it, smashing the glass. He stomped out of the room and down the corridor.

In his own room he opened the middle drawer of his old chest and removed a couple of pullovers that were covering a tobacco tin. He prised the lid off, took out a tiny block of hash in silver foil, an orange packet of Rizzla cigarette papers and a half-empty packet of dry tobacco.

Later, much later, he lay on his bed in the glow of the single red light bulb in the paper globe above him, a Pink Floyd record playing, and smoked the fourth joint of the evening down to the butt. As he crushed it out in the ashtray the room swayed, and for a moment he thought he was on the ferry coming back from Spain.

The room pitched. He waited to fall back against the springs of the bed, but instead he carried on rising, floating now, floating out of his body, out of his sadness and confusion and anger.

Below in the red haze he could see his body, still wearing his desert boots, slumped on the bed, arm out by the ashtray. He watched for a moment. Could see everything intensely clearly. There was dust on top of the lamp shade and he made a mental note to tell Mrs Mannings.

A voice whispered in his ear: 'Everyone's humping her.'

He turned; there was nothing but the dark walls of his room, the red glow of the light bulb, the motionless shadows, smoke from the dying butt of the joint in the ashtray rising like a trickle of water falling the wrong way.

'Everyone's humping her, Harve.'

'She's a great lay!'

'Know what she likes? She likes me putting it in her ear!'

Dark shapes danced on his walls; shadows of people who were rocking backwards and forwards with laughter. Shadows of his classmates and shadows of others, strangers.

He could hear the laughter, guffaws, sniggers echoing around him through the darkness. Shadows bobbing on all the walls now, surrounding him.

The laughter was getting louder. He tried to back away. Shadows filled the room, blotting out the red light. He felt cold, icy, felt the walls of the tunnel sucking, drawing him in.

'She doesn't ever want to see you again!'

'Who?' he screamed.

'Your mother,' said a voice.

'Angie,' said another.

He was spinning, swirling, hurtling towards a pinprick of light. 'Let me back. Leave me alone!' he shouted, but no sound came out.

Then he heard voices, his schoolmates chatting, loud but faintly muffled as if he were standing outside a door.

'Everyone's humping her,' Walls Minor said shrilly.

'Harvey hasn't worked out what his prick's for yet,' said Horstead.

There was a roar of laughter.

'Harvey should try sticking it in her ear,' said Reckett. 'Take them by surprise. They love it.'

The pinprick of light ahead was getting larger, coming closer. He was slowing down.

'It's true from what I hear,' said Powell. 'Everyone's banging her except Harvey. Hey, Harvey, why don't you go round there, grab her and bang her, like anyone else?'

'Bang her, Harve!' Dacre said.

'Yeah, shaft the pants off her,' Horstead shouted.

'Put it in her ear first,' said Reckett.

'Bang her!' squealed Walls Minor.

'Bang the bitch!' said Powell.

The light was enveloping him, but it was murky, diffused, too dark to see clearly for a moment. He was floating up on the ceiling of a room. But it was not his room.

The light brightened. He could see a Simon and Garfunkel poster on the wall, a neatly made bed with several soft toys on it, and jeans, a T-shirt, knickers and a bra strewn untidily on the quilted counterpane. A bottle of cologne lay uncapped on a dressing table. A wardrobe door hung open.

Angie's room.

Angie's room in her parents' house in Barnes.

Her shoes and slippers lay untidily on the shag carpet.

The bitch had gone out.

# *Chapter Thirteen*

*Monday, 22 October*

The rain fell on to the white satin frill that lined Sally Donaldson's coffin, making tiny dark patches. It fell on the dead woman's face, too, each drop sliding slowly like melting wax.

In the eerie silence the small knot of people inside the canvas screens stood frozen, as motionless as the woman in the coffin. Goosepimples rippled down Kate Hemingway's neck, and convulsions of shock spread through her body as if a dam containing them had burst.

In the distance the generator rumbled on and around her the canvas flapped in the wind like a backing sail. Dr Sells moved forwards, glancing around for approval, but no one was capable of shaking their head. He went through the motions of checking Sally Donaldson for signs of life.

Kate watched as the grotesque charade was acted out. Kevin Donaldson stood with his head bowed and his face blindfolded by his hands. The girl in the coffin could have been a waxwork, a hideous waxwork; some bizarre tableau from another century.

Kate closed her eyes but could still see her. She turned her head, as if looking in a different direction might make the image that burned through her skull go away; but she could see the tiny baby, the mess of the blood clot, the umbilical cord.

The doctor parted the front of Sally Donaldson's blue nightdress and listened to her chest with his stethoscope; he checked her pulse, stared into her eyes with a small torch, then tickled the back of her throat with a flat probe. Kate wondered how he managed to avoid gagging from the smell that she was finding unbearable several feet away.

The doctor carefully checked the foetus, too, then turned finally towards Kevin Donaldson. He did not need to make any gesture. Instead he laid a hand on his shoulder and tried to lead him away.

The coroner's officer, the environmental health officer and the funeral director had a brief discussion which Kate could not hear. The funeral director spoke to his colleagues and they replaced the lid, without screwing it shut, lifted the coffin into the chipboard box, swung the hinged top shut and bolted it. Then they hoisted it on to their shoulders and began walking carefully on the slippery mud out through the screens and the churchyard to the street.

'That's it,' Judith Pickford said to Kate.

'Can I buy you a drink?' Kate asked.

'Thank you, but I have to get home. It's my husband's birthday.' She turned and walked off.

Kate followed. Ahead she could see the pack of reporters besieging the police spokesman with questions. She kept her head down as she passed through them. Flashbulbs strobed the wet haze of the sky.

'Mr Falk, can you tell us whether Mrs Donaldson is alive or dead?'

The spokesman's slick hair was matted over his forehead by the rain, and his new raincoat had lost its sharp creases. 'I can confirm that she is dead.'

'Was she alive when she was buried?'

'The coroner's officer attended the exhumation. She will be making a report to the coroner who will decide whether a post mortem is required.'

Kate heard a voice she recognised, Shane Hewitt from the *Evening Argus*. 'Can you tell us what condition the corpse was in?'

'I'm sorry, I was not present.'

'Mrs Donaldson's husband came by looking very distressed,' the *Argus* reporter continued insistently. 'Can you explain that?'

'How would anyone feel to see their husband or wife exhumed?' Falk said.

'Are you saying she was definitely not buried alive?' asked Rodney Sparrow of the *Mid-Sussex Times*.

'Was there anything in the coffin, Mr Falk?' Kate heard Gail Cohen from Radio Sussex ask.

'Mr Falk, could you tell us whether there is any evidence the woman had been buried alive from what you have seen so far?'

'Mr Falk, could you describe to us exactly what is in the coffin?' said Gail Cohen.

'I wasn't present.'

'If there is nothing suspicious, why is the coffin being removed?' asked Shane Hewitt.

'I cannot make any further statements or comments at this time. There will be an announcement in the morning after the coroner's decision. All right? Let's go home now, shall we?'

Dissatisfied, the pack turned on the undertakers carrying the coffin.

Kate found Shane Hewitt walking alongside her, trying to get her to say something, and she went bright red, terrified he was going to recognise her in spite of the darkness and her hat pulled down over her face. She did not dare speak because he would know her immediately from her accent; she shook her head and turned away.

Clear of the pack, she walked up the pavement towards the car. A howl was hammering inside her stomach.

Not real; not real; tell me it wasn't real, someone, please.

She stopped, dropped her head and supported herself against a brick wall, feeling the tears streaming down her cheek and the strength draining out.

Christ, pull yourself together, girl. You saw it. Scoop. You got it, you got it. You got what you wanted.

She felt the damp brick against her cheek and she pressed against it as if it were the only thing she trusted in the world, and saw Sally Donaldson's face again, eyes open, staring.

Staring at her.

The floodlights in the churchyard went out. She heard an engine start up and smelled warm diesel fumes. Her stomach heaved. Several reporters hurried past her, heading for the pub. The television crew and the radio crews were packing up their gear. It was over, they assumed.

They were wrong, Kate thought grimly, unlocking the car door. She switched on the engine and the heater and waited for Eddie Bix.

After a couple of minutes the photographer climbed in, slamming the door behind him. 'Jesus, filthy night. You must be soaked. Been out there all that time?'

She nodded.

'Can I buy you a drink?' He checked one of his cameras' lens cap.

'Thanks,' she said dully. 'But I have to get on. I want to write the piece tonight.'

'Not much to say, is there? Did Falk give anything away?'

She pulled out of the parking space into the melee of departing traffic, not sure she wanted to talk about it at the moment. 'How did you get on?' she asked.

'I couldn't see much, and that woman kept coming in wanting to talk. I think she fancied me or something.'

Kate drove back to the paper. She felt scared and immensely weary. Eddie offered to put the car away. She got out in the dark side street and went through the staff door of the *News* into the dingy lobby.

The night security man looked up from behind his metal grille. 'Evening, Miss Hemingway. Damp one,' he said in a gruff voice, followed by a fit of coughing. 'Going to be working late?'

'An hour or so.'

'I'll be off at eleven; lock up, will you, if you're the last one?'

'Sure,' she said, barely registering his remark, and walked up the stone steps. Behind her she heard another fit of coughing which faded into the echo of her own footsteps.

The landing above her was dark. As she pressed the wall switch a fluorescent buzzed, fizzed, shot a streak of light down the corridor ahead for a few seconds, went out, came back on again more steadily.

She went past the windows of the accounts department, the desks empty, computers switched off, the screens blank; the rooms were dark, filled with silhouettes of filing cabinets and desks and VDU screens. Her own shadow moved silently along the wall beside her.

The aroma of greasy food that lingered on the landing at the top of the stairs in the daytime had been replaced with the smell of lavatory disinfectant and damp mops. She went past the notice boards, and pushed open the double doors into the newsroom.

It was dark and silent. The doors swung back behind her with a squeak and a clunk. Inky pools of shadow lay between the metallic shafts of light that pierced the windows from the street lamps outside. A stark white flash bounced off the ceiling from the headlamps of a passing car. The room smelled of carpet and newsprint, tobacco smoke and cleaning fluid; there was a background hiss from the heating system which stayed on all night.

A sudden, sharp whir and a clatter startled her. A fax machine, its green light glowing in the distant gloom, began spewing out paper. Kate put her hand on the wall panel and pressed a couple of switches. Half a dozen strip lights flickered and came on, including the one above her desk.

The place looked the way it always did at night, as if it had been abandoned in a panic following a fire alert or a bomb scare.

Kate slumped wearily down into her swivel chair and leaned back, hugging her coat around her body. Rain water trickled down the back of her neck. Shivering, she stared at her blank screen. Sally Donaldson's glazed eyes stared back.

The fax machine gave a beep and was silent.

Calm down.

A taxi accelerated down the street below. Her heart raced like its engine, knocking hard. It was unusually quiet tonight. Normally there were one or two others around, often Howard Michael, the suave movie critic, working on reviews, and a copy taker, and there was a reporter always on duty until eleven who was probably out at the moment covering something.

She stood up, walked back out through the doors, across the hallway and into the empty library, and switched on the lights. All six editions of today's paper lay on top of a metal cabinet, ready for filing. She removed the top five editions, then perked up a fraction as she saw the headlines of the first edition of the day, which came out at around eleven o'clock: 'EX-MAYORESS DEFIES MUGGERS.'

It was her story. She had forgotten that Geoff Fox the news editor had told her she was getting the front page splash. And a byline. She saw her name inset: 'Kate Hemingway. Staff Reporter.' She flicked through the rest of the paper, scanning each page. Nothing else of hers in it. Her mayoress story stayed on the front page for the midday edition, but was reduced from the splash to a secondary headline, and her byline had gone. By the sixth edition, the mugged mayoress had shifted to page three.

Kate found her fourteen-line story on the exhumation on page five of the midday edition. It remained unchanged until the fourth edition when it was modified slightly and expanded to eighteen lines. By the final edition it had grown to two columns and there was a photograph of Sally Donaldson on her wedding day. A pretty girl with long fair hair who looked out at the world with a confident 'life's good to me' expression.

Kate shuddered as she thought about what she had seen in the coffin and another shock wave of revulsion stormed through her. She went back to her desk, sat down and switched on her VDU screen. She tapped the command keys, then waited whilst the screen went blank and a clear page one appeared.

She rummaged her fingers through her hair and squeezed the sides of her head. Tears were running down her cheek and she wiped them with the sleeve of her jacket. Her breathing was fast and she was gulping back sobs. The screen blurred; she hit a key, the wrong one, started with a lower case *v* instead of an upper case *B*, and deleted it. Her fingers were numb with cold, numb with shock, like her brain.

The light above her buzzed like a bluebottle. She typed the first line of her story, deleted it, typed it again. She closed her eyes and tried to clear her mind, but the delete key inside her head refused to move. Just another story, she thought, gritting her teeth and attacking the keys; that's all. Just another story.

She finished it quickly, corrected it, then filed it through to the news desk, and followed it with a memo to the news editor: 'Got in there. Saw it all myself.'

She stood up, drained, switched off her machine and went home. In her flat, she poured herself a large neat Scotch and ran a hot bath. She had no appetite and no energy to cook. She heated up some tinned tomato soup, made a piece of toast, then curled up on the sofa in her dressing gown in front of the television.

Later in bed she slept with the light on for the first time since she was a child.

# *Chapter Fourteen*

Angie's laughter carried through the night as clearly as breaking glass.

She was laughing at him.

Harvey Swire stared down at her empty room. Bitch. The laughter was coming from some way off, beyond the rooftops across the street. He felt himself moving, across the room, out through the window, out into the dark night; heard the laughter again, reeling him in.

Reeling him over the rooftops of the houses on the other side of the street. Below he could see a swimming pool shimmering with its underwater lights, could hear conversation, laughter, the sound of a spoon clinking against a saucer.

He slid across more rooftops, another street, moving towards it, towards the laughter. Below him was a cul-de-sac he recognised. At the end was a gate that was always open and a rough track on to the common. He could see the track clearly, followed it round a small electricity sub-station and on across the scrub of the common into the trees. Another even rougher track forked right and down into a small clearing. It was where he always brought Angie after a night out, before dropping her home.

In the distance he could see a faint light; then he realised it wasn't in the distance at all, but only a hundred yards or so ahead, the weak yellow light from a car's interior. The light went out. He heard another giggle.

Music was playing tinnily through a car speaker. It faded into crackle; voices; more music; the jingle of a commercial; more crackle; a radio being tuned. Music again, clearer now, the Beach Boys singing 'Then I Kissed Her'. He felt the unease growing inside him; and anger growing with it. The giggle again.

'Tim! No! God, your hands are so cold! Ow, yes!'

A murmur.

As he sank down towards the car he heard the tearing of foil.

'I'll put it on,' Angie said. 'I like putting it on.'

The car was a large, shiny Rover. Angie and a boy he hadn't seen before were sprawled across the rear seat. The front seats were right forward, their backrests kicked down almost flat. The boy's black hair, in a Beatle cut, flopped over his forehead. His trousers and Y-fronts were round his ankles. Angie's dress was half off, hitched up underneath her breasts which bulged out over the top. They were bigger than he had ever realised, her nipples red, hard, pointing straight ahead. Her knickers were off and as she kneeled he could see up her bare legs into the downy blonde triangle, and the pink lips of her vagina.

She held the boy's erect penis in one hand, a huge penis. Harvey was surprised by its size. With her free hand, in a movement that was too practised for Harvey's liking, she placed a pink Durex over the end, leaving the teat well clear. Slowly, sensuously, she unrolled it down the shaft, playing it up and down gently as she went.

'Careful,' the boy said. 'You'll make me come.'

Anger twisted like a knife inside Harvey. 'Cow,' he wanted to shout out. The anger grew, pulsed through him, made him giddy. The light was fading. 'Bitch!' he yelled but no sound came out. Nothing. Could see nothing.

Then suddenly he was on the ceiling of his own bedroom, staring down at himself lying on his bed, still clothed, still in his desert boots.

Christ I'm stoned, he thought.

He tried to sink down, to get back into his body, but unseen hands held him firmly, relentlessly, pinioning him to the ceiling. Beneath him he saw his body sit up, saw himself rub his eyes, run both hands through his hair. He tried to sink down, to get back into his body again, but he could not; the hands held him up.

Curious and afraid he watched himself get out of bed, go across to the basin, run the cold tap and slosh water on his face. He could feel nothing. He struggled again. Let me back, he murmured. The dread inside darkened further. He was scared suddenly, scared he would be pulled up into the ceiling and the atoms and molecules would close around him, and he would be there for ever.

He watched himself go out of the bedroom, along the landing and down the stairs. Staying above his body he saw himself open the left-hand drawer in the hall table, lift out a set of car keys, pick up his house keys and go out of the front door.

No. Don't do that.

Helplessly he watched himself walk down the drive towards his mother's Mini, unlock the door and climb in, push the seat back, switch the ignition on and pull the choke out.

Don't start. Please don't start. Jesus. The tyres were soft, sagging under the rims. Don't start.

The engine turned over weakly; the battery, nearly flat, faded and there was a dull whine. He saw himself try again and there was a sharp clicking sound. He waited, then tried once more. The engine turned once and fired unevenly. He revved it hard; there was a staccato crackle, several backfires; black oily smoke came out of the exhaust. Then he reversed out of the drive on to the road and put the lights on.

Harvey watched, clenched in frustration. Go back. Go back. The Mini accelerated down the road, then braked sharply at the junction with the main road, slewing out to the right on the soft tyres. It pulled out recklessly, swerving as the front driving wheels momentarily lost their grip and a truck hooted angrily, braking sharply, then overtaking it.

Helpless, he watched the car below him driving crazily fast, then turn off sharply into a side road. It skidded across the dry tarmac and missed a line of parked cars on the other side of the road by inches.

Slow down, idiot. For God's sake.

The Mini shot straight across an intersection. He tried to force himself down, into the car, into his body; but he could not close the gap. He floated above it through the darkness; he could hear the roar of the engine below, the howl of the wind around the car, the squeal of its tyres, but he could feel no sensation of speed himself. Dreaming, only dreaming, going to wake up in a minute.

A car was pulling out of a junction ahead. Slow down, for God's sake, slow down. Instead the Mini was accelerating. It came round the corner, the other car broadside across. Harvey heard the scream of the braking tyres, watched the Mini snaking crazily across the road, swerving to the right-hand pavement then the left. It missed the rear of the car by inches, swerved back across, out of control, came into a bend. The wheels locked, the car went straight on, towards the pavement, towards a tree.

There was a tremendous metallic clang and smashing glass as the passenger-side front wing scraped along the side of the tree and the car slewed, and stopped.

Godfathers.

He looked down at the car. One headlight shone into a beech hedge, the other had gone out; the engine was still running. Lights came on in a house beyond the hedge. There was a howl of tortured metal as he tried to reverse and he got out, went round to the front, braced himself and tugged hard on the crumpled wing. He tugged again, then again, each time the metal giving a piercing creak. Then he got back in the car, reversed, and this time the wheel was clear.

Someone was calling out and running across the garden.

He watched himself back out on to the road and accelerate off, the single headlamp picking out the road ahead like a motorcycle.

He wondered how he was going to explain the damage to his father. Maybe he could get it repaired somewhere before he saw it.

Wake up. For God's sake, wake up.

The Mini raced down the cul-de-sac and on to the bumpy track across the common. It forked right towards the woods and slowed down. The red reflectors shone ahead in the weak beam of the Mini's headlight. He saw himself pull the Mini over to the side, kill the lights and switch off the engine, then get out of the car.

He watched his body start to walk up the track. Panic caught him, swept him like flotsam in a flood stream. No. Stop. Don't! He tried to get back in his body again, threw himself down towards it; but the unseen hands held him relentlessly. Stop, he mouthed. Stop.

Horrified, he watched himself walk on up the track, with a determined stride, his desert boots almost silent apart from the odd loose stone he kicked and which rolled off the camber of the track with a soft crunch.

'In the Midnight Hour' was playing on the car radio; Wilson Pickett's voice echoed through the trees, growing louder as he approached. He stopped and waited for a few moments, a short distance from the car.

Go back.

Through the window he could see a faint red glow; it brightened, then faded. He smelled the sharp, rubbery reek of hash. There was giggling from inside the car, drowning the radio for a moment.

'It was! It was headlights,' Angie said.

'Only another couple like us,' said a voice Harvey did not recognise.

Angie giggled again.

Harvey walked closer. He could see through the Rover's window now. They were curled up on the back seat. Angie's dress was a slack heap around her waist and her naked breasts rested against the boy's chest. The boy toked heavily on the joint, the air hissing into his mouth, then held it to Angie's lips.

She drew on it, then they pressed their mouths together and exhaled into each other.

Harvey watched his body wrench open the car door, and suddenly he felt pleased.

As the boy twisted round, Harvey leaned in, grabbed the boy by the hair and punched him in the side of the face. Angie screamed. He pulled the boy out, dragged him out by his legs, the Y-fronts still round his ankles. The boy thumped face down on the grass, cowering, lashing out, kicking with his jammed legs.

'What are you doing with my girl, you creep!' Harvey yelled, heaving him to his feet, throwing him against the car, punching him in the face again; then he grabbed the boy's balls in his hand and began to squeeze. The boy screamed. The Durex hung limp and saggy from the end of his penis, the small teat filled with fluid. He squeezed harder.

The boy jerked, screamed, tore at Harvey with his fingers, pushed them into Harvey's eyes, but Harvey did not care. As he floated a short way above, watching, he could feel no pain, none at all. He squeezed harder, crushing the slimy, greasy, hairy scrotum tight around the spongy things inside and the boy wriggled, howled like a demented animal, gasping, panting. Harvey saw himself grinning as the boy threw himself back against the car, jerking as if he were plugged into an electrical socket, screeching, pleading; vomit exploded from his mouth, showering Harvey.

Harvey kneed him in the groin in disgust, then again. The boy doubled up. Harvey kicked a door panel of the car in.

'No, don't!' the boy whimpered. 'Me dad's car. Don't kick the car.'

Harvey grabbed the boy by the shoulders and head butted him in the face. The boy crumpled in a heap on the ground.

Angie was trying to get out of the car, screaming at him, 'Harvey, leave him, don't hurt him, Oh God, Harvey, leave him!'

Harvey saw his body grab her throat, push her back into the car, and climb in on top of her, pinioning her down, pressing her back against the seat. He could feel the naked flesh of her shoulders, the soft firmness of her breasts. She was struggling, kicking out at him, shouting at him. He tore at his belt, pulled open his trousers. She wriggled like a mad thing beneath him.

'No, Harvey. Get off, you bastard.'

His zip stuck; he tugged at it.

'Harvey, get off me!' she screamed, fuming. 'Tim, help me!'

The zip opened with a tearing sound. He struggled with the catch on his trousers, holding her down, drowning her screams by putting his mouth over hers and kissing her, pressing his tongue deep in her mouth. She broke free and shouted at him: 'Get off, Harvey.'

He pulled his underpants down, held his hard penis, directed it forwards, felt her slimy wetness, felt the soft flesh of her thighs, the raw scratchiness of her pubic hairs. He thrust in.

'Harvey!' she screamed. 'No. No. Tim, help me! Tim! Help!' She dug her fingers into Harvey's back. He felt them gouging into the flesh, but there was no pain. He could see them from above, digging right in, drawing blood, scoring down under his shirt. He could see his own buttocks thrusting.

Could feel himself deep inside her now.

Could see the look of shock in her eyes.

Could feel himself climaxing. Exploding into her. He clutched her tightly, pulling her face towards him, pressing her cheek against his as convulsions pulsed through him.

Then it stopped. He felt himself slackening inside her. She had stopped resisting now. His back hurt. He smelled her perfume; the same one she always wore, subtle, tangy. He kissed her cheek tenderly. Smelt the rich leather hide of the seats. Felt his penis beginning to slide out.

Then he realised.

He was no longer watching himself from a distance. He was back in his body. In the car. His penis was inside her.

He closed his eyes in horror. Violence. Reckett said girls like to be treated rough. She was quiet, breathing gently; blinking, he felt the tickle of her eyelash on his cheek. She was OK. That's what he should have done all along. Two years ago. He smelled vomit. The boy's vomit that was spattered over him. He kissed her again and held her tighter. 'Love you, Angie,' he said.

She was crying.

'I love you, Angie.'

'Get out.' Her voice was firm, terse.

He kissed her cheek once more.

'Get out.'

'I love you.'

The suddenness of her movement surprised him as she sat up, pushing his head sharply back. 'Get out.' Her voice was deep with hatred. She gripped his neck, shook it hard the way she might have shaken a tree to make the fruit fall. 'Get out. Get out. *Get out!*' Her teeth were clenched; tears were rolling down her cheeks.

He backed away, out of the car, dazed. This is a dream, he thought. I didn't do this; imagining it; going to wake up in a minute. He pulled up his underpants and trousers, stepped back, trod on something soft and nearly fell. It was the boy, stirring, blood all over his mouth, looking up at him with fearful eyes. He stared back into the car, at Angie. Hatred stared back.

He turned away, and walked back towards the car, slouching as if the rods that supported him had collapsed and he was held upright only by his own sagging compacted flesh.

# *Chapter Fifteen*

*Tuesday, 23 October*

She awoke in pitch darkness, drenched in perspiration. Fear pulsed through her. Her room was never this dark; never this silent.

She groped with her right hand for the bedside table, but it hit something soft, satiny. A cushion wedged down the side of the bed, she thought, puzzled, running her hand down it. She could feel quilting and something frilly. Her shoulders were wedged tight and she smelled unfamiliar smells of newly sawn timber and fresh cloth.

The headboard, she realised with a sense of relief; she must have turned sideways in the bed in her sleep. But she didn't have a headboard. She tried to swing herself back, but she could not move. The quilted satin was all around her. It pressed against her right elbow and she pushed back. Nothing yielded.

She tried to shift her position and her face banged into something hard inches above her head. Both her arms were hemmed in; her legs, too; there was barely room to part them. She was cocooned in darkness. Hot darkness.

God it's hot.

She breathed deeply, but the air came into her lungs slowly and she had to draw hard to get enough.

She tried to work out where she was. In a strange hotel? No. She had gone to bed at home – surely – ? The walls seemed to be squeezing in on her and she elbowed them away, irritated, tried to sit up, hit her face, sank back down.

Kick the bedclothes off to get cool; she wriggled her legs, but there were no bedclothes, just something light, a single sheet that had come untucked. She tried to find the light switch again; tried more determinedly. Smooth satin; around her, below her. Like being locked inside a sofa.

Where am I? 'Hallo?' she called. 'Hallo?' Her voice sounded small.

Her head was muzzy with the heat and the shortage of air and she had to fight hard for the next breath.

Car accident; the car had crashed on the way home and she was trapped.

Blind. I've gone blind. She screamed as a terrible panic ripped through her. 'Help! Someone! Help me!' Her knees drummed against the padding. She pummelled with her fists. 'Help me!'

Then she sank back, exhausted, gulping at the air, fighting to suck it in. It was like being in a vacuum; she could almost feel the satin quilting being sucked in around her as she breathed. She pummelled with her fists again, screamed out, kicked, heaved herself up and down, twisted, turned until she did not know which way up she was facing.

'Help!' she cried. She tore at the satin with her nails, felt a tiny strip come away, got her fingers inside and tugged. She heard a rip, felt something cool flop against her face, breathed in fluff and sneezed. She sat up, cracking her head, and cried out in pain.

She dug her hands through the fluff, tugging it away, then reached something bare and hard and slightly rough. Wood. She knocked on it with her knuckles; drummed against it until it was too painful to knock any more and she rested her knuckles and lay back and fought for another lungful of air.

The walls were pressing in. It was getting smaller; she was being squeezed, crushed. 'Hallo?' she cried out. 'Help me! Someone help me!'

Then suddenly the air was cool; she could breathe great gulps of it into her lungs, and see light so bright it was dazzling her. She heard the click of a door, footsteps on the landing outside; her neighbour in the flat across the corridor going to work. Six forty; he always left at six forty.

Jesus.

Kate sat up. Fear surged through her. Her bedclothes had slipped to the floor. She closed her eyes, then opened them again, scared to go back to sleep, and lay motionless for a few moments, collecting her thoughts, ignoring the cold draught that eddied around her, feeling more tired than before she had gone to bed. The light burned above her head; the light she had kept on all night.

She slid her feet on to the shag carpet; they felt as if they were packed in ice. The whole of her felt cold. She stood up, shivering, and made her way to the bathroom and turned on the shower.

The hot water on her body and the scent of the balsam conditioner in her hair could not melt away the horror. She saw Sally Donaldson's face with the hideous rictus grin. She had seen death before, too many times to count; car crash victims and fire victims, a tramp who froze to death in a park, and a floater who was hauled out of the sea so bloated and swollen that his belly burst open and his innards tumbled out when he hit the deck rail of the boat.

But nothing had got to her the way last night had.

Buried alive.

Gave birth.

How long had she been alive for down there? What had gone through her mind? Who had certified her dead? Who the hell had been responsible?

She went through to the kitchenette and switched on the kettle. She poured some muesli into a bowl and diced a banana into it, not hungry but knowing she must eat something, line her stomach, get some energy.

Squares of light were appearing in the black wall of glass across the road; slowly they were joined by other squares like a huge puzzle being filled in. Cleaners were moving through the floors, employees were arriving to set about their insurance business. The drab concrete superstructure was developing like a photographic print out of the blackness of the fading night.

Clearer thoughts were developing in Kate's mind. She had experience in Birmingham of trying to tackle a hospital scandal, a man who died of a heart attack an hour after being discharged. The hospital had closed ranks instantly; the medical profession knew how to look after its own. Every now and then a mistake did happen, but they were rare; they weren't a major problem; unless you happened to be the mistake.

Unless you happened to be Sally Donaldson.

She needed to move fast, to take the advantage she had over the other reporters; after the first edition of the *Sussex Evening News* came out at eleven, every newspaper in England would be getting the story down the wires.

'It is Tuesday, October the twenty-third,' said a voice on the radio.

Tuesday. *Twin Peaks*. She went through and set the video with the same difficulty she always had, knowing more than likely something entirely different would end up on the tape. Then she took her Microfile out of her battered leather handbag, thumbed through the address section at the back and picked up the receiver of the old black telephone she had bought in a car boot sale.

Dr Marty Morgan was a local general practitioner who wrote a weekly column for the *Evening News*, dispensing advice to readers on health and fitness, and was paid a retainer to be available to advise reporters on anything medical. A fitness fanatic, he always spoke fast and slightly breathlessly, as if he had just finished a ten-mile run, or was perhaps in the middle of it. His column had imbued him with a modicum of local celebrity status to which he had reacted by cultivating a mid-Atlantic accent that reminded Kate of a disc jockey.

She had never met him, but had an image of him from his photograph, thin and rather neurotic-looking with short, black hair. 'Sorry to call you so early,' she said.

'No problem, Kate, that's what I'm here for,' he said, a mite too cheerily for the time of day.

'Could you tell me the medical procedure for defining death?' she asked.

'Are we talking about clinical death, or brain death for an organ donor?'

'It's a pregnant woman who's died in hospital.'

'She's not a donor?'

'I don't know.'

'OK, well assuming not, the degree of thoroughness might depend on whether death was anticipated. Basically they – we'd – check for vital signs, for any sign of a pulse. Look to see if they're breathing; we'd look in the patient's eyes. Within a few minutes after death you start getting beading of the veins across the eyeball and they're a pretty fail-safe indicator. Maybe irritate the patient's throat and touch the eyeball to test for a reaction.'

'Is it possible to make a wrong diagnosis?'

'To diagnose someone as dead when they're not?'

'Uh huh.'

'No, I'd say that was impossible. Well, maybe not impossible but very unlikely.'

'If it did happen could that person end up being buried alive?'

'Not if they had a post mortem or were embalmed.'

'If she didn't have either of those?'

'It's possible in theory, but in practice . . . Are we talking about this country?'

'Yes.'

'I think in practice it wouldn't happen.'

'You've never known it happen?'

He gave an uneasy laugh. 'No. Well I did have a close shave once.' He hesitated. 'When I was a houseman in Bristol. We had a girl brought in who'd taken a drug overdose and thrown herself in the Channel. She had hypothermia, wasn't breathing and didn't appear to have any pulse. I was writing out the death certificate when a nurse yelled at me that she'd found a pulse. We put her on the monitor and found she was having one heartbeat every thirty seconds. She survived. In a normal person the heartbeat rate is about eighty a minute.'

'What would have happened if the nurse hadn't spotted it?'

'She'd have been put in the mortuary, and the cold from the fridge would have probably finished her.'

Kate was silent for a moment. 'And she was OK?'

'Yup. Probably still alive now.'

Kate heard the click of the kettle switching itself off. 'That would be a good follow-up. Any idea how I could get hold of her?'

The doctor's voice sounded wary, suddenly. 'It was fifteen years ago. I wouldn't have any idea how.'

Kate bit the top of her pen. 'So there isn't a foolproof test?'

'Normally if the brain is starved of oxygen for more than ninety seconds irreversible damage starts occurring, and after three or four minutes the brain is dead. With hypothermia the body is in a near-freezing state and the metabolism's slowed right down. It's only using a fraction of the energy it normally uses, so the brain only needs a fraction of the oxygen. You sometimes hear of a child who's fallen into an icy pond being resuscitated after an hour and surviving. You can get this very deceptive low pulse. But doctors are more aware of that now.'

'And who issues the death certificate in a hospital?'

'Any doctor who's around on the ward.'

'Have you had any experience of exhumations?'

'No. You'd really need to talk to a pathologist about that area. I can put you in touch with one. Why?'

'Where would an exhumed body be taken?'

'From a graveyard?'

'Yes.'

'In this town it would be to the borough mortuary down on the Lewes Road.'

'Would you mind running me through the procedures from the time someone is declared dead in a hospital to the funeral?'

'Sure.'

When he had finished, Kate thanked him and hung up. She went back to the bathroom and gave her hair a blast with the drier. Her face was white and drawn today and even the freckles were pale; her eyes were tired. She put on her favourite shirt, which had blue and white stripes and always seemed to make her feel fresh, a short black velvet skirt which she'd bought in a closing-down sale in a shop in the Lanes, new black tights, toyed with her lace-up black granny boots, but decided to put on a more conservative pair of black shoes.

She put on her make-up more carefully than usual, trying to look as conservative as was possible with her wild tangle of hair. She shuddered at the memory of Sally Donaldson's teeth last night, and touched her own gingerly with her forefinger then opened her mouth. For most of her teens she had worn a brace over her front teeth and for all that period had cringed at the sight of her open mouth in a mirror. One of the many nicknames Dara called her by had been Rabbit-Face.

She dabbed some Fidji around her neck and behind her ears and as she smelled the rich scent she felt a little cheered and refreshed. Then she rang the news desk and asked what she was down for in the diary. There were a couple of things which she asked them to shift, and told them she wanted to follow something up urgently on the exhumation story which she thought could be big. She'd be in around mid-morning.

Half an hour later, Kate drove her own car, a rusting white VW Beetle, around the busy gyratory system, moved over to the left lane and ignored an angry hoot. A juggernaut chuntered past on her right, its greasy yellow hub nuts inches from her window, then she braked as the rush hour traffic came to a halt.

It was eight fifty. The engine blattered steadily behind her. The car had just been serviced and the speedometer was working for the first time in months. A bill from the garage fluttered on the passenger seat. 'PM Pfeiffer Associates' was printed at the top, and beneath it was typed a list of items that meant nothing to her. Doctors and garages seemed to have their own languages.

The traffic inched forwards along the street, past a row of grimy shop fronts and a builder's yard, then she saw the sign: BRIGHTON BOROUGH MORTUARY.

She turned in between two brick gate pillars, and drove up a tarmac drive, past a gate house towards a long, single-storey building with grey pebbledash walls and a covered awning over one side like the entrance to a hospital. She parked the car, climbed out and locked the door. The sky was an autumnal blue and she could feel the nip in the air through her still-damp hair. The long, low building gave her the creeps. The courage she had plucked up started fading fast as she pressed the doorbell and heard the cheap rasp of the buzzer.

Pushing your luck.

A girl opened the door. She was slightly plump with a pretty, rather jolly face, blonde hair tied up on top of her head with a blue ribbon, and wearing a white apron and white rubber boots. 'Can I help you?' she said.

Kate swallowed nervously. 'Could you tell me if there's going to be a post mortem on Sally Donaldson?' She noticed the girl's flicker of reaction to her accent.

'Who are you, please?'

'From the Environmental Health Office.'

The girl's face relaxed. 'Yeah, right, come in,' she said cheerily, and stepped back, holding the door for Kate. 'I'm Mandy, the assistant mortician.'

Kate walked into a tiny waiting-cum-reception room that was painted a cheery pink, with pink furniture, carpet and cushions. There was a kitchen worktop set into the far wall on which was a recently boiled kettle, several cups, one with steaming coffee in it, and an unopened bottle of milk. An old-fashioned two-bar electric heater with a frayed brown cord blazed on the floor. It felt strangely cosy.

'Actually,' the girl said, 'Dr Wyndham's already started.'

'Dr Wyndham?' Kate said, surprised. Dr Wyndham was a local pathologist. When crime was suspected a Home Office pathologist would normally have been called down from London. 'Is there no Home Office pathologist involved?'

'No,' the girl said. 'They don't consider there's been anything suspicious.'

Kate looked at her, surprised. 'Really?'

The girl shrugged. 'I think there should have been a post mortem originally, strictly speaking.' Her expression stiffened and she looked guarded suddenly. 'Do you want to change, or go in as you are?'

'I'm – er – fine,' Kate said. 'Do you know why there wasn't a post mortem originally?'

'Often happens. Doctors make up their own laws, don't they? Sometimes they don't bother reporting deaths to the coroner, which they should.' She pointed. 'Straight down there, first right. Have you been here before?'

'No.'

'That's why I didn't recognise you. Work for Mr Liverstock, do you?'

Kate nodded, feeling her face reddening.

'Nice man.'

'Yes.' She walked quickly on. There were double doors straight ahead and a passage to her right at the end of which she could see a brightly lit room with some people in it, and a white figure lying face up.

She approached the room slowly, aware of an increasingly vile stench. She could see a smart woman in her late twenties in a neat navy blue two-piece, whom she recognised immediately as Miss Willow, the coroner's officer; there was a uniformed policewoman who was looking green; a uniformed policeman holding his cap, and another woman in a white apron and white boots.

As she walked in the stench became overpowering, and she nearly gagged; it was a more raw smell than the one last night when the coffin had been opened and was sharpened, like seasoning, by the background tang of disinfectant.

She held her breath as she looked around. An elegantly handsome man in his late thirties, with gingery hair and a blue scrub suit tucked into white boots, was standing facing the far wall dictating into a machine he held in his rubber-gloved hand. The coroner's officer was looking at her with pleasant curiosity and Kate avoided her gaze, not wanting to get drawn into a conversation.

'You were at the exhumation last night, weren't you? From the Environmental Health Office?' the coroner's officer said.

'Yes.' Kate saw the pathologist smile distractedly at her, pause for a moment, then continue dictating.

'No sign of old injury, old scars, cuts, grazes, surgical scars . . .' he said quietly into his machine.

The room had tiled, windowless walls and a high ceiling, and reminded Kate of an operating theatre. There was marbled vinyl on the floor and four massive fluorescents hung on metal chains from the ceiling. Along one of the walls were two deep stainless steel sinks with a drain gulley beneath, and a stainless steel work surface on which lay an assortment of surgical instruments and an electric rotary saw. On the opposite wall was a blackboard divided into sections: *Name. Brain. Lungs. Heart. Liver. Kidney. Spleen.* A set of butcher's weigh scales with a digital read-out sat in front of it.

Three oblong steel tables stood in the room. Two were empty and brightly polished. On the third, a young woman lay on her back, stark naked. Her skin looked tallow white under the light. Tresses of blonde hair spilled around the head and her breasts hung at an odd angle, resting squashed on the table top on each side, and a large, slimy, cream and brown object sat on her chest.

Something was wrong, different to last night.

Kate swallowed, trying to fight her queasiness. She could barely look down, felt herself trembling, shaking. Sally Donaldson had been cut open from her neck down to her pelvis and the skin pulled open, exposing her internal organs. Her pubic hair was covered in a large triangle of flesh, like an obscene fig-leaf, and the foetus, still attached by the umbilical cord, lay cradled between her thighs. Two tags, one brown, one yellow, hung from her big toe. Her intestines bulged out of her midriff. The creamy brown lump that was on her chest was her brain.

Kate struggled even harder with her stomach. She felt giddy, tried to concentrate, to think clearly. Something was wrong. Different. Someone had cleaned the dead girl up since last night, had washed away the bloodstains, but it wasn't that.

The pathologist put down his dictating machine, walked back across to the body, picked up a knife in one hand and the brain in the other, placed the brain on a marble cutting block behind the dead girl's head, and sliced into it carefully as if he were a chef preparing a meal.

Blood rushed to Kate's head. The floor swayed. She touched the cold hard metal of an empty slab and steadied herself against it. Don't pass out, don't throw up. Don't.

Must not.

The smell of rotting innards corkscrewed through her. She stared at the stark white flesh and the blonde tresses of hair. The stench was getting stronger. She took a deep breath and stepped forwards.

She had to look away for a moment as the pathologist's gloved hand scooped some of the slippery intestine out of Sally Donaldson's midriff, and then she realised what it was. What was wrong.

The dead girl's fingers. The nails that last night in the coffin looked as if they had been bitten down to the quick.

They were all long, neatly manicured and with a clear varnish.

# *Chapter Sixteen*

Harvey Swire woke up in his bedroom. Rays of sunlight streaked through the curtains. One splayed off a glass jar with a preserved frog; another caught the corner of the glass rectangle with the aborted foetuses. Janet Leigh in his *Psycho* poster was indistinct in the semi-darkness.

The room smelled stale, smoky. He moved his elbow and an ashtray fell to the floor. It felt as if he had a hatchet embedded in his skull. His mouth tasted vile and there was a faint stench of vomit in the room. A bird trilled insistently in the garden.

Last night hadn't happened.

His penis hurt. He snapped on his bedside light and lifted the bedclothes. It lay limp to one side beyond his pubic hairs, looking fatter than usual. He picked it up and rolled back the foreskin; there was a dried film, like a crust, over the end.

His travel alarm clock said six thirty-five. He climbed out of bed and stood in his tangle of clothes which he had no memory of removing. His brain felt as if it had liquefied and was slopping about inside his head.

He walked unsteadily across the landing into his parents' room, fending off the walls which seemed to come at him, and over to the window. He gazed down at the drive; the Mini looked fine, unmarked. It had not been moved; it had not been driven anywhere. He breathed out a sigh of relief. A bad trip, that was all; bum grass.

Heavy.

Freaky dream.

The floor swayed and he sat down on the pink counterpane of the deep, soft bed, hung his head forwards and rested his chin on his chest. His mother's photograph lay on the floor below her dressing table where it had fallen yesterday, the glass covered in a spider's web of cracks, her silver hairbrush beside it. Smells of his mother's perfumes and colognes and talcs rose around him, from the bed, from the bottles on the dressing table. His heart beat a steady boomf-boomf-boomf like a boxer's glove smacking a punchball. Had there been mud on the Mini's tyres? Mud that had not been there yesterday?

He stood and looked at the Mini again. A rattle and a thud beneath startled him, then the postman walked off down the drive.

Last night hadn't happened.

He went back to his bedroom, put on his dressing gown and walked down into the hall. Several letters lay on the floor, but he ignored them, opened the front door and went across the drive to the Mini.

He only had to take a few steps before he could see the far side of it. The wing was crumpled and twisted, the paint flaking off, and the headlight rim and reflector dangled from the empty socket like a gouged-out eye.

The paper boy's bicycle clattered into the driveway, but Harvey barely noticed. The boy jammed the papers in the letter box and pedalled out again, past him. Harvey examined the damage closely, wondering for a moment whether he could fix it himself, then slowly walked back, scooped up the fresh pint of milk from the doorstep and closed the front door behind him. The newspapers fell with a slap onto the parquet floor of the hall. He was surprised his father hadn't cancelled the papers. But he had been distracted and forgetful ever since his mother had died.

He carried the milk into the kitchen and sat on a chair at the formica-topped table. The fridge clicked and hummed. The electric clock on the wall whirred. The tabby cat, Silas, plump and ancient, wandered over and rubbed its head against his bare legs. Absently he dropped his hand and stroked its neck and gazed at his distorted reflection in the polished chromium of the toaster. Outside a thrush pecked at a bread crust on the lawn.

Last night had not happened.

Was not him. Was someone else.

A band of tension tightened around his head. His hands clenched, the knuckles whitening.

His father's housekeeper, Mrs Mannings, arrived and was pleased to see him, asked him if he had had a good holiday and insisted on cooking him a breakfast he did not want; she had not noticed the damage to the Mini.

At ten o'clock he rang Angie. Her mother answered, warm and friendly as ever. She told him Angie was not awake yet.

He drove the Mini to a car repair garage he remembered seeing in Merton. The man said it would take three days and cost a hundred and forty-five pounds. Harvey reckoned he had enough money in his Post Office savings account, left the car and took a bus home.

He got back just after twelve, and explained to Mrs Mannings that the Mini had been leaking oil. She told him she'd have lunch ready at one. Ham and a baked potato. He went upstairs, closed the door of his parents' bedroom and rang Angie's number again. Angie's mother's cleaning lady answered and told him they had gone out. She did not know where and that made him feel panicky.

Police?

If she went to the police his chance of becoming a doctor would be finished.

She would not go to the police. Last night had not happened.

He went into his own room and sat on the chair in front of the small desk with his microscope. Inside were his chemistry set and his instruments, and the pictures that he had collected over the years.

He opened the bottom right-hand drawer and took out his neat file. The first cutting he removed was a full colour page from *Paris Match* magazine of a Volkswagen slewed at a crazy angle at a desert frontier. The car was riddled with bullets and the rear window had been shot out. People were slumped inside the car; a man running towards the camera seemed to have been punched backwards in mid-step. His legs were kicked out sideways, his arms jerked back like a marionette, his face torn into a scream. There was a brown patch in his shirt, about where his heart would be and the material around was exploding outwards into jagged threads.

The camera seemed to have caught the very moment of death. The very instant that the man was both alive and dead. It was one of his favourite pictures. Because it was there, in that moment, that the life force was leaving. The thing that mattered. The essence; the consciousness; the soul.

The bit of him that had left when he had been hit on his bike; the bit that had left and read his exam papers. The bit of him that last night had –

Impossible. Last night had not happened.

He rang Angie again at half past two. There was no answer. He tried at four and no answer again. At six o'clock she answered the phone herself and hung up when she heard his voice.

He rang straight back.

Her voice was taut, like wire. 'I don't ever want to see you again,' she said. 'I don't ever want to speak to you again.'

Mrs Mannings had gone home and he did not have to worry about being overheard. 'I need to explain.'

'Explain?' she said. 'Let me explain something to you. I'm not supposed to be seeing Tim. Mummy doesn't approve of him. If it wasn't for that I would call the police.' Her voice broke and Harvey could tell she was crying. 'And so would he.' She hung up again.

His face in his mother's dressing table mirror was grim, with dark rings around his eyes. Some of his tan seemed to have faded and there was shadowing around his chin and upper lip. He dialled her number again. It rang five times before she answered.

'Do you have a Simon and Garfunkel poster in your bedroom?' he said.

She was silent for a moment. When she spoke her voice sounded cold and composed. 'You raped me last night. Now you want to know if I have a Simon and Garfunkel poster?'

'Do you?'

'This is one hell of a time to start playing mind games, Harvey.'

'Do you?'

'You're schizo, did you know that? I saw a programme on television about schizophrenics. All this stuff about travelling out of your body and getting sent back from heaven by your mother. That's a classic schizophrenia delusion. They were saying that the most common group of people to become schizophrenic are teenagers. And that it was a common occurrence after head injuries. You need to see a shrink, 'cause that's what you are, schizo.'

'Do you have a Simon and Garfunkel poster on the wall to the left of your window?'

'Yes. So bloody what?'

'It's new, isn't it?'

'I put it up two days ago.'

Harvey stared at the tiny holes in the mouthpiece, then put the receiver back on the rest. A bluebottle buzzed in the room. He stood up, and the fear that had haunted him throughout the day sloughed off him like a dead layer of skin. Something replaced it that he could not immediately define.

Got away with it.

He smiled.

Bitch.

He went downstairs to the stale, undisturbed air in his father's consulting room, and sat in his father's chair. The desk was neat and empty. It had on it a black marble pen and pencil holder, a leather blotter and a framed photograph of himself and his mother. There was a shelf on the right containing various surgical instruments and a bookcase on the left, stacked neatly. His heart was beating hard again, the steady boomf-boomf smack of the boxer's glove.

One book, Halland's *Textbook of Mental Illnesses*, opened at the right place as he took it down from the shelf. Page 279. He knew the page number by heart. He had read this section several times since his accident.

*The patient may suffer delusions of passivity, that he or she is being controlled by an external force, such as God or the BBC or a deceased person.*

*'You have to go back, darling.'*

*The patient may hear commentary as coming from a third person from time to time. He may hear people talking about him, discussing him.*

Last night as he had drifted towards Angie's house he had heard his school mates.

*Everyone's humping her.*

*Harvey should try sticking it in her ear.*

*Bang her, Harve!*

*Yeah, shaft the pants off her.*

*Bang her.*

*Bang the bitch!*

Schizo, sure.

Being controlled by external forces. It explained how he had watched himself, helpless, driving the Mini last night. How he had watched himself do what he had done to Angie and the boy.

But it did not explain how he had seen the inside of her bedroom.

# *Chapter Seventeen*

*Tuesday, 23 October*

Kate sat at her desk typing fast. 'Survival expert Doug Ewell told the *News*: "In an airtight coffin survival beyond two hours would be impossible, but if there were a leak, then someone could conceivably live several days before dying from dehydration."'

She glanced down at her shorthand pad, then typed more on to her screen. 'Mrs Donaldson's father, Eastbourne fruit wholesaler Mick Mackenzie, added that the family would be considering legal action against the hospital.'

She turned the page. 'Alan Newcombe, director of Whylies Funeral Service, one of the south's largest funeral directors, said: "Premature burial was a real danger in Victorian England and in many hot countries today where burial is required quickly by law.

"In England with the stringent medical procedures for certification of death it is considered a near impossibility. I have never come across any instance in the past forty years."'

She sipped her coffee. It had gone cold and there was skin on the top; a drip ran down the side on to the brown crackle finish of her desktop. The smell of the mortuary was in her nostrils, in her stomach. Embedded in her brain.

Her cream and brown brain.

Brains weren't grey at all; only when they were pickled in formalin. Mandy at the mortuary told her. Just one more small affirmation that nothing in life was ever how you thought it was.

'What's up? Did you forget to take your happy pill?' Eddie Bix perched on the edge of her desk, his leather bomber jacket resting against her red filing tray.

Kate gave him a weak smile. 'Guess I must have done.'

He dropped a black and white photograph of her interviewing the vicar of St Mary's in front of her. 'How about that? Action girl!'

In the picture she was hunched and stooping forwards with a pious expression on her face, clasping her notepad like a begging bowl. The vicar was staring at her as if she were a dog turd.

Her phone warbled and its light flashed. She picked it up. 'Kate Hemingway.'

It was one of the assistants on the news desk. 'Kate, could you take this? It's a local school and they want someone to cover a cheque presentation.'

Kate took the call. Some kids had raised two hundred and fifty pounds for the Sussex Queen Victoria Hospital's heart unit. They were making the presentation tomorrow at four. She got the diary and saw the event was already marked in. She assured the teacher the *News* would be covering it. When she hung up, Eddie was looking intently at her.

'Your face is a horrible colour. Green. Not feeling well?'

'I have a slight headache.'

'I'll get you a couple of aspirins.'

'No, it's OK, thanks. I don't like taking pills,' she said. On her desk was a copy of the death notice that had been printed in the *News* the previous week.

> Donaldson. Sally Anne. On 14 October in hospital.
>
> Adored wife of Kevin. Funeral service at St Anne's, Brighton on Tuesday, 16 October, at 3 pm. Family flowers only. Donations if desired to Guide Dogs for the Blind c/o Dalby Funeral Service, 311 Lewes Road, Brighton.

'You really don't look well. You should go home.'

She moved her cup out of the way of his jacket. 'I'm a bit freaked out. I went to a post mortem,' she said. She picked up her biro and turned it over in her fingers.

'To a post mortem? Shit! I've been to one. The smell's the worst thing.' He tapped the front of the newspaper on her desk, the eleven o'clock edition of the *News*. 'Good, eh, the splash? How come the exclusive?'

She managed a grin.

'You got in there? Behind the screens?'

'Maybe.' She winked.

'You never told me last night.'

The building was vibrating at the moment from the massive ancient presses in the basement that were churning out the midday edition. She liked it when the presses were rolling; it made the whole process of her work feel complete. She stared at the front page again. At the headline.

BURIED ALIVE.

Beneath was the wedding photograph of Sally Donaldson. Her husband had been cropped out of it and inset, smaller, beneath. To the right was the byline: 'Exclusive by Kate Hemingway.'

Sally Donaldson had been a pretty girl, smiling with happiness, young and fresh-looking. Different, so different to the hideous thing she had seen lying in the coffin and on the slab.

She ran her eye down the opening paragraphs.

> Tragic bride Sally Donaldson, 23, was buried alive, it was revealed last night.
>
> Her coffin was exhumed from St Anne's graveyard in Brighton, where she was buried on October 16.
>
> When the coffin was opened in front of a group that included Sally's husband, insurance salesman Kevin Donaldson, 24, the state of the body revealed that Sally had spent her last desperate hours trying to claw her way out.
>
> The exhumation followed reports of noises from the grave which began on the afternoon of Sally's funeral.
>
> Last night the vicar of St Anne's, the Rev Neil Comfort, was not available for comment.
>
> But Mrs Eleanor Knott, who lives next to the graveyard, said: 'I heard a low moaning as I walked through the cemetery on Friday afternoon. And that was three days after the funeral.'
>
> Sally, who was six months pregnant when she died, slipped into a coma at Brighton's Prince Regent Hospital. Life support systems were switched off after consultations with her family and she was certified dead on October 14.
>
> An inquest will now be held.

The chief sub had cut out her details of the scratched coffin lid, Sally Donaldson's fingernails and the premature birth which he told her would be 'too distressing for our readers'. Subs always managed to cut the best bits she thought, annoyed.

'Getting a splash two days running. You're heading for the big time,' Eddie Bix said.

Normally she would have been thrilled. Today Kate hadn't even yet put the page in her portfolio drawer, as she usually did. Or yesterday's splash, either.

'Hey, there's a gang of us going to see *Ghost* tonight. Want to come? Have a pizza afterwards, or a Chinese? Cheer you up?'

Right now the prospect of going home and reading or watching the box, being alone, did not appeal. She needed cheering up. She liked Eddie, felt comfortable with him; he was like a big brother; like Howie. A caption stuck on the side of a filing tray on a crime desk to her right caught her eye. 'SUSSEX EVENING NEWS – READ BY TOP TURTLES.' She smiled. 'Sure, thanks.'

Her phone rang again. Eddie raised a finger. 'Be back,' he mouthed and disappeared. She lifted the receiver. It was Barry Liverstock, Deputy Director of the Environmental Health Office, wanting to collect his debt.

'Debt?' Kate said blankly.

'I've seen the paper,' he said. 'Great story. Wonder how you managed to get in there.'

'Yes, thanks,' she said. 'It was a big help.'

'Thought we'd try and fix a date for the lunch you promised me.' He was undressing her with his voice and she felt like dumping the receiver on him. Except: he had helped her; he might be able to help her again. The thought of two hours at a lunch table with the big smarmy man giving her the come-on revolted her. She leafed through her diary. Nothing, nothing, nothing. Hardly any appointments at all.

'The next fortnight's a problem,' she said.

'Bad for me, too. How about the first week in November?'

She agreed a date and wrote it in her diary the way she might have written a dental appointment. Then she hung up and studied the list of people she needed to talk to. Some had ticks against them, some had a single mark which meant she was waiting for them to call her back. The phone rang again.

It was Patrick Donoghue, the reporter from the *News* who was now on the *Daily Mail* in London.

Oh God, she thought, closing her eyes. Damn, damn, damn.

'Kate? Remember me? I was the good-looking guy in the graveyard yesterday.'

'I know what you're going to say. I'm sorry. I forgot!'

'I'm getting about seven different kinds of shit flung at me by my editor.'

'I'm really sorry.'

'Great stringer you are. I'm sitting up here like a lemon and your story comes banging down the wires. You were going to call me.'

'I forgot. It was so horrific I – '

She had forgotten her promise to call him if anything came of the Sally Donaldson story. She had also forgotten to call Harry Oakes. Oakes's paper would have paid her for a story like this. Patrick Donoghue could have got a couple of hundred out of the *Daily Mail* for her. 'I'm really sorry, Patrick.'

'I think the least you could do is have dinner with me tomorrow to make amends.'

'Tomorrow?' She felt a beat of excitement.

'I'm down in Sussex. Are you free?'

She swallowed. 'I'll have to cancel Tom Cruse.'

'Pick you up about half seven. Where will you be?'

Kate gave him her address, then hung up and for a moment found it hard to concentrate as she thought about him. His sturdy frame, warm green eyes, strong face and the short brown hair and upright stance that gave him the appearance of a soldier. She smiled, then remembered the open coffin, the post mortem.

Sally Donaldson's fingernails.

She dialled the Prince Regent Hospital's number and asked the switchboard, for the fifth time, to put her through to Brian Merrivale, the general manager.

She got the engaged tone again, hung up, exasperated, and stared at her VDU screen. Her copy stared back, bright green letters on the black background. The sweep second hand on the large round clock on the column to her right slid silently. Twelve ten. Reporters, subs, editors, feature writers were starting to get up from their desks, stretching, walking about. Some were going off for lunch. There were four more editions of the paper still to go to bed, but the morning rush was over and the day was already beginning to wind down.

Two phones warbled out of synch. There was the furious rattle of typing from the crime desk to her right as one of the reporters hammered at the keyboard.

She pressed a key on her own keyboard and the display came up. She typed her ident.

'Repex/Kate/Town – Burial. Memo to Geoff Fox. Awaiting further comments from hospital spokesman. Will try to find medics involved and interview later.

Also awaiting calls back from British Museum and British Medical Association librarians on past instances of premature burials in this country and overseas.

Hospital officials said to me today (Tuesday) there would be an immediate investigation – '

She stopped, flipped back a page of her shorthand notes, deleted the last line she had written, and started again.

'Deputy hospital administrator Derek Gould said they could issue no statement until after they had received the results of the post mortem and at the present time no reviews of the procedures for certification of death were planned.

Pall Bearer Mr Warren Denham, 36, of Dalby Funeral Service, the undertakers, said that he thought he had heard a sound from inside the coffin as they unloaded it from the hearse, but decided he must have imagined it. (I am hoping to interview later today.)

(I'm trying to get interview with SD's husband. Will visit this p.m.)

Need to establish why no post-mortem originally – will contact medical personnel involved.

Her phone rang again. It was Geoff Fox, the news editor.

'Kate, there's a car crash on the A27 near Polegate. One dead, maybe two. Get over there as quick as you can with a photographer.'

'Hey, couldn't you possibly send someone else? I've got a million follow-ups on the burial. I'm sending you through a memo.'

'I'm sorry, you'll have to come back to that.'

She felt a twinge of anger, which she contained as she forced herself to remember she was still a new girl trying to create a good impression, trying to be helpful. The journey to Polegate would take a good half hour each way, but with luck they would be back by two o'clock. She stood up, grabbed her coat and went over to the picture desk.

Eddie Bix was needed to help the darkroom technician sort out an exposure problem and she was sent out with Dennis Rigby, a short, plump, pipe-smoking man in his early sixties who had been with the paper forty-one years and assumed Kate shared his obsession with cricket.

Kate had watched several cricket matches and could not get enthusiastic; she found the game slow and dull, which sometimes made her feel guilty, as if she owed it to her adopted country to be passionate about its national sports.

'I mean, Ian Botham's had a rough time. People don't appreciate how much good he . . .' Rigby drove badly and agonisingly slowly, and talked on incessantly, dribbling down his pipe stem. Kate nodded and made appropriate grunts and 'Uh huhs' and fought the tightening knot in her stomach that was always there on the way to an accident.

A small Toyota had hit a van, rolled over and been sideswiped by a Jaguar coming the opposite direction. A woman had been cut out of the Toyota and already taken to hospital. The police said she wouldn't live. Firemen were trying to free the man. Debris was littered everywhere. Hosepipes snaked across the road. A suitcase had burst open; a nightdress, wash bag, leather slippers, one green patent leather shoe and a blue comb lay in the road amid the torn metal and smashed glass. Traffic crept past the POLICE SLOW ACCIDENT sign, gawping.

Kate felt sick and depressed. The rear window of the car was still in place and on it was written in lipstick JUST MARRIED. Two tin cans trailed on a wire from the rear bumper.

The van driver was in a daze, giving a statement to the police in the back of their car. The Jaguar driver had already been taken to hospital, suffering from shock.

Kate wrote the name of the hospital, Eastbourne District General, down on her pad. The couple in the Toyota were from London, as far as the police could tell. Rigby took his photographs, dutifully, from a distance, careful not to include the dying or dead man behind the wheel, creeping about, crouching down, then standing at full stretch, his camera making a dull clunk every few seconds.

Kate noticed a wedding present, prettily wrapped in white paper and tied with a blue ribbon, lying on the grass verge. The tag hung listlessly. If she had been Rigby, she thought, she would have photographed that and nothing else.

Geoff Fox came on to the landing outside the newsroom holding a cup of coffee at the same time as Kate and Dennis Rigby arrived back, shortly after two o'clock.

'How was it?' he asked.

'Grim,' Kate said. 'A honeymoon couple.'

Rigby went on through; Kate held the newsroom door for Fox. 'Sounds promising. How many dead?' Fox said.

'Two.'

'From this area?'

'No, from North London.'

He screwed up his face in disappointment. 'Injuries?'

'One, minor, from near Eastbourne.'

'See if you can dress it up a bit. We've been short of crashes the last week. You might be able to get the wedding pics – you know the sort of thing. *The wedding photographs they'll never see*,' he said. 'Get the best man. Some of the guests.' He scratched the back of his neck. 'Should be good. Pity they're not local.'

'I've got a lot to chase up on the exhumation. I'll do what I can.'

He turned away rather hastily. 'Sure, work around it,' he said.

Geoff Fox's mild appearance always deceived Kate. The hardness was there underneath; or maybe it wasn't hardness, just a different way of perceiving reality. Whatever reality was.

The early afternoon edition of the paper lay on her desk. A thick stack of messages was beside it, far more than normal. They were almost all from other papers, mostly the tabloids, the *Sun*, *Mirror*, *News of the World*, *Star* and the local news agencies, all wanting her to call back urgently and she put the stack down, feeling a thrill of excitement, and quickly tugged off her coat. She looked eagerly at the two p.m. edition of the *News*.

She frowned. Her story was no longer the front page headline. Instead it was: MAYOR JOINS BYPASS ROW.

The two smaller headlines were BROTHERS RESCUED IN BOAT DRAMA and PRINCESS DIANA COMING TO WORTHING WEDDING.

Her story had gone completely from the front page.

She felt a swirl of confusion as she turned the pages, scanning the headlines. It had been moved to the seventh page, and cut to two small columns. The photographs had gone and the headline changed.

> MRS SALLY DONALDSON.
>
> The body of Mrs Sally Donaldson, 23, who was buried on Tuesday in St Anne's, Brighton, was exhumed last night.
>
> A police spokesman said that a post mortem was taking place to quell unsubstantiated speculation that she had been prematurely buried.

That was all.

Anger rose inside Kate. Her cheeks were burning. She compared the eleven o'clock edition and the midday edition. They both had her story virtually filling the front page. It was common for the lead story to change during the day if something stronger came along, but there was nothing in the other stories remotely as strong.

She hung her coat up and went across to the news desk. Geoff Fox was tapping on his keys and studying his screen intently. His two assistants glanced at Kate then kept their heads down, almost sheepishly, she thought.

She waited until Fox had finished. 'What's happened to my story?'

He had the grace to look embarrassed. 'It's fine.'

'It can't be that fine. You've decimated it.'

'He' – He jerked his head, indicating the editorial desk behind him. 'Terry wants to have a word with you about it. He's in his office.' His left hand rotated ineffectively, like a wheel in mud.

The door to the editor's office was open. It was a large, bland room, with two wing-back leather armchairs in front of an imposing rosewood desk behind which Terry Brent, the editor, slouched, taking his weight on his arms.

He had a boxer's face, tough and streetwise, and his hair was cropped functionally short. The sleeves of his yellow shirt were rolled up, his top button was undone and his striped tie was at half mast; smoke curled from a cigarette in the glass ashtray and he was tapping his desk with the top of a ballpoint pen, scanning through a typewritten sheet of paper.

Kate knocked, her protective coating of anger deserting her and nervousness replacing it.

He waved her in without looking up. 'Shut the door.' He picked up the cigarette between his forefinger and thumb, inhaled deeply then lowered it mechanically into the ashtray. An open pack of Marlboro and a plastic lighter lay on the desk near it, a pile of the day's editions of the *News* beside them.

'Take a seat.' He continued reading.

She sat down. The leather chair was not as comfortable as it looked. Old framed copies of the newspaper's front pages and various awards lined the walls. There were no clues about Brent himself. He looked up at her. 'Getting a lot of flak over this Sally Donaldson piece,' he said.

'Flak?' she said, surprised.

He pinched his cigarette between his finger and thumb and inhaled again, then crushed it out in the ashtray. He exhaled through clenched lips and the warmth faded from his face. 'I've had the police on the phone. I've had the hospital, four vicars, and now I've just had earache from the Bishop of Chichester. He's paranoid that the clergy across Sussex are going to be bombarded with every fucking fruitcake who's heard something in a graveyard. Not bad since the first edition only went out at eleven.'

'Hopefully it's going to make people a lot more careful in the future.'

'More careful? About what?'

'Certifying death.'

He drummed the fingers of his right hand on his desk. 'Kate, before we printed the story this morning you assured me that the woman had been buried alive, right?'

'Yes.'

'That's why we went with the story, because you convinced us. We took your word. You're a bright kid and we want to give you the chances. You hadn't got any corroboration but we thought the story was OK to go with – good and punchy, right?' His face was darkening and Kate was feeling increasingly uncomfortable. 'How do you know for sure that woman wasn't dead when she was buried?'

'I saw her! She'd given birth in there. Her eyes were open. There was blood. Her fingernails were – ' She hesitated. Saw the shiny immaculate nails, felt a prickle of unease. 'The lid of the coffin – there were scratch marks.'

'You an expert on dead bodies?'

'What do you mean?'

'How many exhumations have you been to before? How many dead bodies have you seen dug up?'

'None.' Kate gripped her right wrist with her left hand; she felt both angry and uncertain now. She twisted her silver bracelet, felt a crumb of comfort in the familiarity of the links. Doubt dug away at her.

The editor sniffed. 'Anyone ever explain to you what happens to a dead body after a few days? About the gases inside? How they expand? About how it's possible for the pressure of the gases inside a dead woman to expel the foetus? About how corpses can change positions and their limbs can twitch and jerk?'

Everything seemed to go out of kilter for a moment. Christ. She thought of the consequences if she had got it wrong. The lawsuits from the hospital, the doctors, the undertakers, the husband. Her head swam and she tried to think back. Saw the hands, the fingers, the nails worn down to the quick, the scratched lid. Hadn't there been scratches? No corpse could have twitched that much, surely? And the nails had been worn down.

They had been.

She stared at Terry Brent for a moment in terror. A couple of people had told her he was a woman-hater, that he particularly disliked women reporters. Kate had not sensed it when he had interviewed her; but she did now. His cheek muscles were rippling from the anger simmering beneath them.

'We're a family paper, Kate. We're not some fucking Sunday tabloid. We have a duty to be responsible. Don't want crap like this. Don't need it.'

'Crap?' There was a squeak in her voice. 'It's a horrendous story. It needs reporting.'

He shook his head. 'Even if it's true it's too distressing.'

She stared blankly, numbed for a moment by surprise. 'I – I don't understand. It's OK to show car crashes, but not something like this? I've just come from a car crash. Two honeymooners killed. I don't think what I just saw makes very comfortable family reading – or a very pretty photograph, either.'

'Showing pictures of car crashes helps save lives.'

'Oh, come on! You don't believe that.' She banged her hands together in frustration. Then she felt his silence.

He tugged another cigarette out of the pack. 'I've had my ears bent by the police. I mean really bent. No reporters were supposed to be inside those screens. Did you get inside or did you nobble someone afterwards?'

'It's my job to be in places I'm not supposed to be.'

'Not when it means violating the Press Code and jeopardising our good relationship with the police.' He stuck the cigarette in his mouth and lit it.

'We don't have a good relationship with the police. They are never helpful.'

He shrugged and leaned back in his chair. He rolled his cigarette into the centre of his mouth and held it clenched between his teeth. 'Can you substantiate the story? Get corroboration?'

'I'm working on it now. I mean, I've seen the woman myself, twice. The assistant at the mortuary told me she was surprised there wasn't a post mortem originally. I think there could be a big negligence story in this. There was a doctor there last night. The coroner's officer. An environmental health officer.'

'And you asked them all if they agreed with you?'

'No, I'm planning to talk to them today.'

He took the cigarette out of his mouth and held it as if it were a paper dart. 'You're taking this personally because you're a woman.' His eyes swung at her.

Kate tried not to rise to him. 'I was sent to cover this story by the news editor and that's what I did. I did not imagine what I saw. I didn't need to have been to an exhumation before to see that woman had been trying to get out of there. I mean for real. Someone's been seriously negligent. That woman was not dead when she was put in the coffin, and I think there's a cover-up going on. I know there is.'

'What evidence do you have?'

Through the slats in the horizontal blinds behind Terry Brent she could see a window cleaner working on the building opposite.

The nails.

She stared down at her lap and did not want to tell him; did not want to tell anyone. She listened to the hush of the heating system, then looked back up.

The editor's lips clenched and flattened into each other. He tapped ash off the end of his cigarette. 'We can pick it up at the inquest.'

'But it's hot now! I can get something big if you give me the chance.'

'There'll be an inquest in a few weeks. We'll cover that. Be enough. I need you tomorrow on the Hartley Briggs trial.'

'What?'

'The child sex ring – the satanist lot.'

'It's OK to have news stories about child sex and devil worship; but not about people buried alive?'

'It's in the public interest. Parents need to know about these things.'

'Don't you think that knowing you might get buried alive is also in the public interest?'

One of the early editions of the *News* was on top of the pile on his desk. He scanned the page then read aloud: "Mrs Eleanor Knott, who lives next to the graveyard, said: 'I heard a low moaning as I walked through the cemetery on Friday afternoon. And that was three days after the funeral.'" Coffins don't let any air come in, if they're shut properly,' Brent said. 'Any human being would suffocate after two to three hours. Even if the coffin weren't airtight, if you've got six foot of earth packed on top of you, how the hell's air going to get through that?'

Kate pushed her bracelet around her wrist again.

'Realise what kind of shit we could be in over this?' he said. 'We could end up with libel writs round our necks from the doctors, the hospital, the undertakers, the girl's family.'

The image of Sally Donaldson in her grave flooded through her. The image of Sally Donaldson lying filleted on the mortuary slab with her brain resting on her chest. 'It's true,' Kate said.

'We'll know after the inquest, won't we?'

'I'm going to find out before then. I'll know by the end of today, with luck.'

'Enough,' Terry Brent said. 'I don't want any more about it until the inquest. Understand? Forget it. And I don't want you sniffing about the hospital pissing off everyone there too.'

'Won't you at least let me talk to the doctor, Dr Sells?'

'You're not to talk to anyone. Understand?'

'Are you putting someone else on it?'

'No. It's a load of crap. I'm going to forget about it.'

'And if the inquest shows I was right?'

'That'll be fine, you can go and talk to whoever you want. You'd also better be aware you're going to be in deep shit if you're wrong.' He rummaged on his desk and handed her a sheet of paper. 'If you're so keen on stories about the dead coming back to life, you can do a piece on this tonight.'

It was a press release.

WORLD FAMOUS MEDIUM TO VISIT HOVE

> Dora Runcorn will be holding an evening of clairvoyance at Hove Town Hall on Tuesday, 23 October at 7.30. Dora, author of five international best-selling books, including *The Light at the End of the Tunnel*, will be demonstrating her amazing powers of clairvoyance, spirit communication and healing . . .

'You want me to go to this?' Kate asked.

'Yep. You can say what you like. Rubbish her if you want, they're all charlatans. I don't mind.'

Kate left Terry Brent's office smarting and worried. Worried that she might have got it wrong about Sally Donaldson. Worried that there might be a cover-up. The fingernails nagged her. The fact that there had not been a post mortem worried her. She went back to her desk and dialled Dr Marty Morgan, the paper's medical columnist whom she had spoken to early this morning. When she asked him what she wanted to know he went quiet, pensive.

'I've got a paper on that somewhere,' he said, after a while. 'Shall I dig it out and post it to you?'

Kate asked if she could come straight round and pick it up.

## *Chapter Eighteen*

Dr Iain Cuthby, head of the Department of Anatomy of Queen's Hospital Medical School, stood on the rostrum. A tough little man with neat, sandy hair and a well-groomed smile, his hands dissected the air as he spoke with surgical precision.

Three hundred and sixty students dressed in white coats sat in the room, taking notes and anticipating the end of the lecture with morbid curiosity and an element of nervousness. Most of them had never seen a dead body before.

Each corpse was to be shared between four students. It was theirs to experiment with and to cut up week by week over the next twelve months. Typewritten sheets of paper on the notice board announced the allocations and gave brief biographical sketches of each corpse. Harvey Swire's was number fifty-two. The notes stated he was a man of seventy-six who had died of coronary artery disease. He had been a cival servant and lived in East Anglia. That was all.

The lecture was winding down. Dr Cuthby raised his voice to silence the fidgeting that had begun. 'Now I want you to remember again what I told you before we go in.' His Scottish burr rang across the hall. 'These are people who have donated their bodies to medical science. Every cadaver is willing and happy to be here. But remember these are people, human beings who were once alive like us. Respect them the way you would respect a deceased member of your own family.'

There was a silence.

'And everything stays right with the cadaver, understand? I don't want limbs or sex organs being taken out for practical jokes. When you have finished at the end of the year, their remains will be cremated or buried intact, according to their wishes.'

The Department of Anatomy was at the far end of the college, beyond the kitchens and the laundry and the mortuary. Harvey walked near the front of the army of students, down the grimy corridors, dog-legging left then right, the walls lined with asbestos-clad pipes. It felt like going into the bowels of a ship.

He had the faint headache and muzziness that he woke up with every morning now and knew he had to get used to. In his right hand he held his well-thumbed dissecting manual clamped against the cloth roll that contained his dissecting kit. He felt good in his white coat; confident.

The sign on the pale blue double doors at the end of the corridor said WHITE COATS MUST BE WORN. The right-hand door opened and closed relentlessly as the students filed through. The familiar reek of formalin greeted Harvey, its pungency increasing as he neared the door.

Several students hung back outside, as if they weren't quite ready, needed a final push. He walked contemptuously past them into the room, and stopped, awed by the atmosphere.

The room was cavernous and silent. The cadavers lay in rows, under white sheets on metal benches, each with a brown plastic bucket hooked beneath. His pulse raced. The silence. The complete lack of movement. Like a cathedral or a temple. There were tall, arched windows, the walls in between tiled the colour of tinned peas. Blackboards with badly-drawn anatomical diagrams. Wood and plastic replicas of internal organs sat on plinths on windowsills and shelves. Cracked brown linoleum covered the floor. Along the right side of the room was a bank of metal sinks with hooped taps and paper towel dispensers. Fluorescent lights hung on chains above each cadaver. Above the lumpy white sheets.

Conversations faded; there was the drumming of shoes on the floor, then shuffling, then silence. As if everyone who had come into the room had died for a moment too.

Number fifty-two was down the far end of the room. There was some junk piled beyond, several empty benches, a porter's trolley with a broken skeleton and a large glass tank filled with human organs submerged in formalin.

Harvey watched the motionless white sheet. Beneath it he could see the shape of the head and the body and one foot sticking upright, and waited impatiently for his three fellow students to join him, the excitement growing inside him. He wanted to see the cadaver's face, to touch him. To feel how different the dead were to the living.

Gordon Clifford arrived first, a jokey fellow Harvey did not care for, then a serious boy called Thomas Piper and, finally, several minutes later and apologising for getting lost, a chinless wonder called Hedley Hedley-Weens, whose father had been president – pwesident, as he pronounced it – of the Royal College of Surgeons.

Harvey looked at them in turn. They were hesitant, eyeing the sheet as if afraid it might suddenly rise up. He stepped forwards decisively and began to pull it back.

An even stronger reek of formalin was freed, smarting his eyes. The cadaver's face was covered by a damp muslin mask; where it ended the neck was visible, browny-grey like the scales of a reptile. Harvey lifted the mask away, startled by the cold, moist feel of the skin on his fingers.

The cadaver had a freckled face, the pudginess accentuated by the fact that he was bald, shaved clean of hair. His expression was benign, like someone abandoned in a dentist's chair.

Harvey pulled the sheet down over the man's chest; all the skin was the same constant browny-grey. There was a scar where he had had open-heart surgery. Harvey blinked against the fumes of the formalin, pulling the sheet further down, exposing the navel, then the penis, so shrivelled it was hard at first to tell it apart from the scrotum on which it rested.

He exposed the cadaver's thighs, then its legs. He stopped, surprised to see the left leg had been amputated below the knee.

'Some bugger's been here first!' said Clifford.

Hedley-Weens was a bilious green. Harvey felt tinged with faint disappointment. So discoloured, leathery; it was more like a dummy than a human. Piper was looking numb. Gordon Clifford was grinning twitchily. Hedley-Weens turned away sharply and doused the floor and the front of his white coat in tomato skins, diced carrot, dribble and the rest of the contents of his stomach. 'Sorry,' he said and went in search of a mop and bucket.

Harvey lowered a finger and gently prodded the cadaver's arm. The muscle felt like putty.

'Hey, Harvey!' Gordon Clifford said, feigning shock. 'Don't do that, you'll wake him up.'

Harvey smiled. He thought Clifford was a berk. He thought everyone he had met at medical school was a berk. Play the game, he knew. Show charm, be fun. He had made the mistake at school of telling them too much, of letting them into a secret they were incapable of understanding. And of being too serious. It alienated people, did not help you get on, did not help you get laid. People were pathetic but you didn't let on you knew that.

Piper was studying his text book carefully. 'We start with the back,' he announced. 'Who wants to make the first incision?'

Harvey opened his own book and scanned the index. Thorax.

Abdomen. Heart. Neck. Limbs. He did not need to read any of it; he had studied it so carefully he knew most of it by heart. 'We have to turn him over,' he said.

They rolled number fifty-two on to his stomach. Hedley-Weens had not come back. Harvey took his shiny new scalpel out of his roll, then checked the diagram. He pressed the blade against the skin beneath the cadaver's neck. He had to press hard. It was surprisingly tough and made a faint tearing noise as it cut. He brought the blade slowly down the length of the back, a line of clear, greasy fluid chasing the blade.

He wondered what death had been like for number fifty-two. Had he risen up above his body, swirled down a dark tunnel, seen a bright light and then been greeted by his mother? Had he been allowed to stay or had he been sent back too? Was he floating up there now on the roof of this room, watching him?

Some people believed spirits hung around until the body was buried. That they could not be free to move on so long as there was some life. They could only cross to the next world when there was no body, nothing left.

You weren't necessarily dead when you were buried. Your hair kept on growing. And your nails. Even with their blood drained out and their veins filled with formalin, life was going on in the bodies here; decay; bacteria. It took years for a body to rot. Years in which you could be above it, watching it. In which you might not be freed.

*You have to go back, darling.*

*God is very unhappy with you.*

If you had nothing to go back to? Just a dead, decomposing body, what then? Or if you were cremated?

Was that hell? To be a spirit without a body? Sent back from beyond to drift and watch? For ever?

He raised his eyes, warily, wondering if the air in this room was full of the spirits of the cadavers in here, slithering around above him like fish. Spirits screaming as they realised they were going to have to watch what was going on.

Stuck in a terrible limbo.

Or was there nothing? Nothing at all. Just death, the end? When the brain had gone, were you gone too?

The coldness of the room seeped into him and the smell of Hedley-Weens's vomit brought back the memory that haunted him. Angie.

Out of control.

*Schizo.*

He had been scared since then. Scared of his weird power. The pills had contained it. Chlorpromazine. Twenty-five milligrams three times a day and fifty at night. One of the treatments for schizophrenia he had found in the reference library of the British Medical Association the day after he had last spoken to Angie. He had written out the three-month repeatable prescription from the pad in his father's desk.

Getting access to fresh supplies would be no problem. He had already befriended the dispensing clerk in the hospital pharmacy, told her he was particularly interested in the pharmacological side of medicine; she had shown him the stores. He knew the shelves of psychiatric medication and how the stock records were kept.

The pills gave him a slight headache and muzziness in the mornings but otherwise did not interfere. As each week went by and he had no more recurrences he felt a mounting sense of disillusion that Angie had been right in her diagnosis.

He pulled away the skin, and stared at the web of number fifty-two's spinal muscles. Pickled meat. Like any other animal. He moved to one side and let Clifford have a turn.

This room, of which he had earlier had such high hopes, was not the right place. They were too long dead in here; much too long. He had longed for this day for more than ten years; had dreamed of doing exactly what he was now doing with a real body, a human being. But now he realised that it was the wrong department, the wrong discipline.

It was not the dead who would give him his answers. It was the living.

# *Chapter Nineteen*

*Tuesday, 23 October*

Posters outside the grey concrete building of the town hall showed a photograph of a seventy-year-old woman with bouffed, peroxided hair through which light shone like a lopsided halo. She was wearing a diaphanous gown and had the sort of smile royalty usually bestows from aircraft doorways on to welcoming nations.

DORA RUNCORN – WORLD FAMOUS MEDIUM – TONITE AT 7 p.m. said the caption beneath.

Kate Hemingway stood in the queue. She had never been to a medium, but had a vague idea of what to expect. She was annoyed at having to come and would have preferred to have gone to see *Ghost* with Eddie and a crowd from the office. She was still smarting with anger from the wigging by Terry Brent a couple of hours earlier, and was only just beginning to simmer down. For half an hour she had been so angry she had sat and drafted a letter of resignation, then she had torn it up.

Stupid, she knew. Just a story. Another story. Forget it. But she couldn't. It wasn't just another story. It was a girl a year younger than herself and that had got to her. The fingernails nagged at her. Brent's attitude nagged. Mandy's, the mortuary assistant's, comment that she was surprised there had been no post mortem initially nagged at her. It was wrong. And it was wrong of Terry Brent. Christ, he was a newspaper man; he should have been interested in the story, in the truth.

Then the doubt gripped her again, squeezed her stomach. If she was wrong?

Someone behind her trod on her heel and she winced, stepping forwards.

'Sorry,' said a voice.

She slipped her shoe off and rubbed her heel. The queue moved forwards. She handed her complimentary ticket to the uniformed security man and went into the large hall. It was a typical modern municipal room, bland and airy with an abstract ceiling and bas-reliefs on the walls, and about five hundred hard, orange plastic chairs, of which about two thirds were occupied. Negro spiritual music was playing softly through speakers.

Kate sat down at the back of the hall, surprised by the diversity of the crowd. She had been expecting the blue rinse and hat-pin brigade, but the majority of the audience was young and trendy, late teens to mid-thirties. There was a smattering of older people, done up in their Sunday best, doubtless wanting to look smart for their departed loved ones should they happen to turn up.

On the stage was a white leatherette armchair and a table covered with a white cloth on which was a basket of artificial yellow and white flowers that concealed a microphone. More people filed in. Kate surreptitiously eased her notebook out of her bag and concealed it beneath her jacket. She began to jot down the atmosphere.

The lights on the stage brightened and a tall, blond man with two gold earrings and a yellow tuxedo strode across with a microphone.

'Ladies and gentlemen, some of you may have met Dora already. Those of you who haven't I can promise a unique experience. She is fresh from her recent world tour and her energies are at their peak. She will begin this evening with messages for many of you from loved ones who have departed. Afterwards she will be doing healing and those of you who require it are welcome to remain on.' He held out his hand and beamed a jaw-full of white teeth. 'Ladies and gentlemen, Dora Runcorn!'

As he exited to the left, the medium strode on in a blaze of lights and a fanfare of music from the right. She was wearing a white satin dress with a ruff collar and lace frills.

Kate felt a shiver down the nape of her neck. It reminded her of the white satin and frills that had lined Sally Donaldson's coffin.

The medium smiled her royal smile, bowed and waved to the roar of applause, then sat down in her white chair and coughed. The music and applause stopped and there was a crackle from the microphone, followed by a rumble and another crackle as she adjusted it.

She looked smaller than her image in her photograph and fatter and was caked in make-up like a gaudy nightclub singer.

'Lovely to see you all, darlings.' Her voice was gruff with a rural burr. 'I've just got back from America. Did twenty-seven towns in six weeks. Lovely people, the Americans; they have such a strong spiritual connection with this country. But I'm feeling strong connections here tonight, too.'

Dora Runcorn butterflied her arms outwards, wiggling her fingers, and closed her eyes, breathing deeply. 'There's a lot of energy here tonight. It's going to be a good evening and there are friends and relatives of you all around me, so many I'm not sure where to start. I'm getting the name Wrekin in Scotland.' She opened her eyes. An elderly woman with white hair put her hand up. 'There's a gentleman called Wrekin and he's recently passed on. Would that be right?'

The woman nodded. The audience was silent.

'He wants you to give a message to someone called Farquharson. Do you know someone called Farquharson who's made plans to change home or job in the last six months?'

The woman shook her head.

'I think it's Farquharson,' the medium said. 'No?'

The white-haired woman shook her head again.

'Hold on to it, dear, the meaning'll come clear in a day or two.' She closed her eyes and breathed hard again. 'I'm getting a message for someone called White or Whiting.'

Three people had their hands up.

'This is from a man who tells me he passed on about a year ago.'

Two people dropped their hands. The remaining one was a flinty-faced woman in her late thirties further along the same row as Kate. She had long red hair pulled tight into a barette and wore a green jacket.

'This man was your father, wasn't he?'

'My husband.'

'I'm sorry, dear. I had a bit of interference then, didn't hear him quite right. He tells me you've moved his room around.'

'I've moved house,' the woman said coldly.

Some of the confidence went from Dora Runcorn's voice. 'That's what I mean, dear.' The confidence came back. 'You've moved the position of his chair – in the new house.'

'I've sold his chair,' she said.

The medium smiled triumphantly. 'I think that's what he's been trying to tell me, dear, that you've moved it out of your life and he's a little hurt you've done that.' She beamed, closed her eyes again and sat in silence for a moment.

'I'm getting a message for someone called Parks who comes originally from the West Country.'

A girl with cropped black hair shot her hand up, and an elderly woman raised hers more hesitantly.

'This is from someone called Bill.'

The old lady put her hand down.

The medium looked at the girl. 'I think he's an uncle, would that be right?'

'Me dad.'

'I knew it was either your dad or your uncle. Passed over about five years ago?'

'Ten.'

'He's giving me a warning about your stairs. He's very worried about a loose stair rod, I think it is.'

'We live in a bungalow,' the girl said.

There was a titter of laughter.

'I think he's worried about the lady next door to you. Is there a lady in the street who's got an upstairs?'

The girl nodded.

'He wants you to warn her about her stair rod. He's very insistent about this.'

Kate felt irritated as she scribbled. The woman was twisting everything; it was a glib act and she could not believe how so many seemed to be sucked in and swallowing it.

'Now I'm getting a message from someone who's got an American connection. It's for someone who had a brother in America, who passed on about ten years ago, he's telling me.'

Kate's interest kindled a fraction.

Dora Runcorn was sitting with her eyes shut. 'I'm not getting him very clearly, but he tells me his sister's here tonight.'

Kate saw three hands go up.

'He's telling me he passed in an accident at sea. He was on a yacht. He's telling me he was caught by the sail and knocked overboard.'

Kate felt as if she had been hit in the chest by a sledgehammer. The three hands lowered slowly, reluctantly. The medium continued to talk with her eyes shut.

'He's trying to tell me his name. It might be Harry.'

'Howie,' Kate mouthed silently.

The medium's eyes were still closed. 'Yes, I think it's Harry. He was eighteen when he passed, but you are still his little sister and he wants to look after you. He wants to know if you have a toy called Keith. He's showing me a monkey.'

Feef. Kate stared at the woman, stunned. Her rag doll monkey, Feef.

'He's very distressed about something.' The medium's eyes opened and she was staring straight at Kate. There was no need for her to put her hand up. The medium knew.

Kate gazed at the white satin, at the lace frill, saw Sally Donaldson's face then Dora Runcorn's.

'He's telling me you are in great danger from something that you are doing – or you might be going to do – in your work. You mustn't do it.'

Kate felt her scalp squeezing like a clamp around her head and the skin tightening down the back of her neck.

'He's gone very faint. I'm having difficulty in hearing him. Speak up, dear!' she shouted, then was silent for a moment. 'He wants you to drop it, not get involved.' She closed her eyes. 'He's trying to give me a name. It sounds like wire. Something about wire he's trying to tell me.' She opened her eyes. 'Do you deal with electrical things?'

'Sort of, I guess,' Kate said lamely.

'I think you need to be very careful with wire. I think he's saying that you mustn't touch any wire. Something new with wire. Does that mean anything, dear?'

Kate shrugged and tried to speak loudly. 'Sort of, but not really. Can you give me anything more?'

The woman closed her eyes again. 'I'm losing him, dear, I'm afraid. He's very worried about you. You mustn't do this new thing.'

Kate's brain was spinning.

'Hold on to it, dear. Maybe it'll mean something in a few days.'

Kate sat in silence, watching, listening, her heart hammering, her stomach churning.

Harry. Howie. Ten years ago. Accident at sea. America. Brother. Sister here.

If it was lucky guesses, it was a lot of lucky guesses in a row.

'I've got a message here for someone called Mary,' Dora Runcorn said.

Several hands went up.

'It's from someone who wears glasses. They're showing me a pair of glasses and saying you used to get angry with them because they were always losing their glasses.' She scanned the show of hands. 'It's a woman called Betty, I think.'

Kate sat limply for the rest of the session. The routine carried on. Names, banality. She scarcely heard any of it. Her mind was back in Boston, back to the day her father sat on her bed and told her Howie wasn't coming home any more. Then forwards to now.

*Something with wire . . . He wants you not to get involved.*

She stayed in her seat when the session had ended while people filed out. The man in the yellow tuxedo reappeared and brought two orange chairs on to the stage. A line of thirty people formed. Kate joined the back of it.

The line moved slowly. Dora Runcorn spent a couple of minutes with some people, as much as five with others. Cleaners started work in the hall, stacking the chairs, hoovering. The man in the tuxedo stood in the wings, yawning.

The woman smiled at Kate as she finally approached. She seemed much older close up, and tired.

'I'm sorry,' Kate said, 'I don't need any healing. I wondered whether you could give me any more.' She wasn't sure whether the medium recognised her from earlier or not.

'I'm sorry, dear, not tonight.'

'Could I have a private session or something? I'm happy to pay.'

The woman smiled. 'It's not the money, dear.' She was frowning at something. Kate realised she was clutching her notepad. 'Are you a reporter?'

'Yes,' Kate said, embarrassed, then realised she shouldn't be. 'You sent an invite to the paper, the *Sussex Evening News*.'

'Yes, dear, I read it.'

'You're local?' she said, surprised.

'Born and bred in Sussex.' The medium picked up a card from the table and handed it to Kate. 'Call me next week. I'm touring this week; can't do private sittings when I'm touring. It's too tiring.'

'Thanks, I will.'

'What's your name, dear?'

'Kate Hemingway.'

'Any relation to the writer?'

'No. Wish I was.'

'You're very pretty, dear. You remind me of someone, an actress. Got long blonde hair and a pretty face like yours. I'm no good at remembering things, I'm afraid.'

Kate smiled. 'Thank you. I'll call you.'

'Next week, dear. Call me next week.'

Kate walked through the empty hall, past the security guard who was sitting on a chair by his desk and out into the night. It was eleven o'clock and raining and she had not eaten. And she did not know what the hell she was going to write.

# *Chapter Twenty*

The recovery ward on the third floor of Queen's Hospital was a square, windowless room with white walls and ribbed, cast-iron radiators which were currently switched off against the late spring heatwave. It serviced five operating theatres in which general surgery was carried out. At the moment four patients lay on their trolleys, being carefully watched by recovery nurses and medical students.

Harvey Swire sat by an elderly man who had not yet come round from the anaesthetics after surgery for an abdominal aortic aneurism. There were six weeks to go of the summer term of his third year at medical school. He was hot in the room, had misjudged the weather this morning and had dressed in a warm suit and woollen socks and was now feeling irritable as well as bored. He glanced intermittently at a copy of the *Daily Express* which he had beside him, his eye drawn back constantly to the photograph. The headline read: MASSACRE AT KENT STATE.

Four students, two men and two girls, had been shot by National Guard soldiers at Kent State University in Ohio during a Vietnam war protest. The picture on the front page showed one of the students in jeans lying on the ground, his frozen death mask of a face staring at the camera. A girl knelt hysterically beside him, arms out, screaming for help. Other students seemed to be sleepwalking past her.

It was a good moment-of-death picture. He would put it in his collection.

Harvey was going out with a red-headed student nurse called Gail who was crazy about oral sex. He still took his pills and had managed to keep them a secret from her and from the other girls he'd scored with. Girls came easily now, nurses mostly. He had learned the secret, which was to pretend to care for them, show interest, be charming and witty; that was easy. Work was easy, too.

Life was a game. You had to realise that; you had to be seen to play it by the rules. You could fool anyone if you played it by the rules.

Sometimes he could even fool himself that he was normal; that he did not have the power. That he did not need the pills.

For a few nights before the exams he had stopped taking them, had tried to travel out of his body again and read the exam papers. But nothing had happened. Maybe it was the withdrawal symptoms. The power seemed to have gone.

Without the pills he felt dizzy constantly. He could not even get erections; his temper became erratic, out of control. He half left his body but could not separate from it completely; it was as if he was conscious of controlling himself from a cockpit attached to his head. Gail became scared of him after he got mad at her one night, told him he must be working too hard, was having a breakdown, had turned really weird.

She told him a lot of the things he remembered his first girlfriend, Angie, telling him. So he went back on the pills again, to the familiarity of the muzziness in the mornings and the headaches which he had long got used to, long understood as reality.

As real as the man in the bed he was sitting beside who was a horrible shade of white, like marble. They always came out of major surgery looking like marble; either that or dead. Often, without the green spikes of the electro-cardiogram, it was hard to tell the difference.

This one was alive. E. Meadway was the name on the plastic bracelet on his wrist. One of the drip tubes was taped to the plastic cannula in the back of his hand just below it. ECG pads were taped to his chest below which was an eight-inch line of fresh stitches. The tubes ran up to the saline and adrenaline solutions hanging in their plastic bags from the drip stand; the wires from his chest were connected to the electro-cardiograph monitor. He lay on his back, hands straight out beside him, eyes shut, mouth open, unaware of the brass plaque on the side of the monitor above him which read "In memory of Louis Silverstein, 1968". Unaware of Harvey seated beside him, whose duty was to stay with him until he had come round sufficiently from the anaesthetics for it to be safe to send him back to his ward.

The man's chest heaved weakly but rhythmically. Breathing on his own. The anaesthetist had removed the breathing tube twenty minutes previously. Harvey glanced at the blood pressure monitor. 148/70. That was OK. E. Meadway had survived the operation and the anaesthetics, and was coping on his own.

Heavy anaesthetics. Twelve cc of Brietal to knock him out and 1%

halothane to keep him asleep because there had been complications and the operation had lasted nearly four hours. Eight milligrams of Pancuronium to paralyse the muscles to allow the surgeon to cut through the abdomen without reflex actions. Fifteen milligrams of Haloperidol and forty milligrams of Pavaveretum to control the blood pressure so as to minimise blood loss during the operation. Harvey was intrigued by the chemistry of anaesthetics.

The man stirred; coming round soon now, Harvey thought, glancing again down at the photograph in the newspaper, then at the black-stockinged legs of a nurse across the ward called Anthea, who he fancied. Thomas Piper was seated by the trolley next to him on which lay a man in his forties with a Zapato moustache.

Harvey had spent a year working with Piper, dissecting their cadaver, yet had not got to know him. Piper was OK, serious, diligent, charmless. Hedley-Weens had dropped out, because he had been unable to cope with the sight of blood. Gordon Clifford had been killed this spring in a skiing accident.

There were anxious voices around the trolley across the ward on which lay an elderly woman. The nurse, Anthea, called out to someone urgently, 'Could you get Mr Crymble quickly?'

He looked over his shoulder. An anaesthetist was lancing a vial with a hypodermic, and a junior anaesthetist called Roland Dance, a pompous man who liked to show off to the students, was struggling to force a breathing tube down the woman's throat. There was a clatter of footsteps, then Harvey's attention was distracted back to his own patient who gasped suddenly and decisively. He spun round, scared for a moment that the man had died on him and he had missed the moment.

So far he had only caught it once. It was in similar circumstances to this morning's, with a patient who had also undergone major abdominal surgery like E. Meadway, who was lying there, off the ventilator, when he had suddenly stiffened and the spikes of the monitor had flattened into a continuous straight line.

Harvey had known he was dead then; knew it at that moment; had almost been able to feel the life force leaving him. He had stood back whilst the crash team had tried to get him going, but it had been no good; in seconds the colour had drained out of his face. Something else had drained out of him, too. Harvey wished he had been able to weigh the man before it had happened, the instant before. He was certain something had left his body. Positive.

E. Meadway had already died once. An hour ago in the operating theatre. His heart had stopped and the surgeon and nurses had struggled for almost two minutes to get it going again. They had tried the defibrillator, without success, then they had injected adrenaline into one of the heart chambers. That had worked, but they could not be sure the patient had not suffered sufficient oxygen starvation to cause brain damage. He was an elderly man, seventy-seven, with little resilience to anything. They would not be able to tell for a couple of days, until he was reasonably lucid.

Harvey had watched him whilst he was dead, spreadeagled under the layers of green cloth on the operating table. It had felt strange.

E. Meadway gasped again. His eyes sprang open and he made a movement as if he were trying to sit up. Alarmed, Harvey jumped to his feet and stood over him, watching intently. The man stared straight up at Harvey, who was amazed to see anyone come so suddenly and acutely awake like this.

'Cor, blimey!' E. Meadway said in a croaky whisper, whether to himself or to Harvey, Harvey was not immediately sure. He checked the monitors. The spikes were strong. The man spoke again, still in a whisper with a cheery East End accent: 'Lumme! I saw you all. Saw the whole bloody operation! I saw you pick your bloody nose! I was up there on the ceiling of the bloody theatre. When the surgeon said I was gone, I tried to tap the bugger on the shoulder and tell him I was all right, but he couldn't bloody hear me.'

E. Meadway's eyes closed. He slept some more.

Harvey stared, transfixed. The spikes on the monitor weakened a little. During the operation he had been standing behind E. Meadway's head with the anaesthetist and the junior anaesthetist monitoring the anaesthetics machine. As was normal during major surgery, a screen of green cloth had been raised behind the patient's head to minimise any possible risk of germs transferring from the anaesthetics machine to the patient.

He had dropped his mask and picked his nose. He remembered doing it in the heat of the excitement. He had picked it whilst the man, E. Meadway, was clinically dead.

Impossible. E. Meadway could not have seen him.

It was as impossible, he realised, as what he had seen when he had been run over on his bicycle.

# *Chapter Twenty-One*

*Wednesday, 24 October*

Summer seemed a long time ago; a vague memory that was already getting confused in Kate's mind with other summers, the way images slid into each other and got buried under the stack that was for ever mounting up.

There were days only a month ago that had been so hot it had been impossible to imagine ever feeling cold or damp again. Now the heat was little more than an illusion, and reality was a damp autumnal morning with deep puddles across the pavement, angry water sluicing down the gutters, and a sky that was a silent rotating vortex of grey on darkening grey.

Kate stood in the jostling scrum of people outside Lewes Crown Court house, and vaguely wondered whether the ancient building was capable of swallowing everyone. Sex offences always drew crowds and this was a particularly horrific case: a forty-seven-year-old self-professed satanist called Hartley Briggs and four others were accused of abducting and performing ritual sex acts with sixteen children over the past five years.

Court rooms, like railway compartments, were either baking hot or freezing cold. The trick, Kate had learned, was to wear layers of clothes you could peel off. She liked to look smart when she went to court; it helped with interviewing witnesses who were often in a state of confusion about who were officials and who were not, and tended to be under the impression that people in smart clothes had court sanction.

She was wearing a black and white herringbone wool suit which she had bought in a Fenwick's sale the previous January, a white blouse with a small floppy black velvet bow and her best coat which she knew looked stunning on her; it was navy wool and cashmere, calf-length, which she had also bought in the sale, and she had draped a large Cornelia James wool shawl, which matched perfectly, over her shoulders. She was wearing plain tights and polished black shoes with low heels.

Her shoes were looking a bit scuffed. They were several years old. But trade was bad in the shops this year and a lot of sales would be starting before Christmas; it was only a few weeks to wait. Kate bought most of her clothes in sales; she liked nice materials and good quality shoes and it was the way she could afford them.

A solitary band of pain ran somewhere inside her forehead as the result of a sleepless night. She had lain in bed thinking and fretting about everything, scared and confused. She saw Sally Donaldson with her torn and jagged fingernails in her coffin, and Sally Donaldson on the mortuary table with her nails immaculate, saw the fury on Terry Brent's face, heard the words of Dora Runcorn.

*He's telling me he passed in an accident at sea. He was on a yacht. He's telling me he was caught by the sail and knocked overboard.*

So accurate.

Harry. Less accurate. Harry, Howie, the sound was close. Too close.

*He wants to know if you have a toy called Keith. He's showing me a monkey.*

Feef. Christ.

*He's telling me you are in great danger from something that you are doing – or might be going to do – in your work . . . He wants you to drop it, not get involved. Something about wire he's trying to tell me.*

Wire. Stories came down the wires; half her leads came that way. It was too vague. Ambiguous. It was like articles she had read on mediums: they impressed you at the time, but afterwards you realised what they were telling you could be interpreted hundreds of different ways. There was nothing specific. Except. Feef. Harry. The yacht.

She shivered as she thought of the medium's stare. As if the woman knew, was being directed.

The fingernails. Maybe it was just bits of lining, or dried placenta that had made them look broken. Maybe.

If she was wrong she was going to be sacked. Sued. Career kaput. She could imagine her sister Dara's snarky comments. *Twenty-four and the idiot can't make a go of anything. Hasn't got a career, hasn't got a boyfriend, can't hold a job down.*

She remembered at four o'clock there was a presentation to a girl pianist at a school in Brighton she had been told to cover and wondered if she would have a chance to get to that. She liked to cover things involving children, to encourage them.

The scrum moved slowly, like toothpaste trying to get back into a tube, towards the narrow door to the public and press galleries. Police stood on the steps of the court, keeping a passage clear to the main entrance. People were scurrying in, heads ducked against the rain. There were a wigged and gowned barrister, several men and a couple of women in smart clothing, solicitors, probably. A scruffy handful of people, shouting and holding up a banner on which was scrawled HARTLEY INNOCENT, hung around on the pavement.

Kate felt the prod of a finger in her back and heard a clipped voice say: 'Aren't you meant to be out digging graves?'

She turned. Patrick Donoghue was standing behind her, greatcoat collar tucked up, eyes twinkling merrily. 'I'm beginning to despair of you as a stringer. You got the hottest story that's happened down here in years and instead of chasing it you're spending a day in court.'

'Not my choice.' She was glad that she was dressed so well; the *Daily Mail*'s reporter glanced down at her approvingly. He was in his usual gear, clothes that looked a little battered, but never scruffy. Bottle green corduroy trousers, brown brogues, a Vyella shirt under a ribbed jumper, and a tweed jacket that looked as if it might have been a hand-me-down from his father, and his ramrod straight stance. Kate felt a thrill of excitement at seeing him, felt cheered and safe and comfortable with him.

They moved forward a few more paces. 'So what's the news on the great exhumation?'

Kate shrugged. 'I'm off it,' she said, and tossed a stray strand of hair away from her face.

'What do you mean you're off it? You got the scoop.'

'I nearly got the sack.'

He looked concerned. 'What's the problem?'

'Terry Brent seems to think I made the story up. The rantings of female hysteria. Nobody will substantiate the story and apparently it's perfectly normal for dead women to give birth in the grave.' She tilted her head to one side and waited for his reaction.

'What? Give birth in the grave? You don't mean – ?'

Kate nodded.

'That wasn't in the piece.'

'Dick Wheeler, the chief sub, thought it would be too distressing,' she said, rather cynically.

'She'd actually delivered her child in the coffin?'

'Perfectly normal, so Terry Brent tells me. Stiffs do it all the time, if you believe him.'

'The dead do move about a bit. Rigor mortis setting in then easing off again; they make moaning sounds when they're moved sometimes – from the gases getting squeezed out of their stomachs. A dead body's a very disgusting thing.'

'Do they really move?'

'Yes. Sometimes they clamber out of the grave and come running after you.' His eyes widened.

Kate grinned. 'Terry Brent tells me I've upset half the clergy in Sussex. I have to drop the story until the inquest.'

'The story's all over Fleet Street.'

'I know. I was rung yesterday afternoon by the *News of the World*, the *Mirror*, the *Sun* and about a dozen other papers.'

'And what did you tell them?'

'I haven't called them back yet.'

'Good contacts, Kate. Get you out of the boondocks and into the big time.'

'So I can get sent back to Sussex to cover exhumations and satanists, like you?'

'Get better paid for it in London,' he said.

Kate dug her hands into her coat pockets. She scraped some fluff from the bottom of the lining with her nails; there was a scrap of paper in her left pocket, folded and crumpled and she was distracted by it for a moment, trying to remember what it was. 'No one's going to be too impressed with me if I've goofed.'

'Do you really think you have?'

The bit of paper was nothing, she remembered; just a receipt for some shampoo. 'No,' she said. 'I don't. But I don't know what's going on. I was convinced yesterday and now' – she shrugged – 'I don't know. I had experience in Birmingham at dealing with a hospital scandal. Everyone closed ranks pretty fast.'

'The medical profession always does,' he said. 'Most professions try to look after their own. But they won't easily be able to cover up a pathologist's report to the coroner.'

'The girl at the mortuary said she's surprised there wasn't a post-mortem done originally. And they're using a local pathologist rather than a Home Office one, which means they're not treating it suspiciously.'

'How do you know?'

'I went to the post mortem.'

'They let you in?'

She smiled and blushed. 'Yes.'

'I won't ask how,' he said.

'It was easy.'

'How did you get on?'

'I nearly passed out.'

'I went to a post mortem once and did pass out. It was when they cut the top of the skull off with the rotary saw – '

She raised her head and swallowed. 'I don't need to know any more.'

'Guess what they fill the skull with after they've taken the brains out?'

'Don't!'

'Old newspapers. Remember where what you're writing might end up.'

'Thanks, Patrick.'

'You'll get used to it.'

'I don't think I want to. Would the pathologist look at everything?'

'They're pretty thorough.'

'How about fingernails?'

'The pathologist's job is to find the cause of death. He'd look at anything that was relevant to that.' They moved closer towards the entrance. 'So you're not out doing any door-stepping? Getting comments? You should be right in the thick at the moment, badgering the hospital.'

'You don't have to tell me.'

'Are you convinced enough about what you've seen?'

'Yes, in my heart. At least I thought I was.'

'Well, it doesn't need both of us here all day.' He looked at her. 'I'll phone your reports through for you. OK? What are you waitin' for? Buzz off.' He winked.

'Are you serious?'

'Yes, dead serious. Provided one thing.'

'Uh huh, what's that?'

'That you don't forget our date tonight.'

She grinned. 'Deal! And you'll phone my reports through to the copy takers?'

'Yes. And unlike you, I won't forget.'

'If Brent finds out what I'm doing I'll – '

'Brent's an asshole. Don't worry about him; he always blows hot and cold.' He gave a single jerk of his head. 'Go on, piss off and do a day's work.'

# *Chapter Twenty-Two*

The Rolling Stones' 'Satisfaction' pounded in the hall outside and red and blue lights flashed on and off in tune with the beat. Harvey stood in the cramped kitchen under the stark glare of a naked white light bulb. The mottled Formica worktop behind him was littered with bottles of cheap wine, tin pipkins of beer and plastic beakers.

A drunken girl in a miniskirt above her crotch sat on the draining board, her fishnet-clad legs dangling, her lipstick smeared across her face, arguing with an equally drunken medical student called Ted Blake, who was wearing a red corduroy shirt and a floral tie, about whether circumcised women could have orgasms.

Harvey Swire hated parties; particularly this sort of Saturday night student crush box. It was hot and he was sweating just standing here. Gail, his girlfriend, was in another room, dancing with some tall prat. Harvey didn't care; dancing bored him. He sipped his tepid metallic beer, thinking about E. Meadway, the abdominal patient who told him he had watched his own operation whilst floating on the roof of the operating theatre. He had visited the old man several times since, but he had suffered post-operative complications and had either been asleep or too confused to talk.

Someone thumped him heartily in the back. 'OK, old boy?'

He turned and saw Roland Dance, the junior anaesthetist, in a polo neck sweater and tweed hacking jacket. Dance was sloshed, and uncharacteristically jovial. 'Fine,' Harvey said. Dance picked up a heavy beer tin and clumsily refilled his plastic tumbler. Froth rose up and beer slopped over the rim and down to the sticky lino floor. Harvey did not like Dance much. He thought he was pompous and arrogant. Word was that Dance was exceptionally bright; that he was going to make a brilliant anaesthetist. He was already young for his position. Harvey resented him for his achievements. He was surprised to see him here.

'S'great party.' Dance's slippery lips puckered and he attempted to focus. A reedy, funnel-nosed man, with short, limp hair, a round mouth, virtually no chin and tiny, sharp-looking teeth, he reminded Harvey of a pantomime rodent.

'No woman could come without a clitoris, sh'impossible,' the drunken girl by the fridge slurred.

'Surely it would depend on the depth of the penetration?' said Ted Blake.

Roland Dance's concentration was deflected to the couple; he frowned disapprovingly, tried to focus, then leaned over to Harvey. 'I say, that's a bit fruity, isn't it?' He tipped some beer down his throat.

Harvey wasn't sure whether he was talking about the girl's miniskirt or the conversation. He glanced at the girl, then at the white flesh of her slightly plump thighs through the netting of her tights, and felt a flash of randiness. He wondered if he could muscle in on the conversation. 'Some of the African tribes do that, don't they?' he said.

'S'not true,' the girl said aggressively to him. 'Not all black men have big pricks.' Her head lolled forwards and she squinted. 'Anyhow, shish a very personal conversation.'

'Are you planning to specialise in anything?' Roland Dance said to Harvey, trying to change the subject.

'I haven't decided,' he said tersely, annoyed for a moment at the interruption. Then he realised his opportunity and smiled at Dance. 'Actually, I wanted to ask you something. About a patient earlier this week, name of Meadway. Mr Wendell operated on him on Tuesday. You were there.'

'Meadway?'

'The second op on Tuesday morning. An elderly man; abdominal surgery. Had a cardiac arrest.'

The decibels of the music increased, drowning his words.

'Sorry,' shouted Dance. 'Have to speak louder.'

Harvey repeated what he had said.

'Ah – the aortic aneurism.'

'I was with him in the recovery ward,' Harvey said. 'When he came round he told me he had been conscious during the operation.'

'Conscious?'

Harvey stared into his beer. 'Not exactly awake. He said he had been floating on the ceiling of the operating theatre and that he had seen everything going on. He described where everyone was standing, what everyone was doing.' Harvey looked up. 'He told me what I was doing.'

The junior anaesthetist nodded dismissively and his aloofness returned. 'Happens quite often, old boy,' he said.

'Really?'

'Absolutely.'

The fishnet legs distracted Harvey momentarily. 'You mean people leaving their bodies?' Another medic and a nurse he recognised came giggling into the kitchen and rummaged around amongst the wine bottles. 'People can actually float out of their bodies and drift around?'

'Yes, it's very common. It's all an illusion.'

Harvey felt the lance of disappointment. 'What do you mean?'

The anaesthetist stared at him as if he were an idiot. 'I do it with my drugs. Neuroleptic anaesthesia. I suppose you haven't got on to that area yet?'

'No.' The music stopped, giving a brief respite. 'You're saying it's drugs that create this effect?'

'Of course. Disassociative drugs. Butyropherones like Haloperidol. Ketamine, when you want to keep the patient semi-conscious. Good for trauma situations, when you have to cut someone out of a car or from under a building without dropping their blood pressure.'

'And they think they've left their body?'

Dance nodded.

'Doesn't that feel pretty freaky for them?'

'Yes, it does. Especially Ketamine. It produces dreadful post-op nightmares which can go on for days, weeks; pretty hairy stuff.'

Harvey sipped some more beer. He had to be careful with the pills. More than a pint and he started feeling strange. 'Do you believe anyone could really leave their body?'

'The soul, you mean?'

'Soul – or consciousness – or some energy mass.'

'Load of bollocks. Did you know that one of the biblical temples where miracles took place had an underground gas leak of nitrous oxide? Anyone in there would have been tripping out, high as a kite. All these hallucinatory things have chemical explanations.' He held up his beaker and squinted at the beer.

'How do you explain this patient, Meadway, describing what people were doing in the operating theatre when he couldn't see them?'

Dance was getting bored of the subject; his eyes slipped furtively to the girl on the draining board.

'Men don't understand about orgasms,' she slurred and glared at Dance and Harvey.

Dance winced. He looked at Harvey and tapped his left ear. 'Hearing, old boy; it's the last sense to go under anaesthesia. That's why you never discuss a patient in the operating theatre. If one's a shade too light on the anaesthetics they can hear what's going on. Combine that with a disassociative drug which makes you feel you are out of your body and that's it.'

Harvey cupped his beaker in his hands. The girl on the draining board was now snogging with the man in the red corduroy shirt and his hand was buried up to his wristwatch inside the waistband of her tights. 'That would be a hallucination. What I'm saying is how do you account for someone describing exactly what is going on? Surely if it was just a hallucination you wouldn't be able to.'

Dance leaned towards him and waggled his ear. 'These things, old boy. Blind men can see with these. Bats can see with these; all sorts of insects. You make do with what you have; when your other senses get shut down what's left becomes heightened. Your ears become like radar.'

Harvey thought back to the operating theatre. Could E. Meadway have heard him picking his nose? He remembered clearly doing it, turning away, pushing his mask down his chin. 'Have you ever heard of anyone having this sort of experience when they haven't been out under anaesthetics?'

'History's full of them. Plutarch. Caesar. The Bible. Sudden stressful situations or trauma can cause them.'

'How come, without drugs?'

The anaesthetist belched and stared accusingly at his beer. 'Know where the best drugs factory in the world is, old boy?' He tottered and steadied himself against a cupboard.

'No, where?'

Dance tapped his chest. 'Our bodies. Bloody magic. Can make up anything. We make our own hallucinogens at times – deliberately when we go to sleep, accidentally when we have a bang on the head, or a disease or a shock.' There were beads of perspiration on his forehead and his nose was shiny. 'Bloody hot in here.' He took out a yellow polka dot handkerchief and dabbed his brow.

'Could someone with a head injury hallucinate?' Harvey said.

'It depends what else was going on. This business of floating. It often happens after the heart's stopped. The brain goes into a sort of shut down. Hallucinogens get released – endorphins. People get an image of floating above their bodies, then going down a tunnel, seeing dead relatives.' He gave an asinine grin. 'They're convinced they've died, and been over to the other side.'

Harvey stared at him numbly. 'Is that a common experience?'

'No, it's pretty rare,' Dance said.

'And you don't think there's any more to it than that?'

'I know there isn't, old boy.'

'Could you prove it?'

'Prove it? Yes – ' He hesitated. 'I suppose it would be possible.'

'So you could make someone have that experience?'

'Deliberately?' Dance looked at him oddly.

'Yes.'

'Technically it would be possible,' Dance said and leaned closer to Harvey. 'I can do anything I want with my anaesthetics machine to a patient. No one realises the power anaesthetists have. All the surgeons are interested in is that the patients don't move, that muscles don't go into spasm or have reflexes. Surgeons are just a cross between glorified carpenters and plumbers. Anaesthetists are the ones who have the power in operating theatres. What I do with my anaesthetics machine, the drugs I use and the amounts I put in is what decides whether a patient lives or dies.' He drank some more beer. 'Do you know the psychiatrist, R. D. Laing?'

Harvey nodded. The snogging behind Dance was getting heavier. The girl had the man's red shirt tails out and her hands down inside his trousers. 'I've read one of his books, *The Divided Self*.'

'Good study of schizophrenia.'

Harvey blushed.

Dance did not notice. 'Ever hear about his dilemma?'

'No.'

There was a crash of scattering glasses. The girl on the draining board had her legs scissored around the student's waist and they were writhing against each other. Dance frowned in disapproval. 'Laing says he had a patient who was an anaesthetist. The chap told him that every now and then he used to kill a patient for fun. Apparently Laing could never decide whether the man was a psychopath and really did do this, or whether it was his guilt – his way of justifying himself when he did lose a patient.'

Harvey glanced down at the brown marbled lino; there was a hole from a cigarette burn near his foot. 'What was the outcome?'

'Oh, well, Hippocratic oath and all that. He felt he was not able to reveal the chap's name – apparently he's dead now, anyway. Bloody difficult thing to prove, you know. You get some patients who are borderline. Give them a bit too much of something and that's it. Anaesthetic drugs give a pretty good insult to the body. Some people can't take them. You are going to lose a percentage of patients, particularly in emergency situations. Get a crash victim come in – the poor sod's internal organs buggered up and the body's chemical balance haywire – the anaesthetist has to make a lot of quick choices and sometimes pure guesswork. Be bloody easy to kill someone deliberately without even the surgeon knowing, if you really wanted to.' The anaesthetist's eyes flicked away suddenly, as if disturbed by something they had seen.

'Have you lost any patients?' Harvey asked.

'Yes. From time to time,' Dance said. 'Had a woman a couple of weeks ago, who was only twenty-eight. Came in for a minor exploratory op. Stupid woman hadn't put down on the form that she was asthmatic.' He shrugged and checked the inside of his mouth with his tongue. 'The drugs we pumped in gave her an anaphylactic reaction. By the time we realised, it was too late.'

They stood in silence for a moment.

'Oh, well,' Dance said, draining his glass, 'better go and check out the talent, I suppose.'

'Bye, Bye, Miss American Pie' was pounding in the next room. 'There's something I don't understand about what you're saying,' said Harvey.

'Uh?'

Harvey waited for a moment as the snogging couple squeezed past him and went out into the hall. 'These disassociative drugs, this feeling of floating, that's fine if the patient is alive. How do you explain someone like Meadway who was clinically dead whilst this was happening? It was during the two minutes that his heart had stopped. He was dead. How could he have had any consciousness then?'

'Ah!' Dance looked smug. 'It's the big fallacy. I wrote my PhD thesis on this. I'll let you have a copy. People define death as when the heart stops, but the heart's just a pump. All it does is shunt blood to the brain. It's the old brain box that matters, not the heart. The brain can carry on for ninety seconds – two minutes at the outside – after the heart has stopped beating. The potential for regaining consciousness is still there. Death only occurs when the oxygen's eaten up and the brain becomes irreversibly damaged. It can take five or six minutes for the electrical activity in the brain to cease. Then consciousness can never be regained.'

There was a loud crack. Dance's eyes shot to Harvey's plastic beaker. Harvey's hands felt wet. He had squeezed the beaker so hard it had split and the beer was running out on to the floor. Flustered, he put it on the table. A brown puddle spread from it. Harvey turned away, ignoring it. 'Could you simulate brain death with anaesthetics?' he said quietly.

'Simulate? I'm not with you, old boy.'

Harvey was trembling. His own internal chemical balance was going haywire. He could feel adrenalin pumping into his bloodstream. 'Making someone brain dead and then bringing them back. Give them disassociative drugs, then stop their brain activity, and see afterwards if they could remember anything during that time.'

Dance frowned. 'Brain death is not reversible. When the squash has gone, that's it.'

'Aren't there any drugs that could simulate brain death? Shut down all brain activity?'

'Why would you want to do that?'

Harvey clenched his hands together. 'Don't you see? If you could get someone to float out of their body, then stop their brain activity completely and talk to them afterwards . . . don't you see what that would prove?'

'You've lost me.'

'It would prove whether there is life after death!'

The junior anaesthetist shook his head, bewildered. 'Why?'

'You've just said that floating out of the body is an illusion. If someone was brain dead and still floating out of his body then that couldn't be an illusion, could it?'

'They'd be bloody dead!'

'Isn't there any drug that would damp down brain activity, stop it completely without damaging the brain?'

Dance thought for a while. 'I suppose there's the new generation of barbiturates,' he said then. 'We sometimes use them on epileptics, for *status epilepticus*. It's pretty tricky. Quite an insult to the brain, but it does sometimes work.'

'Have you ever tried monitoring anyone it's happened to?'

'No.'

'Next time you have someone with that condition, I'd like to watch the treatment.'

'*Status epilepticus* is pretty rare. We only get one every few months.'

'I'd be interested. Would you let me know?'

Dance said he would.

# *Chapter Twenty-Three*

*Wednesday, 24 October*

Kate felt low as she drove away from the courtroom, leaving Patrick Donoghue to cover for her. Standing there with him she had felt good and strong, but now doubt tapped her again. The mind played tricks; sometimes you could see things in movies that weren't there because you were too scared to look properly.

*He wants you to drop it, not get involved.*

This? Was this what Dora Runcorn meant? What Howie had been trying to tell her? If it was, then maybe he was right. She had loused it up right down the line, missed her chance. Her one golden chance.

The trick was to catch bereaved spouses quickly, during the first three hours whilst they were numb with shock, off-guard. They would often open up because it was good to talk, talking kept their minds off the pain, off the reality, made it seem as if it were happening to someone else, not to them. After that the bedrock of grief and resentment would set in and the shutters come down. Their families would close ranks, answering their front doors and their telephones for them with guarded stiffness.

If you were sharp you got inside the house and borrowed the photo albums to stop other papers getting any pictures. And if you were hard enough you got them to make a cup of tea and whilst they were out of the room you swiped the photographs off the mantelpiece. You sent them back, of course, after a few days, with a lame apology. It was part of the game.

Kate cursed herself for not having taken her chance to interview Sally Donaldson's husband in the cemetery in those first few minutes after they had opened the coffin. He would have talked, given her everything she needed.

But she hadn't because she had been too shocked herself. Or perhaps that was just her excuse, and the truth was she was too soft, did not have what it took to go in for the kill. She had felt sorry for the man and did not want to intrude on his grief.

Maybe Dara, her sister, was right, and she was always going to be a failure, did not have the right stuff, whatever that was.

Sunlight startled her, appearing ahead through a sudden blue hole in the cloud and glinting off the chrome strip on the bonnet. Slicks of flooding lay across the dual carriageway. She hit a patch of water too fast and the Volkswagen slewed, water drumming on the underside. The steering wheel jerked in her hand, then became slack, useless for a moment; her chest tightened and she panicked that the car was going to cross the central verge or roll over; it plunged forwards like a boat into a wave.

She eased her foot off the accelarator as the front wheels hit tarmac briefly then ploughed into another puddle. A truck thundered by on her outside, blinding her with spray, the slipstream swaying the car wildly, the wipers humming and thudding, etching two smeared arches in front of her eyes.

She dropped her speed down to below thirty, gripped the wheel, checked in her mirror then pulled out past another sweep of water. On her right was the red brick complex of Sussex University, and she wondered as she often did whether her life would have been different if she had gone to university instead of bumming around the world for a year after leaving school.

*He's telling me you are in great danger.*

She had not written the piece on Dora Runcorn yet. She was not sure what to write.

*He was eighteen when he passed on, but you are his little sister and he wants to look after you.*

The medium had been playing a game with her; the same game she had played for everyone else. Kate had spotted those tricks and twistings of meanings easily enough. She tried to work out how she had missed the ones the medium had played on her.

Must have played on her.

As she drove on into Brighton, she drifted off into her own thoughts. A twinge of guilt tugged at a nerve. God. Religion. She did not believe in God, not really, but there were some nights when she prayed still, as she had done as a child, because deep down she knew she would like to believe.

The traffic stopped. Across to her right now were the domes and minarets of the Royal Pavilion rising out of the lawns beyond the roofs of the vehicles, a wild extravaganza of a palace. Built by George IV for his mistress, Mrs Fitzherbert, when he was Prince Regent. Kate wondered what kind of a woman Mrs Fitzherbert had been. There were pictures in the Pavilion of a tall, elegant lady in a hat, keeping the world at bay with a needlepointed fan. She wondered if Mrs Fitzherbert had felt the same having her affair with the Prince Regent as she had felt having hers with Tony Arnold in Birmingham. She wondered how it felt to be visited by your lover in a palace instead of in a grotty flat on a ring road. Nice to be pampered. She hadn't felt pampered for a long time.

She drove slowly along Brighton seafront and lucked upon an empty meter bay opposite the grey edifice of the Old Ship Hotel. The wind was blustery, caught at the car door as she climbed out and then at her hair. An old lady walked by in an expensive coat with a shitzu straining on its leash.

The sea was a churned-up brown; lumpy waves broke against the girders of the Palace Pier chucking spray up against the walls of the helter-skelter on the Palace of Fun at the end. A tanker was turning in from the horizon towards Shoreham Harbour three miles to the west.

Kate loved the tang of the sea air, the salt, the putrid seaweed, the tar, the rust. A tin can rattled along the promenade below her. The paddling pool was empty, abandoned for the winter; a cluster of motor boats rocked about, roped together under tarpaulins in the next pool; an ice cream kiosk was boarded up, fishing boats rested on rotting davits in the shingle well back from the high-tide mark. She caught, fleetingly, the smell of chips.

Memories of childhood came back. The pontoons of Mamaroneck. Cruising up the New England coastline. The smart quayside of Rhode Island. Barbecues on deserted beaches. Sitting alone in the warm summer evenings on the teak deck of *Sloop Doop*, crabbing with chicken bones tied to string, shrieking as a big one came up, greeny-black and shiny and pissed off as hell, its legs flexing, its eyes swivelling and its pincers angrily clacking towards her.

She pulled herself away reluctantly and, buttoning her coat, crossed the wide, busy road. She turned right and hurried around the corner into the lee of the wind, behind a crescent of Regency houses that faced on to a bus station and badly needed a lick of paint.

The Register of Births and Deaths was housed in the ground floor of the same building as the Environmental Health Office. Kate walked under the imposing but tatty glass awning and into the wide lobby. She followed the sign down a corridor, past a large no smoking sign and a row of chairs and heard the echoing sound of typing.

The corridor led through into a small reception area with a large wooden counter, behind which sat a fair-haired girl in a neat green suit. There was a colour poster of a seal pinned to the wall above her.

'I'd like to have a look at a death certificate,' Kate said.

'Do you have the date and place of death?' The girl's voice was crisp.

'Yes, it was October the fourteenth at the Prince Regent Hospital.'

'There's a fee of two pounds for a copy.' The girl looked at her quizzically.

'That's fine.'

'Could I have the name of the deceased?'

Kate told her and she disappeared. Several more people came in and stood behind Kate, forming a queue. Then the girl reappeared and handed Kate the copy. She paid the fee, waited for the receipt, then walked over into a corner and studied the certificate carefully.

It had a crest at the top with a Latin inscription and an illegible signature at the bottom. She read down it. Name and surname. Sally Mary Donaldson. Sex. Female. Maiden surname of woman who has married. Mackenzie. Occupation and usual address. Secretary. Ten, Ryland Close, Brighton. Cause of death. Cerebral oedema. Certified by H. Matthews, MB.

Kate folded the photocopy and tucked it into her pocket. Then she went back to her car, did a U-turn and headed for the Prince Regent Hospital.

# *Chapter Twenty-Four*

The thirty-five-year old woman had been admitted to the gynaecological ward of Queen's Hospital for an operation to remove ovarian fibroids. With a pre-med of twenty milligrams of Valium working on her central nervous system, her apprehension had been turned to a faint sensation of euphoria. She felt only mild curiosity as the whistling orderly wheeled her on the trolley down the corridors and in through the double doors of the cramped, white-painted anaesthetics room.

Stan Meers, the anaesthetist, a short, gingery man with a freckled, slightly pudgy face, turned round. 'Hallo,' he said breezily. 'How are we?'

As the woman mouthed 'Fine,' he tapped the back of her hand, looking for a vein. Her eyes stared up at the anaesthetist in his green pyjamas, surgical mask tied around his neck but at the moment loose beneath his chin, green hat and white clogs. They moved to the nurse, similarly dressed, then to Harvey Swire and two other medical students who were doing their four-week stint on gynaecology. Harvey smiled his well-practised sympathetic smile.

On the worktop behind the patient were five plastic trays for the five patients for this morning's list. Each tray was laid with a disposable hypodermic syringe in a sealed plastic wrapper, ampules of anaesthetic agents, and a typed sheet, giving the patient's name, details, ward, brief medical history and list of any allergies. The type and dosages of drugs on the trays varied for each patient according to the surgery they were having.

Harvey knew the drugs; they were all variations on the three basic components of anaesthesia. Hypnotic drugs to induce sleep and keep the patients asleep, analgesic drugs to prevent pain, and muscle relaxants to paralyse the patients, preventing reflex jerks when muscles were cut and easing the surgeon's access to the internal organs.

'All right?' said Meers.

She nodded.

'We're going to pop you off to sleep in a few seconds.'

The room was warm, smelled of sterilising fluid and the faint stringent odour of disinfectant. The double doors opened and the surgeon came in, fully gowned.

'Hallo,' he said to the patient. 'I'm Mr Emmerson. We've met before, but you probably don't recognise me in my funny disguise. I'll see you tomorrow after you've had a snooze.'

The woman's lips started to form a smile. The anaesthetist poised the syringe. 'Just a little prick in the back of your hand,' he said, sliding in the cannula.

The smile did not get completed. As he continued to press the plunger she took a deep breath, then her whole body stiffened as if she had been set in cement. Her eyes glazed over, frozen open in mid-blink. For a moment Harvey thought she was dead. Then she exhaled; her breathing had altered to the long slow breaths of the deep asleep.

The anaesthetist carried on pressing the plunger until all the Brietal in the syringe had been injected into the woman, then held the cannula in place whilst the nurse taped it to her wrist. Meers's stubby fingers closed her eyelids.

It was like watching someone die, Harvey thought. There was a moment, almost a precise moment that you could measure, at which a patient changed from a conscious thinking being into a vegetable. Fast. Rarely more than thirty seconds.

The anaesthetist replaced the first syringe with another, containing a muscle relaxant. Methodically, the anaesthetist tilted back the woman's head, inserted the curved steel laryngoscope, then pushed the endotracheal tube past the white triangle of her larynx and down the bright red tunnel of her throat. It stuck, and he struggled with the tube, poking it harshly, jigging it around, pulling it out and ramming it back in, increasingly anxiously and impatiently, the way an angler might struggle to extricate a hook from deep in a fish's gullet.

The tube slid into place, and Meers pushed it down until just the nozzle protruded from the woman's mouth like an infant's dummy, then he inflated the cuff and connected the breathing system.

Two orderlies wheeled the trolley through into the operating theatre; Harvey followed. They slid wooden poles into hoops on either side of the mattress, and lifted the patient on to the metal table. She lay motionless in her cotton hospital gown beneath the brilliant glare of the overhead lamp, helpless, unable to do anything on her own except breathe, and she would be incapable even of that in a few minutes.

There were two other students in the theatre, also gowned up, and two nurses, the sister, the operating theatre technician, the obstetrics surgeon and his junior, the anaesthetist and his junior, and Harvey himself. All wore pyjamas or gowns, rubber gloves, clogs or rubber-soled boots, their masks pulled over their mouths and noses now so that only their eyes were visible.

The anaesthetist worked fast. The junior anaesthetist wound a blood pressure cuff around the woman's arm and Stan Meers switched on the gas valves on the anaesthetic machine and connected the breathing hoses to the endotracheal tube.

The nurses untied the tapes of the woman's gown and pulled it away, leaving her naked except for the plastic name tag on her wrist. The two orderlies each hitched up one of her legs and strapped them into the stirrups. Harvey's eyes ran over her large, sloppy breasts, and her plump, shapeless stomach with its stretch marks, and the glow of light on the stark white skin where her pubic hair had been shaved.

One of the nurses began swabbing iodine on to the woman's stomach using a brush that she dipped into a tin. The fluid ran in messy rivulets down each side of her abdomen. She daubed the woman's pubic area and the insides of her thighs as if she were painting a damaged shop window dummy. Another nurse arranged the surgical instruments in a neat row, the clatter reminding Harvey of his mother laying the table for lunch.

Stan Meers logged the woman's blood pressure on his anaesthetics chart; he would do that every three minutes, and her heart rate, and the exact doses and times of the drugs she would receive. It gave him an instant reference if there were any sudden complications. And it covered his back against any recriminations.

The oscilloscope on the ECG display on the anaesthetics machine was showing low, even spikes. A nurse hitched a plastic bag containing clear fluid on to the drip stand. Meers said something to the junior anaesthetist which Harvey missed; the junior turned a knob on a flow meter and an alarm bleeped on the machine for a second. The nurses pulled the white anti-thrombosis stockings on to the woman's legs, the cellulite flab on her thighs bulging at the top, and the operating theatre technician tied blue diathermy plate around the woman's ankle.

'I see this lady's had a laparotomy,' the sister said, looking at a scar on the woman's abdomen, then painting over it.

Hartmann's solution dripped intravenously into the back of the woman's hand. The anaesthetist checked the gauges on the oxygen and nitrous oxide. The nurses began covering all the exposed parts of the woman's body except her midriff in green cloth, and they erected a screen behind her head to shield her from the anaesthetics machine.

Operating theatres awed Harvey. His eyes ran across the pristine tiled walls and ceiling; across the high, frosted-glass window, the electric sockets, the recessed scrub-up area with its shiny steel sinks and lever taps; across the anaesthetics machine with its flickering dials and silently winking lights, and the colour-coded cylinders of oxygen and carbon dioxide and nitrous oxide. He looked at the shiny metal slab of the operating table beneath the huge kettledrum light. Like an altar.

Operating theatres felt like temples. Temples of knowledge. He breathed in the smells. Clean. Everything clean, walls, floors, ceilings, light fittings. He could smell the crisp green cloth and the disinfectant and the anti-static fluid, and heard the occasional squeak of a rubber sole on the terazzo floor.

The nurses were finishing laying the green covers; the final preparation, like a silent religious ritual. The laying of the cloth, he thought. Ceremony. Like communion. Celebration.

The search for knowledge.

Only the woman's face and a rectangular area of flesh in her midriff were visible now. The strip of exposed flesh stained brown by the iodine glowed almost ochre under the light that shone through the thick lenses above. The light that shone down on to the altar.

The surgeon pressed down on the woman's abdomen with his gloved fingers. 'OK, Stan?' he asked the anaesthetist.

'She's nicely under.'

The surgeon pressed down again. 'Abdominal muscles feel a little tense.'

'I'll give some more curare.' Meers also swiftly rotated the knob on the halothane vaporiser.

There was silence as the surgeon picked up his scalpel and made a steady, slow incision down the centre of the woman's abdomen. The skin parted behind the blade, like lips opening, a thin ribbon of blood quickly filling them.

*Surgeons are just a cross between glorified carpenters and plumbers. Anaesthetists are the ones that have the power in operating theatres* said a voice Harvey recognised. He glanced round. But no one seemed to have spoken.

Roland Dance, he remembered, had told him that. He watched the carpenter now, working on his bare patch inside the green covers, freeing the tissues around the woman's uterus as the nurses clamped back the flesh and sucked up the blood with a hissing vacuum nozzle. Distanced. Down there was a disgusting slimy mess. It was up here by the woman's head that mattered. Here with the tubes and the valves and the gauges and the blips chasing each other across the monitors of the anaesthetics machine that the woman's life was controlled.

He watched the black concertina bag of the respirator crush, expand, crush, expand. Stan Meers marked his chart. The junior anaesthetist checked the blood pressure. The woman's face was motionless, expressionless, her jaw distorted by the breathing tube. Further down, a hundred miles away, the surgeon worked away at his carpentry and his plumbing, happy so long as the woman's muscles did not twitch and her blood stayed red.

Dance was right. The anaesthetist controlled the woman's life. One switch, one rotation of a valve; one failure to notice something or to take the right action if she reacted against the drugs. That was all it needed.

The surgeon removed two fibroids, small, bloody objects the size of golf balls, then slowly and neatly sutured his incision down her stomach with zig-zag lines of black thread. Plumber, carpenter, tailor, Harvey thought. The operation was finished.

The orderlies lifted the woman back on to the trolley and wheeled her through into the recovery room. She was fine, already breathing unaided as the curare which had paralysed her lungs wore rapidly off after reversal.

The anaesthetist and his junior stayed by her until her eyes opened. 'OK? Awake?' said Meers.

The woman mumbled incoherently.

'She's fine,' Meers said to his junior and to Harvey and the two other students, then walked through into the anaesthetics room. As the door opened, Harvey could see the next patient lined up. He was about to follow when a nurse startled him.

'Mr Swire?'

Harvey turned. In a few years she would be calling him Dr Swire. He looked forward to that. 'Yes?'

'Telephone call for you in sister's office.'

Surprised, he went through into the tiny office and picked up the black receiver which was lying on the desk. 'Hallo?'

'It's Roland Dance. You said you were interested in seeing a *status epilepticus* patient.'

Harvey's mind jolted back to the conversation six weeks or so before with the junior anaesthetist in the kitchen of someone's flat during a party. He remembered it well. His girlfriend, Gail, had gone off that night with another medic. The bitch had not even said goodbye. 'Yes.'

'One's just been brought into the ITU. Like to come and see her?'

Harvey hadn't been given any specific duty to do. No one would miss him. 'Yes. Very much,' he said.

He changed swiftly out of his scrub-up gear back into his linen trousers, striped, button-down shirt from Lewins in Jermyn Street, silk tie and white coat. He weaved his way down the congested corridors, through the trolleys and staff and lost visitors and confused patients, the buzz of excitement carrying him faster than he usually moved, and up four flights of stairs.

The intensive care unit was hot, as it always was, and quiet, much quieter than the other wards, with its sound-deadening tiles on the ceiling and grey-carpeted floor. Each bed was in a recess affording its twelve patients a degree of privacy. Not that many of them were aware of that as they lay plugged into their winking monitors, their bodies wired with electrodes and punctured by tubes like tap-roots from the forest of drips and machinery around them.

If they were awake, it was just their eyes that moved, wary coloured beads following the incessant traffic of staff who were trying to raise the percentage of survivors. It stayed relentlessly the same, week in week out. Eighty per cent of the patients would go from here to one of the main wards or private rooms. Twenty per cent would go to the mortuary.

In spite of the warmth of the summer's day outside and the constant eighty degrees heat of the unit, Dance wore a heavy tweed jacket, a thick shirt with a green woollen tie, and cavalry twill trousers. He was in conversation with two nurses, and ignored Harvey for several minutes as he kept talking, discussing treatment of a haemorrhaging patient who was not responding. Beads of sweat lay on Dance's angular face and they irritated Harvey; he wished Dance would mop his brow.

'Ah, hallo,' Dance said, finally turning to him. 'Right. It was *status epilepticus* you were interested in, wasn't it?'

'Yes.' Harvey smiled. 'I'm impressed that you remembered.'

'Oh – well – ha!' Dance took him down to the far end of the small ward where a young woman lay in the most secluded bed. She was slender, willowy, with high cheekbones and a delicate face that was stunningly beautiful, even though now puffy and distorted from the endotracheal tube protruding from her mouth, and rippling every few seconds like a cornfield in the wind. Her limbs were making small jerks. Every few moments her stomach distended and her back arched. Her teeth bit on the tube, she made low moans and froth oozed out of the corners of her mouth.

On the table beside her were two greetings cards and a large vase of flowers. Small black electrodes were taped to her forehead, her temples and her scalp, their wires meeting in a neat clip above where they fused into one thick multi-coloured strand which plugged into the electro-encephalogram. Erratic spikes danced on the green oscilloscope screen. Peaks, troughs, flat spells. There was no regularity. Her brain was short-circuiting. Every muscle in her drugged, unconscious body was twitching in spasm.

'She's twenty-five,' Dance said. 'Fashion model. Got thrown from a horse three months ago and suffered a depressed fracture of the cranium causing haemorrhaging into the brain. The damaged brain tissue has become electrically unstable and that's causing her epilepsy. It's classic post-injury epilepsy situation. She was admitted yesterday by her doctor after complaining of an increasing number of fits. She started fitting again this morning in the ward and did not respond to intravenous diazepam. We tried large doses of intravenous phenytoin and that did not work either. *Status epilepticus* was diagnosed, so we decided to bring her into the ITU. She's now on thiopentone infusion.'

Harvey studied her face, then the equipment.

'If we were to leave her untreated,' Dance said, 'she would start to suffer brain damage and her muscle coordination would break down to a point where she would stop breathing and could be left a vegetable or even die. The way we are trying to reverse this is by damping down the electrical activity of her brain. Over the next half hour we'll be closing down her brain activity completely.'

Harvey watched the flow of the drug down the clear plastic tube and into the back of the woman's hand through the plastic cannula that was taped in place. The spikes of the EEG slowly became smaller, less uneven. The drug was working, bringing her down. As the spikes shrank, his own excitement grew. Just himself, Dance and the woman. Dance, the junior anaesthetist, in total charge of this woman's life.

His eyes caught the nurse's. Sandra Lock. He felt a frisson of arousal. He looked down at the patient, not wanting to be distracted, not now. Then he looked back at Sandra. She was smiling at him.

She had a turned-up nose and a large, generous mouth. Her black hair was cut short in a Sassoon style. Her face did not look that great and the skin was coarse, but something about her turned him on. She was in her early twenties. Large breasts, long, slender legs in her black stockings, and he imagined them being white, marble white, when they were bare.

'Like his mother's,' said a voice, sharply, into his ear.

He blinked, startled, and spun round. There was no one behind him. Sandra smiled again. Her? Had she said that? He heard the flat puff of the respirator. People speaking to him. Voices. People speaking about him. They did that occasionally. He did not mind. People had whispered about him at school and he'd shown them.

One day he would show the world.

The bellows inches above the girl's head contracted and expanded robotically, forcing air in and out of her lungs. Clunk-puff . . . clunk-puff. Flat, bright lighting shone down from the fluorescents and clean filtered air slid noiselessly in through grilles in the walls.

'Responding?' said a voice. It was Dr O'Feral, the anaesthetist in charge of the ITU.

'She's coming down,' Dance replied.

O'Feral glanced at the drip then at the EEG oscilloscope. 'Five cc?'

'Yes.'

'How long?'

'Fifteen minutes.'

'What's her pulse?'

'Fifty-five,' Sandra Lock said.

'Increase to seven and a half. We need some help on Mr Wendell in bed seven,' he said to Sandra. 'Could you give a hand for about five minutes?'

The nurse followed him. Dance adjusted the drip controller. 'Seven and a half,' he announced. Dr O'Feral came back. 'Roland, could you have a quick look at Mrs Gaffrey? I've got an RTA downstairs.'

Dance turned to Harvey. 'OK on your own for a moment?'

Harvey nodded.

'Check her pulse every three minutes. Shout if it goes below forty-five. She's coming down nicely, shouldn't be any problems.'

Suddenly Harvey was alone. He stared at the woman, then at the EEG. The spikes were dropping. Her jerks and twitches were weakening. He felt the pulse. Forty-eight. The barbiturate was slowing down everything. He knew it was fine for the heart rate to slow because the woman's metabolism was slowing and she needed less oxygen.

Her wrist was cold, damp, limp, the pulse beat like a tiny frightened animal. Yet her face now was starting to look calm, serene. The warning buzzer on the monitor sounded. The spikes on the oscilloscope had almost flattened. Harvey pressed the override switch and the noise stopped.

The last blips faded from the screen and there was now just a steady green line. Her brain was shut down completely. There was no activity at all. It was exactly as if she were dead. Her pulse had slowed to forty-five. Harvey listened to the puff of the ventilator, smelled the stale, rubbery air, felt his own heart racing.

Brain dead. No activity in there; no thought; nothing. She could not see or hear or feel. Until the barbiturate dose was switched off and spikes started to jump back out of the green line, she was a vegetable.

The ventilator hissed again; flat, stale air. If you stopped someone's brain activity completely, did you stop their consciousness? Or did you squeeze the consciousness out? Out somewhere? Like out on to the ceiling of the operating theatre?

Ernest Meadway, the cardiac patient who had told him that he had watched everything from the ceiling of the operating theatre had not been brain dead, merely drugged. Dance could have been right there, that it was a hallucination. Possibly.

But what if this woman was aware of what was going on now? Aware even though she was brain dead: then that would be different. It would be better still if she wasn't breathing at all; if her heart and brain were both dead, and afterwards, when she had been brought back and woken up, if she could recall what had been going on . . .

Stopping her breathing would be simple. One switch, inches from his hand. He turned, listened for footsteps, stared down across the ward. No one was near, no one was looking.

Just for a few seconds to see.

His hand went out, rested on the switch. He felt his adrenalin squirting, sweat ran down inside his shirt. Footsteps were coming down the ward towards him, fast, anxious; they stopped by the next bed and he could not see who it was. Nervous, he took his hand away. Somewhere in the distance he heard Dance's whinnying laugh. Damn. If the patient's consciousness was up on the ceiling and she was watching him, maybe she would remember afterwards. Maybe.

Give her a sign, he thought. Do something she could remember; something that would prove if she was watching from above.

He moved a few steps until he was out of her line of vision, to make completely sure. Then he raised his arms above his head and gave victory salutes with both hands. As he did so, he sensed someone standing behind.

'OK?' Dance said.

Harvey lowered his arms, feeling foolish. 'Stiff,' he said.

Dance glanced at the drip stand, then the EEG. 'How's the pulse?'

'Forty-five,' Harvey said.

'Getting what you wanted?'

'Yes, thank you.'

'Are you doing a thesis on epilepsy?'

Harvey hesitated, then nodded.

'Much more common than people realise,' Dance said. 'Affects about one in twenty of the population.' He yawned. It was like watching a horse yawn. 'Actually, I'm involved with an experiment that would interest you.'

'Oh, yes?'

Dance yawned again and tapped his mouth with his balled fist. 'Sorry, been on nights for the last week.' He put his hands into his jacket pockets and stared at the carpet as if he had dropped something. 'We're doing lab work on heavy barbiturate dose treatment for epilepsy. Quite interesting results on rats and cats. We've been tying off the arteries in the necks of cats – strangling them if you like – just enough to cause severe oxygen starvation to the brain, then we've been giving one group of them deep barbiturate therapy and the other group nothing and seeing which group had the greater brain damage. Quite impressive results. The rats are interesting. We've been having positive results on epileptic rats.'

'Do rats get epilepsy?' said Harvey.

'We're giving them GW 2937.'

'I don't know that drug.'

'You wouldn't. It's an experimental drug from Grauer's. It was developed for insomnia but they found it induces epilepsy. Bloody awful thing, epilepsy. Particularly what this poor girl's got.'

'*Status epilepticus* isn't that common, though,' Harvey said.

Dance gazed at the patient thoughtfully. 'Shame. Such a beautiful girl.'

'Shame there aren't more like her,' Harvey said.

Dance frowned dubiously at him, then his slippery lips curled into a grin. 'Pretty girls, yes of course! Thought you meant *status epilepticus* patients for a moment.'

Harvey said nothing.

# Chapter Twenty-Five

*Wednesday, 24 October*

The Prince Regent Hospital was on high ground half a mile back from the cliffs at the eastern end of Brighton. The rooms to the south had fine views across the rooftops of the Regency and Victorian terraces and out over the English Channel, and those to the north had views across the Downs and Brighton racecourse. As was typical with bureaucratic planning, most of the windows faced west into an industrial estate and east on to the hospital's multistorey car park.

The hospital had begun life in the early nineteenth century as a home for disabled sailors. With constant additions over the decades it had grown into one of the largest provincial hospitals in England, and with the Princess of Wales student wing under construction was soon to become a fully fledged teaching hospital annexed to the University of Sussex.

The hospital's central core was a grimy, grey stone building with a slate roof and a palladian portico flanked by a tarnished copper statue of the Prince Regent and an equally tarnished statue of Queen Victoria. Spread out on either side was a sprawling hodge-podge of buildings interconnected by windowless corridors and sloping walkways containing most of the firms, the older wards and the administration offices.

Pebbledash-rendered offshoots behind contained the laundry, mortuary and pathology departments, as well as the research laboratory block and the discreetly unmarked animal house, and behind them was the Queen Elizabeth II wing, a grim twelve-storey 1950s tower block containing general wards, intensive care, maternity and a suite of nine operating theatres.

Kate was disturbed by hospitals. They touched off memories and fears that she preferred to leave buried; they reminded her of her own mortality and she found life insecure enough without that. She did not like the buildings, nor their smells, nor the helplessness of the patients in them. She had been in hospital twice as a child, in Boston; once when she was seven to have her tonsils out, and when she was ten to have her appendix out. The doctors had been nice and so had the nurses, but they hadn't made the pain any better or the fear any less.

As Kate drove the VW up the ramp of the car park, the glove locker lid fell open. She slammed it shut, it opened again and a clutch of parking tickets fell out into the footwell.

The first level was full and the next three, and she drove on up the last ramp out of the darkness into the blustery sunlight and found a space. The wind screamed at her up here and she had to lean to walk against it, her coat pulling away from her like a sail, her hair whiplashing her face, the roots straining painfully.

She went down a stone stairwell that smelled of urine, past a spraygun graffiti saying SADDAM FOR PM and through a heavy fire door. There was a barrage of signs. Mendelssohn Ward, Victoria Ward, Chemotherapy, Microbiology, Histopathology, Day Care, ITU, Obstetrics, Casualty, Enquiries.

She pushed open a massive rubber-flanged door into a long dark corridor that smelled of mincemeat and cabbage and heating oil; steam coiled out of an open door. She realised she had come a floor too low. An orderly trundled a metal laundry trolley past her, a bunch of keys swinging from a ring clipped to a belt loop. She walked on, came to the bottom of some stairs, and saw a hive of activity down another corridor to the right, piles of laundry being sorted, loaded on to trolleys and trundled away.

She climbed the stairs, went through more double doors, and found herself in the enquiry and waiting room. The girl behind the reception desk was perky and efficient. Kate asked her where she could find Dr Matthews.

'There are two Dr Matthews here,' the girl said. 'Dr William and Dr Howard.'

Kate unfolded the copy of the death certificate and checked. H. Matthews. 'Dr Howard,' she said.

The girl glanced at something Kate could not see below the counter. 'He's in ITU. Level six.'

Kate thanked her, went down the corridor to the elevators and pressed the button. There was a smell of disinfectant and some chemical she could not identify. A cork notice board hung on the walls with a poster tacked to it advertising for blood donors. The metal door of the lift slid jerkily open. Two nurses were in there chatting, and a middle-aged man in a red paisley dressing gown holding a rolled-up newspaper. As she stepped in, a young porter pushed in a small tray stacked with surgical instruments. He greeted the nurses cheerily.

Kate got out at the sixth floor and followed the arrows to the ITU down a grey carpet-tiled corridor, and in through double wooden doors with safety glass panels to a small empty reception area. There were some comfortable-looking chairs behind a bamboo screen, a vending machine, a drinking water fountain and a payphone in a perspex cone. Through an open door Kate could see a tiny, empty bedroom with a single bed covered in a purple candlewick spread.

The counter was unmanned. A cursor blinked on a green computer screen on which were rows of technical jargon that made no sense to her. The place had a hushed, private feel, as if it were removed from the hustle of the rest of the hospital. Warm air hissed softly down from metal grilles in the styrofoam-panelled ceiling. Staff walked noiselessly along the passageway; no one was rushing, but no one looked slack. It felt similar to the newsroom of the paper; a sense of being at the centre, having the inside track, making the pace. There was even a similar institutional clock with a sweep second hand on the wall.

After about a minute a nurse saw her and came up to the other side of the desk. She was black with starkly brush-cut hair and a soft, warm face. A chromium watch hung on a chain from the lapel of her blue and white uniform and she held a clipboard in her hand. 'May I help you?'

'I'd like to see Dr Matthews,' Kate said.

'I don't think he's here. He's on nights at the moment.' Then she frowned and glanced down at a list. 'No, wait a minute, the roster's changed. I'll go and see.' She was about to walk off, to Kate's relief without having grilled her, when she stopped. 'Are you a relative of a patient?'

Kate smiled, glad she was looking smart, and shook her head.

'Who shall I tell him?'

'My name's Kate Hemingway.' The nurse did not ask her any more questions, but turned and walked off. After a few paces she stopped a man striding the opposite way who exuded an air of both authority and arrogance, and showed him something on the chart she was holding. He studied it carefully. He was expensively dressed, and the nurse looked nervous as if she were in awe of him. Kate wondered who he was, finding herself oddly unsettled by him.

He had a squat, rather bull-like frame. He was no more than five foot seven or eight, but held himself very erect, with his head tilted up, making him seem taller. His face was flaccid, with a pallid, indoors complexion, a stubby nose, tiny rosebud lips and small, icily cold eyes set deep behind doughy cheeks. His hair was light brown, thinning, and carefully groomed, not a strand out of place.

He was wearing a double-breasted blazer with naval buttons, grey flannel trousers and shiny black loafers with gold chains. His shirt was cream with a cut-away collar, and his tie was vulgarly jazzy. All his clothes looked as if they had been taken fresh out of their dry cleaner's bags that morning.

He pursed his lips and clasped his hands together as he spoke and Kate noticed he wore a gold ID bracelet, a gold watch and a Wedgwood signet ring. He talked on, unsmiling, as if he were contemptuous of the black nurse. There was something eerie about his face, she thought; it had the ruthless quality of a man who could be capable of running a concentration camp.

His eyes suddenly stared at her as if he had known she was watching him, and she turned away feeling at the same time a flush of embarrassment and a wintry chill inside her. She looked back. He was still staring at her. She gazed down at the counter, then at the flashing green cursor.

Out of the corner of her eye she saw the nurse walk off and the man stride on. He was looking ahead, his attention elsewhere now, she assumed. But just before he disappeared he stared at her again. There was no hint of flirtation. It was more contempt and hostility.

Being paranoid, she thought. Guilty about being here.

The nurse was walking back followed by a man in a white coat. His expression was aggressive as if he had been interrupted in the midst of something important. His rough skin, purposefully cropped blond hair and full but equally purposefully cropped beard, gave him the air of a zealous student leader.

'Yes?' he said in a hard, bland voice.

'Dr Matthews?'

His eyes, hard and bloodshot, scanned her as if she were a malignant biopsy and she knew, even with her suit, that he could see *reporter* written all over her. He gave a single nod.

'I wondered if I could talk to you about a Mrs Sally Donaldson. You're the doctor who signed her death certificate, I believe.'

His mouth tightened. 'Are you a relative?'

Kate hesitated, then shook her head.

The last vestiges of courtesy faded from his expression. 'I'm sorry, who are you?'

'I'm – ' she hesitated. 'A newspaper reporter.'

A muscle in his cheek began to quiver. 'God, you people make me sick. I'm trying to save lives in here and you hound me non-stop. I'm working nights and days because we're short of staff and I don't have time to talk. I've had three hours' sleep in the last three nights. All press communications are done through the unit general manager's office. You should know that.'

The nurse was standing a couple of paces back, looking faintly apologetic. Kate met Dr Matthews's eyes. 'You say you are trying to save lives. But you signed a death certificate on a woman who wasn't dead.'

He nearly rose to the bait. Kate hoped he was going to, prayed he would; his mouth opened, his knuckles clenched; she felt his breath as he exhaled. He was rattled, a nerve touched. 'You'll find the general manager's office on the second floor of the Jubilee Wing. I suggest you go and talk to him. I have seen no evidence to suggest Mrs Donaldson was not dead.' He spun round and walked off, his white coat flapping.

Kate turned away, annoyed at herself for how she had played it. She had got nothing from the meeting. She did not even know where Sally Donaldson had died, whether it was in this unit or in another ward. Dr Matthews was rattled. Guilt made people rattled; so did tiredness. There was no conclusion she could draw.

Sally Donaldson had been on life support so almost certainly she would have been in here. There were other doctors in the unit, nurses. Someone would know, might talk. She walked out into the corridor, tried to decipher the battery of signs on the walls, then began to navigate her way through the maze of corridors.

Dr Matthews said he was tired. Three hours sleep in three nights; even if that was an exaggeration, he was clearly grossly overworked and when you were like that you made mistakes. Yet he was still there, had obviously not been suspended or even had his workload lightened. If he was under any sort of suspicion, surely he would have been suspended?

Therefore he wasn't under suspicion. Either because the final diagnosis had been made by someone else and he was merely the pen pusher. Or because the hospital management weren't concerned because they knew that Sally Donaldson had not been buried alive. It was a terrible libel by a hysterical journalist. Herself.

Or the cover-up had started.

The general manager's office was a tip. There were two desks buried under paper, a word processor and a couple of ancient manual typewriters, a weary-looking photocopier and a fax. The walls were plastered with press cuttings, headlines, cartoons. A grimy blind had been lowered against the sunlight. Beneath, through the large window, she could see the masts and pilings of Brighton Marina, and the Channel beyond.

A girl was seated at one desk talking in a brittle way into one of three telephones on her desk. Kate recognised her voice. Her name was Susan Malden and they had spoken several times in the past, and once the previous morning when Kate had been told, tartly, that the hospital 'would be investigating'. She had long brown hair, a flat nose and round metal granny glasses. She hung up and swore under her breath.

'Is Mr Merrivale in?' Kate asked her.

'He's busy at the moment. Can I help you?'

'Yes. Do you have any new information on Sally Donaldson?' Kate asked.

'Who are you, please?'

'Kate Hemingway, the *News*.'

Susan Malden looked as if she had just broken a tooth on something. She sifted through some paper, tugged a sheet out and held it to Kate at arm's length, as if worried she might catch something if she came any closer.

PRINCE REGENT HOSPITAL – PRESS RELEASE – URGENT was printed at the top. Kate read it.

> 24 *October*
> A newspaper report that Mrs Sally Donaldson, who died on 14 October in the Prince Regent Hospital, had been prematurely buried is wholly without foundation.
>
> The deceased woman spent five days on a life support machine in the hospital's intensive care unit after she had been diagnosed brain dead from cerebral oedema following uncontainable epileptic fitting. Full diagnostic procedures were carried out, and life-support machinery was switched off after consultation, and with the full consent of, the deceased's family.
>
> The newspaper's reporter, who was not present at the exhumation, appears to have misinterpreted accounts of the natural biological processes which occur after death in a non-embalmed corpse as evidence of premature burial.
>
> The hospital will make a further statement after the inquest.

Kate looked back at Susan Malden. The smugness on the girl's face churned her stomach. The two roundels of glass glinted victory.

She left the room, not wanting to give the girl any more opportunity to gloat, not wanting to risk flying off the handle herself and saying or doing something she would regret. The cover-up had started. If it was a cover-up.

# *Chapter Twenty-Six*

'You've got a great cock, did you know that? Really great.' Her fingers moved up and down his limp, slimy shaft, rubbing gently. 'Really great,' she whispered into his ear, her breath hot and coarse, like her skin.

Harvey Swire felt himself hardening again. Sandra kissed his neck, then his nipples, still rubbing gently and steadily, long, slow strokes. 'So great.' She ran her tongue down his chest, pressed it hard against his belly button, rolled it slowly around. Then she worked her way further down, took him softly in her mouth and caressed the shaft with her lips. She played her tongue around the swelling head, then lightly probed with the tip inside the slit at the top.

Harvey clenched his fists in pleasure and drew in air sharply. Then she licked the shaft up and down in slow, steady strokes, slithered still further down and closed her mouth gently around his balls. He felt a tug of apprehension, and tensed as they squeezed together and a faint twinge of pain shot up into his stomach. He was tired, did not know what time it was. Two, maybe three in the morning. It was a balmy summer night; perspiration was still drying on his body from when they had made love half an hour or so ago.

He could see flashes of her breasts each time she raised her head; they were large, white, translucent in the stark glare of the street light through the open window. And he could see flashes of the white skin of his own hardening shaft as she worked her mouth up and down it, and was aroused again.

It was their first date and would be their last. They had made love twice in his bed in his cramped flat near the Elephant and Castle which he had bought with his inheritance from his mother.

He had been right in his view that Sandra would be a good screw; so good that as she ran her tongue back up his stomach, rolled his nipples between her teeth, then arched above him and began to mount him again, pushing him inside her and sliding slowly down inch by inch, he was tempted to delay his plan and have another session or two with her first.

He had invited Sandra out after meeting her in the intensive care unit at the bed of the willowy model with *status epilepticus*. The beautiful blonde whose brain activity had been damped with barbiturates to stop her *status epilepticus* attack. Maddie Stelman.

Roland Dance had given him the job of monitoring her and turning her. He had stayed at her bedside, watching the line on the oscilloscope, staring at her motionless body. Brain dead. If she had any awareness, any thoughts, they had to have been taking place outside her brain. Maybe outside her body.

Three times, when he had been confident no one was close, he had switched off the ventilator; the longest he had kept it off was just over a minute; he was too nervous of being caught to leave it any longer. He did not want to blow his career before it started; there would be time in the future. Plenty of time.

But even those three brief periods had been intensely exciting; the knowledge that he was in the presence of someone who was dead and would come back to life. It was three hours before Dr O'Feral, in charge of the model's treatment, allowed the barbiturate infusion to cease. During the next hour, as its effects had begun to wear off, Harvey had watched the spikes on the EEG monitor start to rise again. Steady, even spikes. Normal brain pattern. The epileptic fitting was over.

When her eyes finally opened in the late afternoon, he had waited for the flicker of recognition. Waited for her to say, 'Hey! I was up there, on the ceiling of the ward. I saw you raise your hands in the air and do V-signs!'

Instead she stared at him blankly and asked him in a voice that was mumbling at first and then became frosty and arrogant where the hell she was. When he explained that she was in the intensive care unit of Queen's Hospital, she looked at him in accusatory disbelief, as if she held him personally responsible for her being here.

If her consciousness had left her body, she had no memory of it and got increasingly irritated as Harvey questioned her more, and when Roland Dance came up to the bed she told him to stop Harvey pestering her with damn fool questions.

Harvey asked Dance to let him know if she had another attack. Dance said the consultant neurologist had decided she should be put on regular anti-convulsant medication for her epilepsy. Harvey was disappointed. Dance promised he would let him know if another *status epilepticus* patient was admitted, but did not anticipate one for several months.

The light played on Sandra's white breasts; he caught glimpses of her red nipples as her stomach contracted and expanded as she slid down on him and lifted up, saw her white thighs, smelled her animal smells.

She slowed, lifted herself gently up high so that he almost came out of her, then slid back down, staring him in the eyes, smiling almost demonically, down over the swollen bulb of his cock, down the shaft, thrusting her black pubic brush hard into the soft flesh of his navel.

'Oh, Harvey, yes, Harvey!'

As she slid back up his shaft he began to climax. She sensed it, gripped his wrists, and he felt his sperm squirting inside her, sensed the pumps in the glands working, tiny spasms, getting smaller, his balls which had already emptied twice, draining themselves dry.

He went limp almost immediately and a wave of disgust began to replace the surge of pleasure. Her weight was crushing his thighs. Her hot breath was sour and garlicky, from food, cigarettes, booze. Her sweat rose up through her sharp, cheap-smelling perfume, sour also, acrid. The musky smells that had turned him on in the intensive care ward had gone. Her skin was wet, slippery. She kissed him tenderly. He could feel the prickle of hair on her upper lip that she had concealed with make-up instead of removing.

She arched back and the glare of the street lamp shone on her breasts. Large breasts that had excited him, but were spoiled by flat, ugly, indented nipples. She kissed him on each eye. He tried not to take in the smell of her breath. His cock shrank further and slid out of her. He felt his sperm drip on to his thigh.

She rolled off him and curled up beside him and began to caress his limp cock. It tickled, irritating him, and he pushed her hand away. She moved it back playfully and kissed him again. He wished she would lie still. She lightly brushed some stray strands of hair back from his forehead.

'Do you like medicine?' she said.

'Yes.'

'When you've qualified, are you going to specialise in neurology?'

'Neurology?' he said.

'Isn't that why you were in the ward with that epileptic woman?'

'No, I'm going to specialise in anaesthetics.'

'Oh, right. That's why you were there.'

Harvey said nothing.

'Somebody told me you're very brilliant. Didn't you get top marks last year?'

Before the start of the third year prelim exams the previous summer, Harvey had tried coming off the chlorpromazine pills he still took four times a day, to see whether he could repeat what had happened when he had taken his A levels. But it had not worked; for several days he had felt disoriented, had the same experience as the previous time he had tried coming off pills, the uncomfortable sensation of being partly in and partly out of his body.

He hadn't needed to cheat; he knew he would walk the exams; exams were easy. Doing his experiments was harder. Doing them without having to explain them. Without getting found out.

'What's your ambition?' she said. She entwined a finger in his pubic hair. 'Is there something you really want to achieve? Do you have some personal Holy Grail? You know, to do something you could be remembered for?'

'Like inventing penicillin?'

She grinned inquisitively. 'Something like that?'

He stared at the bare light bulb hanging from the ceiling. The glare from the street lamp made it look as if it was on. 'Yes,' he said.

'What is it?'

He lay still for a while, feeling calm and serene. 'I'm going to be the man who proves to the world that there is life after death.'

'Wow!' she said, then was quiet for a moment. 'That's quite an ambition. Do you believe in God?'

'God's an arrogant bastard.'

'Why do you say that?'

'How about some more champagne?' he said.

'Why not?'

Harvey slid out of the bed, picked up the two champagne flutes from the bedside table, and walked, naked, out of the room, along the corridor and into the kitchen. He closed the door behind him, turned on the light and pulled down the roller blind. He took the uncorked champagne bottle out of the fridge, filled the glasses and set them down carefully on the small butcher's block table.

He glanced cautiously at the door, then knelt and pulled out a small polystyrene box from the rear of the fridge, removed the lid and lifted out a tiny glass vial with a quarter of an inch of fine white powder at the bottom. He removed the cork stopper and tipped the contents into the left-hand champagne glass on the table. Then he replaced the box in the fridge and took the drinks back to the bedroom.

As he went through the door and towards the bed, he dropped the glass in his right hand. It shattered on the floor. 'Bugger,' he said, stepping around the shards of glass. He handed Sandra her glass. 'I'll open a new bottle.'

'We can share this.'

'Swill it down. It will give you strength. We'll share the next one.'

She sat up. 'How decadent! Four in the morning and we're drinking champers in bed!'

'I'll sweep up the glass,' he said.

Shortly after two o'clock the following afternoon, as she was setting up the saline drip for a cardiac patient in the intensive care ward, Sandra had her first epileptic fit.

# *Chapter Twenty-Seven*

*Wednesday, 24 October*

Kate filled her Volkswagen with petrol, and bought a tuna and cucumber sandwich and a tiny carton of apple juice from a rack inside the garage shop. By the door she noticed a bundle of the midday edition of the *Evening News*. The headline read OUTBURST AT SATANIST TRIAL.

Christ! If she'd missed something . . . She knelt down. In smaller type were the words, 'by Kate Hemingway, staff reporter'.

She smiled with relief. Patrick Donoghue had done what he had promised and phoned copy through to the paper for her. She hoped he was still there and had not been called away for something more important.

She scanned the story. Ugly scenes outside the court. Members of the families of some of the children the accused men were charged with raping or sexually assaulting had tried to attack the men as they were brought into court. Inside, some had shouted abuse at the judge and police and jeered at the defendants. Some had been evicted. Preliminary submissions by the prosecution were under way.

The sky was blackening and the wind had a cold bite as she walked across the forecourt and jumped gratefully back into the warmth of her car. She again checked the address on the photocopy of Sally Donaldson's death certificate, opened the glove locker and took out the street map of Brighton.

Ten Ryland Close.

She memorised her route, put the map back in the locker and shut the lid. It fell open. Irritated, she slammed it shut again.

Spots of rain thudded on to the windscreen. The forecourt was empty apart from an old van parked by the tyre pressure gauge. A bus thundered past down the road. She slid her fingernail into the plastic wrapping of the sandwich, but failed to open it. It was stuck down. The label on the pack said "Mr Tasty – fresh daily!" There was a date stamp. It was yesterday's date.

Even more annoyed she yanked the door handle to take it back, when there was a sudden drumming of rain on the roof of the car. Slivers of water shattered on the imitation brick surface of the forecourt.

Probably all yesterday's, she thought, turning the pack round and trying to find another point of entry. There wasn't one. She stabbed the cellophane with her nail and it broke through, piercing the dry bread and the soggy filling. She made the hole bigger, eased the sandwich out and took a bite. The bread had a strong, harsh flavour that reminded her of the smell of dog biscuits, and the filling tasted like putty.

She twisted the ignition key. The engine turned over slowly at first, then fired with a shrill clatter; a puff of blue smoke drifted across the windscreen. The wipers smeared the water into a ribbed film. She blipped the accelerator and turned on the heater; her feet were cold; she wiggled her toes inside her thin tights in her black shoes.

Doubt etched into her.

*Follow your heart, Shrimp*, her father used to say to her when things were rough, when Dara sneered at her for not going to college. He'd say it again now if she rang him and told him the story.

Ryland Close was on the outskirts of Brighton, in the labyrinth of quiet streets that had spread back from the sea up to the foot of the Downs. It was a close of small houses with mock Georgian façades, no more than two or three years old, Kate judged from the staked saplings in the flat grass verges and the immature shrubs in the beds.

Number ten had carriage lamps on the wall and a grandiose varnished oak front door with a brass lion's head knocker and ornate letter box which Kate thought looked naff. There were two cars parked on the narrow hard in front of the garage, a modest Toyota and a small Ford with a black spoiler and boy-racer stripes.

The curtains of the downstairs window were drawn. The sign of a family closing ranks around the bereaved. Kate walked down the crazy-paved path, ducking her head against the sheeting rain, and pressed the door bell. It rang with a deep chime. The curtain twitched and Kate was glad of her smart clothes, knowing she wouldn't immediately be taken for a reporter, that she might have a chance of getting to speak to Kevin Donaldson if she kept her cool.

The door was opened by a brassy blonde woman in her late forties, who looked as if she normally wore a lot more make-up than she had on now. 'Yes?' she said wearily, her skin pallid and shiny in contrast to the matt black of her baggy blouson jumper. Her eyes, strained and wary under long curled lashes, looked Kate suspiciously up and down. Deep pouches hung beneath them. She wore sparkly rings on several of her fingers, and a rhinestone bracelet rested halfway down the back of her bony hand. Below her jumper she wore brown ski pants tucked into leopard skin slippers. She reeked of tobacco.

'Is it possible to have a word with Kevin Donaldson?' Kate was conscious of the blast of heat coming out of the door.

'He doesn't want to see anyone.' Her voice was flat, final.

'It's very important.'

'He's had a bereavement and is in very severe shock. I'm afraid you'll have to leave it for a few weeks.'

'I was at the exhumation when they opened Mrs Donaldson's coffin,' Kate said.

The woman hesitated. 'Are you from the police?'

Kate was pleased. The woman hadn't twigged her. 'I was there at the request of the environmental health officer.'

'He doesn't want to see anyone.' She wore metallic blue eye shadow; her hair had grey roots. The rain was coming in the front door, wetting the woman's feet. 'I'm his mum. Can I help you?' She retreated a few inches from the weather.

'May I come in for a second?'

The woman stepped back further; Kate felt the claustrophobic heat and the cloying cigarette smoke ingrained in the air as the woman closed the door behind her. The hall was tiny and looked new, as if its contents had only that day been removed from their wrappings. The paintwork was fresh, unchipped; the doors glistening with varnish, the brass handles and striker plates seemed freshly minted, the thick twist pile carpet seemed never to have been walked on. The new home for the newly-weds.

It was the smells and the heat that gave it away. The smell of grief she encountered almost daily in her work; it was always the same; the slack, stale air from the windows being closed and the heating turned up too high; the rank smell of unchanged clothes; the greasy pall of uneaten food gone cold.

A cat came out of a doorway and miaowed mournfully. An ivory and black Burmese. Not an ordinary cat. Showy, like the black and white patterned, too-loud carpet, the hall table with its flashy tropical hardwood veneer and brass handles, the gilded frame around a cheap print of Sorrento on the wall, the elaborate fibre-optic lamp hanging from the ceiling. Trying to impress, like the flashy Ford in the drive.

Kate realised, uneasily, that she was searching for things to dislike about Sally Donaldson. She knew that would make the horror somehow easier to bear. As she stood sneering at someone else's taste she despised herself for her arrogance and for thinking that way.

Sally Donaldson had been an ordinary girl, pretty, with the excitement of a new home, married life, a baby on the way. Upstairs the baby's room would already have been decorated, the cot bought, a mobile hung. Ready.

Ready for the shrivelled foetus that had lain in the bottom of the coffin.

'What was it you wanted?' the woman asked, kicking off one of her slippers, leaning down and scratching the sole of her foot.

'Does Mr Donaldson believe Mrs Donaldson had been buried alive?'

The woman balanced herself with a hand on the wall and pushed her foot back into the slipper. 'What do you mean? Of course he does. She was.'

'I know she was, but the hospital are denying it.'

The woman gave a bitter laugh. 'They would, wouldn't they? I mean, that's just typical.' She shrugged. 'Everyone saw it. My son saw it. The vicar saw it. They all saw it.' Lines creased her face. Her hands shook. 'Let anybody try and say they didn't.'

'They'll have their reasons. The vicar won't want to be accused of burying a living person. Nor will the undertakers. The hospital doesn't want to be blamed.' Kate looked down at the carpet. 'I'm sorry. I know this is very distressing for your family, but don't worry. I'll talk to everyone over the next few days.'

'They done a post mortem. They won't be able to lie about the findings of that at the inquest.'

'A good lawyer will make mincemeat of the pathologist's report.'

'Not the time of death, though; he'll be able to prove that. They always can. I've seen it on telly enough times. That Poirot the other night – they knew to within half an hour the time of death of a three-week-old corpse.'

'They do on the television because it's convenient for the stories,' Kate said. 'But it's not like that. Pathologists cannot diagnose time of death at all easily.' She opened her handbag and took out the stapled sheets of photocopies she had collected from Dr Marty Morgan, the *News*'s medical columnist, the previous evening. She showed it to Mrs Donaldson.

The top sheet was headed '*Time Since Death and Decomposition of the Human Body*'.

Below, Kate had marked a red line against one paragraph:

Much of the difficulty in determining the time since death stems from the lack of systematic observation and research on the decomposition rate of the human body. Neither body weight nor temperature can be reliable guides, particularly when temperature is fluctuating. Metabolic rates of absorption and breakdowns of toxins can only be used as a measure if the original dose is known. *Where time of death is critical to court evidence, relevant forensic evidence should be treated with extreme caution.*

The woman's heavy lashes beat against each other. In the silence Kate could hear the scratching as they meshed. The rain drummed outside. From the back of the house came a click and a whir as a washing machine started a new cycle. A curtain of doubt drew across the woman's face. 'And what's your interest?'

'I want the truth to come out. Kevin's the only person who can help me.'

The woman raised a hand, indicating Kate should wait, opened a door to her right and leaned in. 'You asleep, love?'

There was a murmured reply.

'There's a lady come about the inquest. I think you ought to have a word with her. Do you feel up to it?'

No response.

'It would be best if you did,' the woman said and nodded for Kate to go in.

Kate's feet sank into thick carpet in the darkened room. Gold curtains with rope tassels were drawn and the only light was from two table lamps, smaller versions of the fibre-optic one hanging in the hall, and the huge television which was on, but mute. A three-piece suite and two stereo speakers either side of the fireplace, like sentry boxes, dominated the room. Three bars of an electric heater burned in the fireplace, with flickering lights dancing over plastic coals. A model Ferrari stood on the mantelpiece beside a framed wedding photograph of Sally and Kevin Donaldson.

He was almost unrecognisable from the photograph now. He was slumped in one of the chairs, a hand resting on each of its arms, his black hair dishevelled, his face white and drawn with massive bags below his eyes. He was like a living corpse.

He was wearing a crumpled business shirt incorrectly buttoned over a grimy T-shirt, and creased suit trousers with woollen socks and grey slip-on shoes. It looked like he had not slept, or removed his clothes, or shaved for several days, and he seemed barely to be aware of her.

'I was with you at the exhumation,' Kate said gently.

He did not respond. His eyes gave her a passing glance before turning back to the silent *Neighbours* on the screen.

'Have a seat, love,' Kevin Donaldson's mother said, her attitude softened towards Kate now.

Beside the other armchair was an ashtray filled with lipsticky butts, a pile of women's magazines and a paperback Robert Goddard novel lying face down, open halfway through. Kate sat on the sofa.

'The lady's worried that the hospital might be trying to cover up what's happened to Sally,' the woman said. 'She thinks they're going to try to deny the truth.'

He spoke slowly, his voice a deep slur like a tape cassette with the battery running down, and Kate decided he must be on tranquillisers. 'The coroner said he would ring me.' He fell silent again.

'With the results of the post mortem?' Kate prompted, her hands instinctively reaching towards her bag for her notebook. She restrained herself in time.

'They did the post mortem yesterday. He hasn't rung yet.'

His mother sat down and shook a cigarette out of a pack. 'There's going to be a major law suit,' she said. 'That's what they're scared of, in't it?' She put the cigarette in her mouth and clicked a shiny metal lighter. 'They got every right to be. We're going to sue 'em.' She lit her cigarette and inhaled deeply. 'Hundreds of thousands, my husband reckons.'

Kate looked at Kevin Donaldson. 'Could you give me the background to what happened? If that's not too painful?'

He watched the television for several seconds and Kate thought he wasn't going to reply. Then he started speaking, still watching the screen. 'How far?'

'How far back?' Kate said. 'Whatever you think is relevant.' Decisively, she opened her bag. 'Do you mind if I make the odd note?' she said, trying to sound innocent, and caught a flicker of suspicion on Mrs Donaldson's face. 'I need to make a report,' she added.

The woman nodded understandingly.

'It was the gynaecologist,' Kevin Donaldson said. 'Mr Heywood. Said she ought to go into hospital.' He stopped and stared at the screen.

'When was that?' Kate asked.

'Had to go for monthly check-up; she was twenty-four weeks.'

Silence again.

'Why did Mr Heywood want your wife to go into hospital?'

His mother answered for him. 'She had high blood pressure. The doctor thought she ought to go in for observation.'

'Pre-eclamptic toxaemia,' Kevin Donaldson suddenly said, clearly, without slurring, as if he were reciting to a class.

'She developed complications,' his mother explained. 'Her blood pressure continued rising and she got a swelling on the brain. Then she started having epileptic fits.'

'She was an epileptic?'

'No, it's a side effect of this toxaemia thing.' She knocked the ash off the end of her cigarette. 'They couldn't reduce the swelling on the brain and the fits got worse. They gave her all the drugs and things they could. Mr Heywood seemed very attentive.' She drew on the cigarette and blew the smoke out again quickly. 'Then she went into a coma. They had to put her on life support. She was there five days – '

'Six,' interrrupted her son.

'Six.' She crushed the cigarette out into the pile of butts and coughed. 'He was sleeping there – they have a bedroom for relatives. In the middle of the night the doctor on duty told him there wasn't no chance; said she was brain dead and had been for several days and they might as well turn the life support off and end the agony.'

'The baby was abnormal,' Kevin Donaldson announced.

They both looked at him, but his face showed nothing. His mother took another cigarette out of the packet. 'Mr Heywood had told him that once a mother is brain dead there's very little chance of the baby surviving, and if it did it might well have some kind of abnormality. We all went to see Mr Heywood. He was very nice, very kind, went through everything in great detail. Kevin and Sally's parents agreed there wasn't any point in attempting a caesarian.'

'And they switched the life support off?'

Kevin Donaldson nodded sadly. 'That night; there was a new duty doctor. He said they needed the bed. It was quick. She stopped breathing and they said she was dead.' He looked at Kate almost for the first time.

'Did they do any tests?'

'I don't know. I was crying too much. They asked if I wanted a taxi. Then I saw them wheel her off covered in a white sheet.'

Tears were streaming down his face now. Kate felt tears in her own eyes too. She took a breath. 'Did you see her again?'

'No. The undertakers said I could, any time.'

'So you didn't see her again until . . . the coffin? The exhumation.'

He was silent again. Back in his shell.

'And it was you who requested the exhumation?'

He said nothing.

'He had a hard time,' his mother said. 'The police didn't want to know. Coroner didn't want to know at first, told him it was impossible and he was probably a bit' – she tapped her head – 'you know, doolally because of her death. The vicar wouldn't help. Kevin had to get witnesses, get their phone numbers, have the coroner talk to them. He nearly got arrested one afternoon when he went up there himself with a spade and started digging.' She looked at him. 'Didn't you?'

He did not respond.

Kate bit her lip nervously. She was wringing wet from the heat and from her nerves. 'Kevin, you and I both saw the same thing when they opened up your wife's coffin. Have you any doubt at all that she was alive at some time whilst she was in there?'

'Dead people don't give birth to babies,' said his mother.

'It can happen, apparently,' Kate said.

'Rubbish. I'm not having that.'

'They'll argue that at the inquest.'

'Kevin said her fingers – the nails was broken; worn right down like she'd been biting them. There was scratch marks on the lid of the coffin. She'd been scratching it, clawing it like an animal.'

'They're going to argue that corpses move around in coffins as rigor mortis sets in,' Kate said.

'And score grooves in mahogany? Come on, girl!' his mother said.

'What about your Dr Sells? He was there. What has he said? He must agree,' Kate said.

'He doesn't. He says we should wait for the pathologist's report. He says he didn't notice any scratches on the lid. Says that we're all being misled because of the baby being expelled.'

Kevin Donaldson spoke, startling them. 'She was always doing her nails. Took care of them. Always doing them,' he said.

There was silence; Kate felt an updraft of hope as she wrote down what he had said, slowly, in longhand, to keep up the pretence of not being a journalist.

His mother smiled bitterly. 'I may not be that bright about medicine, but I'll tell you one thing I do know. Dead people don't bite their nails.'

# *Chapter Twenty-Eight*

It was three days after Harvey Swire had given Sandra twenty-five milligrams of GW 2937, the reference name of the drug that was produced by the Swiss pharmaceuticals giant Grauer Meyerhoffen for non-human laboratory experimentation only.

He had obtained it easily. As part of his research for his term paper on epilepsy he did animal experimentation at the medical school's animal laboratory. Rats, cats and chimpanzees were given GW 2937 to induce severe epileptic fitting, which was then halted by massive barbiturate doses.

The GW 2937 tablets were round and white, similar in size and shape to aspirins, but clearly identifiable by the letter *GW* stamped into them. Harvey had to grind the tablets in a pestle to a chalky powder which he then mixed into the animal feed; the drug had no taste and traces of it were normally metabolised by the energy in the fits.

He had to feed forty animals in total with the substance; it had been easy to replace a small amount of the drug with plain aspirin. When he had ground it into the feed, neither the animals nor the neurologists in charge of the experiments noticed any difference that day.

He did not know how to calculate a human dose, and worked it out on brain capacity. He calculated the weight of an average human brain, of one thousand, two hundred and forty grammes, against a chimpanzee's.

On the Sunday evening he had rung the nurses' home where Sandra lived, and was told by a sour girl that she was not back from work. He had left no message. On Monday evening he rang again and a different girl answered the phone. She kept him hanging on for several minutes then came back breathlessly and apologetically to tell him that Sandra was not well and was being kept in a ward overnight for observation.

On Tuesday morning Harvey was among a pack of students following an obstetrician and his junior on a maternity ward round. Swollen, milky-skinned women lay in the metal beds in their pink sheer nightgowns surrounded by flowers and cards. Disoriented husbands perched on hard chairs, and female relatives were stuck in for a siege. Outside the weather was cooler than it had been, but this ward was kept at greenhouse temperature. Harvey loathed the smell of the maternity ward, a sickly sweetness that permeated his skin and stayed with him for hours afterwards.

A fat woman poked a finger at a pink mite in a wool shawl. 'Peekaboo! Ahhh! Peekaboo! Ahhh!' The mother lay back against the propped pillows, too tired and too polite to tell her to go away.

'Paging Mr Harvey Swire. Internal phone call for Mr Harvey Swire.'

Harvey went to the black phone on the wall at the entrance to the ward. It was Roland Dance. Another *status epilepticus* patient had been admitted to intensive care. He thought he'd let Harvey know in case he'd like to pop over and see her.

Harvey played it cool. He told Dance he was tied up at the moment, but would come in his break. Then he continued with the ward round, but it was a blur. He could concentrate on nothing as excitement uncoiled like a spring inside.

It was half past one when he walked into intensive care, which was as hot as the maternity ward he had just left, and waited by the nursing station whilst a nurse went to find the junior anaesthetist.

Up on the wall to the right was the ward list, a large, white plastic notice board with the number of each bed printed on the left and the patients' names written beside in blue chinagraph pencil. Against number six was the name *S. LOCK*.

Sandra Lock. He could feel her slippery wet skin now, see her white breasts above him, smell her body, her hot breath. Roland Dance was walking towards him, in his shabby tweed jacket with its leather buttons, cavalry twills and a drab tie. He'd had his hair cut, a severe short back and sides and the harsh stubble did nothing for his equine face.

'Oh, hallo,' he said as if he had not really expected Harvey to appear. He clasped his hands behind his back and rocked to and fro on the balls of his scuffed suede brogues. 'Yes. Most interesting. A bit like buses, isn't it?'

'Buses?' Harvey repeated, baffled.

Dance had nicked himself shaving and there was a small square of elastoplast stuck to his neck. 'You hang around for ages waiting for one, then four come along all at once.'

'I try and avoid going on buses,' Harvey said.

Dance's expression became pained, then froze, as if a battery powering his facial muscles had suddenly gone flat. 'Quite.' His mouth flickered. 'That *status epilepticus* case you saw a couple of weeks ago, the model with the head injury. If that had been viral epilepsy one would be jolly worried to have a second case so soon, particularly as it's one of the nurses on the ward who was looking after her.' He shook his head. 'But it wasn't. There doesn't seem to be any connection.'

'What's caused it?' Harvey was distracted by the sticking plaster which was about to fall off.

'Too early to say; this could be encephalitis, but she's not running a temperature and she ought to be if it's an infection. Possibly a brain tumour, although we already know that her CT scan is normal. We're going to do a lumbar puncture and have a look at her CSF – to exclude infection – as soon as we have her dosed. The girls in the unit are pretty upset.'

Harvey wondered if the GW 2937 might be detectable with a blood test. But he knew that blood tests were specific and laborious. You could only find traces of a drug if you were looking for it. To have looked for GW 2937, someone would have had to suspect. There was no reason why Sandra Lock should suspect. It was unlikely that many people, if anyone at all, knew he had taken her out, and even if they did the chances of them connecting her attack with his few days of laboratory research work were remote. And unprovable.

'It could, of course, be an overdose of anti-depressants. That can bring this on. But the other nurses are being a bit defensive, saying she was jolly and outgoing, a bit of a raver, apparently.' He rocked backwards and forwards pensively. 'Mind you, those are the types who can become depressives. Interesting case, though. Particularly interesting, in fact.'

'Why?' Harvey asked, the remark making him uneasy again.

'The severity of the attack. She's not responding to barbiturate treatment so far. Come and have a look.'

The bed was next to the one in which the model had been, and recessed for privacy like all the beds in here. Sandra was unconscious, a ventilator tube in her mouth, the black concertina bag inflating and deflating above her matted hair, and a drip was attached through a cannula to the back of her hand. Her back was arched, her stomach lifting the sheet up, her arms and legs outstretched, making tight puppet-like jerks. Her teeth were clenched around the breathing tube and she was making incoherent grunts and moans. Sputum frothed from the corners of her mouth.

A plump, round-faced nurse with short red curls was standing by the drip stand and seemed distressed. The badge on her lapel said Elaine Foster. 'She's worsening, Dr Dance,' she said in a Scottish accent.

Roland Dance looked at Harvey. 'Down on the ward they injected five cc of diazepam, which had no effect. Then they tried intravenous phenytoin, which didn't work either. When she came up here we put her on thiopentone infusion – a heavy dosage.'

'Thirty-five milligrams,' said the nurse.

'See the problem? If we leave it uncontrolled it's going to give her brain damage. If we put much more barbiturate in, I don't think her body's going to be able to cope with it.'

Wires ran from Sandra Lock's forehead to the two oscilloscopes on the shelf above the bed. Harvey watched the spikes on the electrocardiograph. Her heartbeat was already weak and irregular from the damping down by the barbiturate. On the electroencephalograph the peaks showing her brain activity were off the screen. He stared down at her face. Her eyes were open, staring straight at him. He thought he saw an impossible fleeting hint of recognition in them before they rolled up, the pupils disappearing into the lids, leaving only the sightless whites. Her arms flailed wildly. The drip tube severed from the cannula fixed on the back of her hand and the drug sprayed on to the bed.

Dance grabbed her wrist and the nurse pushed the tube back on. 'Have to strap her,' Dance said.

The blood oxygen monitor alarm bleeped. 'We need assistance,' Dance said. 'Call Dr O'Feral. And get an ampule of curare.'

The nurse ran out.

Dance turned to Harvey. 'She's fighting the ventilator. We'll have to paralyse her. Can't increase the barbiturate any more.'

Dr O'Feral, the head of the unit, walked swiftly over followed by two more nurses. They injected the curare, but it did not work.

'Give her another twenty-five milligrams of thiopentone,' Dr O'Feral said urgently.

The EEG monitor bleeped its staccato alarm. The spikes of the oscilloscope had gone haywire, like a mass of wriggling worms.

Harvey sensed the flurry of panic around him.

'She's arrested,' O'Feral said, laying his hands on her chest and pressing hard. 'Get the cardiac unit,' he said. 'Need the defibrillator.' He pressed down again, then again, rhythmically.

One of the nurses was already sprinting across the ward.

The spikes on the EEG screen were beginning to calm, to weaken, but it wasn't the barbiturate that was doing that. It was oxygen starvation of the brain.

It took less than ninety seconds for the defibrillator to be brought in. Dance ripped open Sandra's hospital gown, and Harvey saw her large breasts with the flat, indented nipples. They placed the electrodes over her heart, O'Feral shouted 'OK!' and one of the technicians pressed the button. There was a loud electronic clunk, Sandra jerked up in the air in a massive convulsion, then lay still.

The spikes on the electrocardiograph were getting weaker. They tried again, then again, each time the convulsion flinging her up in the air and each time she fell back, motionless, limp as a rag doll.

After three more minutes the spikes had gone completely and there was a solid unflickering line accompanied by the steady rasp of the warning buzzer, which no one, for a moment, moved to switch off.

Sandra Lock was dead.

## *Chapter Twenty-Nine*

*Wednesday, 24 October*

The wipers clouted away the rain, and mottled water slid relentlessly down the Volkswagen's misted side windows. Kate drove towards a narrow railway bridge, relieved to be away from the claustrophobic heat and grieving of the Donaldsons' house, and irritated by a car that sat on her tail.

She moved over as close to the kerb as she dared but it made no effort to pass. Her concentration wavered as she glanced repeatedly in her mirror. On the far side of the bridge she slowed to let it pass, but it slowed too. She reached the T-junction with the busy shopping street she had been aiming for and turned right, beginning to wonder if she was being followed. The car behind turned left. 'Jerk,' she said.

The premises of A. Dalby and Sons were a couple of hundred yards along, on a street corner next to an ironmonger. They looked suitably sombre and unobtrusive, with the words *FUNERAL DIRECTORS* in gold letters on a black hoarding, and the name of the firm below in smaller letters across the curtained window.

She parked in a side street and walked back down. The rain was easing, but the cold wind and the bleakness of her thoughts chilled her. She felt again the anger of Terry Brent, her editor, heard the words of the medium, Dora Runcorn, last night; saw the image of Kevin Donaldson slumped in his chair. Maybe the funeral director had been right when he'd said in the graveyard that the vicar had a lot to answer for. It seemed to Kate almost as if the lifting of Sally Donaldson's body from its place of rest had thrown the slender balance of her own world into turmoil.

She had seen a movie where people fooling around in a burial ground got possessed and destroyed by the spirits of the dead. But that was just a movie, it wasn't real. Things like that did not happen really.

Dead brothers didn't send messages, really.

She shivered.

Just before the main road she passed a wide gate in a brick wall. A notice said:

A. DALBY & SON, FUNERAL SERVICE. DO NOT OBSTRUCT.
24 HOURS ACCESS REQUIRED.

She swallowed nervously as she stood at the front door, realising she had never been inside a funeral director's premises before, and rehearsed her story. She hoped she wasn't going to see the same undertaker she had met in the graveyard. Hopefully he would not recognise her but would notice her accent and might think it an odd coincidence to see another American woman. Then she took a breath, put what she hoped was a suitable expression on her face and went in.

She had been expecting to find a shop counter with a solemn, cadaverous man behind it. Instead, she was in a room that felt like the lounge of a tiny, rather exclusive hotel. It was L-shaped, with two comfortable seating areas separated by a reception desk at which sat a mild-looking woman in her fifties with short grey hair, a blue cardigan and a string of tiny pearls. She smiled at Kate. 'Good afternoon.'

The furniture was reproduction Victorian mahogany, with green velour upholstery. There was a thick gold carpet, gold flock wallpaper, ornate chandeliers with pink lampshades and matching sconces on the walls. All that was missing, Kate thought, was a fireplace. 'I have two elderly aunts who live together,' she said; 'one of them's in a hospice and likely to pass away within the next few days, and her sister's asked me to come and see you. There are one or two things she's worried about so I thought I'd try to ease her mind a little.'

'Of course.' The woman gave her another smile, full of deep sympathy, not all of it fake.

'She's had previous experience of your company and has a very high opinion of your services. But she's been distressed by an article in the newspaper about a woman who was buried alive – and you were the funeral directors.'

The woman blanched. 'Yes. I think it might be best if you had a word with Mr Morris Dalby. I'll just go and get him for you.' She went out through a door at the end of the room.

Kate had a craving for a cup of coffee. She'd drunk nothing hot since breakfast. She glanced around at the two groups of chairs. Cosy, like the pink parlour in the morgue. Like the frilly lining of Sally Donaldson's coffin. On the wall was a framed certificate from the British Institute of Embalmers. Then the receptionist came back.

She was followed by a small man who carried about him the contrasting auras of quiet dignity and assertive self-importance. He wore a charcoal suit, a starchy white shirt, and a black tie that was unfashionably wide. His threadbare greying hair was raked back and Brylcreemed down to his scalp. His skin was pale with dark creases, and his cheeks were like the pouches of a small rodent. There was a streetwise wariness in his eyes and a gravelly unctuousness in his voice. 'I'm Morris Dalby, madam, can I help you?'

She was relieved it was not the same man she had seen in the graveyard, and repeated what she had told the receptionist. The undertaker motioned her to a chair, sat down opposite and laid his small hands on the polished veneer of the table. 'It's always sad to lose an auntie.'

'Yes,' Kate said.

'They're special people, aunties.'

'Yes, they are.'

'I'm sorry her sister's been upset by that piece she read. It's understandable, of course. A very irresponsible article, that. Upset a lot of people, I'm afraid. One of these clever journalists trying to score points. Local papers should be more responsible.'

She felt her face reddening, wondering for a moment if he had sussed her out. She tried to remember if she had seen him at the exhumation. Maybe he had seen her. 'Is there no truth in the story?'

'None at all, madam. Your poor aunt has nothing to worry about. Would it be burial or cremation?'

Kate reddened further, unprepared for the question. 'Burial.'

'Public cemetery, or does she have a plot in a church? Or a family vault?'

Kate hesitated. 'Public cemetery.'

He looked at her oddly and her discomfort grew. 'If the lady's worried about her sister coming round in the coffin there's two services we can offer to give her peace of mind. We can either open up a vein if she's not going to be on view, or we can embalm her. Are you familiar with the embalming procedure?'

'No.'

'It's very straightforward. We replace all the blood in the veins with a preserving fluid. It has colourings which make the departed appear completely natural, and, of course, it eliminates any possibility of being buried alive.'

Kate felt a sudden panic. 'This woman in the paper, had she been embalmed?'

He took a leather notebook from his jacket pocket and laid it on the table. 'I wouldn't want to betray any confidentiality, but if it will ease your auntie's mind, no, she wasn't. We only embalm if the person is going on view. This particular lady had been on life support for several days and when it was switched off the family wanted a quick funeral. The newspaper article was rubbish. The poor woman had been clinically dead in hospital for several days, then spent over twenty-four hours in our refrigerator here. No one could survive that, let alone anything else.'

He glanced away from her intense stare too fast, she thought. Too shiftily. He burrowed in his pocket again and retrieved a silver fountain pen. 'Now I'll just jot down a few details. If I could have the lady's name, and an address for the – ah – account? Then we can discuss the choice of coffins and trims. Would you like us to place the death notices in the papers? We could draft them now so they're ready for insertion when you have the death certificate signed.'

'I don't suppose it would be possible to have a quick look around. My aunt is one of these rather particular people and will probably ask me loads of questions about what will happen to her sister's body when it leaves the hospice.'

'Coppercliffe, would that be? We have a good relationship with them. May I have a note of her name?'

Kate's mind raced. 'Mrs – er Miss Vining. Miss Alice Vining.' She spelt it for him and he wrote it down.

'And an address? Would that be your own?'

'I would like to see round before we go any further; it will have to be her decision. If she's happy with what I tell her, I can come back tomorrow.'

'Of course, madam.' He stood up. 'We'll start with the chapel of rest.'

Kate followed him through the door at the rear into a tiny marble-floored hall, and up a carpeted staircase. On the landing at the top was a red velour-covered banquette and an oak door, which he opened reverentially and held for her.

She went in first, into a dark, church-like atmosphere with a smell that disturbed her: a combination of pine and chemical preservative that was not unpleasant, but reminded her of hospitals and of the mortuary.

The undertaker turned a dimmer switch and the light increased. On the wall at the far end was a crucifix and a backlit mosaic of coloured glass. 'We have a twenty-four-hour service for visiting loved ones. You can pop in any time you'd like to see your auntie; if you want to come at night or at the weekend you just call us.'

They went back out on to the landing, and she was glad when he had shut the door. A dark-haired man in his late twenties came up the stairs. He was smartly dressed in a formal black mourning jacket and grey trousers. 'Harry and Jane are doing a pick up from the Prince Regent,' he said to the older man. 'You won't forget the five o'clock?'

'I'll be with you in ten minutes, Bill.'

They walked down the stairs. 'My son,' the undertaker said. 'We're a family business. Wife and daughter in it also.'

Kate heard a door open upstairs and a voice she recognised.

'Morris?'

Dalby stopped. Kate saw the tall man who had been at the exhumation. He looked at her briefly but there was no hint of recognition. 'Yes, Reg?'

'It's that chap from the *News of the World* again on the phone.'

Dalby threw an awkward glance at Kate, his face reddening. 'Tell him there's going to be an inquest and we cannot comment.'

They crossed the hall, went along a corridor that was dingy and old-fashioned, with a wooden floor and yellowed walls, stopped and Dalby opened a door cautiously. 'That's all right,' he said. 'You can come in.'

She walked into a small room that smelled more powerfully of the same pine and chemical preservative. The walls were tiled and the floor had a hard, non-slip surface with a shallow gulley cut into it and a small drain. There was a metal table similar to the one she had seen in the mortuary, and a wheeled stretcher with straps hanging loose. There were racks of shelves stacked with plastic bottles containing a pink fluid, glass pots of jelly, tubs of make-up, and various surgical instruments.

'This is the embalming room,' the undertaker said with a certain amount of pride. 'My daughter does the embalming.' He opened the door on the far side of the room and Kate heard an electrical whir. 'The fridges are here.'

Kate followed him into a concrete-floored alcove, and stared uneasily at a bank of metal doors, each about two and a half foot square, that completely filled one wall. On the front of each door was a handle and a square slot for a tag, some of which were empty, some containing a buff ticket on which names were written in clear black handwriting. Kate read them.

Mr T. Hake. Mrs E. Millbright. Mr A. Reece. Mrs S. Donaldson. Mr N. –

Her heart crashed against the walls of her chest.

Mrs S. Donaldson.

She was in here. Which meant she had been released by the coroner. She read the label again, to make sure she was not mistaken, trying not to look too obvious.

'If you don't plan to view your auntie, then we would keep her in one of these,' Morris Dalby said chirpily. He leaned forward, grabbed the handle of one of the doors that had no ticket and swung it open.

A blast of cold air engulfed Kate. She gazed in horror into the deep, dark interior, feeling the cold air rolling out and holding her breath against the rancid greasy reek of dead human flesh. To the right, in the dim light in there, she could make out the silhouette of a body encased in white plastic.

Goosepimples prickled her. Sally Donaldson. Lying in there. In the dark, the cold. The undertaker pulled out the empty slatted tray a few inches; it rolled silently on well-oiled castors. 'Forty degrees we keep these. There's no one could survive more than an hour or so in here.'

'Why is there a handle on the inside of the door?' Kate said.

'In case someone cleaning them gets shut in by accident.'

Kate tried to imagine spending a night in one of the fridges. Christ, death seemed lonely. You really were alone, in one of these. She reassured herself, as she did often, that when you were dead it did not matter any more. You were gone. That was it; either oblivion, or your soul or life force or whatever it was had moved on, gone to heaven or hell, or come back as something else. Your body was a carcass; something you sloughed off the way a butterfly sheds its chrysalis or a crab its shell. It was nothing.

Nothing.

But if you woke inside that fridge? If you woke in the night and it was cold and you were wrapped up in plastic and you were too weak to move, too weak to open the door, and no one heard you shout for help?

'Can't people who have hypothermia sometimes be mistaken for dead?' Kate asked.

'I've heard that's possible.'

'Couldn't it happen in here?'

'No, dear.' His voice was losing a fraction of its patience. 'People are already dead when they come in here, with doctors' certificates.'

She sensed the tetchiness and did not like it. He closed the fridge and they went back through the embalming room and walked to the end of the corridor. The door was old-fashioned, with two small glass panels and secured by a modern mortice deadlock which was on latch.

Outside was a cobbled yard with a row of garages, from one of which protruded the nose of a white Volvo and from others the tailgate of a hearse and of a black limousine. 'Daimlers,' he said. 'They're very comfortable.'

As they went back inside, Kate glanced up at the rear windows and noticed they were barred. The undertaker opened a door to the right and a strong smell of fresh timber came out. 'This is our workshop and store.'

Half the room was filled with coffins. They stood upright, stacked shoulder to shoulder like a platoon of soldiers, graded back in height and width. Partially blocked by them was a large green fire exit sign on the wall. Beyond it was a small wooden door. A rusty brass key hung on a hook beside it.

'We hold three qualities of coffin in stock: solid oak, solid mahogany, or chipboard with oak veneer, but if your auntie would like anything different we can get that for her,' Morris Dalby said.

An ancient first aid poster curled away from a wall. The room was poorly lit by a bare, dusty bulb and a small frosted glass window beneath which was a workbench covered in tools and rolls of cloth. An elderly man in brown overalls was stooped over a coffin on a wooden trestle, tacking in a cream lining with a small hammer. He carried on without acknowledging them.

'Oak's the most expensive,' said the undertaker. 'But it's durable, lasts for ever.'

Kate was not listening. In the far corner to the left of the coffins was a large chipboard box. A similar chipboard box to the one in which the undertakers had placed Sally Donaldson's exhumed coffin at the cemetery. There were mud stains on the base.

It was the same box, she realised.

'Brass handles are traditional,' the undertaker was saying. 'If budget's a concern you can have plastic with brass coating, but they're really for cremations.'

Kate touched one of the coffins. 'Is this oak?'

'Yes.'

She glanced again at the brass key on the hook, then down at the chipboard box. 'Which is the mahogany?'

'I'll show you.' The phone rang. He hesitated, then turned and walked to the work bench and picked up the receiver. 'Morris Dalby,' he said.

Kate sidled closer to the key, watching him. He seemed irritated.

'Better put him on, I suppose.' He covered the mouthpiece. 'Won't keep you a minute,' he said to Kate. 'Mr Webb, good afternoon. No, no truth in it at all. I think you'll see that at the inquest. The husband, did you say you spoke to? Well the poor gentleman's demented with grief. This exhumation should never have happened.'

The workman's head was inside the coffin. Kate unhooked the key, clasped it tightly in her hand then sauntered as casually as she could away from the coffins over towards some Dexion shelves, and dropped it noiselessly into her pocket.

# *Chapter Thirty*

The mortuary of Queen's Hospital was deep beneath the main building, at the end of a dark corridor beyond the kitchens. It was a large, dank room with a vaulted brick ceiling, tiled, windowless walls, a green marble floor and a draughty corridor that led off to the fridges where both bodies of patients awaiting post mortems and bodies donated for dissection were stored.

There was a stone sink, a Formica-covered work surface laid with surgical instruments and glass vials, old-fashioned weigh scales below a lined blackboard chart, and a row of tiered wooden benches capable of seating fifty students. In the middle of the floor was an oblong metal table on which lay the naked, stark white corpse of Sandra Lock.

Her face rose like an alabaster bust out of her short black hair, her cheeks indented, mouth open, and sightless eyes staring upwards, oblivious to the glare of the large overhead lamp. Behind her head was a blood-stained wooden block resting on four stubby legs on the end of the table. The room was full of the same vile stench of human innards that always filled the mortuary during autopsies, drowning the disinfectant.

The pathologist, whose name was Percy Higgs, was a stocky, blunt-faced man, with salt and pepper hair and a toothbrush moustache. He stood over the dead nurse in his green surgical gown, apron and gloves, squinting through the stream of smoke from the untipped cigarette between his lips. His hands, buried to the wrists inside her chest, worked a sharp knife to release the heart and lungs.

Only a handful of students sat on the observation benches. There were none of the usual bravado wisecracks. Today's autopsy was too personal, too close to home. Sanda Lock was no older than themselves, an attractive, lively girl who had been one of their crowd. In the carcass that lay on the slab in front of them, and the grim butchery that was taking place inside it, they were experiencing an unwelcome glimpse behind the thin curtain that screened them from their own mortality.

All of them except Harvey Swire.

The breasts that had for a short while turned Harvey on in bed lay flattened, hanging sideways, distorted by the incision from her neck to her groin, her large indented nipples resting on the metal slab either side of her. Her thighs were too pudgy and her feet seemed too small and were oddly bent in towards each other on the end of the metal tray. A buff tag was tied with a piece of string around her big toe. The nail had been recently varnished and Harvey thought what a waste of time that had been for her.

Death did strange things to people. A few days ago in bed she had been a wild energy force of muscles, glands, pumps, emotions. Now she was nothing. The thing had gone and there was no hope of getting it back. Past the point of no return.

The pathologist severed the last membrane, lifted out her lungs with bloodied gloves, laid them with a wet slap on his wooden dissecting board and prodded them with his fingers.

The lungs were dark red and brown with a spongy texture like foam rubber, and indented as he pushed them, releasing watery black dribbles. 'See the fluid retention?' The pathologist spoke with a nasally Yorkshire accent. An inch of ash wobbled precariously on the end of his cigarette then dropped to the floor. 'You'd expect that in an old person, but not someone of this girl's age. I should think she was quite a heavy smoker.' A drip was forming on the end of his nose.

*She was*, Harvey nearly said, but bit his lip in time and merely nodded.

The mortuary assistant, a silent, flimsy-looking slip of a woman in her fifties, lowered a metal ladle through the incision in Sandra Lock's chest as if she was about to dish out soup. There was the slop of blood, she lifted the ladle out filled to the brim and tipped the contents with a sloosh into a gulley beneath the table. She scooped the ladle in again.

'It is also a symptom of suffocation,' the pathologist went on. 'The barbiturate dose needed to stop the fitting relaxed the lung tissue muscles so much they couldn't function; it looks like they've collapsed and couldn't reflate.'

'Do you think it's the barbiturate that killed her, Dr Higgs?' Harvey asked, trying to mask the anxiety in his voice with an air of student inquisitiveness.

'Human organs can only take so much chemical insult. It's always a danger when treating *status epilepticus*.' He wiped his nose on his sleeve, picked the lungs up and dropped them in the metal basket at the end of the table.

The assistant left the ladle obscenely sticking out of Sandra Lock's chest, carried the basket silently across the room and placed it on the weigh scales below the blackboard. She chalked '750g' under the words 'left lung', and '850g' under the words 'right lung', then tipped them out into a white plastic bag and brought the basket back over.

The pathologist nodded at the chart. 'For a normal, healthy woman of her age they ought to weigh about three to four hundred grammes. Fluid retention is the extra weight; this is a clear pointer towards suffocation.' He pulled off his gloves, laid his cigarette in an ashtray on the worktop near a metal sink, wiped his hands on a cloth and picked up a ball-point pen.

Harvey relaxed a little as Dr Higgs wrote his notes on the lungs. It was going to be OK. It was going to be fine. The assistant ladled more blood out of Sandra Lock's midriff. The blood of a dead person who was horizontal always drained down into the chest, like a sump.

Vehicles. That's all human bodies were.

The pathologist put down his pen, took another drag on his cigarette and stubbed it out. As he walked back to the cadaver, a student called Brian Kirkland said: 'Dr Higgs, is the purpose of this autopsy to establish that Nurse Lock died of *status epilepticus*, or to discover the cause of the epilepsy?'

The pathologist took a linen handkerchief from his pocket, shook it open like a conjurer, then blew his nose into it with a loud trumpet. He balled the handkerchief up with one hand, stuffed it back in his pocket and looked at the group. 'The purpose of a post mortem is to establish the cause of death and to satisfy the coroner that there are no suspicious circumstances. The law in this country states that if a person dies more than twenty-eight days since last seeing a doctor, or within twenty-four hours of an operation, there must be a post mortem. If there is any doubt about the cause of death, there must be a post mortem. In this situation here we know the mode of death was *status epilepticus*, but we don't know the cause of that epilepsy in an apparently healthy young woman with no history of epilepsy.'

Anxiety returned. The pathologist went over to his jacket, which was hanging on a hook. 'I have already examined the brain for indications of a tumour or other damage and have found nothing. From the slight inflammation, all things point at the moment to a viral infection, but we must never make assumptions.' He took a packet of Player's cigarettes from the jacket pocket.

Harvey caught the pathologist's eye and nodded attentively. That's what you'll find, he thought smugly. Viral symptoms.

'Dr Higgs,' said another student, 'will you be sending the bodily fluids to toxicology?'

The pathologist shook a cigarette out of the pack and tapped it on the glass of his wristwatch. 'Viruses are hard to identify. We will be taking blood and fluid samples for the laboratory, but it's unlikely they will be as useful as the samples that would have been taken when the woman was still alive.' He lit his cigarette and pulled his gloves back on.

Two hours after rats had been administered the equivalent of four times the dosage Harvey had given to Sandra Lock, there was no trace of GW 2937 in their systems. Harvey knew that even if the drug had not fully metabolised they would have to test specifically for it to find it. It would be like looking for a needle in a haystack.

The pathologist picked up his knife and began to remove the girl's liver. With her belly open and half an inch of white flesh tinged with blood down the incision line, she could have been pork on a butcher's block. Dead. Empty. The driver had gone; the pilot; the soul, or spirit – if there really was one. Gone too far to be able to ask her about it.

Stupid bitch. He glared at her. But it was himself he was angry at. He had guessed wrongly. Too much of the drug. He looked at the chart on the wall where the weight of her brains, heart and lungs were already chalked up, and noted them down in his diary.

Next time he would reduce the dosage. But he was going to have to wait, he knew. Two *status epilepticus* cases within a fortnight of each other was an acceptable coincidence. Three would look strange. Leave it a couple of months or so. He had given Sandra Lock thirty-five milligrams of GW 2937. Next time, on a girl of Sandra's height and weight, he decided he would try twenty-five.

# *Chapter Thirty-One*

*Wednesday, 24 October*

'If the coroner's released the body,' Patrick Donoghue said, 'it means they'll be burying her again within a few days. Maybe even tomorrow.'

There was only one other table occupied in the restaurant and Kate regretted choosing to come; she had been here a couple of weeks previously at lunch time and it had been crowded and lively; now in the emptiness the smart black and white decor merely added to the stark chill of nervousness she was feeling.

The waiter hovered, anxious to please, and she wished he would leave them alone to the privacy of their conversation.

'A couple more minutes,' Patrick said to him.

Kate twisted her wine glass in her hand. Patrick was wearing a beat-up corduroy jacket, and a tieless blue denim shirt buttoned to the top which gave him an air of rebellious directness that she liked.

She scanned the menu, wanting something light that would give her some energy and not make her sleepy. Parma ham with melon, then grilled monkfish, she decided. 'If he's released the body, presumably he thinks there's nothing suspicious.'

'Not necessarily. It means he's satisfied that he has all the information he needs from the pathologist's report. Has the coroner spoken to the husband?'

'I rang this evening and spoke to his mother. The coroner had just rung and said the pathologist is waiting for the analysis results of the bodily fluids, but his initial report says that the cause of death is as per the original clinical diagnosis.'

'Epilepsy, wasn't it?'

'Swelling of the brain related to it.'

'So no sign of suffocation?'

Kate leaned forwards. 'I talked to Dr Marty Morgan, the *News*'s medical columnist, and he said that in someone who's been dead over a week suffocation is a very hard thing for a pathologist to ascertain. Virtually impossible, in fact.'

'How did the coroner explain the blood in the coffin?'

'Amniotic fluid and other substances that came out when the foetus was expelled.'

'What's the mother's view?'

'That it's bullshit.'

He interlocked his fingers; sturdy, manly fingers, which were nicely cared for without looking pampered. He studied her face.

'You probably think I'm nuts,' she said. Her grey-blue eyes looked pleadingly at him.

'No, I don't.'

'Do you still believe me?'

'Yes.' He drank some more of his wine. 'I think you'd better get Donaldson to request a private post mortem.'

'Would the coroner allow that?'

'He should. It would help if you had some evidence of things the pathologist has overlooked. What about the other people at the exhumation? The grave diggers?'

Kate sipped her wine. It was an Australian Chardonnay, oaky and rich, and she would have liked a whole lot of it and to have got roaringly drunk tonight, instead of having to stay sober, drinking enough to take the raw edge off her nerves, enough to give her courage, but no more. 'I'm going to speak to them all – that's what I'm planning to do tomorrow.'

'I'm not going to be able to cover for you tomorrow,' Patrick said. 'I'm being sent to Brussels.'

'Brussels? Hey, that's good news for you,' she said, trying to hide her disappointment.

'Yup. I have to do a story on Euro-MPs' lifestyles.'

'That's great!'

Their eyes met for a moment. Kate glanced down at the menu then back and smiled. In his own expression was a tenderness that touched something in her. Her throat dried and a tremor of excitement rippled through her and stayed, churning like a trapped creature inside her stomach as she realised the feelings for him that were kindling in her. She noticed the wiry hairs on his wrist coiling around the bevelled winder of his watch; ran her eyes down his strong hands with their long fingers and flat tips with clear, sturdy nails. Sturdy. Everything about him was sturdy, indestructible and she felt anxious that he was going away. She wondered whether he had a girlfriend or a fiancée. He was still looking at her, and a warmth was infusing into her, giving her courage. 'I'm pleased for you,' she said. 'Really pleased.'

'There were dozens of reporters at the trial today. You'll probably get someone else to cover for you fairly easily.'

'Sure.' She remembered she had forgotten about the presentation of the music award at the Lady Gosden Primary School, and felt bad; she hated to let kids down. She'd pick the story up later by phoning the school.

It was shortly after midnight when Kate drove the Volkswagen slowly down the road past the front of A. Dalby & Son. She was relieved to see the premises of the funeral directors were in darkness. A taxi hooted her then passed with an irritated roar of acceleration. The traffic was light and apart from a couple of takeaways, everything else around was closed too.

She turned up a side street, then into a terrace of small run-down Edwardian houses, and parked between a motorised caravan and a rusting Jaguar. She switched off the ignition, unbuckled her belt and climbed out. The night was wintry, black, thick with cloud; a strong damp wind blew across her cheeks and tore at her hair.

Patrick had dropped her home, given her a light peck on the cheek, and promised to call when he got back from Brussels in a couple of days. She had not invited him up because she needed to get on, and had not wanted him to know what she was going to do tonight. She was worried he might have insisted on coming too, and she did not want to risk getting him into trouble. It was her problem, her mess, and she had to sort it out herself.

She had changed into jeans, a thick black jumper, rubber-soled boots and her dark blue imitation Barbour jacket, and had put on a new pair of thin, black leather gloves she had bought that afternoon after she had left the undertaker's. Into the jacket pockets she had crammed a torch, a penknife, a pair of pliers and her small Minolta automatic camera. As she walked back down to the main road, trying to hook the two parts of the zipper together, she felt cumbersome and nervous as hell and tired, and she wished she were sitting at home in her living room, talking with Patrick, drinking a glass of wine and playing some music.

Patrick. She was tingling with a high from being with him; had watched the tail lights of his battered Alfa Romeo disappear down the street with a deep sense of longing she could not remember feeling before.

The gates were lit by the glare of a street lamp across the street and by the light that spilled through from the main road, and as she neared them they seemed increasingly conspicuous.

A. DALBY & SON, FUNERAL SERVICE. DO NOT OBSTRUCT.
24 HOURS ACCESS REQUIRED.

A police Panda car drove past and she watched it warily until it had disappeared. The wind gusted fiercely. Across the road a loose door banged. Kate stared at the upright wooden slats of the two gates. They were about six foot high, with eyes through which the chain was looped at about four foot. In daylight they had looked easy; now in the darkness they seemed to tower above her like the ramparts of a fortress.

An old white Chevvy on jacked suspension rumbled by, rock music blaring from its speakers. The front door of a house up the road opened; a couple came out, turned and walked away.

She looked around again carefully, raised her arms then jumped and grabbed the top of the gates with both hands and hauled herself up, the soles of her boots scrabbling for a grip on the slippery wet planks. Her right foot found the chain, her toe jammed in the eyehole, she levered herself up higher, slithered over the top of the gate and dropped down.

It felt as if she was dropping for ever. Her feet hit the hard cobbles with a jar that snapped through her and she fell forwards, bashing her knee painfully, her gloved hands thumping on to the wet, hard stones, the torch and pliers clattering in her pocket.

She stood up unsteadily and took her torch out, looking nervously around the dark yard, listening. All the garage doors except one were shut and the windows at the rear of the premises were dark. She flashed the beam of the torch in through the open garage door; an oil stain lay on the concrete floor.

*We have a twenty-four hour service for visiting loved ones.*

She hoped no one was intending visiting a loved one in the next few minutes, and that no one had gone off to collect a corpse. The beam slid over the dark, frosted glass of the workshop window, over the black windows of the chapel of rest above, then scooped the darkness out of the far end of the yard. All that overlooked them was the windowless wall of the ironmonger beyond. No one could see her.

No one who was alive.

She shivered. Tried to get rid of the thought even before it had developed.

*He was eighteen when he passed on but you are his little sister and he wants to look after you*, the medium had told her.

Don't believe in ghosts.

She walked up to the small wooden fire exit door at the end of the workshop and pulled the large brass key she had taken earlier out of her pocket. The beam lit up the deep keyhole.

*He's telling me you are in great danger from something that you are doing . . . in your work. You mustn't do it.*

Don't believe in ghosts.

The lock was stiff and for a moment she thought the key was not going to turn. Half hoped it was not going to turn. Then it made a single snap as loud as a gunshot and the door moved a few inches as if some enormous pressure on it had been released. She turned the handle and the door swung outwards with a clatter from the bottom.

The shadows of the coffins took a step forward towards her. Then they rocked as she moved the beam. Her throat tightened as she stepped in, shut the door behind her and locked it, and suddenly felt very alone and very scared. She played the beam around the room, on to the work surface, the curling first aid poster on the wall, the coffin on the trestle, the Dexion shelves stacked with handles and plaques and plastic caskets for ashes.

The beam picked up a bump on the floor and she looked down at it for a moment in horror. It was a tiny grey mouse, furry with a long tail, the back of its head flattened by the metal spring of a trap and a trickle of fresh blood running down its back. A piece of cheese lay on the bare boards a few inches away.

Shadows followed the beam, slipping out of the walls one by one like phantoms come to greet her and she shone the torch back at each one in turn, afraid, turning it back into a coffin, or a filing cabinet or a table.

Calm down.

The window rattled in a gust. She walked past the coffins, with their intense smell of raw timber, knelt and opened the chipboard box, then shone the torch down at the coffin inside. The sides were crusted with mud and dry leaves and there were streaks of white lime. The brass handles and plaque on the lid glinted dully.

The lid was oddly clean, different to the rest of the coffin. She raised it up, surprised by its weight, and a strong smell of new plastic engulfed her. The lining inside the coffin looked as if it had been renewed. White satin and white lace frills without a mark on them. New white plastic liner at the bottom. She studied the inside of the lid inch by inch, but nothing marked the smooth finish and the natural grain of the mahogany.

She thought back to that moment on Monday night when the lid had been raised and she'd seen what she thought were scratch marks; had shifted her position in case it was a trick of the light, but was still sure she had seen them, shallow grooves, some criss-crossed, some, the deepest ones, in the same place, as if someone had ground at them, determinedly, with the only thing she had. Her nails. She studied the grain of the wood, wondering, as she did constantly, whether she had been mistaken, had confused the grain for scratch marks. She turned the lid around now in the beam of her torch, but saw nothing that looked like scratches.

She put the lid back on and closed the box, disappointment seeping through her, then walked across the workshop to the open door to the passageway. She had hoped that the scratches would still be there, that she could take a photograph, or maybe even call the police and have the lid analysed. Then fear blotted out her thoughts as she stepped into the dark passageway.

She stood still and listened, playing the beam up and down the flaking yellow plaster on the walls. The building creaked, rattled in the wind, and a cold draught eddied around her. A floorboard cracked sharply, making her jump. Something ran across the floor above, light, scampering; a mouse, or a rat. Then silence. For a moment the only sound was the pounding of her heartbeat. It was cold in here, bitterly cold, but Kate barely noticed.

*He's telling me he passed in an accident at sea. He was on a yacht. He's telling me he was caught by the sail and knocked overboard.*

Don't believe in ghosts.

She took a few steps, then stopped outside the door of the embalming room and hesitated as she thought she heard voices. Nothing. Just the faint whir of the fridges beyond. Goosepimples chased each other down her arms as she turned the handle and went in. Then she froze.

A man was in there.

She backed away, smacked into the wall, the beam still on his face, his white face, motionless like the rest of him lying on the metal table.

His mouth was indented from the slackening of the jaw muscles which gave him the appearance of yawning; his silvery hair, which was straight and cut short, was tousled as it might have been after a night's sleep. He was naked, stretched out on the steel bench, his skin the colour of moonstone, his penis lying in his grey pubic hair. His feet with blue toes and scaly shins were splayed out, and his thin, bony arms lay folded on his large stomach.

Sorry, she wanted to say, sorry to intrude. A tap dripped. She kept the beam firmly on him as she stepped forwards, watching for a twitch of skin, a flicker of an eyelid, the curling of a finger. The smell of formalin seemed to ooze out of the walls at her. The black shadow of the alcove loomed closer, the whir of the fridges was increasing, the air was getting colder.

She swung the torch away from the corpse to the alcove. It was OK, just beige tiles. Nothing else.

No ghosts.

Then a floorboard cracked behind her and she spun round. The beam struck the face of the corpse and a strangled croak of terror tripped out of her throat. On this side, the side she had not been able to see from the door, the man's face was stoved in, lumps of splintered bare bone sticking out of what remained of the cheek and forehead, and the flesh missing completely from the top of his scalp. The eye was distorted, crushed and swivelled round, half gouged out and staring sideways out at her.

She turned away, swallowed hard, then walked resolutely into the alcove and up to the wall of fridges. The beam ran across the small square doors; grey metal; cold, claustrophobic. People were in there, someone was behind each door that had a tag in the slot on the outside; in there instead of their snug bed at home.

Alone.

Mrs S. Donaldson.

Kate put her gloved hand on to the handle and pulled. It pivoted backwards with a metallic clunk and the crack of a rubber seal releasing, and the door swung open. Cold air poured out, enveloping her.

She was conscious of the deep thumping in her chest as she stared into the darkness, the darkness in which lay a human form wrapped like a mummy in white plastic sheeting.

Sally Donaldson.

She gripped the handles of the tray with hands that were almost paralysed with fear and pulled. It slid noiselessly, effortlessly out.

It's not real, she thought, none of this, just dreaming. Barely able to hold the end of the sheeting in her trembling gloved fingers she slowly lifted it up off the face. The dead girl's eyes stared back up at her out of the alabaster whiteness of her flesh. She had the same grin that had been on her face when the coffin had been opened; a grin formed by the flesh receding, shrivelling away from a mouth that was frozen in a scream of despair.

It was the complete absence of movement that spooked her the most. Still. Motionless; waiting for her to wake up and knowing she never would. There were small brown patches, like liver spots, where the flesh was beginning to putrefy. Against the carefully brushed tresses of her blonde hair, it looked even more obscene, even more scary. Kate placed the cover back over the face. 'Doing what I can for you,' she said quietly. 'I'm trying for you.'

She freed Sally Donaldson's left arm and lifted up her hand. It was stiff, firm. She examined each finger carefully in the beam of the torch. They were a dark blue colour and the flesh had shrunk. The nails were clear, unvarnished, long and perfectly formed. Immaculate. Too immaculate.

She removed a glove, pinched the end of the nail of Sally Donaldson's index finger between her own forefinger and thumb, and twisted it. Nothing happened. She tried again harder, and felt her own nail bending. She pulled. Nothing. She tried the next finger, then the next without success.

Then she took the pliers out of her pocket, gripped the index fingernail with those and pulled hard. There was a slight tearing sound and the nail and part of the flesh came away.

Christ.

She stared down in horror at the raw torn flesh. At the nail she gripped with the pliers with tendrils of flesh hanging beneath it. Her stomach turned over a revolution. She held the nail up in the torchlight; it looked real, horribly real, not like the false nail she was expecting. She wrapped it carefully in her handkerchief, folded it tightly, pushed it into an inside pocket and zipped it shut.

She closed her eyes, almost weeping in disbelief, and thought again of the moment in the cemetery when they had lifted the lid. The foul stench that had risen. The scratches on the lid. The coppery stains of dried blood on the blue nightdress. Sally Donaldson's eyes open wide, filled with despair. Her skin glaring in the arc lights. The white immaculate teeth protruding from the blue lips in that hideous rictus grin. Her long thumb nails. The rest of the nails bitten or worn down to the quick.

Worn from scratching.

They had been.

It wasn't her imagination, any more than it had been when she'd watched a policeman lift the leg and half the lower torso of a Conservative MP out of a rose bush thirty yards from the car bomb that had killed him. Any more than dozens of other horrors that she had seen in the course of her work.

The alcove suddenly brightened. She snapped the torch off and turned round. Light spilled through from the embalming room. She tiptoed into the doorway, her heart punchballing inside her. The light was on in the corridor outside. She felt a howling draught of air, heard voices, cheery male voices.

'Got him?' said one.

'Yes.'

'I'll just shut the door.'

Fear slid between her skin and her muscles like the cold blade of a knife. The body. Get it away, out of sight.

She ran back, bundled the wraps over Sally Donaldson, working in the faint light, then pushed the tray in. She pushed too strongly and it hurtled forwards, crashing with a dull clang into the rear of the fridge. She shut the door then turned, about to run out when the light came on in the embalming room.

'He's a heavy bugger!' one voice said.

She scanned the walls in desperation. Nothing. No windows, nothing but tiles.

A shadow fell across the alcove. She heard shuffling footsteps.

'Didn't ought to lie around like that with no clothes on – might catch cold,' said another voice, a younger man. One of the men sniggered.

Fridge.

The shadow got bigger. Then she could see an anorak; a man walking backwards.

She stuffed her torch into a pocket, crouched on to her knees and pulled open the fridge door nearest the floor, out of sight of the alcove. She pushed her feet in, and they hit something firm, but yielding. She looked round in horror. There was a body, wrapped in white plastic.

Oh Christ.

She began scrambling back out but the man was starting to turn.

No time.

She heaved herself backwards in over it, feeling its lumpiness beneath her, her back pressing against the empty tray of the compartment above, wriggled herself backwards, deep into the compartment, struggling, then she grabbed the inside handle, pulled the door and shut it as quietly as she could.

She squeezed her eyes shut, cursing, and waited.

Silence.

Cold.

Ice cold; so cold it hurt to breath, hurt her nose, her teeth. She smelled plastic. Her cheek lay on the skull of the corpse below her, her hair tumbled down over her face and the familiarity and the texture gave her a fleeting moment of comfort. She could feel the contours of the scalp, then something soft, an ear. She tried to alter her position and her hands brushed against the nose through the sheeting.

Then she heard footsteps, dull, muffled, echoing. It was pitch black except for a tiny band of light around the door seal in front of her. She shivered, her teeth chattering from the cold, from her fear, her nerves shaking like loose rigging in a wind, so cold it was numbing her mind. The smell was vile in here. Plastic and formalin and pine and rancid grease and rotting flesh.

There was a click like a pistol shot, and light flooded in. She stared, terrified, through the slats. Inside it was one huge open fridge. She could see other horizontal white shapes. The light was coming in down the far end of the fridge. She heard a tray slide out, a grunt, a thump, then the younger voice, which she recognised now as Morris Dalby's son.

'Dad's ordering a second fridge. Capacity for another nine.'

'About time.'

Kate tried to lie still, to breathe quietly, to stop her whole body shaking, the plastic beneath her rustling, crackling. Her ears were hurting with the cold; any moment they would see her, would shout, drag her out. She waited for it; hoped for it now, anything to be out of here, off the thing beneath her, out of this cold.

She heard the sound of the tray sliding again, heard a deafening echoing clang and she was in pitch darkness again. The footsteps receded. Then the narrow band of light through the door seal went out.

Pitch darkness.

They hadn't seen her. Something thumped below her and she was scared for a moment it was the body she was lying on trying to move. She felt the head, hard against her cheekbone, and lifted her own head up. There was pain and an echoing clung as she hit a slat of the metal tray above her, and she laid her head back down and rested her cheek again on the bony skull of the dead man or woman beneath her.

Its heart was beating.

Then she realised it was her own. Thumping, powering through the silence; through the cold that was getting worse, sucking all the warmth out from her, pouring cold air like liquid down her neck, through her hair, soaking her gloved hands and her booted feet in coldness. She was shivering. Shaking, crushing the thing beneath her.

She took out the torch and switched it on and wished she hadn't. It had been better in the darkness, better when she had not been able to see the tight white bundle beneath her, the tight white bundles that were laid out, silent, motionless all around her. The cold was getting worse and she could not take it for much longer. Morris Dalby was right, no one would survive for long in here. She listened to the hissing echo of her own breathing, glanced at her watch. She had been in the premises for nearly half an hour.

She pushed open the door a few inches and waited. Silence. She crawled out, inching her way forwards, sliding over the body beneath, feeling the head bobbing, then she hauled herself to her feet, shivering uncontrollably and stood, listening. She could hear nothing except the wind. Another drip fell from the tap next door. She closed the fridge then hurried out, almost running, through the embalming room, through the workshop and past the coffins. She opened the fire exit door and peered out. The garage door that had been open earlier was shut now.

She closed the door quietly behind her, crossed the yard and heaved herself up on to the gates. The street was deserted. She dropped down to the pavement then ran back to her car, ran to get warm, to get away from the horror. Then she remembered she had forgotten to replace the key. She hesitated, wondering whether to go back, but decided it was too risky. She took it from her pocket and dropped it into the gutter.

She climbed with relief into the driving seat, switched the engine and the heater on and a radio station, any station, just to have some noise, normality.

Then she closed her eyes and fought the tears of disappointment, and tried to think, to clear a path through the tangle of confusion and numb horror in her mind, through the growing despair that was sapping her.

Something niggled. Something she had overlooked. Something that was not right in the undertaker's. She tried to think but she was too cold. Nothing. Probably wasn't any good. A straw, whatever it was.

Christ. Other people had been there at the exhumation. Other people had seen inside the coffin when it had been opened; it hadn't been just herself and Kevin Donaldson and the gravediggers. The coroner's officer had been there; and Judith Pickford, and a doctor.

Then the despair again. Perhaps none of them had said anything because it wasn't unusual, because that was the way coffins often looked when they were opened after a short period of time. Perhaps Terry Brent was right. Perhaps everyone was right. It was a grief-stricken husband clutching at straws and a stupid reporter clutching at a cheap story.

She drove home with her head low. In her flat, she tossed her coat on to the sofa, and had a long, hot shower in which she managed to wash most of the reek of death out of her skin and her hair. But not the reek of failure.

# *Chapter Thirty-Two*

*Thursday, 25 October*

The atmosphere in the court was sombre. In the morning, the press had been allowed in, but not the public. The five defendants, all bland-looking middle-aged men, stood in the dock. Behind a screen near the wigged and gowned judge, a ten-year-old girl was relating what had happened to her in precise detail in a composed and often cheery voice. Kate admired her guts.

After lunch, the public were admitted. The girl's parents gave evidence. Then a motor mechanic who had sold one of the accused men a car. The courtroom was grand and theatrical, with a high ceiling and a ballustraded gallery. It was packed with reporters, with the families and friends of the victims and the accused, with law students and with the inquisitive. Artists from three newspapers sketched the proceedings.

Mechanically, Kate scribbled page after page of shorthand notes, her mind straying all the time back to Sally Donaldson. She had lain in bed, unable to sleep, churning the same thoughts over and over. The fingernails did not make sense. On Monday the nails had been worn right down; last night the nails were perfect. Real nails.

But that did not alter anything. Did not alter the fact that Sally Donaldson had been buried alive.

It was hot and stuffy in the court today; she was wearing the same smart black suit as yesterday, but with a fresh blouse. She took her Microfile diary out of her bag, flipped it open at the mark she had made, and checked through her notes of the people she still had to see. The verger who had first heard the rappings she wanted to talk to again. The pall-bearer who had admitted hearing something move inside the coffin; another of the residents who claimed to have heard cries. The mortuary attendant at the hospital. Judith Pickford. But they would all be a waste of time if the pathologist's report was dismissive. And it was going to be, from what Donaldson's mother had told her over the phone last night, unless the analysis of the bodily fluids showed anything. And Dr Marty Morgan had cheerily told her that unless specific chemicals or drugs were being looked for in the analysis, it was unlikely to show anything.

They had to get a second post mortem.

She tried for the hundredth time to piece the elements together, to work out the scenario from the time Sally Donaldson had been admitted into hospital to the time she had been buried. Who had been involved? How many at the hospital? Dr Matthews's name was on the death certificate, but was he the one who had certified her death?

But again it came back to the pathologist's report. Medical facts. That's what would be believed at the end of the day at the inquest. No amount of eye-witness accounts of wailing and rapping would amount to anything if the cold facts did not support it.

She felt trapped in the court. She'd rung Kevin Donaldson's mother first thing this morning and told her what to say to the coroner, and under no circumstances to allow the reburial to take place yet. She did not tell her about her visit to the undertaker's last night.

At lunchtime she'd gone to a pub with the pack of reporters, drunk two glasses of a heavy red wine and eaten a microwaved moussaka that had scalded the roof of her mouth. She regretted now having eaten such a filling dish and drunk the wine and she yawned, finding it hard to keep her eyes open.

Harry Oakes, the tubby reporter for the *Eastbourne Gazette*, was still annoyed because she had forgotten to phone him through with the details of the exhumation as she had promised. She had finally mollified him by explaining how she had been pulled from the story and promising faithfully she would call him if she came up with anything – if he would cover the trial for her tomorrow. He agreed, reluctantly, leeringly adding the rider that she should have lunch with him one day. Kate decided that men had the words *lunch* and *foreplay* inseparably linked in their brains.

The counsel for the defence sprang to his feet. 'Your honour, this evidence is not – '

'Sit down! Let the witness continue.'

There was a ripple of angry voices and Kate looked up with a start, realising she had missed something completely. Then Morris Dalby's son's voice, and the man with him.

*Dad's ordering a second fridge. Capacity for another nine.*

*About time.*

Kate trembled. She felt a surge of excitement as she realised now what had been niggling her all night.

*About time.*

Did that mean that the one she had been in was sometimes full up? That there wasn't room for all the bodies?

Was it A. Dalby Funeral Service where the buck started and stopped? Had they been aware Sally Donaldson was still alive and gone ahead with the funeral anyway, scared of losing the trade?

No. More likely they would have been concerned about their reputation. Covering their tracks afterwards.

*The poor woman had been clinically dead in hospital for several days, then spent over twenty-four hours in our refrigerator here. No one could survive that, let alone anything else.*

Maybe not. But if Sally Donaldson's body had not been put in the fridge? And instead of dying when the life support had been switched off in hospital had started to recover and the undertakers had not spotted the faint pulse?

It could easily have happened. They would have collected the body from the hospital mortuary in the early morning bound in a white plastic shroud, changed her into the blue nightdress – or perhaps that was the one she was wearing in hospital – put her straight in the coffin and closed the lid. Probably barely even glanced at her face.

Kate's fingers drummed on the wooden rail in front of her in her excitement. She wondered if anyone had spotted that the fire exit door at the undertaker's was unlocked. She wanted badly now to go back there tonight and have another look around. A much better look around.

The judge said, 'Court adjourned until ten thirty tomorrow morning,' stood up and walked out of the court.

'Coming for a drink, Kate?' said Gail Cohen from Radio Sussex as they filed out of the courtroom.

'Sure.' Kate felt in need of a drink. In need of some courage. 'I'll phone the afternoon's proceedings through first – might make the final edition – and catch you up.'

The rain was sheeting down outside, and it was already dark. As she ran down the steps, she saw a small, dark figure moving across the pavement towards her and felt a stab of fear. A man in a shabby mac with the collar turned up against the rain staring directly at her, his face lit by the sodium glare of the street lighting, his quiet dignity of yesterday changed into something altogether more urgent and menacing.

'Miss Hemingway.' The gravelly voice of Morris Dalby, the funeral director, rang out through the babble around her and the din of the rush-hour traffic.

For a moment she thought she was imagining him. He looked out of place. Confusing him with someone else. Then he took a determined step towards her and panic for a moment seized up her coordination, her eyes staring at him wildly, her brain unable to communicate any sound to her mouth.

Terry Brent, was all she could think. The undertaker complaining to Brent that she had been to see him when she should have been in court. When Brent had instructed her to do nothing further. She mustn't answer Dalby, he mustn't know for certain who she was.

She turned away, her face burning red, and pushed through the crowd leaving the court, in between two barristers, past some people with placards and a line of photographers.

'Excuse me, Miss Hemingway.'

She walked faster, dodging through shoppers, sprinted across the road, ran down the pavement the far side, half blinded by the driving rain and by fear. She tripped over a wheeled shopping basket, ran down a hill, off the pavement and on to the road to avoid the thick wedge of pedestrians, past a newsagent and sprinted down a narrow side street and into the car park.

She unlocked the VW and dived in, her lungs aching, slammed the door, and pushed the key at the ignition. For a moment she could not get it in, struggled with it. The car smelled damp and the windows were misted. The engine turned over sluggishly and she wondered, alarmed, if the battery was charging properly. Come on, come on. It fired and she revved, wiping the condensation off the inside of the screen with a duster. She pressed the clutch down with her left foot and her knee ached from when she had bashed it falling last night. Then her foot slipped off the clutch and it sprang back up with a klunk.

Shit.

She pressed it down again, pushed the gear lever and drove forwards. As she waited at the car park exit for a stream of traffic to pass, looking nervously around for sight of the undertaker, she was startled by headlights that suddenly appeared in her mirror, as if they had come out of thin air.

She bit her lip and pulled out into the one-way street, and the vehicle followed with a loud roar of its engine, then stopped behind her a short way on at a red light. Under the glare of a street lamp Kate could see in her mirror that it was a white car. She stared into the mirror trying to see the driver but could only make out a silhouette through the windscreen.

She turned right, heading for a back road out of Lewes she had discovered a few weeks ago, to avoid getting stuck in the rush-hour traffic. She wanted to keep moving. To get away. The car followed. She concentrated on trying to see through the smeared interior of the windscreen and the driving rain outside.

Mr Dalby. What the hell did he want? Except she knew what he wanted. Knew why he had come. The demister whirred busily, but seemed to be making the fogging worse; she leaned forwards, wiping the screen again with the duster, and trying to see ahead through the rain that was coming down faster than the wipers could clear it away. Her hands were shaking. Come on, no proof. Got no proof.

None.

She hoped.

She accelerated, driving too fast up a dark road, and the car behind accelerated too, sticking resolutely with her. She saw lights ahead and slowed as she approached a busy main road, indicated left, and stopped at the T-junction on a long curve. The car pulled up behind her as a seemingly endless line of cars, travelling fast, flashed past. Her wipers, which had been clacking busily, slowed suddenly and the speedometer light faded as the engine faltered. She blipped the accelerator; the wipers speeded up and the light brightened. She engaged first gear, kept the clutch pressed down and the engine racing as she waited.

There were half a dozen more cars to come, then a gap that was long, but not long enough, before the battery of lights of a long-distance truck. Could be long enough if she went quickly. There were more vehicles behind the truck. If she could get in front of it she'd lose the white car. She revved again, raised the clutch pedal and felt the clutch bite.

Now.

As she shot forwards into the path of the truck's headlights, the engine died and the car jerked to a halt.

She twisted the ignition key frantically. The lights were towering above her, bearing down, raking one way then the other across the road. Skidding, she realised. Then they fixed on her, blinding her. Above the lifeless clattering of her own engine as she turned the key again, stabbing at the accelerator with her foot, she heard the hissing of air brakes, the slithering of tyres.

Saw the blinding light.

The silhouette of the driver high in his cab.

The engine fired; she scrabbled with her gear lever, tried to find reverse, to back away.

There was just a tiny jolt at first. Then a dull boom that came in at her from every side as if she were in the centre of a bell. A screaming tornado followed it. Something kicked her stomach, slamming the air out of her lungs. An agonising pain seared through her right side. Then she was hurtled into the air. Floating. Weightless. Floating as if she had all the time in the world; as if time did not matter any more. Lights drifted by on either side, above her and below her.

In the distance she heard a sound like a metal dustbin rolling across concrete. A jarring crunch compacted her body; the seat belt tore into her shoulder. A dull boom reverberated inside her head. In slow motion the glass of the windscreen crazed over, then swung inwards as if it were hinged, bending like a snake, and smacked her across the side of her face. The dashboard buckled then snapped free, curling like burnt paper. She heard screams, howling. Rolling now. Over. Over. Hit something. Over.

Then silence. Gentle rocking; a ticking sound; a hiss. The stink of petrol.

She was dimly aware of hanging upside down and her neck hurting. A light was coming, getting brighter, brighter. Tyres slithering on wet tarmac. Then a jarring boom, like being on the dodgems, she thought, spinning round helplessly, like a top, getting giddy, lights blurring into one, then snapping out as if someone had pulled a switch.

'She's breathing,' said a voice.

'Just pulled out in front of me, pulled out right in front of me and stopped,' said a man's hysterical voice.

'Someone halt the traffic that end,' shouted another.

A siren wailed; getting louder. She was shaking. Dimly lit faces looked down at her. She was cold, there was pain down her side. She tried to speak but nothing came out.

Metal doors clanged shut. Bright light; a man in a blue uniform was looking down at her; he had a soft black beard; the road drummed beneath her and a siren seemed to be chasing them. 'Won't be long,' the man said. 'You lie there and relax.'

The siren stopped. Cold air swirled around her. She felt rain on her face, then motion, trundling wheels, a door swung open, people were running, shouting, there were more lights now, passing by over her head, several fluorescents in a row, then a long dark corridor. Tunnel. It seemed to go on for ever, she was moving fast, heard footsteps running beside her, another corridor, then another, then a room with bright lights.

Two men stood over her. A woman wielded a pair of scissors, Kate was vaguely aware she was cutting away her clothes. Her best suit. 'You don't have to do that,' she said, but heard no voice.

'Head injuries, possible spinal damage. Suspected ruptured spleen,' a man's voice said. He was looking at her but sounded as if he was talking about someone else. There was a prick in her left hand.

The pain was getting worse; she felt sick. A nurse smiled. 'You're going to be all right, you'll be fine.' She hooked up a packet of blood.

'Her name's Katherine Hemingway,' said another voice.

'Lost a lot of blood,' said another.

A woman was peering down at her in a white coat; she had short, silver hair and a rubbery nose. 'Next of kin?' the woman asked her urgently. 'Who is your next of kin?' Blood ran down a tube.

'Mother,' Kate said, but did not hear the word come out. She was moving again. One of the wheels below her had a slight squeak. The ceiling slid by above her, walls were moving past either side, people slid past, shiny trolleys, doorways, pipes.

A door closed. She was in a room that was white and felt small. White shelves lined with vials, bottles, syringes in plastic bags. There was a smell of disinfectant. A nurse in a blue scrub suit was looking down at her; then another. Then a man who seemed familiar, also in a blue scrub suit with a blue hat, his mask hanging loose on its tapes below his chin. His face was flaccid, with a pallid, indoors complexion, a stubby nose, tiny rosebud lips and small icily cold eyes set back behind doughy cheeks.

She had seen him before but was confused, could not work it out. She did not know him, but he was smiling and drawing fluid out of a glass vial into the hypodermic syringe in his rubber-gloved hand.

And suddenly she felt afraid of him. She did not know why, but she did not want to be here. Did not want to be injected. She struggled, screamed out. Someone was holding her wrist.

'It's all right,' a nurse said soothingly, placing an oxygen mask over her face.

The man attached the syringe to the drip on her left hand. 'You'll be asleep in a few seconds,' he said. His voice was warm, suave, and just a fraction high-pitched.

His name was Harvey Swire.

## *Chapter Thirty-Three*

*Thursday, 25 October*

'No!' Kate screamed. 'No! Let me – '

The ketamine coursed through the vein, into her main bloodstream and up into her brain. Within thirty seconds of the injection of the induction agent, it had begun suppressing Kate's conscious systems.

She was helplessly aware that everything was slowing, getting heavier. Her eyes closed; she was receding into her body, shrinking away from the drug, hurtling backwards through her own tunnels, trying to find a place it had not reached that was safe. But it raced relentlessly, like an incoming tide, into each of those places too, pushing her back, further back, deeper and deeper into darkness.

But not silence.

She could hear.

Voices. The sounds were a long way away, as if they were coming from another room.

'Can't get the bloody thing in,' said a young man.

'I'll show you,' said a woman. 'You have to be quite firm. See the little white triangle of the larynx?'

Then she knew she was moving again because she could hear wheels and footsteps. There was a clatter of instruments being laid on a tray.

Hey, I'm still awake. Please.

She tried to signal, to move an arm, to speak, to open her eyes. In the room, somewhere beyond her silence, she could hear people talking. There was a hiss of air, then another.

'I can't, I'm going on nights again from tomorrow,' said a young woman.

'I want to buy it for my son,' said a man with an Indian accent.

'Get the AA to look at it.'

'What do we have here?' said an acid-sounding woman.

'RTA,' said another woman with a young voice. 'Suspected ruptured spleen. Severe bodily bruising on her lower left abdomen, and her blood pressure's low and falling. Concussion; superficial head and facial abrasions, possible internal head injuries. Bodily lacerations and possible further internal injuries.'

'Pretty girl, isn't she?' said another voice.

There were clunking sounds. A sharp hiss, then another. Squeeze-clunk. Squeeze-clunk. Echoing air. It sounded as if she were breathing through a snorkel.

'Anyone know what happened?' said another woman.

'Yeah,' said a man's gruff voice. 'She was in a Volkswagen Beetle, got hit broadside by a lorry; knocked the front of her car off, apparently. Rolled over several times. The ambulance man said that's what it looked like.'

Then the man with the Indian accent again, courteous, quiet, authoritative. 'What is her blood pressure, Harvey?'

'Eighty systolic, and falling.' She recognised the suave, slightly high-pitched voice of the man who had given her the injection.

'And her pulse rate?'

'One hundred and twenty, but faint.'

Hey, I'm conscious.

'Has she received any blood?'

'Two pints of O-negative, with six pints on the way up.'

'What have you given her so far, Harvey?'

I'm conscious. Please, I'm conscious.

'I've put her under with one hundred and fifty milligrams of ketamine,' said the suave voice. 'She's had one hundred milligrams of suxamethonium, six milligrams of vecuronium, fifteen cc rhesodioxepan; she's on four-two nitrous oxide and oxygen ventilation.'

'Rhesodioxepan? That's that new drug from Grauer's?'

'There's a lot of brain activity on the EEG,' said the Indian accent.

'Might be the ketamine. But I also think she could be fitting from damage from the head injury.'

'Is that why you're giving her the rhesodioxepan on drip?'

'Yes. I'll increase the dosage if the fitting doesn't stop.'

'That's a neat appendicectomy scar,' said a woman.

'Yes, it is a good one,' said the Indian. 'Right, are we ready now? I think we should put in some antibiotic.'

'Of course,' said the suave voice.

She tried to scream. Nothing. There was a sharp pain, then her arm felt as if it were being inflated.

'I'm going to open up the abdomen. Is she fully prepared, Harvey?' said the Indian. Kate realised he was the surgeon.

'Yes.'

I'M AWAKE.

'Blood pressure's still falling,' said a young man's voice.

She was cold with fear. Was this what it had been like for Sally Donaldson, trapped inside her body but alive? Was this how Sally Donaldson had felt when she was taken out of the fridge and put in her coffin?

'Does this AA examination of motor cars cost much?'

STOP TALKING ABOUT GODDAMN MOTOR CARS. I'M AWAKE, CAN'T YOU SEE?

'About ninety pounds, but it'll pay for itself.'

Panic was seizing her. She had once told her mother she wanted to be cremated. Christ, what if? If she was declared dead, but was still alive? The way Sally Donaldson had been? No chance of being rescued after the flames started eating the box.

Then the pain struck. A red hot poker melted its way through her stomach and deep into her internal organs.

She bellowed in agony, tearing her lungs out, thrashing her balled fists, twisting in agony. The heat burned inside her, cauterising her stomach lining, her liver, her kidneys. Searing, unbearable pain that tore up through her chest, shot burning lances into her shoulders. Getting worse. Worse. She shook, tossed herself from side to side, clenched her fists, smashed her head back against the table, trying to escape from it, but it kept on going, burned through her insides like a blowtorch.

She threw herself up, crashed down. It was worse. Up again, down, even worse.

GOD HELP ME.

A wave of nausea engulfed her.

'She is not bleeding much,' said the surgeon with a tinge of concern. 'Probably the blood loss, I expect.'

HELP ME, she screamed.

'And the rhesodioxepan,' said the man with the suave voice.

'You're keen on that.'

'It's good for both epileptic fitting and trauma; constricts the capillaries.'

'Yes, there's less blood loss than I would expect from this incision. Mind you she's pretty low on blood. She's very calm.'

'It's good.'

Calm? Sweet Jesus please HELP ME. She felt the fingers like white hot stilettos driving deep into her; metal clamps pinching her skin. She screamed in pain as her stomach was pushed aside and the fingers touched a nerve. Pain careened up her spine into the base of her skull. She screamed again.

But they could not hear her. Could not sense her moving.

She was not moving. Her lids lay closed over her eyes like lead weights.

Like coffin lids.

'So you think the AA would be a good idea?' said the surgeon.

'They're very thorough. Old Fiats are prone to rust. Unless you really know what you're looking for.'

'No, I don't, I'm not good with motor cars.'

She cried dry tears, beat against her prison walls, turned, turned, but the fingers kept on digging, digging. Oh, sweet Jesus, I can't bear any more. PLEASE HELP ME.

She heard a sharp beep-beep-beep. Then a young man's voice, urgent. 'Dr Swire, look at the EEG. Her brainwaves are ceasing.'

'That's good. The effect of the rhesodioxepan and the low blood pressure. Switch the alarm off. Concentrate on the EEG and the blood oxygen.'

A shrill whistle rang out.

The poker broadened into a red-hot shovel scooping out her insides. She screamed again, clawed at her cell, clawed at the inside of her own body, tearing at it with her nails.

'Blood oxygen's dropping,' said the young man, sounding edgier.

The pain again, exploding like white-hot shrapnel inside her.

A piercing staccato buzz rang out. There was an instant hubbub of panic.

'Christ, she's arresting!' said the young man.

'What is going on, Harvey?' said the surgeon.

'Allergic reaction. Either to the anaesthetic or the antibiotic,' said the suave voice, unflustered.

'Heart's stopped!'

'Oh God!' shouted the surgeon. 'Get some adrenaline into her. Quick, man! Someone get the defibrillator!'

A bell rang out. Kate heard footsteps. A klaxon was sounding; a voice on a tannoy was echoing around.

The pain stopped.

The release was ecstatic; Kate wanted to shout for joy; to tell them the pain had gone. That she was OK, her heart had not arrested, she was fine now.

THE PAIN HAS STOPPED!

She could see again. Blurry light. A strange round object, light glowed around it, out of focus at first then getting clearer. A flying saucer. Dreaming, she realised, suddenly recognising what it was: the huge round kettledrum lamp above the operating table. Except she was looking down on to the top of it from above.

She was on the ceiling of an operating theatre.

She was dreaming or hallucinating and it felt great. She stared down at the circular metal casing of the lamp, and could see the bolts where the steel spaceframe strut was clamped to it. Could see plastic flex. The chrome hand-rings. The ventilator slats cut into the cream casing for each of the ten bulbs. There was a curious symbol that had been drawn with a black marker pen on the casing, a triangle with a squiggle inside like a road sign warning of bends ahead.

A young woman lay on the operating table beneath the lamp, swathed in green cloth up to her chin except for a large exposed area on her abdomen. People in blue theatre gear, blue hats and masks, worked frantically. A buzzer rasped, and there was a bleeping. The woman's head protruded from the cloth. She had long ragged blonde hair, two cuts on her face, and there was a ventilator tube in her mouth. The girl looked like herself. Incredibly like herself.

It was herself.

She stared in amazement, not scared, just curious. She looked at the cuts on her face; one on her forehead, and another on her cheek below her eye.

Down the centre of her exposed abdomen was a long, deep incision, the raw flesh held open by metal clamps. Smooth, glistening organs covered in veins were pulsing inside. A nurse tore the green cloth away from her chest, exposing her breasts; they looked flat and distorted. Another nurse began to pump her heart with her hands. The surgeon, a short man with a brown face, was barking out instructions.

The man with the tiny rosebud lips, whom she had seen earlier and recognised, the anaesthetist, she guessed, was tearing a syringe out of its wrapping. Beside him, the younger man was checking the oscilloscopes.

A nurse ran into the room and handed a glass vial to the anaesthetist. 'Lignocaine,' she said.

Kate watched him turn away. Instead of plunging the needle into the vial, he was glancing around shiftily at the others in the theatre. Then she saw him slip the vial inside his gown and pull out another one that looked identical and push the needle into that.

Hey, hey! Anger and panic rose in her. She watched the surgeon place a large lump of white wadding into the incision and hold it with his bloodied, gloved hands.

The scene below her was getting smaller; she was moving away, could see the whole room now, the terrazzo-tiled floor, the spotless pastel green-tiled walls, the frosted-glass windows, the screened-off scrub-up area with twin stainless steel sinks and lever taps and the double doors to the anaesthetics room, the blue, white, yellow and black gas and oxygen lines hanging from the ceiling.

A screen of green cloth had been erected behind her head. Lights, dials, digital printouts and display screens flickered and pulsed on the anaesthetics machine and on dials on the steel master panel on the wall. There were two round clocks. One said seven ten, the other was a timer, registering just over five minutes. There was a blood pressure cuff on her right arm, a plastic name tag on her left wrist and a plastic needle on the back of her hand with a line running into it from an inverted plastic bottle on the drip stand, and a small black clip on her middle finger, with a wire running up to a digital meter. Two rubber tubes from the anaesthetics machine ran to the head of the operating table, and a clear plastic tube from that into her mouth. The bellows on the ventilator flattened, then expanded, flattened, expanded. Higher above it, on top of the anaesthetics machine, was an oscilloscope with short, steep erratic green spikes.

The anaesthetist pushed the empty vial into a waste box below the anaesthetics machine, then injected the fluid straight in through the port on the cannula.

What the hell are you doing?

He sidled back to the machine and again seemed to be watching the others, not her. Almost imperceptibly he pressed a switch on the side of an oscilloscope, moved to the drip stand, adjusted a drip controller below a plastic bottle, then wrote some notes on a sheet of paper attached to a clipboard. Double doors opened and three men wheeled in a large machine, with paddles dangling on the end of rubber tubes.

The people were getting smaller still. Something was pulling Kate steadily upwards. She fought it. It pulled harder and her calm fascination suddenly turned to deep terror.

Dead.

No. Not dead. Please not.

She rose further, feeling cold now.

I'm OK. Please, I'm OK.

She felt as if she were being sucked by a giant vacuum. The scene below her was still shrinking.

Please, someone.

The sound below went dead. She could hear nothing. Silence. The void.

Dread filled her. She scrabbled with her arms, legs, trying to fight the vacuum. Don't take me away. No. Please leave me.

Her body was getting smaller. Smaller. She grasped at the air. Don't want to die. Not yet, not like this, not over, please, it hasn't started.

She imagined the funeral. Her mother. Father. Dara and the kids in the crematorium. Maybe Patrick. Watching the coffin slide off through the curtains.

With herself inside it screaming at them.

Dara leading the kids back out, standing looking at the labels on the flowers. She could hear her saying, *Poor little thing, always found life a struggle, never really got her act together*.

Below her, the operating theatre faded into a white dot of light, like the shrivelling picture on a television screen that had just been switched off. It became a tiny white speck, but it did not vanish, it stayed, steady, a pinprick of light in the distance.

Then she was travelling fast, but she could not hear any wheels. As if she were in an insulated glass box. Hurtling towards the pinprick of light, accelerating, but it was not getting any larger. Darkness hurtled past, occasional flecks of light, like travelling through a tunnel in a train, except she could hear no roaring or thundering or echoing. It was cold, cold as a freezer.

Her fear worsened. Help me. Her voice sounded small, lost. She was shaking with terror. Could still see the pinprick of light, could still feel the acceleration, going faster all the time, so fast the darkness blurred into a solid mass, and she could no longer tell whether it was moving or stationary. There was a roaring in her ear, a buzzing, getting louder.

A dream, the alarm, waking now.

The buzz got louder, then began to fragment, to break away like a swarm of bees separating. The speck of light began to grow. To get brighter, intensely bright, like a headlight coming at her, except it did not dazzle. It was warm, welcoming as a sun-drenched beach. Drawing her towards it. Drawing her unhurriedly. She could feel her speed dropping. She was drifting gently towards it, rays of velvety heat playing on her face, caressing her body, filling all her pores, seeping through her, dissolving all the pain and her fears, drawing her steadily in.

Then slowly, as if a button had been pressed, her life began to replay in front of her. Images and memories and emotions tripped through her mind. She saw herself at six, locked in her bedroom, crying because she had been smacked for punching Dara; she was opening and shutting the drawers in her wardrobe, taking out the tiny objects she had collected, a piece of smooth glass from the beach, a lucky quarter stained brown from a Christmas pudding, a tiny grubby fossil that felt rough as she rubbed her thumb along it.

Howie chasing her with a crab in his hand, screaming, running away down the beach. Later they had put it on the bathroom floor before Dara went in.

Dara's ninth birthday party. Dara was at the head of the table, puffed up importantly in her party frock. Kate watched her mother kiss her, then her father. Dara always seemed to have birthday parties; she never did. The only one who did not kiss Dara was Howie, her brother.

Kate saw the pride on her mother's face as she held a slip of paper in the air. 'Dara's got into college! She's going to Berkeley!'

Dara's wedding. The last time Kate had been to America. Photographs of Dara's three children arrived regularly every few months with smug progress reports that Kate felt like a slap on the face. Testaments to Dara's success as a whole human being, and to her own failure.

Howie in tattered jeans curled up on the foredeck of her father's old yacht, reading a book. Howie, with his freckled face and blond curls and big grin, who didn't get on with Dara either. Her ally.

Her dad coming to her bedroom one autumn day when she knew there was something wrong just from the greyness of the sky and the wind and the cold, and he sat down on her bed, his black curly hair untidy the way it always was, his eyes red with crying, and moved Feef over, straightened Feef's leg, put his arm around her and told her Howie had had an accident on a boat at night, he'd been caught by a wave trying to untangle a sail and been taken overboard and they'd found him in the morning on an empty beach.

Tony arriving at her apartment in Birmingham on a Sunday morning in his jogging suit, with flowers he'd bought at a gas station. Tony coming out of the supermarket with his arm around his wife, and the three kids laden with packages, and his fleeting, sheepish glance before turning away.

The memory of ringing a front door bell in Birmingham and a rosy, cheerful girl of twenty opening the door with a two-month-old baby in her arms which she tickled and nuzzled. And the girl's expression changing to puzzlement as Kate told her how sorry she was to hear about her husband.

'My Billy? Why? What's happened?' The happiness dropped away from her face as if it had been sheared off with an axe.

Kate had stood paralysed, realising the police had made a mistake. They had released the man's name and address to the newspaper before his wife had been informed. On his way to work, his motorcyle had slid under a truck and he had been incinerated by its fuel tank.

The brilliance of the light absorbed the guilt and the horror and the embarrassment, freeing her from it, absolving her. All that was behind, did not matter any more. She was going to move on now, move through the light, charged with a new energy. She could feel the light telling her she would receive a new understanding.

In the distance she could see a silhouette. It was getting increasingly clear because she was moving towards it, moving through the light and out of the other side, out into a huge green field on the edge of a wood. The sky was cloudless, rich deep ultramarine, and beyond the wood she could see the ocean, flat, like a lake, spangled with light.

The silhouette was watching her. A boy, leaning on a gate.

It was Howie.

Her heart leapt. Howie, the same as the last time she had seen him, his blond curly hair long and shaggy, his T-shirt with the motif I'M NICE TO DOLPHINS, his torn jeans, his grimy bare feet, and his tanned face, grinning, covered in freckles.

She ran towards him, leaned over the gate and they hugged and held each other tight, and she started crying and felt wet tears on her face, and he ruffled her hair, the way he always used to. They stood in silence for a while, holding each other, and she did not know it was possible to feel this good.

'Hey, Shrimp, you idiot!' he said gently. 'Why did you do it? I told you, didn't I?'

'Told me what?'

'To leave it alone. To drop the story. To keep away from him.'

'I didn't understand the message. And I guess I didn't believe it really was you.'

He ruffled her hair again. 'You're a klutz.'

She hugged him harder.

A trickle of cold air eddied through her, and she sensed the sky darkening. Then his hands slipped away. 'You have to go back now,' he said.

'I don't want to do that,' she said. 'I want to stay.'

'There's a lot of things you have to do.'

'What do you mean? What things?'

He grinned again and shrugged his shoulders. 'You know, things. Stuff.'

'Why can't I stay here with you?'

'Because they're restarting your heart, Shrimp. You have to go back.'

They were separating. Except Howie was not moving. It was herself being pulled backwards. She clutched at him.

'You have to keep away from him, Shrimp!'

'From who?'

'Drop your story.'

Rushing wind filled her ears. The light was fading. She was being powered backwards. Howie was receding fast. 'I want to stay here!' she shouted, 'I want to stay here with you!'

The light went completely. Pitch darkness raced past her. Her ears went numb.

Then silence.

She felt heavy, too heavy to move.

Cold eyes stared down at her.

They faded. A while later they were back again. Rosebud lips tightly shut, expressionless. They went. A woman's voice she did not recognise, somewhere a long way in the distance said: 'She's breathing on her own now.'

She heard people walking quietly. Heard coughing and distant telephones and rattles of trolleys and trays, then nothing again. She opened her eyes and it was dark.

Then she opened them again and there was warm daylight. Everything flickered like an old movie projector. Dull yellow light. Hazy. She smelled fresh laundry and lint and antiseptic. Her body felt leaden and there was a fierce pain in her stomach. Dimly, in front of her, she saw a nurse in a white tunic with a blue belt. She was not in the theatre any more.

The nurse was smiling but it was hard to focus on her face. It kept changing shape, elongating then shrinking as if it were liquid, not flesh. A watch hung on a chain from her lapel. The chain stretched then shrank and the watch bounced up and down like a yo-yo. The tunic shimmered.

'Back with us?' the nurse said cheerily.

# *Chapter Thirty-Four*

*Thursday, 25 October*

The rain was still falling at twenty past nine, raked at a steep angle by the sou'westerly that blew in off the Channel and was funnelled down through the dark terraced streets into fierce howling vortexes. Harvey Swire drove his Range Rover slowly in through the open gates, pulled up in the yard of A. Dalby & Son and switched off his lights. The car rocked in the wind.

A figure emerged from the rear door, hurried through the rain and shut the gates, then ran back to the door. Harvey Swire followed him into the shelter of the dark hallway and smoothed his hair back into shape.

Morris Dalby closed the door and turned the key. 'Thank you for coming, Dr Swire.' Rain dribbled down the undertaker's threadbare scalp as he proffered his small bony hand. He seemed agitated.

Harvey Swire stood in his Burberry and hogskin gloves, eyeing the small man in his starchy white shirt and wide black tie with distaste, and shook his hand with the minimum of contact, the way he might have pulled the chain in an unsavoury lavatory. 'I couldn't come any sooner. Busy evening in theatre and we're short staffed at the moment.'

'No, of course,' the undertaker said in his gravelly voice, taking a packet of Benson and Hedge's out of his pocket and removing a cigarette. As an afterthought he offered the pack to the anaesthetist, who shook his head.

The undertaker was blinking fast and his hands were shaking. 'I thought I'd better call you. We've got a bit of trouble.'

'What do you mean?'

'We had a break-in last night, you see.'

Harvey Swire stared at him in the weak light from the naked bulb. 'What was taken?'

'That's the point,' the undertaker said, his unlit cigarette bobbing in his mouth. 'There wasn't nothing taken.'

'Someone snooping?'

'My son discovered the fire exit door in the workroom was unlocked this morning and the key gone. He knows it was locked because he'd loaded in some coffins through it yesterday morning. I reckon I know who it was, too.'

'Who?'

The undertaker clicked his lighter then lit his cigarette. 'I had a smart young lady here yesterday. Gave me a cock and bull story about an aunt in a hospice. I checked up afterwards and the aunt didn't exist.' He drew on the cigarette. 'Journalist, I reckon.'

'She took your key?'

'She wanted me to show her around yesterday. That's quite common – people feel a bit reassured when they see what goes on. We was in the workroom and I took a phone call. I thought I noticed her do something a bit strange but I couldn't work out what it was. She must have taken the key off the hook.'

'Nothing at all was taken?'

'Not that we've been able to find. I – I had a hunch about her, you see. That piece in the *News*. I thought maybe it was her – don't ask me why. She was American, this girl yesterday. They printed the reporter's name on the headlines on Tuesday, so I rang up the *News* and they said that reporter was American.'

Harvey Swire's eyes widened.

'Someone in her office told me she was in court in Lewes all day. I went over there this afternoon. Thought I'd have a word with her.'

'Are you mad?'

'Thought I'd confront her,' Dalby said defensively.

'What happened?'

'She ran off when she saw me.'

Harvey Swire studied Dalby. 'What about the body? Is that all right?'

The undertaker's face blanched. 'I don't imagine anyone would take that.' The light bulb swung on its old flex as the wind gusted outside.

'Have you looked?'

'Well, not specifically, no –'

'Where is it?'

Dalby put the cigarette in his mouth, walked down the corridor, turned left into the embalming room and switched on the light.

Harvey Swire followed him through the spotless tiled room, his leather soles echoing on the hard floor, his coat rustling, rivulets of water running off his polished black Oxfords, past the shiny steel embalming table, through the alcove and along to the fridges.

Half the slots on the fridge doors had name tags. The undertaker opened Sally Donaldson's and pulled out a metal tray with a body wrapped in white plastic sheeting. 'This is her.' He peeled back the sheeting from her face and stood aside.

Harvey Swire looked down at her. 'Had me worried for a moment,' he said. He tugged the sheeting away from her face, and as he did so her right arm fell free. He lifted her hand, and froze. Then he raised the hand closer, inspecting the index finger. He turned the dead girl's hand over as if somehow expecting to find something clenched in her palm.

'Where the hell's this nail?' He rummaged in the sheeting.

'Nail?' The undertaker squinted down through a stream of smoke at the bobbly torn skin where the fingernail had been. 'Bloody hell.'

'There's no possible way it could have fallen off,' Harvey Swire said. 'You can see it's been torn off. When did this happen?'

Fear was growing on Dalby's face. 'She didn't come back from the mortuary like that. I checked her carefully.'

'This is what your intruder came for, isn't it?' Harvey Swire stared at the undertaker with undisguised fury, then let go of the dead girl's hand and paced around the concrete floor. 'Don't you have any bloody security here?'

'Well, we've never felt the need to.' The undertaker picked up the dead girl's hand and focussed on the finger with frightened eyes. 'No one's going to be able to prove anything from just a nail, surely?'

'They can get a DNA print from it. Match it to the rest of her body tissues.'

There was a silence for a moment. Dalby inhaled then removed his cigarette with his forefinger and thumb, breathing out smoke as he spoke. 'Dr Swire, I appreciate that the hospital doesn't want a scandal, which is why I went along with you in the first place, but I think it's time I informed the police. I've had enough, being bombarded by the press all week and now this. I don't find having the reputation of my business on the line very funny.'

Harvey Swire angrily yanked open another fridge door. A parcelled body lay on the middle shelf, the others were empty. 'Plenty of room tonight, haven't you?' he said. 'If you hadn't taken on more than you could handle, this wouldn't have happened.'

'There's no legal requirement for us to keep bodies in the fridge, Dr Swire. It happens to be our practice to do so normally. Mrs Donaldson was in the fridge for quite a bit of the short time she was here. We took her out early because we needed the fridge space. Same as you switched off the life support because you needed the bed,' he said. The undertaker sucked his cigarette down to the butt. 'Are you trying to imply we wouldn't have had this problem if she'd been in the fridge all the time, because she would have died then from the cold?'

'Of course.'

'I thought doctors tried to keep people alive.'

'Only when the potential quality of life warrants it.' He shut the fridge door. 'She was brain dead. If she started breathing again it was not important. She was a vegetable.'

'Was she really, Dr Swire?' The funeral director gave him a penetrating stare.

Harvey Swire's face reddened. 'We're not infallible. We try to do our best for our patients, but medicine is a very inexact science. Sometimes we make mistakes,' he said bluntly. 'What's happened with this woman is a freak situation; it's never happened before and it won't happen again. You're not going to the police. You're not a bloody fool. You didn't go along with this because you cared about the hospital's reputation, you did so because you're terrified about your own firm's reputation. It would destroy your business overnight if this got out. You've just got to keep calm.'

'What do you suggest we do?' Dalby said.

'Find whoever took the nail, fast. You think it might be this reporter?'

'I've got no proof, but it was strange her running off like that.'

'Could be her. We need to find out what she's done with the nail – and who she's told about it. Do you know where she lives?'

Dalby was silent for a moment. 'I think she might be dead.'

'You said you saw her this afternoon.'

'I did. I followed her when she ran off. Back to her car. We was in the same car park so I followed her out. I dunno if she got twitched or something, but she pulled straight out in front of a lorry.'

Harvey Swire frowned.

'It was a pretty bad mess.' Dalby chewed the inside of his mouth.

'What did this reporter look like?'

'Pretty. Long blonde hair – that raggedy look. Sort of fashionable. Freckles, about five-foot five, slim – '

'What car was she in?' Harvey Swire interrupted.

'Volkswagen Beetle thing.'

'She's not dead,' Harvey Swire said. 'She's fine. Except the little bitch won't be able to talk for a couple of days.'

## *Chapter Thirty-Five*

*Saturday, 27 October*

Kate was woken by a metallic rattle. There was a smell of mashed potato that made her queasy. She felt as if she had been kicked in the stomach and the neck. Her mouth was parched and her jaws ached. Her throat was raw. Going to be sick. She opened her eyes, panicking, and bright light dazzled her. People moving around. Shapes in front of her. The smell of mashed potato was getting stronger. Lavatory. She tried to move, to sit up, to get out of bed.

She retched. Nothing came out. She retched again. Someone was holding a metal bowl in front of her. A young nurse in a pale green uniform with a starched apron; a watch hung on a chain from the lapel and there was a plastic badge beside it with Belinda Tindall printed on it.

She retched again and a few droplets of saliva fell into the pan. The nurse was smiling. She had a pretty, open face with a mole above her lip, and short brown hair.

'Sorry,' Kate slurred.

'Don't you worry.' Her voice was young and cheery. 'You've been having a rough old time. Like to try and sit up?'

'Yes,' she said. 'Thanks.' There was a cranking sound and she felt her back being raised, heard the thump of a pillow being plumped. The nurse crooked her hand under her armpit and heaved her up. A sharp pain twisted in her abdomen and Kate sat still for a moment as the pain subsided. 'Sorry.' She smiled weakly, trying to work out her bearings. Something was pulling around the back of her neck; the tapes of the cotton hospital gown she had on. Then she noticed there was a drip line attached to the back of her hand.

'Bit sore?'

Kate grimaced.

The nurse lifted the sheet; Kate saw a catheter tube and a bottle half filled with urine.

'I'll change that for you. Would you like to try a drink? Some water or juice?'

The room seemed to sway as if she were in a boat and her stomach heaved. 'I'm – yes – I – what's in my arm?' Her voice sounded oddly gruff and her throat felt as if it had been rubbed with sandpaper.

'Just saline and dextrose to give you energy. You've been asleep for a long time – a day and a half.'

'A day and a half?' Kate raised her hands, wincing at another twinge in her abdomen, and checked her hair. It was tangled. She touched her face and felt a sticking plaster on her cheek. Memories were stirring. 'Christ.' There was another plaster on her forehead. 'Am I OK?'

The nurse smiled. 'Yes, you're fine. You had a bad car accident and the surgeon had to make a cut in your tummy to see if everything was all right in there. You'll be a bit sore for a few days and you've got a couple of small cuts on your face. They won't scar.'

'Where am I?'

'You're in the Prince Regent Hospital in Brighton. Have you been here before?'

'Yes,' Kate said.

'Hey, Shrimp, you idiot!'

Kate looked around, startled, as she heard Howie's voice, crystal clear.

'Why did you do it? I told you, didn't I?' Howie said.

'Told me what?' Kate said.

'To leave it alone. To drop the story. To keep away from him.'

'I didn't understand the message – ' Kate stared bewildered around her. A large ward. A woman with ginger hair was in the bed opposite; beside her sat a stooped man with his coat folded on his lap, and a bored-looking boy who was playing with an electronic game. To the woman's left was a tall window with blue curtains that looked out on to the grey concrete wall of a multistorey car park. The person in the next bed along had a cage carrying the weight of her bedclothes and Kate could not see her face.

*You have to go back now . . . because they're restarting your heart.*

She felt drained. The nurse was watching her with a trace of anxiety in her face. 'What day is it?' Kate asked.

'Saturday.'

Saturday. She wasn't sure what month it was. Saturday. Easter soon. No, it wasn't Easter. Christmas was next. Then she remembered. 'I should have been in court yesterday. Hartley Briggs. Lewes Crown Court. I need to phone. I have to tell my editor. They won't know – '

'Are you a journalist?'

'Uh huh.'
'My brother wants to be a journalist. Which newspaper are you with?'
'The *Sussex Evening News*.'
'It's a good paper. I read that. Is it your boss you want to get a message to?'
A woman wheeled a meal trolley past the end of her bed. A doctor strode by in his white coat, stethoscope bulging from the pocket. Two nurses walked by talking to each other. A gaggle of people in coats stopped in the doorway by the nursing station. 'There she is!' said one of them, waving down towards the far end of the ward.
'What's the time?' Kate said. Tinny music was leaking from headphones somewhere nearby.
'Half past twelve. Shall I have someone phone your boss? Don't look so worried. He'll understand.'
'I'm covering a trial, you see.'
'You give me your boss's name and I'll take care of it.'
'They cut my clothes off. I remember them cutting my clothes off.'
'They thought you were in a pretty bad way when you came in. I've put your things in your locker. Is there someone we can phone who can bring you night clothes and washing things?'
Patrick.
Kate touched her lower lip with her tongue.
'Husband? Boyfriend?'
She shook her head.
'Your parents?'
'They're not in England.'
'You haven't got a flatmate or anyone?'
It was starting to come back. Fear rumbled through her. The undertaker. The truck. She became silent, trying to work out her thoughts. Lapsed back into a doze then snapped out of it. Howie. Weird dream. Some people were walking towards her, a short Indian man in a neat grey suit who looked familiar, and behind him was a younger man in a white coat and two nurses, a tall, elegant woman with long dark hair, and a thinner, younger one with a pinched face.
'Geoff Fox,' Kate said. 'The news editor. Could you have someone phone him?'
But the nurse wasn't there any more. The light was different; the blue curtain was drawn across the window. She frowned, confused; it was midday – had just been midday, surely?

'Well, good evening. Awake now, are we?' The Indian spoke, and with a start she recognised the voice.

It was the voice of the surgeon.

He stood at the end of the bed looking at the chart, a small man, with an intelligent, finely chiselled face and alert brown eyes. 'How long have you been awake?' he said.

'I think – a while ago I – ' She stopped, disoriented.

He was wearing a gold Rolex watch and had a shiny black tie with red and yellow hexagons. Or maybe they were octagons, Kate thought, distracted by them. She tried to count the sides.

'And how are you feeling?' he said with a smile, walking up the side of the bed to her.

'A little groggy, I guess; some pain in my stomach.' She tried counting the sides on the motif again. There were seven this time.

'I'm not joking when I tell you this. You died in the operating theatre, did you know that? For three minutes you had no heartbeat and no brain activity. You are the most dead person I've ever managed to bring back to life.'

The man in the white coat behind him was peering at her as if she were an exhibit in a museum. The memories shuffled, arranged then rearranged themselves. Buzzers ringing. The brilliant light. Howie.

*She's arresting!*

'I saw you all,' Kate said. 'I was watching you.'

The Indian raised his eyebrows politely.

'Are you the surgeon?'

'Yes, I am Mr Amritsan.'

'I saw you. I watched you from above.'

He smiled benignly. 'You were having a good hallucination, I think.'

'I could hear you when I was brought in. You were talking about motor cars. You were asking whether you should have an AA test on a Fiat, or something.'

'I was talking about a car for my son who is going to university, yes. I wonder when that was.'

'In the operating theatre,' Kate said.

'No, it was – ' he hesitated. 'Ah, yes, you are quite right.' He stooped down, his face crinkling into a frown. 'But you were anaesthetised then, surely?'

It was weird, as if Kate was dreaming this conversation. 'I felt you cutting into me – and your fingers.'

His eyes widened. Deep brown pupils, but whites that looked yellowy compared to his brilliant white shirt.

She was tired, felt herself slipping back into sleep, but she wanted to tell him. Had to tell him. 'I was screaming, but you couldn't hear me. I couldn't move, or anything. I was going out of my mind with pain.'

He sat down on the chair beside her and placed his hands neatly together as if he were closing a book; they were large hands, out of proportion to the rest of him, with slender, well-tended fingers. 'Catherine, isn't it?'

'Kate.'

'Nice name, Kate. You are American?'

'Yes.'

'Your spleen is fine. We had to perform a laparotomy because we suspected it was ruptured, but it turned out to be only heavy internal bruising of the mesentery. This together with shock had the effect of drawing your blood to it and reducing blood pressure dramatically, giving the symptoms of a ruptured spleen. And you have also two fractured ribs. You will be sore for a couple of weeks, but that is all.'

She was trembling; there was a strange urgency inside her that was rising and falling.

'Unfortunately you suffered a dangerous allergic reaction to one of the anaesthetic agents, or the antibiotic, resulting in a cardiac arrest, and you must have allergy tests in case you ever need another anaesthetic. Honestly, I thought we had lost you.' He parted his hands then brought them slowly back together. 'You are a strong girl and we were lucky to have Dr Swire in the theatre. He is a very brilliant man, the best anaesthetist in the south of England. But you gave us a shock. It is fortunate you are young and fit. You will recover quickly.'

'How long do I have to stay in?'

He was evasive. 'We'll have to see how you are. One or two weeks, I expect.'

A wave of panic ploughed through her. Sally Donaldson.

'I have to get up now. I have a real problem. I – I can't stay a week.'

'You will have to, Kate, and I honestly don't think you are going to feel like doing anything for a few days. Do you have any headache now? Or dizziness?'

'No. I mean some, I guess.'

'We need to make sure you have suffered no permanent internal head injury, either from your accident or from your cardiac arrest. You did, unfortunately, have some symptoms of fitting during the operation?'

'Fitting?'

'Epileptic fitting. It can indicate internal injury. I think it probably is only part of the allergic reaction and nothing to worry about. We are going to do an EEG – electroencephalograph – on your brain. If you experience any memory loss or any other problems like that please contact us immediately. I will ask our neurologist to come and have a look at you.'

'Thank you.'

The surgeon adjusted the already perfect knot of his tie. 'This pain you felt in the operating theatre . . . you must understand it is very difficult with road traffic accidents. You are brought in and there is sometimes no opportunity to prepare. We don't know what you have been eating or drinking, or what drugs you might have in you. Decisions on anaesthetics and surgery must be quick.' He pulled his suit jacket down. His shoes were small and rather dainty.

'You hear us talking in the operation; then you see us from above. One of the drugs you have been given is ketamine which is good for reducing haemorrhaging but it has a side effect of making the patient feel disassociated from the body – that you are floating above it. Sometimes also the sense of hearing does not go completely, and perhaps you are putting the two things together in your mind. Creating a hallucination. From the ketamine you may unfortunately have hallucinations for several days to come. Anaesthetics do very strange things to the mind. They are powerful substances. If you add to this the trauma of being in a road accident.' He shrugged his shoulders.

'It felt very real,' Kate said.

'I am sorry if you experienced pain. Possibly there was too weak a dose of anaesthetic at the start, so you were paralysed by the vecuronium but the ketamine wore off. It can only have been for a moment until Dr Swire deepened the anaesthetic, because you had no brain activity at all for several minutes. It would have been impossible for you to have seen or heard anything during that time.'

'Was that during the period my heart stopped?'

He thought for a moment. 'Yes.'

'I saw and heard everything. And I met my brother.'

'Your brother?'

'He's – ' her voice tailed off. 'He's dead.'

He smiled. 'You would be a miracle woman. I'm afraid hallucinations can be very confusing. And cardiac arrest tends to obliterate all immediate memory. I think you will find it is just hallucinations that are going to continue for a little while.' He glanced at his watch. 'I'll pop by to see you tomorrow.'

'Thanks,' Kate said.

His mind already moved forward on to something else, he walked off; the doctor in the white coat and the nurses followed.

Then the bolt of fear slammed her like the truck. She felt a trickle of cold fluid spreading through her stomach as if it had just been injected into her.

*Hey, Shrimp, you idiot! I told you, didn't I? To leave it alone. To drop the story. To keep away from him.*

From who?

*You have to keep away from him, Shrimp! Drop your story.*

Her mind drifted. From Howie to Dora Runcorn.

*Something about wire he's trying to tell me. Do you deal with electrical things? . . . I think you need to be very careful with wire . . . You mustn't touch any wire. Does that mean anything, dear?*

Then tiredness soaked up the fear and Kate slept for a while. She dreamed she was in a dark box that was rolling forwards, and that curtains were sliding shut behind her. The box got hotter and hotter. The sides exploded, fell away and she was surrounded by burning gas jets like candles around an altar, except they were burning sideways, pointing at her.

Burning her.

Her eyes sprang open.

The lights in the ward were on and it was quiet. Someone was walking towards her. Another nurse, holding a paper cup. 'Some pills for you. Like anything to drink?'

'Some water, please.'

'How are you feeling?'

'OK. A bit tired.'

'Dr Swire popped down to see you a couple of times but you were asleep. He said he'll come back in the morning.'

# *Chapter Thirty-Six*

*Sunday, 28 October*

Kate lay awake, wide awake now, in the ward, absorbing her strange new environment. Unfamiliar sounds. Noises of beds being cranked, rattling trolleys, cutlery and crockery; constant footsteps and the starchy rustle of uniforms. Murmured conversations. The ward was dingy. The metal beds looked old, the lime green walls in need of replastering, the window frames in need of a new coat of cream paint. The unframed posters randomly stuck to the walls, mostly of endangered species, had curled at the edges like old sandwiches. Even the morning light through the windows seemed sapped of vitality. Figures lay listlessly in the beds or moved in slow motion across the ward in dressing gowns and casual clothes. Someone coughed. Kate smelled toast which gave her a faint stirring of hunger. The drip line had gone and there was a strip of plaster taped over the back of her hand. Higher up, around her wrist, was a clear plastic bracelet with her name typed in the centre. Like a luggage tag, she thought, then stared at her slender fingers and her long nails, two of which were broken, she noticed, annoyed. She was aware of a dull pain in her ribs as if a hand were pressing down on them.

The scene in the operating theatre played back in her mind. The sight of her own body below it. She had read about people that had happened to. It was usually after a trauma, or an accident.

She saw her body below her on the operating table. It was so clear in her mind she could paint the scene. The colours of the tiles and the floor of the operating theatre. The strange triangular symbol that had been drawn with a black ink marker on the casing of the lamp. The anaesthetist switching vials of something, slipping one into his pocket.

Hallucination. The Indian doctor was right. Had to be right.

'I've brought you some biscuits.'

Belinda Tindall, her nurse, was standing in front of her holding a white plate with four plain *petit beurre* biscuits, and a huge bouquet of flowers. 'These have just arrived for you. I'll get a vase, shall I?' She put the biscuits on the table and laid the flowers on the bed.

Kate touched the cellophane, ripped open the tiny envelope stuck to it and took out the card.

'Get better quickly. From Terry,Geoff and all at the *News*.'

She set the card, which had a bunch of daffodils printed on the outside, beside the biscuits and her empty water glass. A plump girl on crutches hobbled past her, giving her a cheery nod. Kate smiled back.

A shimmer of heat rose from the cast-iron radiator beneath the window across the ward. Belinda came back with a large blue vase. 'Someone rang you last night, very anxious about you.' She took a slip of paper out of her tunic pocket and unfolded it. 'Patrick Donoghue telephoned. He'll call again this morning.'

Hearing his name made her feel a little stronger, and a flood of emotions suddenly distracted her, taking her concentration away from the nurse. Patrick. Then she felt foolish, wondering what he'd think of her looking like this. A nurse was pushing in a payphone on wheels behind Belinda, and she wanted it desperately to be Patrick, but she headed on past and called out to someone further down the ward.

'Is it possible to get a newspaper?' Kate asked.

'I'll pop down to the shop for you in my break. What would you like?'

'It's Sunday, isn't it?'

'Yes.'

'Could you get me the *Sunday Times*?' Kate said. 'And if they've got one of yesterday's *Evening News* left, I'd really like one.'

'Mr Amritsan wants you to get out of bed and walk around the ward a bit. Think you're up to it?'

'Sure.'

'I'll remove your catheter.' The nurse drew the curtain around the bed.

Kate gritted her teeth in pain as the catheter slid out. Then she experienced an intense sense of relief; a step back towards independence. She ate a biscuit, tasted the sweet crumbling texture gratefully, and immediately wanted another as she swallowed it. Then slowly and painfully she swung herself out of bed, and her feet touched the cold brown linoleum floor. Belinda opened the curtains again, then hurried away and came back with a dressing gown and slippers which she helped Kate put on. Kate walked for a few stiff paces with the nurse holding her arm, then managed on her own. There was a sharp pain in her stomach, but it was bearable.

They walked over to the nursing station and into the sister's office, a cubicle with a small desk, two telephones and sheets of paper pinned to the walls and laid on every flat space. The sister was a fat, matronly woman with her hair raked into a bun and a jolly Welsh accent.

'Here's our little angel, back from the dead!' She rummaged through a drawer and took out a plastic bag with a toothbrush, a tube of toothpaste and a flannel, and gave Kate a white towel. 'You'll feel better after a good wash; everyone does.'

Belinda pointed to the washroom a short distance down the corridor. Kate shuffled towards it, towel over her arm, and felt a sudden sense of freedom as she went in and closed the door behind her. Privacy. It was good not to have anyone else around. Then she looked closely in the mirror, horrified by the reflection of her puffy, bruised face and matted hair.

She leaned against the washbasin, exhausted by the effort of getting here, turned the lever taps and put the plug in. As the basin filled, she was conscious of the reek of chlorine in the water and the bland institutional smell of the soap; she had to sit on the stool for a few minutes before she had the energy to wash her face.

She walked slowly back down the corridor. Belinda was holding a cup of tea and chatting with a group of nurses outside the sister's office. In gold letters above the double door was written 'Princess Margaret Ward'.

'Feeling better?' Belinda asked.

'Thanks,' Kate said.

'I got your papers. I'll help you back to bed.'

The flowers were on her bedside locker along with the crumpled message from Patrick, the folded copy of yesterday's *Sussex Evening News* and the thick, fresh wodge of the *Sunday Times*. There was an Anglepoise lamp above the bed, a set of headphones and an alarm light.

'I haven't shown you the remote control,' Belinda said, picking up a gadget on a stalk. 'This is for the radio and your light and the alarm.'

'Neat.'

'We've got your valuables in a sealed envelope in the safe. If you want anything at any time let me know.'

'Sure.'

'And here's a menu. Fill in what you'd like for lunch and dinner.' The nurse put it on top of the locker.

Kate eased herself painfully back into bed and the nurse pulled the sheet and blanket over her. 'Like the backrest up?'

Kate nodded then yawned, heard the crank of a lever and felt her back being raised. She smiled her thanks at the nurse then closed her eyes for a few moments. But thoughts whirred through her brain.

The triangle on the lamp.

She shivered, picked up Patrick's crumpled message and read it. 'Patrick Donoghue telephoned. Will call in morning.'

Just seeing his name written down cheered her. She picked up the *News*. There was a boxing story as the splash on the front page and a smaller story on the trial. She wondered who had covered it on Friday. She flipped through the pages, looking for anything she had written. As she reached the leader page she was surprised to see a feature she had written three weeks ago occupying the whole page except for the editor's opinion column.

ANIMAL RIGHTS SAVAGES by Kate Hemingway.

She read the article, startled by the venom in it that she had never intended; it had been created by a sub-editor taking more liberties than usual with her text. She had written the piece after an animal rights group had firebombed a local furrier and had meant the article to be critical of their tactics whilst sympathetic to the principles of animal rights, which was a subject she cared about.

She folded the newspaper smarting with anger, determined to speak to the chief sub about it when she got back to work. She picked up the typed menu card, took her handbag out of the locker of her bedside table and rummaged in it for a pen. She chose celery soup, grilled cod and a fruit salad. As she marked the final box, she noticed someone standing motionless at the end of her bed. Someone who looked familiar, but whom she could not immediately place.

A man of about forty, expensively dressed with a squat rather bull-like frame and a head that seemed big for his body. His face was flaccid without being fat, with a pallid indoors complexion, a stubby nose, small rosebud lips and tiny eyes recessed deeply behind his doughy cheeks. His hair was light brown, thinning, and carefully groomed. He was wearing a navy double-breasted suit, shiny loafers with gold chains, a blue and white striped button-down shirt and a yellow tie with violins on it. He had a gold ID bracelet, a gold Rolex on the other wrist, and a blue and white Wedgwood signet ring.

She caught his eye, but for a moment he did not respond, just continued to study her coldly, the way he might have studied a piece of furniture.

Then his whole persona changed and he smiled gently, taking her by surprise. 'How are you feeling?' His voice was suave, just a fraction high-pitched and inflected with a warmth she suspected was not genuine, and she realised who he was immediately. She had seen him on Thursday, standing over her in the anaesthetics room, his mask dangling below his chin. And in the operating theatre. And somewhere else.

'Like I've been kicked by a horse,' she said.

'A big iron horse with sixteen wheels, wasn't it?' He continued smiling as if they were sharing a secret together, but there was still a cold glint in his eyes. 'I don't know if you remember me. I'm Dr Swire. I was your anaesthetist.'

'I gather I owe you a big thank you for saving my life.'

'I did what any anaesthetist would have done in the circumstances. Although I understand from Mr Amritsan that I didn't put you to sleep terribly well?' His face adopted a pained expression. 'I'm really terribly sorry; how awful for you. Kate, isn't it?'

She nodded.

He sat down beside her, carefully tugging the crease lines of his trousers over his knees. His hands were fleshy and rather shapeless, his nails immaculately clean and manicured.

'I thought I was going to die of pain,' she said. 'I could feel the scalpel cutting me open, and the surgeon's fingers prodding around inside me.'

'Awful. You poor thing. It does happen sometimes. I did wonder. I noticed your pulse rate rising as Mr Amritsan was making his incision, so I deepened the anaesthetic. Then I'm afraid you had a massive allergic reaction to one of the anaesthetic agents or the antibiotic.' He stood and moved the chair forwards a few inches. 'I'll give you something tonight to help you sleep. Mr Amritsan mentioned that you'd had some rather unpleasant hallucinations.'

'I'm not sure that they were hallucinations. I – I think I may have had one of these things I've read about – an out-of-body – or near-death experience.' She looked at him cautiously. 'Have you ever heard of them? When people leave their bodies? They see themselves on the operating table or in the wreck of a car, travel down a dark tunnel into a bright light, then they get to meet some relative who's dead, who tells them they have to go back?'

She caught a strange flicker in his eyes, like the shadow of a bird flying across the window, then it was gone.

'Yes.' He was wringing his hands in a slow soaping motion.

'That's what I had.'

'Tell me about it.' His hands continued their soaping.

She hesitated. The memory of him switching vials in the operating theatre came back clearly. She saw the nurse giving him a vial of lignocaine. Saw him switching it with the one in his pocket. Maybe that was just hallucination. Maybe it had all just been a hallucination, and she was about to make a fool of herself. There was a sharp rip of velcro as a nurse removed a blood pressure cuff from the woman in the bed on her right. She lowered her voice. 'I – I heard someone say, "Dr Swire, look at the EEG. Her brainwaves are ceasing." And you replied, "That's good," then you said something like rhesodox and blood pressure. I heard you say "Switch the alarm off. Concentrate on the EEG and the blood pressure." Then I suddenly found myself floating on the ceiling of the operating theatre looking down.'

His eyebrows raised. 'Floating?'

'Sort of weightless.'

'How did you feel?'

'Great, because the pain had stopped. You were all getting really agitated, trying to resuscitate me. I wanted to tell you I was OK, but I couldn't.'

His eyes raked her. She could almost feel them scoring her flesh like diamond cutters on glass. 'What else did you see?'

She looked away, not wanting to tell him about the lignocaine. Not yet. 'There was another man standing beside you. I think he was your assistant, looking at the dials and things. I saw you tear a hypodermic needle out of its wrapper. I saw a clock on the wall that said ten past seven. You injected me through the thing on my hand, then you adjusted some valves and wrote something on a clipboard. The nurse opened the green covers and started pumping my heart with her hands. Three men wheeled in the – I guess – the defibrillator. Then I was being pulled away.'

Something came into his eyes that scared her, chilled her. An expression of excitement that was almost child-like, except there was no child-like innocence with it. It was cold; greedy; shifty. She swallowed a lump in her throat that had not been there a moment ago and glanced down at the menu. Braised beef with dumpling. The normality of it comforted her. Kate noticed the anaesthetist's peppery cologne. It smelled expensive; flash.

'Go on.'

'I was kind of enjoying it because I was free of pain, then I started to rise up higher and I was being pulled away into a dark tunnel. I didn't want to go. I was frightened.'

'What of?'

'That if they took me away I'd be dead.'

'If who took you away?'

'Spirits, I suppose,' she said, feeling silly. There was gentle interest in his eyes now and a mild smile on his face and she wondered if she had imagined the chilling expression that had been there a moment ago. 'I sort of swirled down this tunnel and at the end came out into a brilliant light. It was like a living thing – a being – as if it was a person, or an entity.'

'Was it friendly?'

'Yes.' She shrugged. 'Kind, understanding.' She felt the glow again now, a deep warmth melting away the pain inside her. 'It felt good, incredibly safe and secure and loving. I didn't ever want to be in any other place. Then I saw my brother, Howie – he died when I was fourteen – and he told me I couldn't stay, that you were getting my heart started again, so I had to go back to my body.'

'How did you feel about that?'

'I didn't want to do it. I felt bad about having to go back. I didn't want to. It was such a better place where I was, and there was so much I wanted to ask him but he didn't give me any time. He was a bit mad at me, said I had to get back, that I had a lot of things to do. Then I heard someone say "She's breathing on her own now," and I was back in my body again.' She waited for the ridicule. Instead, he sat in silence.

'Do you understand what death is, Kate?' he asked at last.

'Yes. I guess.'

'There are a lot of fallacies about death. The legal definition is brain death. People can be kept alive for years – decades – on life support, but if they have no brain activity the legal view is they have no consciousness. Like vegetables. Did you know that?'

'Sort of.'

'The heart's a pump; the other organs are filters and chemical production plants and waste disposal systems.' He seemed to come alive. There was passion in his voice. Excitement. 'Your brain was shut down by the anaesthetic agents during the operation. It had been shut for about five minutes so there was no possibility you could have had any activity going on in there. Then your heart stopped. To all intents and purposes, you were clinically dead. A vegetable.' He studied her face carefully. 'Your heart stopped for three minutes. Normally if someone's heart has stopped for more than ninety seconds the brain is starved of oxygen and you get irreversible brain damage. But yours was protected because it was shut down by the anaesthetics and it didn't need its normal supply of oxygen.'

'Like with hypothermia?'

'Similar.'

'Why was my brain shut down?'

'You were showing symptoms of epileptic fitting consistent with internal head injuries. And it reduces the risk of cerebral haemorrhaging.'

'Do you mean I have internal head injuries? Epilepsy?'

'I doubt it. Let's hope not. Often they are merely a symptom of trauma.' He said it in a tone that made her feel foolish for having asked. 'When you were up on the ceiling of the operating theatre your brain had been shut down completely. It is totally and utterly impossible that you could have seen anything during that period.'

Coils of ice unravelled through her. 'So how do you explain what I saw?'

'Cardiac arrest and barbiturate cessation of brain activity both normally wipe out immediate preceding memory. So you shouldn't have remembered anything.'

'But I did.'

'You have typical post-operative hallucinations brought on by the anaesthetic agents. The brain releases nice hallucinogenic chemicals when it's dying, it's part of the shutting down mechanism. Sometimes people close to death who are brought back report communications with deceased relatives, and these are part of the transition into death. The last thing the brain does is to make it pleasant for us to die. There's no way you could actually have seen anything. You were gone, shut down. You had no brain activity.'

Kate shook her head. 'It was really weird.' Dora Runcorn's voice came back into her mind. Then Howie's. The operating theatre. The strange triangular marking on top of the lamp.

'What do you do for a living, Kate?'

'I'm a journalist, a newspaper reporter.'

'Which paper?'

She pointed at the one beside her bed. 'The *Evening News*.'

He smiled. 'Good paper. Can be quite controversial sometimes.'

Kate shrugged. 'Not really. It doesn't have any balls.'

'Why do you say that?'

'It's too influenced by the need not to offend the community.'

'There was a pretty controversial piece on Tuesday about an exhumation.'

His eyes were staring directly into hers. She looked away

uncomfortably, wondering if he knew it was her piece. 'It was pulled in the later editions because the editor got twitchy.'

'What was he twitchy about? Upsetting people?'

'Partly that.'

A sequence of rapid pips startled her. He pulled a bleeper out of his jacket pocket and squinted at the display. 'I'm sorry, I have to deal with an emergency.' He stood up abruptly. 'I'll come and see you later.' He turned and strode quickly away.

Kate's mind swirled. She lay back against the pillow for some minutes, drained. Scared.

The triangle on the lamp stuck in her mind.

Howie.

Dr Swire switching the vials. Something shifty about him, something not right. Not right at all.

*You have to keep away from him, Shrimp!*

*From who?*

Dr Swire?

'Done the menu?' Belinda Tindall reached forward, picked the card up and scanned it. 'He's a nice man, Dr Swire, isn't he?'

Kate nodded uncertainly.

'He runs the intensive care unit, you know. You couldn't have had a better anaesthetist.'

Kate remembered now. That was where she had seen him before, when she had gone to the intensive care unit to talk to Dr Matthews. She had seen the anaesthetist walk by.

'Did you know a woman called Sally Donaldson, a patient who died in this hospital a couple of weeks ago?'

'Yes,' Belinda said. 'She was in this ward. She was a lovely person. So looking forward to her baby.' The nurse was crestfallen. 'I felt so sorry for her, and for her husband, poor man. I couldn't believe it when they told me she'd died.'

'What exactly did she die of?'

'She developed *status epilepticus*, sort of non-stop fits from a swelling on her brain. It started off with blood pressure – pregnant women often get it – and sometimes it can develop into this.'

'Is it fatal?'

'No, not often. But the drugs treatment is very heavy. Most people do recover, but sometimes their systems can't cope. Dr Swire did everything he could for her.'

'Was she under Dr Swire?'

'Oh, yes. Dr Swire's meant to be the best in the country. Written books and loads of papers on it.' She lowered her voice. 'It's just as well. We've had a spate of them since he's been here. Five *status epilepticus* cases, I think it is.'

'How long has he been here?'

'He joined us about four months ago. We wouldn't normally expect to have more than a couple of cases in a year. Funny how things go.'

'Always in waves,' Kate said.

'Yes. Do you know what made him take such an interest?'

'No.'

'His fiancée died of it, apparently, some years ago. The poor man's never got over it. He's dedicated to finding a cure because of that. Sad, isn't it?'

# *Chapter Thirty-Seven*

*Sunday, 28 October*

Kate woke with a start from a light doze.

'Catherine Hemingway?'

She heard a tentative, leaden voice and looked up. A sturdy, square-shouldered police constable stood awkwardly above her, wearing a bulky wet-weather coat and holding his cap.

The undertakers. A. Dalby & Son. Someone had seen her, reported her. 'Yes,' she said warily, gathering her thoughts.

'Constable Stroud, East Sussex Police. I'm sorry to trouble you. Would this be a convenient moment to have a word?'

'Sure,' she said, trying to get her bearings and work out what time it was. A nurse strode by carring a large bouquet of flowers. A chaplain wandered past smiling inanely and fingering his dog collar. A serious young man in a white coat stood in the middle of the ward in deep conversation with an older man in a tweed suit.

Constable Stroud unpopped a button on his breast pocket and eyed the chair beside Kate. 'Do you mind if – ?'

She shook her head. He sat down and tugged his notebook out. 'How are you feeling now?'

'OK, thank you.'

'You probably don't remember me,' the policeman said. 'I was one of the people who helped get you out of your car.'

She felt a flicker of relief. He hadn't come about the undertaker. 'No, I'm sorry, I don't.'

'I thought you were a goner, to be honest. I'm amazed to see you sitting up. You were lucky, if I can call it that. The lorry sheared off the front of your VW. If it had hit you a few feet further along, in the door, it wouldn't have been so clever.' He opened his notebook and felt in his pocket for a pen. 'I'd just like to make a few notes if you feel up to it.'

'Is the lorry driver all right?'

'Yes. He wasn't hurt, but very shaken.'

'Was anyone else hurt?'

'No.'

'Thank God.'

He removed the cap of his ball pen and tested the nib on his finger. It made a short blue line. He rummaged through the pages of his book, until he found a clean one. 'Now, can you tell me what happened?'

'Where do I start?' She caught an expression in his eye that made her blush with guilt. As if he knew she had broken into the undertaker's premises; that there was going to be more to what she was about to tell him than she was letting him know. There was a weariness in the expression. The weariness said that there was always more than people let him know.

She kept it brief; told him there had been a white car behind her, but did not say that it had been following her, merely that it had been behind her at the junction, and she had pulled out more rashly than she might have done because it had seemed in a hurry.

He wrote slowly in longhand, and told her he would make enquiries about whether the driver of the white car had come forward. He said he did not recall seeing a white car at the scene. Then his eyelids closed and opened again revealing a new expression, like a scene change on a stage. 'Miss Hemingway, I'm afraid that we will require you to come in and make a formal statement and we will have to pass the evidence forward for consideration for prosecution for driving without due care and attention.'

'Thanks a lot,' she said.

He stood, nodded his head and had the grace to look embarrassed. As she watched him walk out of the ward, she felt an acute twinge of pain deep inside her stomach. She raised the sheet, pulled up the flimsy hospital gown and looked at the dark blue stitches in her abdomen, wondering how thick the scar would be. The wound twinged again as she shifted her weight. She heard a squeak and a clatter and looked up.

A pretty nurse with beech-brown hair was wheeling a yellow payphone over to her bed. 'Long distance call for you.' She plugged the jack into a socket above Kate's head and handed her the receiver.

Her mother, she thought, lifting the receiver to her ear, bracing herself to dish out the reassurances that she was fine.

'Kate?'

It was Patrick. His clipped, warm voice sounded close. 'How are you?'

She felt as if she had known him all her life, as if he were her best friend in the world, and a surge of weepiness swept through the thrill of hearing him. She wished he was here in the ward with her, sitting beside her. 'I'm OK,' she said.

'What's happened?'

'Where are you?'

'Brussels. I have to stay on a few more days. What's happened to you?'

'I'm a bit bashed about.' She hesitated. Morris Dalby. The white car. Except there wasn't any point in explaining to him, not now, not over the phone. She wanted to talk to him about her out-of-body experience too, but wondered if he'd think she was nuts.

'I rang the office and a colleague told me. He saw a piece in your paper. I couldn't believe it. I phoned your office yesterday and they said you were here. I've tried calling you about four times, but you've always been asleep and they won't give me any information. You're really OK?'

'Yes, though rather sore.'

'You sound pretty down.'

'I am.'

'How long are you going to have to be in?'

'They said about a week.' She lowered her voice a fraction. 'I'm in the same ward where Sally Donaldson was.'

'You're kidding! Have you found anything out?'

A doctor and a nurse walked past the end of the bed and she was silent as they passed. 'I'm working on it.' She thought of Dr Swire. In charge of intensive care. His strange expression. He knew about Sally Donaldson. Had to. 'I can't really talk here.'

'I'm in a payphone and running out of coins. I'll call you this evening when I'm back in my hotel. What's the latest I can call?'

'I'm not sure.'

There were some bleeps, a loud clunk, he said something she didn't catch and then there was a flat hum. She put the receiver back on to the hook, cheered, feeling good. She closed her eyes and savoured the image of his rugged face which she could picture clearly in her mind, his short, dishevelled brown hair, his clear green eyes, the slight kink in his nose where it might have been broken once, the firm chin that he always held up, his earnest, caring expression, and the twinkle of warmth that lay beneath the surface. The image clouded and she panicked as she suddenly could not remember what he looked like any more and wished she had a picture, a photograph, anything.

Then she saw the gangly hulk of Eddie Bix, the *News* photographer, striding across the ward in his jeans and Timberland boots, clutching a basket of fruit and an enormous envelope.

'Hey!' he said. 'You look great! Thought you were going to be lying with your arms and legs up in traction.'

She blinked at the mountain of pineapple, bananas, grapes, kiwis. The card seemed to have been signed by the whole paper.

'Thanks,' she said. 'That's really nice.'

'You OK?'

'I have some internal bruising.' She touched her face. 'And a few scratches. They have to do some tests, but they don't think there's a problem.'

He sat down and gave a sharp sniff. 'Tell you, I'm glad it wasn't me had to take the pictures of your car.'

'Did someone?'

'Dennis Rigby. He said it was quite a mess. I brought the piece for you.' He took a copy of the *Sussex Evening News* from under his arm, put it down in front of her and turned a couple of pages.

Her eyes were drawn to a photograph of a mangled car, starkly floodlit against the blackness of the night. A policeman with his back to the camera stood in a fluorescent jacket, directing traffic. Kate read the article.

REPORTER IN MIRACLE ESCAPE

*Evening News* reporter Kate Hemingway was rushed to hospital last night after her car was in collision with a lorry near Lewes.

PC Derek Stroud said: 'Her Volkswagen was mangled almost beyond recognition in the accident which happened during heavy rain. Her survival was a miracle.'

Kate, 24, suffered internal bruising and cuts. Her condition was described as fair this morning.

'How are things at the office?' Kate said, sickened by what she was looking at.

'OK, no great dramas.' He grinned. 'Not since your exhumation story, the one Terry Brent did his tank on.'

'Could you do me a favour? I need some clothes and wash things from my apartment.'

'No problem. Geoff Fox already asked Joanna. I'll take her your keys.'

Kate opened her locker drawer and pulled out her handbag. She opened it, but her keys were not there. Nor was her purse. Then she remembered and waved at Belinda who was emerging from the curtains around the next bed.

'Your keys'll be with your other valuables in the safe. I'll get the envelope for you,' the nurse said.

As she walked off, another nurse was wheeling the payphone towards her. 'A call for you.'

'Want to be private?' Eddie Bix said.

Kate shook her head and took the receiver. There was a click as the nurse plugged in the jack. 'Hallo?' Kate said.

'Kate Hemingway?' She recognised the sharp voice of Kevin Donaldson's mother. 'It's Beth Donaldson here.'

'Oh, hallo.'

'Sorry to hear about your accident. Are you all right?'

'Yes, thank you.'

'Been trying to track you down. It took me a while.'

'What's the news on the second post mortem?' Kate asked.

'There isn't going to be one.' There was a finality in the woman's voice that was ominous.

Kate swallowed. 'Why not?'

'I had a phone call from Mr Dalby, the undertaker, on Friday night. All apologetic, he was,' she said with bitter sarcasm. 'His lad had made a terrible mix-up. Sally's been cremated.'

# *Chapter Thirty-Eight*

*Sunday, 28 October*

Joanna Baines brought Kate's clothes and washing things in a small holdall. She stayed and chatted for a while, then left shortly before three and Kate dozed again.

She woke to find herself being lifted in the air and placed on a trolley by a nurse and an orderly. She stared around, bewildered. 'What's happening?'

'You're being moved to a private room,' the nurse said rather sulkily, as if she did not approve.

'I haven't got private insurance,' Kate said.

'The instructions are to transfer you,' the nurse said. 'I'll bring your things over.'

The orderly pushed Kate out of the ward and down a long corridor. The trolley vibrated slightly as the wheels rolled on the lino tiles beneath her; she watched the fluorescent lights slide by overhead. They passed some vending machines then stopped outside the steel doors of an elevator.

'On whose instructions am I being put in a private room?'

'I dunno, Miss. I just get the orders. Maybe you got health insurance at work?'

'I don't think so.'

The elevator travelled slowly upwards. It was gloomy, like her thoughts. Sally Donaldson had been cremated. Gone.

The doors opened and she was wheeled out into an area that immediately felt plusher. The paintwork was fresh and there were abstract pictures of Brighton on the walls. A sign above the door said 'Leggett 1'. They stopped at the nursing station. 'Catherine Hemingway,' the orderly said. 'Which room number?'

'Eleven,' said a voice. Kate turned her head and saw a tall and rather aggressive-looking woman in a blue sister's uniform. She had straw hair cropped like a mop and large, marbled eyes.

They travelled down a long, narrow corridor, the wheels silent now on the carpet pile, past several evenly spaced doors, most of which were open. Through them Kate could see little snatches of the interiors. Figures in beds. A newscaster on a television screen. Flowers. Cards. An elderly lady eating off a metal tray. The orderly opened a door and they went into a small room that was like a bland hotel room except for the high metal-framed hospital bed. A door led through to what she presumed was a bathroom.

A slender, dark-haired nurse came in and helped the orderly lift Kate into bed. The nurse had a quiet convent air about her. The name on her badge was Margaret Watts. 'Have you eaten yet?' she asked Kate.

'No.'

'Would you like supper?'

'Why have I been transferred?'

'There's a shortage of beds in the main wards tonight and I think they're transferring one or two who don't need such constant supervision,' the nurse said. 'This is your remote control for the television.' She lifted the gadget. 'You've got the four television channels, three radio channels and the call button if you need a nurse. There's a toilet and bathroom through there.' She left quickly.

Kate lay back, puzzling over the sudden transfer. The room was pleasant and it was good to have privacy, a telephone and television, but she was uneasy. Something about the transfer seemed too smooth, too well-oiled. Then she had a stab of fear that the phone had been bugged when she'd spoken to Patrick. Except she had said nothing to him. Being paranoid, she knew. More likely the hospital management was uncomfortable about her being here and wanted to put her somewhere where she wouldn't have so much contact with other people. Where she couldn't so easily ask questions.

A young, unsmiling houseman popped in, read the notes at the end of her bed, asked her if she was comfortable and left. The dark-haired nurse came back, took her temperature and blood pressure and noted them on the chart. A slim oriental nurse brought her a bowl of pea soup, some grilled chicken and a mango yoghurt. Kate wondered whether it was her imagination, but all the staff seemed frosty towards her. Maybe word about her had spread.

She ate slowly, not hungry but knowing she needed to build up her strength, and watched *Only Fools and Horses* on the television. But nothing lifted her feelings of gloom and anger. Sally Donaldson had been cremated. Gone. She thought of smug Morris Dalby. Running across the road towards her. She should have stood her ground, she knew, bluffed it out; and she cursed herself again for panicking, for ending up here because of it.

All that was left of Sally Donaldson was one fingernail and whatever bodily fluids the forensic scientists had. She did not know whether the nail would be any good. There was a tiny bit of flesh attached to it. Forensic scientists seemed to be able to tell a lot from very little. Her eyes closed; she felt drained again. She pushed the trolley away and rolled on to her side. It was too painful and, carefully, she eased herself on to her back. She slept.

Some while later she was dimly aware of the tray being moved and the headboard of the bed being lowered and the door being closed. She dozed lightly and saw Dora Runcorn running towards her, screaming at her, and Kate could not hear what she was saying. The medium held up a huge placard and Kate could see it was a triangle with a squiggly line down the centre, like a road sign.

Then someone was holding her arm; she felt pressure tightening around it and opened her eyes with a start. Dr Swire was standing over her, in the same smart clothes and yellow tie he had been wearing this morning, winding a cuff around her arm. She stared at him, alarmed, and he gave her a reassuring smile.

'Just a little something to help you sleep tonight. Stop your ribs from hurting.' He held up a needle and she saw a dribble of fluid drop from the end, then felt a prick.

Something pumped into her arm, swelling it up. Heavy, cold fluid pushed through it and the expression in the anaesthetist's eyes frightened her. She felt a burst of terror and pulled away. But the pain in her ribs startled her and she gasped. The anaesthetist kept the needle in.

'Relax,' he said.

Then she realised there was no need to be frightened. His smile was warm, kind, he wasn't going to hurt her. He had come to help her. Stupid to be frightened. He was her friend. His smile broadened, told her she was safe, so safe and she lay back as euphoria flooded through her, intoxicating her.

'How are you feeling, Kate?'

His voice was distant and she rolled her eyes slowly towards his mouth to check that he had spoken. His rosebud lips moved again and his voice came at her from a distant part of the room. 'Are you feeling relaxed?'

'Great,' she said. 'Really great.'

'Good, I'm pleased. No pain now?'

He seemed a long way off and there was no hurry to answer him. The euphoria deepened. He was wonderful and she realised how wrong she had been to mistrust him. He cared for her, really cared for her. She could see it in his face.

'That was a great piece you wrote in the *News* on Tuesday about the exhumation.'

'Did you like it?'

'Brilliant.'

She giggled and her ribs did not hurt any more.

'Why did your editor pull it?'

'He hates women. That's part of it. Didn't trust my judgement.'

'You were right, weren't you? You know you were right.'

'Yes.' She felt a thrill of excitement as she realised he was going to help her. That he wanted to help her.

'You had proof, didn't you?'

'Yes.'

'The fingernails. You saw that the fingernails were worn down and broken.'

'Yes.'

'Did anyone else?'

'Her husband.'

'Anyone else?'

'They must have done. I haven't spoken to everyone yet. And someone had replaced them by the next morning.'

'Were they false nails, or real ones, Kate?'

'I don't know. That's what I want to find out.'

'Do you want someone to test the one you took for you?'

'Yes.'

'If you let me have it, I'll test it for you.'

'It's at home. I'll have to get it.'

'I could get it for you if you like. Whereabouts would I find it?'

Through the haze, Kate saw two dark circles; they tightened, darkened. A voice screamed out and she looked around but could see nothing except the two circles. She was conscious of someone smiling, leering. She could no longer hear her own voice and was afraid for a moment. Then she felt the euphoria again, rippling like warm waves through her stomach and she said something, but did not know what; did not know whether anyone else could hear. Did not care. She lay on warm sand and basked in sunshine.

There was a swish and a rattle, then bright light. Kate opened her eyes and blinked at a dark shadow that stood in front of the window. The shadow moved across the wall and turned into a tall woman in a white uniform. She had a wide blue belt and black stockings, one of which was laddered. Her face was bony and pasty, with a large nose, thin lips and narrow nervy eyes. Her greying hair was untidily pulled back into a pony tail. 'Good morning.'

Kate blinked again at the brilliant sunlight flooding into the room. Through the window she could see part of a yellow crane and a row of chimney pots. The view had changed from the wall of a parking lot. The ward was small.

'Would you like anything? You're late for breakfast, but I could get you some toast.'

The colours in the room seemed intense. Kate stared at the bare cream walls; at the television set; at two bunches of flowers by her bed; one was shiny, glowing, and she realised it was wrapped in cellophane.

'Those just arrived for you.'

'What's the time?'

'Ten to eleven.'

'I – I – ' Her voice tailed away as she gazed around, disoriented. She wondered why she wasn't in the ward; she had been in the ward yesterday afternoon. Her brain was clogged, heavy; a piece of logic was missing somewhere. The woman was a nurse, so she was still in hospital. A different hospital. Head injury; possible brain damage. She began to panic. They had transferred her to a neurological hospital. Brain damage.

Going mad.

'Where am I?'

'In hospital.' The nurse had a tart voice.

'Which one?'

'The Prince Regent.'

'I was in a ward.'

'You were moved last night.'

Kate frowned. The memory was dim. A porter wheeling her along a corridor; lights sliding by overhead. Dr Swire injecting her, or maybe that had been a dream. Dora Runcorn was in there somewhere; maybe that had been a dream too. She rolled over and let out a gasp of pain as she felt an acute twinge inside her stomach then an even sharper pain from her ribs. She pulled her left arm free from the bedclothes and pushed up the sleeve of her nightie. There was a tiny roundel of elastoplast on her forearm. She prised it up and saw a minute clot of blood.

'Did Dr Swire give me an injection last night?'

'I'll have a look on your notes.' The nurse went to the end of the bed and studied them for a moment. 'You're down for a rib-block injection every twenty-four hours, in the evening. But no one's marked down that you were given it last night. It must have been forgotten in your transfer. Very careless. Are they hurting now?'

'A bit.'

'I'll get you something.'

'Thanks.'

Kate tilted her head back, trying to think clearly. Something lay beneath the surface of her mind, bothering her. Something had happened that wasn't right. Dr Swire. He had been in the room a moment ago, surely? Given her an injection. She tried to remember, but it was like trying to read writing that was no longer there.

She tugged the small envelope off the cellophane wrapping around the flowers and took out the card.

'Keep out of the way of fast-moving trolleys. Love, Patrick.'

She smiled and lay back holding the card, then heard a knock on the door. 'Come in.'

It opened tentatively and a woman stood there whom it took a moment for Kate to recognise. She was short with wavy peroxided hair and her face was heavily caked in make-up. She was wearing a smart black coat with an astrakhan collar and a cream blouse beneath closed at the neck with a turquoise brooch, and black suede gloves. 'Hallo, dear,' she said. 'All right if I come in?'

Kate heaved herself up, wincing against the pain, staring in amazement at Dora Runcorn.

The medium closed the door then sat down on the chair beside the bed. 'Took me ever so long to find you. Reception had you down as being in the Princess Margaret ward and no one in the ward seemed to know where you'd gone.' She removed her gloves, carefully peeling the fingers over two ornate rings. 'How are you, dear?'

'I'm OK, thanks.' Kate smelled a sweet, pungent perfume.

'I've been trying to reach you since Friday. You are the reporter who came along to my evening at the town hall last Tuesday, aren't you?'

'Yes, I'm sorry. I haven't done the piece on you yet.'

'Don't worry about that. I keep getting a message for you. I've been told I had to come and find you. Your brother has been most insistent. Keeps pestering me.'

The feeling of disorientation returned. Kate wondered if she was still asleep and was dreaming the conversation.

'The boy who was drowned on a yacht, dear.'

'Howie.'

'He says you didn't listen to him. That's why you're here. He's got another message for you, but it's not very clear. That's the problem with these messages, dear, they're never very clear. I don't know why the spirits never say anything clearly – always in riddles, always just bits of messages. I suppose we don't realise how much difficulty they have getting through to us.' She smiled. 'You probably think I'm batty as a fruitcake.'

'No, I don't. Really.'

'I don't mind if you do, dear. Lots of people do.' She patted her chest. 'It's my calling and the spirits are grateful to me, and so are lots of people on the earth plane. I've had thousands of letters over the years. It's the healing that's most important. You'll put that in your article, dear?'

'Yes, of course.'

The door opened and a cleaning woman with a broom stuck her head in and retreated apologetically.

'Did you enjoy your evening in the town hall?'

'Yes, but I don't know if I believe in it. Do you really think the spirit world communicates to you? It's not you picking anything up telepathically from the audience?'

The medium seemed hurt. 'I don't pick up healing by telepathy, do I?' she said huffily. 'It's the spirits that give me the healing. They look after us, they're around us all the time, our spirit guides. They want to help us. I think your brother is your guide, but he can't help you if you won't let him. That's what he's so angry about now. He says you didn't listen.'

'Angry.'

The medium closed her eyes. 'He's trying to tell me something now. The same thing again. Cats. I'm being shown cats. There's great danger with cats.'

'It was wire before,' Kate said.

'I'm being shown a cat. Something strange with a cat.' She opened her eyes and stared, frightened, at Kate. 'He says you're not to do anything when you see it.'

'When I see what?'

'The cat, dear. The cat he's showing me.'

Kate wondered whether the woman was perhaps slightly deranged. 'How will I recognise it?'

'Oh, you'll know it when you see it, dear. He's telling me that you'll know it.'

'Do you believe people can have out-of-body experiences?' Kate asked.

'Travelling on the astral, dear? Of course. Our bodies are only vehicles for the earth plane. When we die we go back to the astral.'

'Can we see other spirits on the astral? Can we meet our guides?'

'Oh yes, dear, but not for very long; that's for when we move on – to the greater understanding.'

'What happens when people have near-death experiences, when their heart stops and they travel down through the tunnel and then get sent back? Is that hallucination, or travelling on the astral?'

'That's not hallucination,' the medium said. 'That's not hallucination at all. It's the spirit world preparing to receive us.'

'Can you prove it?'

'What proof do you want, dear?' She closed her eyes again. 'He's telling me something now, your brother. He's drawing something for me. It's like a roadsign. A black triangle with a squiggly line down it. And there's a light shining around it. He says it's something you've seen recently and you'll know what it means.' She opened her eyes.

Kate's heart thudded inside her chest with a dull boomf-boomf-boomf. She pushed her fingers into her ears to stop the sound but the beat became louder, deeper, like a huge drum. The massive stick swung through the air and struck the taut skin with a deep, echoing boom.

Then it swung slowly through the air again and hit the side of the drum and she waited for the boom. But instead she heard the tortured shriek of a cat in agony.

She sat up, terror surging through her. Perspiration torrented down her body. Dora Runcorn had gone. Her bedclothes were stuck to her body. She swallowed, wondering if she had dreamed her visit. There was a faint smell of perfume in the room, sweet, pungent and she wondered if she was imagining that too.

Her heart was racing.

*He's telling me something now, your brother. He's drawing something for me. He says it's something you've seen recently and you'll know what it means.*

She did. She knew what it meant. And she knew exactly what she had to do.

# *Chapter Thirty-Nine*

*Monday, 29 October*

The nurse brought some toast and Marmite. As she was finishing it Patrick rang. He had phoned last night and no one knew where she was. She thanked him for the flowers, said they were beautiful. He told her he had to stay on in Brussels for a couple more days and he'd call again tomorrow.

She got out of bed and showered and felt brighter. She'd asked the nurse who brought the toast whether she'd had a visitor earlier and the nurse looked at her as if she were loopy. As she came out of the bathroom wrapped in a towel, the sister came into the room.

'How are you today?'

'Better, thank you.' Kate found the woman daunting. 'I was a bit woozy when I woke up a while ago. I can't remember whether I had a visitor or just dreamed it.'

'What did she look like?'

'About seventy with dyed blonde hair, short, in a black coat.'

'Is she a relative?'

'No, a friend.'

'I haven't seen anyone looking like that but I've been out of my office a few times this morning. How's the pain today?' She studied the chart at the end of the bed. 'Didn't you have your injection last night?'

'I – I thought – '

'It must have been overlooked. Still, you slept for long enough. Bowels opened?'

'Yes.'

'Good. Mr Amritsan would like you to walk around so get dressed and have a wander. There's a day room on the next floor up, in Leggett two.' She left abruptly and closed the door.

Kate opened her cupboard door, took out her holdall and found in it some underwear, leggings, a blouse, a grey knitted shirt-waister and a baggy pullover. It took her several minutes to get dressed, and when she had finished she sat down on the bed, tired from the effort. Then she put on her boots and went out.

She stood in the corridor for a moment feeling strangely lightheaded, wondering which way to go, when double doors at the right-hand end opened and an orderly pushed through a trolley, came a short distance down the corridor towards her, then wheeled the trolley into one of the private rooms.

She walked down the corridor in the direction the trolley had come from, past the nursing station, through the doors, into a small foyer in front of a single lift. There were abstract prints of Brighton on the walls, which she vaguely recognised from last night. There was a door to the right with a sign reading 'Emergency Stairs'.

Kate toyed with taking them, but she felt tired from the walk to here and knew she had to conserve her strength. She pressed the square metal button for the elevator; a plastic strip above that told her she was on level ten. She leaned against the wall, feeling giddy. The lift announced its arrival with a dull clung and the doors slid open.

Inside was a black doctor in a white coat, wearing thick rimmed glasses and talking earnestly to a nurse. Kate shuffled in, feeling self-conscious. The doctor put his hand on the panel and looked at her quizzically.

'Ground floor, please,' Kate said, unsure where she had to head.

He pressed the button and the one above it.

The ground floor was plushly carpeted and there was a barrage of signs and arrows.

Jubilee Wing. Straight ahead.

Queen Elizabeth Block. Temporary entrance on level two.

A man in a blue boiler suit came through swing doors ahead holding a pail and mop. A cold draught of air wrapped round her. 'Excuse me,' she said. 'Can you tell me how to get to the operating theatres?'

'Level six in the Queen Elizabeth block,' he said cheerily.

She got lost three times and had to ask. Each time she avoided anyone who looked like either a doctor or a nurse, not wanting to arouse any suspicion. Several times she sat, exhausted, until she got her strength back. Perspiration was pouring down the back of her neck and she felt queasy. Her stomach hurt like hell and she hunched against the pain in her ribs. She shuffled down a long, draughty interconnecting corridor with overhead fluorescents, which she thought she vaguely recognised from the previous night, trying to think back all the time. Dr Swire last night. Something bothered her. Something had happened that she could not recall. Dora Runcorn this morning. She was scared and confused.

At the end of the corridor was a sign to the lifts. She rested again, then walked on, pressed the button for the lift and waited.

As she stepped out on to level six she noticed a smell of sterilising agent and disinfectant. Ahead of her white letters on a green board on a door with two small glass panels said 'Theatre Staff Only. No Entry'.

Kate opened the door and the sterilising smell was immediately stronger. The floor was covered with grey industrial carpet. She passed the window of a small common room where several gowned nurses were sitting drinking tea or coffee; there was a row of gas cylinders and then another green board with white letters indicating theatres five to nine.

She stopped again. In the distance she could hear the clatter of what sounded like someone stacking chairs. Then she carried on down the corridor and saw a window to her left which looked into an empty operating theatre. It was clean and bare, the metal table in the centre shiny and pristine. The floor had the same speckled tiles she had seen from above. Similar, it looked so similar; but not the same. Something was different.

She realised what it was. The wall tiles were battleship grey. The ones she had seen were pastel green. She felt faint and her forehead was clammy. There were a couple of plastic chairs ahead and she sat down in one and dabbed her forehead with her handkerchief. The chair swayed. There was a twinge of pain from her stomach.

She heard voices and saw a group of people gowned up and wearing white boots or clogs walking towards her. Three men and four women. She watched them warily, afraid one of them might be Dr Swire, and was relieved to see it wasn't. They passed, followed by an orderly wheeling an elderly man on a trolley. She lowered her head as an overwhelming tiredness engulfed her.

A door opened and shut and rubber-soled shoes squeaked on the corridor. Then a voice: 'You all right?'

A young man in a boiler suit was carrying a plastic bucket. He had fair hair with a short pony tail and a cluster of gold rings in each ear. 'Yes, thanks.' Her voice sounded strange, squeaky and gruff at the same time, and it hurt to speak. 'I'm looking for an operating theatre.'

'Are you sure you're all right?' he said.

'Yes, I'm fine.'

'Should you be here?'

'I had an operation and I wondered if I could see the theatre I was in.'

'You'd have to talk to a theatre nurse about that. I'll take you along.' He crooked his hand under Kate's armpit and helped her to her feet.

'Thanks,' she said.

They walked slowly down the short corridor and turned right into a wider area, where there were several more empty trolleys and a small window to the right, with a sign above saying 'Theatre Nurse Manager'.

'Mrs Pearse,' the young man leaned in and called. 'Lady here'd like a word.'

A woman peered out of the window. She was wearing blue pyjamas with a soft blue hat like a J cloth over her head. Her face was plump and creamy, with rounded contours. 'Yes?' she said in a French accent.

'I was operated on here a few days ago. I wondered if it was possible to see the theatre.'

'What for?' The woman's face softened into a smile. 'Most people usually want to see the back of operating theatres.'

'I'm just curious.'

The woman stared at her for a moment, then smiled again. 'Well, I suppose there's no harm in a quick look if it's not in use. Do you know which one it was?'

'No.'

'Who was the surgeon?'

'Mr Amritsan. It was Thursday evening. I had a car accident.'

'I'll just check. I was away last week.' She consulted a book. 'Are you Miss Hemingway?'

'Yes.'

'Theatre four. That's empty at the moment. You'll have to put on a gown and some overshoes.'

She took Kate into a changing room, helped her into blue pyjamas and gave her a pair of clogs that were too large. Then they went down the corridor.

'You didn't lose a contact lens or your false teeth or something? If it was Mr Amritsan he probably stitched them back inside you.'

'Great. Is he a bad surgeon?'

The nurse gave a childish giggle which surprised Kate since she looked well over forty. 'No, I am only joking. He's good. Very thorough. Here we are.'

They stopped outside double doors and she pushed one open, holding it for Kate. They went into a small anaesthetics room, painted white, with shelves stacked with bottles and ampoules and boxes of hypodermic syringes in sterile wrappers. Then through a second double door into the operating theatre itself.

As Kate stepped in she instantly knew it was the one she had seen.

The shadow of fear slid through her again, and she hesitated, afraid to go too far in, stared at the speckled terrazzo floor, the pastel green tiles on the walls, at the massive kettledrum lamp, at the steel table beneath it, the screened-off scrub-up area with the twin steel sink and the paper towel dispenser; the electrical sockets; the coloured gas lines suspended from the ceiling; the two clocks, the robot-like anaesthetics machine with the silent monitors and their dark screens; at the frosted-glass windows high up. Her eyes were drawn back to the lamp. The nurse was watching her.

She heard Dr Swire's voice echoing in her head.

*When you were up on the ceiling of the operating theatre your brain had been shut down completely. It is totally and utterly impossible that you could have seen anything during that period . . . You have typical post-operative hallucinations brought on by the anaesthetic agents . . . there's no way you could actually have seen anything.*

Kate reached up to touch one of the handrails around the lamp and a sharp pain shot through her stomach. She winced. 'I want to see what's on top of the lamp.'

The nurse looked at her as if she was mental, then tilted the lamp completely upside down. 'Nothing at all.' She gave Kate a quizzical grin.

But Kate did not notice her. She was staring in numb silence at the domed cream casing: at the triangle that had been drawn on it with a black marker pen. A large, bold triangle with a curious squiggly line inside it. Like a traffic sign.

When Kate got back to her room, she was exhausted and rested in the armchair before removing her clothes and getting back into bed. A short while later the nurse she had seen the previous evening brought her in a tray with lunch.

'Does the hospital have a reference library?' Kate asked.

'Yes, in the Fitzherbert wing. But it's only for medical staff and students. There's a small library in one of the day rooms in the Queen Elizabeth block if you want something to read.'

Kate gazed at her food after the nurse had left. Celery soup. Braised beef. Blancmange. Her heart was pounding and she could feel the blood coursing through her veins, tingling. The triangle. She had asked the nurse in the operating theatre what the sign was for and she had shrugged her shoulders, mystified, and said it was probably to do with the electricians. Kate had not wanted to question her too hard, had not wanted to draw attention to her interest.

But she knew for sure now that she had not hallucinated. She had been up there, out of her body. And she had seen Dr Swire switch vials. And when he had told her it was a hallucination, he had lied.

Kate stayed in bed all afternoon, too tired to make another trip anywhere. Eddie Bix and Joanna Baines came to see her and brought a copy of the paper and some magazines and chocolates, and Howard Michael, the movie critic, brought her a pile of review books he'd been given by the books reviewer.

She rang Dora Runcorn's telephone number, got an answering machine and left a message asking her to call. In the evening a nurse took her temperature and blood pressure, and gave her an injection. The serious houseman visited her again, and Mr Amritsan came to look at her stitches. There was no sign of Dr Swire.

The following morning, after breakfast, she got up and dressed again, checked her notebook was in her handbag and set off to find the Fitzherbert wing. She had more energy today and had to stop less often. She asked the way twice and eventually found the curious Odeon-style building in the shadow of the massive scaffold and breeze-block shell of the student wing that was under construction.

A brass plaque at the entrance to the Thomas Stanmore library stated that it had been built from a bequest made by the late Sir Thomas Stanmore Bt. Immediately inside the entrance to the library was housed a small exhibition of Roman artefacts and pieces of pottery which, according to a sign behind the plate glass window, had been unearthed during the excavation of the foundations for the wing in 1928. Inside, the library was bigger than she had expected, with a central atrium and two floors of galleried bookshelves and a spiral staircase in each corner. There were oak tables with upright leather chairs, a number of which were occupied by students in casual clothing like her own, young medics in white coats, a whiskered man in a tweed suit who had the air of a university lecturer, and an elderly man who might have been a retired consultant. A. J. Davey's *Anaesthesia Explained* lay beside him.

The librarian, a woman in her sixties with tight silver curls, was seated behind a microfiche screen, and surrounded by metal filing cabinets and wooden index card holders.

Kate had always like libraries and immediately felt at home here. She went up to the woman, keeping her fingers crossed that she wouldn't be grilled on her identity. The woman gave her a pleasant smile.

'I'm doing a project on Dr Swire,' Kate said. 'Do you have any of his works?'

'Yes. You'll find them down at the far end on the left under Neurology. Is there anything in particular?'

'I'm interested in his studies on epilepsy.'

'Oh yes, all his works are on that. Do you want his papers too?'

'Please.'

'I'll get them out for you.'

Kate walked down to the shelves and saw the section heading. Neurology. She checked the numbers, then ran her eyes along the rows. After a moment, she saw the anaesthetist's name on a battered spine on the second shelf down: *Status Epilepticus. New Advances in Diagnosis & Treatment*. By Dr H. Swire. MB. BS. FFARCS.

She pulled the book out.

# *Chapter Forty*

*Sunday, 4 November*

Outside, the fields and the sea lay battened beneath a flat carpet of mist. Flocks of migrating starlings flew south, high above the cluttered rooftops of the buildings of the Prince Regent Hospital and out over the English Channel. Beneath them gulls circled, their cries hanging in the windless morning like echoes from the deep. The window of the small room was lightening, and the chimney pots and the yellow crane were again becoming visible.

Kate had cornflakes for breakfast, and hungrily spooned the last drops of sugary milk out of the bowl. Then she sliced off the dented top of the boiled egg and spread Flora on to a slice of soggy toast. She was feeling stronger now, in spite of having slept badly the past few days, woken by her fears and her churning thoughts.

She had spent most of the time during the last week in the library, and on the telephone. Dr Marty Morgan, the *News*'s medical columnist, had been invaluable. He did not understand why she wanted the information she had asked him for, but he had managed to get all of it. Dr Swire had not been back to see her, and she had the impression that the nurses had been instructed not to talk to her about him. She had tried to quiz all of them in turn about Sally Donaldson and the anaesthetist, and each time they had made excuses and hurried off.

Dora Runcorn had rung her back. She told Kate that yes, she had visited her on the Monday morning, and that she thought Kate had seemed very dopey. Kate thanked her, said she'd remember the message but it didn't make much sense. Dora Runcorn assured her it would. Kate said that when she was out of hospital she'd like to do an interview with her for the paper, and the medium seemed pleased.

Mr Amritsan had removed the stitches yesterday. She was going home this morning. Patrick was due back in England from Belgium last night. He would be here in a couple of hours to collect her. Had insisted on collecting her.

After breakfast she was visited for the third time that week by the neurologist, Dr Nightingale, a man of about forty, with a quizzical rather handsome face, who reminded her of Harrison Ford. Earlier in the week he had given her an EEG scan and several other tests. He tapped her reflexes, pricked her toes, fingers and forehead with a pin, asked her a short sequence of questions then assured her with a fine bedside smile that everything seemed 'absolutely tickety-boo'.

A houseman she had not seen before came in shortly afterwards and told her not to go back to work for two weeks. He handed her a prescription for painkillers which he said she could have made up at the hospital pharmacy. Then she had a shower and washed her hair.

She pulled back the plastic curtain, stepped out of the deep enamelled tub and towelled her hair in front of the steamed-up mirror, studying the two cuts on her face. They had scabbed and were healing well. Her skin was pale and she could barely see her freckles, and her eyes were puffy. A large bruise on her left breast had started to fade. The skin had been skimmed down the right side of her rib cage and there were other bruises and marks on her thigh and down her legs. The incision in her abdomen was now a rubbery black line.

She plugged in her hair drier and switched it on. The hot air felt good; her hair scattering into fine wisps and the smell of drying lanolin shampoo felt good too. She brushed her teeth carefully, the way she always did, put roll-on deodorant under her arms, dabbed Fidji cologne around her neck and some on her hips and thighs for good measure. The smell cheered her, made her feel more normal, blasted the sanitised smell of the hospital out of her nostrils.

She put on her make-up, running through a list in her head of things she needed to do. Notify the insurance about the Volkswagen was one she hadn't done yet. She wondered whether the car was repairable, whether there was anything she needed in the boot or the glove compartment. She had no idea where it was, she realised.

The clothes she had been wearing when she had the accident had been neatly folded into a grey plastic bag. The bloodstains on her blouse, the crudely cut open suit top and skirt made her shudder, but her warm camel coat had only suffered one small rip and would be OK to wear home today. She dressed in fresh underwear, her pullover, jeans and boots, checked her appearance in the mirror again then sat in the armchair by her bed, took her Microfile out of her bag and began to look through her notes.

The quiet, dark-haired nurse came in and asked if there was anything she needed and Kate, suddenly feeling as if a colony of butterflies was hatching in her stomach, suggested she gave the flowers to someone who didn't have any. Then she turned back to the Microfile, but the knowledge that Patrick would be here any moment was too distracting and she could not concentrate.

She had a sudden panic about her appearance, decided to go back to the bathroom quickly and try to improve on it a bit, and made a move for her bag, but it was too late. There was a rap on the door.

'Come in,' she said.

Patrick Donoghue pushed the door open and strode in. 'Hi!' he said tenderly. He was wearing his tweed greatcoat, a blue turtleneck pullover, jeans and scuffed black boots, and looked better even than she had remembered during the past ten days. He stopped for a moment, and his face dropped a fraction as he registered her cuts and bruises.

'Hi.' Kate gave him a lame smile, and shrugged, tossing her hair back nervously and feeling tongue-tied and vulnerable and scared that the hope she had been harbouring was going to fizzle to nothing. 'Thanks for coming,' she said. 'You really didn't have to. I – '

He took the few steps over to her, laid his hands lightly on her shoulders and kissed her on each cheek. Without moving his hands he stared approvingly at her face and into her eyes. 'You look beautiful.'

'I'm a wreck!'

'You're the nicest looking wreck I've ever seen.'

Kate watched his face in silence for a moment. He moved closer, his eyes riveted to hers. She felt a tightness in her throat and swallowed involuntarily. Her lips touched his; they were soft and warm and gentle. They kissed lightly, then again, much longer, and she closed her eyes, wanting never to stop.

Their mouths parted slowly, reluctantly; she opened her eyes and saw one large eye looking at her, and she wanted to stand here like this with him for ever. Their cheeks touched and they hugged each other; his rough shaved stubble felt good and manly and she immersed herself in his scents and textures, in the warmth of his skin and the fresh lemony shampoo of his hair and the wool of his jumper and the rich tang of the cologne or talc he was wearing. Some of the strands of his tweed coat were tickling her neck but she did not care.

He stood back and held her at arm's length, his strong hands on her shoulders, and carefully examined her face with his clear, green eyes, then he balled his fist and touched her cheek lightly. 'I don't believe you've been in here. You look as if you've had a week's holiday.'

Her eyes felt moist and she did not want to cry, not now. She pointed at the flowers. 'Thanks, they're gorgeous.'

'Good.' He indicated the holdall and the grey plastic bag. 'Is this your luggage?'

'Yes.'

'I'll bring the car round to the front.'

'It's OK. I can walk.'

'I've parked in the car park. It's miles away.' He picked up the two bags. 'Meet me at the front entrance in about five minutes.'

Kate watched him leave and the room seemed empty suddenly. Just the unmade bed and the morning newspapers. She went out into the corridor and walked slowly towards the elevator.

Patrick's car was in the crumbling portico beside a No Waiting sign and in front of a parked ambulance. It was a battered orange Alfa Romeo two-seater, with rust holes in the door and a soft top patched in several places with black carpet tape.

'It's not much of an ambulance, I'm afraid,' Patrick said as he opened the door for her.

'It's really nice of you to come.'

She eased herself into the low, hard seat, stretching her legs out over a fire extinguisher; they did not reach the end of the deep footwell. She pulled the seat belt across her shoulder and clicked the buckle home while Patrick dropped the bags into the boot, climbed in and closed his door. The car smelled of hot oil and damp canvas. The interior was purposeful, with small round dials angled towards the driver, and there was plain rubber matting on the floor. No frills; like him. The engine made a sucking sound, then started with a gruff roar; pop music blared loudly from the radio, which he switched off. The gear stick shook from side to side.

'So how are you feeling?' he said.

'Great.' Her heart was thrashing like a trapped bird inside her chest.

He covered her hand with his, squeezed it, then gently traced his fingertips over her knuckles. 'I was worried when I heard about your accident.' He squeezed her hand again, then lifted his away reluctantly and pushed the gear lever forwards. He released the brake, gripped the thick wooden steering wheel, drove down the ramp marked Exit to the main road, and indicated right.

Kate leaned her head back against the rest and looked at him. His collar was turned up and his face, under the dark canopy of the roof, was silhouetted against the side window. His short brown hair was dishevelled the way it always was. He exuded strength, physical and inner, and she felt safe with him; immensely safe and secure.

'So tell me what happened?' he said.

The sun was warm through her side window. A guy in a leather bomber jacket was walking arm in arm with a girl in a thick jumper. Normality, she thought, watching them stop and kiss, the girl saying something teasing and trying to run off, the guy hanging on to her arm, dragging her back; the guy kissing her again.

'Do you believe in life after death?' she said.

'I'm a Catholic,' he said 'At least, I was brought up as a Catholic until I was fourteen.'

'You didn't stay a Catholic?'

'My uncle, my father's brother, died of cancer. He suffered for a long time and my father was really chewed up by it. A few nights after the funeral my father came in and sat at the kitchen table and he said: "God, I've tried hard to believe in you all my life, and if you really exist you're going to have to explain why you took Sean away. I'll give you twenty-four hours to give me some sign that you're there, otherwise I'm going to have to stop believing in you."'

'And did he get a sign?' she said.

'No.' He drove in silence for a few moments and she saw something in his face that seemed either to be sadness or regret. 'How about you, Kate? Do you believe?'

'I don't know.' Then she heard Dora Runcorn's voice.

*He was eighteen when he passed, but you are his little sister and he wants to look after you.*

Then Howie's.

*Hey, Shrimp, you idiot! I told you, didn't I?*

The triangle on the lamp. Floating up there. Out of her body.

Impossible.

Except she had seen it. Unless the lamp had been turned upside down in the operating theatre. Unless . . .

She told Patrick what she had done after they had had dinner together; how she had broken into the funeral director's, and taken the fingernail. How she had suggested the Donaldsons got a private post mortem and that Sally Donaldson's body had been 'accidentally' cremated within hours of their making that request.

They drove round a roundabout, past the Palace Pier and along the seafront. The sun had dissolved the mist into a watery haze beneath which the sea lay flat and shiny as if it had just been polished. A gull perched on a marker buoy. The promenade was crowded with strollers and she envied them their carefree Sunday, envied them because maybe they'd never seen the face of a girl who had tried to get out of a coffin. Envied them because maybe they had never left their bodies and floated up on the ceiling of an operating theatre and stared down at the kettledrum lights and their own bodies.

She opened the window a little and for a brief moment smelled the tang of salt and rusting iron and rotting seaweed. The sea always brought her a feeling of deep emotion, of sadness and happiness at the same time. Then the smell became saturated with the reek of frying food, which made her queasy. Travelling in the car was making her queasy too, she realised, and she fell silent, concentrating on trying to settle her stomach.

She was conscious of the car turning and going up a hill. 'You OK?' Patrick said gently.

'Fine,' she said. The kettledrum light was beneath her, and her own body lay under green covers beneath that. The nurse ran into the operating theatre and handed the glass vial to Dr Swire. 'Lignocaine,' the nurse said. Then Dr Swire shiftily slipped the vial into his pocket and took out something different.

Dr Marty Morgan had told her over the telephone that lignocaine was used for cardiac arrests in operations. It was the standard drug for getting the heart restarted.

So why the hell had Dr Swire deliberately not used it?

There was a jolt and a ratchety click. They had stopped, double parked, outside her flat.

'Jump out and I'll go and find a space,' Patrick said.

'I'll come with you.'

'No, you go inside. It's not that warm.'

She climbed out and opened the downstairs door. The lobby floor was littered as usual with post and newspapers and mailshots and menus from local takeaways. There were several letters addressed to Kate, and her copies of the *Independent* were strewn around. She scooped everything up, carefully to guard her wound. She put the front door on the latch for Patrick, then climbed the narrow staircase to the landing. From the floor above she heard the thumping beat of music.

She inserted the key in her lock, turned it and pushed the door open. As she stepped into the narrow hallway that opened into her living room something dark leaped at her, clawed at her face, tore into her hair.

A cold down-draught of terror tumbled through her as she recoiled, crashing against the doorpost. The newspapers and post fell to the floor but she barely noticed as she windmilled her hands above her and felt a sharp pain like a knife slash in her wrist and heard a venomous hiss.

Her scream got tangled in her vocal chords as she stepped backwards, goggle-eyed, through air that was thicker than water, forcing her way through it until she was out in the landing again, away from it, away from the horror, choking on her own scream, trying to spit it out, but it would not come.

She stepped further back, away from the sleek black cat that raced dementedly around the hall floor then leaped on to the small table and sat motionless, like a hideous ornament. The top of its skull had been neatly sawn off between its ears, and she could see its brains through the cavity, raw, glistening, creamy white with blood vessels like red threads. Excrement and urine lay streaked on the floor.

She watched it, paralysed by horror, dimly aware of footsteps coming up the staircase; the cat arched its neck and head slowly, as if responding to a snake charmer's tune, twisted round, its eyes locking on to her for a brief moment during its rotation. Then it convulsed, jerked wildly, dementedly, and began to twist and thrash, hissing, frothing at the mouth until its burst of energy was spent and it sprawled, limp, giving only a tiny judder every few seconds as if an electrical current were being passed through it.

## *Chapter Forty-One*

*Sunday, 4 November*

'There's some real rubbish out there,' the policeman said. He stood in his blue serge uniform, legs apart, hands behind his back holding his cap, a solidly-built thirty-five-year-old with a blunt nose and short-cropped hair. His face was sour with shock. 'Whoever did this isn't part of the human race.'

Kate pressed her fingers around the fresh elastoplast on her wrist, trying to ease some of the stinging from the deep scratch. She had not caught his name, nor the name of the policewoman who sat facing her, pretty, in her early thirties with her brown hair pinned up and large blue eyes. There was a childlike gentleness to her appearance which contrasted with her quiet determination when she spoke.

*I'm being shown a cat. Something strange with a cat. He says you're not to do anything when you see it.*

They had tried to get the cat down off the table, but it had clawed at them as they neared it, and they had not wanted to throw a blanket over it for fear of damaging its exposed brain. The police had not wanted to touch it either and had radioed for a vet.

Everything had been pulled out of her drawers and lay strewn around the floor. Her knickers, tights, stockings, suspenders, some of which had been Tony, her lover's, choice. There was a kinky black bra and panties he had bought for her. The centres of the cups had been cut away and so had the centre of the crotch. He had made her put them on once and she had been embarrassed then, as she was now seeing them again. She did not know why she had kept them, maybe some dim hope that he might turn up one day and they'd get back together.

There were old letters, handkerchiefs, bank statements, pullovers, a gift pack of Crabtree and Evelyn soaps she had been given and hadn't used, and a box of table mats with scenes of Victorian London. Stuck to the mirror of her dressing table was a crude note made from words and letters cut out of a newspaper: THIS IS WHAT YOUR FRIENDS DO.

'Do you have any problems with neighbours, Miss Hemingway?' the policewoman asked.

'Not that I'm aware of.'

'No domestic disputes?'

'Domestic?'

'You haven't got an ex-boyfriend with a grudge, or anything like that?'

She glanced at Patrick then out of the window at the windows of the office block. 'No.'

'Has anyone got a key apart from you?' The policewoman's eye fell on the cut-away bra.

Kate cringed. 'No.'

'There's a window catch open, but that's at the front in full view of the street. It seems more likely that whoever it was came in downstairs through the front door – could have done that easily enough, then either picked your lock or had a key. It's an old Yale and the lip's been fitted the wrong way around. Anyone could open it just by sliding a credit card down the side of the door. Do any of your neighbours have a key?'

The gloomy office block was closed for the weekend, the windows dark, chains padlocked along the row of poles across the parking lot. 'No,' Kate said.

'Do you have a cleaning lady?'

'No. A friend of mine at work, Eddie Bix, had the key for a while last Sunday. He and another colleague came to get some clothes and wash things for me.'

'How well do you know them?' said the policeman.

'Not well, but we're friendly. There's no way either would have done anything like this.'

'We'll talk to them,' the policewoman said. 'They might have seen something.'

The doorbell rang. To answer the door Kate had to get past the cat and it was clawing at the air again. Patrick motioned to her to stay where she was and squeezed past the cat, keeping his back pressed against the wall.

A small man was standing outside in a shabby blue anorak, holding a metal briefcase. He had a bald dome that rose from a tangle of wiry hair like an egg in a nest, and a beak of a nose that curled down into a scrubby little moustache. His eyes were telescoped into black beads by the thick lenses of his glasses. 'Oh dear,' he said, looking at the cat. 'I'm Dennis Yapton, the vet.' He set his briefcase down, kneeled and clicked it open. He pulled out a hypodermic syringe and a small vial, drew some fluid into the barrel of the syringe, and grabbed the cat by the scruff of the neck. As it thrashed ferociously but helplessly, he deftly injected it beneath the tail. In a few seconds it went limp.

'I've just tranquillised her for a few minutes.' He looked at Kate, then at the police. 'This is from an animal laboratory.'

The sight of the cat now completely inanimate suddenly seemed even worse to Kate. She stared at the hideous incision and the raw glistening brains, and had to turn away, rapidly, swallowing bile.

'Is this what they do to them?' the policeman said.

'Yes.'

Kate noticed her small automatic camera lying on the floor, beneath her old wind-up gramophone stand, its back open and the film removed. Someone had wanted the film. Except there had not been anything on it; she had put in a new very fast film Eddie Bix had given her before going to the undertaker's, but she had not taken any photographs.

'They cut the tops of their skulls off?' the policeman asked.

'Yes, to expose their brains so they can place their electrodes accurately.'

'What sort of tests do they do?'

'Oh, testing drugs, reactions to stimulae, experimental surgery. Cats are good subjects – they have well developed brains.'

'Miss Hemingway, you said you were a newspaper reporter on the *Evening News*,' the policeman said.

'Yes.'

'You haven't written anything that – er – might have got the backs up of the animal liberation people?'

She was silent for a moment. 'Yes,' she said then. 'Last Saturday there was a piece in the *News* I wrote. Except it wasn't very well edited.'

'And what was that?'

'It was a follow-up after that furrier in Brighton got firebombed. I wrote a piece criticising the animal rights people's methods and it came out much more vitriolic than I'd intended.'

'I read it,' the policewoman said.

The policeman rubbed the side of his nose. 'Have you discovered whether anything is missing yet?'

The film. Would have to explain what the film was for.

'No.'

'I don't have to tell you the animal rights lot are fanatical,' the policeman said.

'Sure,' Kate said lamely.

'It would explain the note, wouldn't it? You'd better give me the details about this article. I remember the firebombing. I don't think anyone was arrested. We can check that up, and we'll see what the CID come up with on fingerprints.'

The vet was examining the cat's skull. 'I'm going to have to put this to sleep. It would be kinder.'

'What about protecting this lady?' Patrick looked at each police officer in turn. 'I think she's in very serious danger.'

'We'll ask the local patrols to keep a watch.'

'Isn't there anything else you can do?'

'It's more like someone's angry at the young lady, sir. Trying to frighten her, warn her off writing any more pieces like that.'

'I'll remove the cat. Will you be needing photographs?' the vet asked the policeman.

'Possibly.'

'I'll put it on ice.' He unfolded a blue plastic bag from his case and pulled the zipper with a sharp crackle.

'Can't you do anything for it?' Kate said.

'It's probably been reared in a laboratory. Even if we could fit an artificial skull cap it couldn't survive outside.'

'Now, young lady,' the policeman said to Kate. 'I would advise you to have the lock changed to something much more secure and be extra vigilant. Call us immediately if you see anything suspicious – or even if you're the tiniest bit worried. Perhaps you should have a spy hole and a safety chain put on the door. But I think you'll find it's just a warning.'

'And if you come back tomorrow and find her crawling around with half her skull missing?' Patrick said angrily.

'Patrick, it's OK,' Kate said.

'I don't think it is OK at all.'

'There are private security firms,' the policeman said. 'Perhaps the lady's newspaper might be prepared to provide something.'

'You obviously haven't met my editor,' Kate said, mustering a grim smile.

They left along with the vet, saying the fingerprint people were on their way and for them to touch as little as possible in the meantime. Kate closed the door on them. Patrick looked at a mess of excrement on the floor. 'I'll clear it up. I don't imagine they need to fingerprint that.'

'I'll do it. And I want to see if there's a locksmith with an emergency service in the Yellow Pages.'

'I'll clear it. You're meant to be resting,' he said firmly.

'I've been resting for ten days.'

'Then phone the locksmith. I'm clearing up.'

She went to her imitation Barbour which was hanging on the hook where she had left it after coming back from the undertaker's, and slipped her hand into the inside pocket.

It had gone.

The skin down the back of her neck felt like cloth being gathered in for a pleat. A memory crystallised in her head. A voice that was quiet, suave.

*You saw the fingernails were worn down and broken.*

*I could get it for you if you like. Whereabouts would I find it?*

It was coming back now. She could remember him in the room, putting the cuff around her arm.

The needle going in.

The smile.

She checked each pocket in turn, pulled them inside out, but she knew it was a waste of time, knew it had gone. Knew who had taken it.

She closed her mouth, clenching her teeth and lowering her head in bitter anger at herself, feeling what strength she had left sapping away.

'What are you looking for?' Patrick said.

'What the person who came here was looking for,' she said. 'And found.'

'What?'

'The nail.'

'Sally Donaldson's nail? You're joking? What have the animal rights people got to do with – ?' He stopped, frowning. 'I don't understand the connection. Was Sally Donaldson something to do with them?'

'There is no connection with the animal liberation thing. It's the hospital that's the connection.'

'The hospital?'

'The policeman said whoever it was either picked the lock or used a key. I'm the only person who has a key.' She lifted a saucepan off the top shelf and shook it. Something rattled and she removed the lid. A key lay there. 'That's my only spare one. I think someone either made a duplicate of the one in the hospital safe or borrowed it.'

'When? That cat had only been here a few hours.'

'Yes. It must have been put there during the night. By someone who knew I was coming home today.'

'Whole thing's crazy. It doesn't make any sense.' Patrick put his arm around her and held her. 'It doesn't make sense,' he repeated.

'It makes perfect sense,' she said. 'Someone who's smart enough to manipulate the coroner, the pathologist and the undertaker is smart enough to do his research on me and come up with a believable decoy to cover his tracks when he raids the apartment.'

'There must be something very special about that nail,' he said. He kissed her lightly on the cheek. 'You're damned plucky, you know that?'

She smiled, feeling helpless and weak.

'I have to go to London this evening. There's a press conference at Heathrow Airport I've got to cover. Why don't you come and stay for a few days, get away from this?'

She stared at his green irises and could see for the first time tinges of brown that seemed to soften them, warm them, and she saw the reflection of her own face in the black pupils. She put her arms around him and hugged him. 'I'd like to,' she said. 'I'd like to very much. But I can't. I'm not running away from this.'

He held her more firmly. 'You're dealing with someone crazy.'

'No. Very smart.'

'Come to London.'

'I can't.'

'Why not?'

She nestled against him in silence for some moments, strengthened by him, protected from the horror of what had just happened. Then she pulled back a few inches until she could see his face. 'Because I've always run away from things. It seems it's my family trait to run away from things. I don't want to do that any more. I'm going to stay.'

'It's a story, Kate, that's all. Forget it. Come back when you've convalesced and you're feeling stronger.'

'It's more than a story, Patrick. It's my job on the line.'

Again there was silence. Then Patrick said: 'Let me help you.'

'I got myself into this mess and I have to get myself out of it. I know what I have to do.'

'What?'

'I'm going to go back to the hospital and confront him.'

'Who?'

She smiled mischievously. 'Uh oh. This is my story.'

He looked at her reproachfully. 'I don't care about the story, Kate. You can have the story – but if you're going to confront anyone in your condition, I'm coming with you.'

'I'm only going to the hospital.'

'Sally Donaldson only went to the hospital.'

'I have a couple of questions to ask him, then I'll know for sure. He's not going to attack me in the middle of the hospital. I have to do it quickly – he may still have the nail.'

'I'll come with you.'

'I want to go this afternoon. You said you have something important to cover in London.'

'I can forget that.'

'No way. You are not risking screwing up your new job over my mess.'

'OK. Listen, I'm clear all tomorrow. Why don't we go and see him together tomorrow?'

'Sure,' she said wearily. She gave him a kiss then turned, went into the living room and found the telephone directory. She looked up the number of the Prince Regent hospital and dialled. When the woman on the switchboard answered, Kate asked to be put through to the ITU.

'Intensive care unit,' said a young girl's voice.

'Is Dr Swire working today?'

'Yes, but he can't be contacted. He's in theatre doing emergencies.'

'When will he be finished?'

'Not before eight, I shouldn't think. Probably later.'

Kate thanked her and hung up. Patrick walked in, carrying a bucket and a cloth.

'Get through to a locksmith?' he said.

'No luck. I'll try another.'

He went out to the hall. She picked up the telephone and dialled a number she knew. A woman's voice answered: 'Streamline, good afternoon.'

'I'd like to order a taxi for seven thirty this evening,' Kate said quietly.

## *Chapter Forty-Two*

*Sunday, 4 November*

A low had moved in from the Atlantic during the afternoon, and the weather had rapidly deteriorated. A force eight gale now screamed down Brighton's seedy terraces, rattling hoardings, scattering litter, ripping the last of the autumn leaves from the trees and peppering the dark pavements with buckshot volleys of rain.

As the taxi pulled up under the glass portico at the front of the Prince Regent hospital it was buffeted by a gust like a boat at anchor. Kate paid the driver and hurried into the dingy reception area, back to the familiar, dreary smells of mashed potatoes and disinfectant and polish.

She passed the empty counter, an untidy stack of collapsed wheelchairs and a battery of signs, walked up a steep ramp and through rubber-flanged double doors, following the signs to the Queen Elizabeth block, although she did not need to read them.

The hospital had a desultory Sunday evening feeling about it and there seemed few staff around. Kate was glad of the warmth of her blue cashmere coat as she waited at the bank of elevators. The horror from the cat was burning in her mind and the shock was still there in her system, but she contained it. At the moment she was driven by a silent fury and determination, and she felt no other emotion.

As the empty elevator scuffed its way upwards, her stomach fluttered with a sudden attack of nerves. Dora Runcorn's words rang inside her head. She ignored them. She did not care about anything right now except what she had to do. She took her tape recorder out of her coat pocket, tested again that it was on standby and checked the wire that ran through the tiny hole she had cut in the pocket, up through the lining of the coat to the microphone she had sewn in place inside the lapel.

She stepped out on the sixth floor, walked through the double doors with the glass portholes marked 'Operating Theatre Staff Only' and across to the theatre nurse manager's booth, but no one was there. A door opposite opened and shut with a squeak and two gowned nurses came out.

'Excuse me,' Kate said. 'Do you know where Dr Swire is?'

'Yes, he's in Theatre four.'

She sat down on a hard chair feeling thirsty and tired, and realised her energy was draining fast. There was a flurry of activity as a man with a chalk-white face, on a ventilator, was wheeled past her followed by several staff running, then silence. Her mother had phoned earlier, anxious because she had had no reply the previous Sunday and had tried several times during the week. Kate told her she had been busy working around the clock. She had been too tired to talk about the accident. After she had hung up, she had suddenly felt very alone.

She studied her notes, then wondered if there was a vending machine or a drinking fountain. As she was about to explore, some double doors opened and a man in a green gown and white boots and two women, similarly dressed, came through, laughing about something. Another woman followed. Then Dr Swire, tugging off his mask.

He noticed her almost immediately, walked across and greeted her warmly. 'Kate! Good to see you. I've been meaning to pop by but I haven't had the time. It's been one of those weeks. How are you feeling?' He removed his cap and smoothed down his hair.

She was surprised by his greeting. 'Better, thanks.'

'Great. When are you going home?'

She looked for a flicker, a hesitation, but there was nothing except kindness; doubt began to tap inside her. 'I've been allowed home today.'

'Gosh! So soon? You must be a fit girl to have recovered so quickly.' He looked at his watch and frowned. 'It's rather unusual to discharge a patient at this hour. It's normally done in the morning.'

'I was discharged this morning. I've come back to see you. I was wondering if I could have a word with you, somewhere private. It's about what we were discussing.'

'Your out-of-body experience?' He raised his eyebrows in amusement. 'Yes, of course. Have to be quick, I'm afraid, I'm due at a meeting. I'll get changed and we can pop downstairs to my office. Won't be a minute.'

She sat down again, puzzled by his reaction to her. He had seemed genuinely pleased to see her, and had not given the slightest hint of having anything to hide. Maybe she was wrong about him.

Except she knew she couldn't be.

He came back a few minutes later, changed into a navy double-breasted blazer, cream shirt and red paisley tie, smart grey trousers and black loafers, hurrying in an ungainly lumber like a charging rhino.

'OK?' he said, rubbing his hands and not stopping.

She hobbled along beside him, taking larger and faster steps than were comfortable in order to keep up, her stomach twinging and straining.

In the lift he pressed the bottom button. 'So how've you found life in hospital, Kate?' he said as the doors closed.

'The food was better than I thought it would be. I got moved to a private room. Overcrowding in the wards or something.' She watched his face for a reaction, but again there was nothing. The lift slid bumpily downwards, passing the first floor, the mezzanine, the ground floor.

'Be better when the student wing's built. They're adding some new wards. Underfunding for years has been the problem. You're a journalist, aren't you?'

'Yes.' They stopped abruptly and the doors opened.

'You ought to do a piece on the National Health one day. It's a disgrace. The budget for the research we do here is pitiful.'

They stepped out into a wide basement corridor that was gloomy and deserted. Kate felt a prickle of unease. Half the overhead lights were not working. There was a row of empty trolleys ranked along the wall. Steam coiled, noislessly, through a vent. An extractor made a loud, reverberating hum. She looked around anxiously for a sign of other people.

The anaesthetist strode off at a pace that was again too fast for her and she struggled, painfully, to keep up, keeping one hand in her pocket on her tape recorder to stop it shaking too much and to stop its weight ruining her coat. Asbestos-clad pipes ran along the walls beside her. The din of the extractor faded into the background and for a moment the only sound was the clacking of their shoes.

They walked up a steep ramp, through a flanged door out into the open, and crossed a dark, almost deserted staff car park. Blotches of light from the hospital's windows lay amongst the shadows. Kate was tempted to stop, not to follow him any further, to head back into the hospital.

To run away, she realised.

She kept on walking, clenching her hands against the pain, anger sweeping away the fear. Anger at the chaos in her apartment, at the treatment of the cat, at the fingernail that had been taken, at the memory of Sally Donaldson's face and her husband's grief, at the smug little undertaker, at Terry Brent.

They weren't going to beat her; no one was going to beat her, to make her run away. Not this time. Dr Swire had the answers she needed. She was going to get them from him.

A nurse hurried by in a coat, her head ducked against the wind and rain, and the sight of another person gave her courage.

Safe here. This is a hospital. People all around.

They passed a row of Portakabins, a shadowy bulldozer, and a pile of building materials under flapping plastic sheetings. Steam poured from a massive pipe like a ship's funnel on the roof of a building to their left. They were approaching a cluster of Nissen huts behind a high chainlink fence. A large red and white sign on the gate said: RESEARCH DEPARTMENT. STRICTLY NO ADMITTANCE.

Kate trailed behind, breathless from trying to keep up, her stomach lanced by fierce rods of pain. She was going to have to sit down in a minute. The anaesthetist pulled a bunch of keys out of his pocket, unlocked the gate, let Kate through and locked it behind her. She was too exhausted to speak. They hurried on, the wind tearing at her hair and the rain stinging her face, past the dark windows of the Nissen huts and stopped in front of a long, single-storey building. There was an unpleasant smell in the air that reminded her of a zoo.

He unlocked the door, held it for Kate, pressed several light switches then closed it behind him, locking it from the inside and pocketing the bunch of keys. 'Security,' he said, with a smile. 'We have a lot of drugs and chemicals here.'

They were in a small, cluttered laboratory, with an acrid reek of chemicals. A strip light flickered, making an erratic clicking like a moth trapped in a lampshade. She followed the anaesthetist through a door at the back.

He switched on another light and the snap echoed sharply. 'These were the air-raid shelters during the war, down here,' he said. 'Labyrinth of rooms going right back into the hillside; used by smugglers in the nineteenth century. It's rather steep, so be very careful, Kate.'

She held on to the rail as she followed him down some almost vertical stone steps into a narrow passageway lit by a weak recessed lamp, with a row of closed doors, each with a printed name card. They passed a small kitchenette, then the next door along had the card: Dr H. Swire.

It was a small, windowless office, functional and basic, with two leatherette easy chairs in front of an old metal desk, a more imposing chair behind, and a door behind that which she assumed was a cupboard. There were three filing cabinets, bookshelves stacked with medical reference works, including his own books, and several curious-looking instruments, but nothing of a personal nature that gave anything away about him. An old-fashioned grey telephone sat on the desk. The air was stale and heavy with the smells of the carpet and the vinyl.

'The National Health doesn't believe in squandering money on flashy offices,' he said, pointing her to one of the chairs, then kneeling and switching on a blow heater. 'Would you like something to drink, Kate? I'm going to make a quick coffee.'

'Please. I'd love a glass of water, too, if that's possible.'

He went out and closed the door. Her stomach felt raw from the exertion. She studied the room and its contents carefully for clues but noticed nothing of interest. She put her hand into her pocket and fiddled clumsily with the tape recorder, switched it on, took it out furtively to check it was running and dropped it back. Through the door she heard a kettle boil, then footsteps and some clattering of crockery.

Dr Swire came in with a tray on which was a glass of fizzing water, two coffee mugs and a bottle of milk. 'Perrier OK?'

'Thank you.'

'Milk? Sugar?'

'Black, please.'

She took the glass and drank it straight down, feeling the warm draught of the heater, the rest and the drink giving her back some of her strength and courage.

The anaesthetist sat down beside her, crossed his legs and put his coffee mug on the carpet. He was wearing blue socks with a piano keyboard motif on them. 'So, you wanted to have a talk.'

Kate stiffened. 'Yes. I want to know what was going on in the operating theatre.'

'Very simple. We were trying to save your life.'

She did not move her eyes from his face. 'No, I don't think you were. I didn't have a dramatic allergic reaction at all. That was bullshit. You gave me something.'

He looked carefully at her. 'What do you mean?'

'The nurse brought in a vial of lignocaine. You switched it for another vial when you thought no one was looking.'

'Kate, you know that it was medically, physically and scientifically impossible for you to have seen anything?'

'Yes.' Steam from her coffee curled up at her. 'So how did I?'

'We were talking last week about death, Kate. About what we understand about it – do you remember? How it used to be thought when the heart stopped death had occurred, but that's no longer considered the case? After the heart has stopped, the brain continues for ninety seconds, sometimes longer, without any impairment in activity. Then it starts quite rapidly to shut down, to die. After three or four minutes it becomes totally inactive. That's when a person is clinically – and in most countries legally – dead.'

Kate drank some of her coffee.

'Brain death is not reversible,' he said. 'No one has ever done that. But the state of brain death can be simulated: by hypothermia which can temporarily shut down all activity, and by some barbiturate drugs.' He intertwined his fingers. Kate noticed his cufflinks, gold coins set in clasps which she thought vulgar.

'During your operation, because of your dramatic allergic reaction to the anaesthetic, your brain activity ceased completely for eight minutes. You were to all intents and purposes brain dead during that period; further, for three of those minutes, your heart had stopped too. You could not have seen, felt, tasted, touched or smelled anything.' He leaned forwards. 'But you did. You saw me. And you saw the triangle, didn't you?'

Kate felt chilled by his eyes. They had lost the warmth of earlier; they glinted with an almost fanatical excitement. 'I didn't tell you I'd seen the triangle.'

'But you did see it, didn't you? That's why you went back to the theatre, to check?'

'Yes,' she said quietly. 'Because I knew that if the triangle was there, it would mean I had not imagined seeing you.'

He smiled broadly, but there was still no warmth back in his eyes. 'Kate, there was a panic on over you in the theatre. You were mistaken.'

She shrugged. 'OK. Tell me how I saw the triangle?'

'I can't conclusively prove how you saw it. What I can tell you is that as long as someone has brainwave activity then there is a valid argument that it could simply be hallucination. Or even telepathic communication with the people around. The only way you can know for sure that there is no brainwave activity at the time is to monitor the brain with an EEG. You are one of the very few people I've come across wired to a monitor showing no brain activity who has been able to recall an out-of-body experience.'

'Why was I monitored?'

'I have an EEG monitor in the operating theatre as part of my research.'

'Research?'

'Yes. This is one of my areas.' He was silent for a moment. 'Don't look so worried. It's exciting because it's so perfect! It's unbelievably perfect for three reasons.' He counted on his fingers. 'Firstly, you were able to remember in great detail things that happened to you whilst you had no brain activity.'

'My journalistic training,' she said wryly.

The anaesthetist did not acknowledge the remark. 'Secondly, you were able to see things it is totally impossible for you to have seen. The activity in the theatre. The triangle.'

His eyes were becoming manic and they made her nervous. 'And the third is because of the pain you felt – and the point at which it stopped – we are able to tell precisely the moment at which your out-of-body experience started.' He paused. 'It was the moment at which your brainwaves ceased completely.'

The heater seemed to be blowing cold air over her.

'There's a fourth factor needed for absolute proof,' he said.

'What is it?'

'Finish your coffee and I'll show you.' He waited as she drained the mug, then stood up and opened the door behind his desk. He switched on a light and gestured for her to go in.

She went through into a room that was several times larger than the office, with another door leading off to the left. The middle of the room was dominated by a wire mesh cage mounted on white insulators.

Kate heard a click behind her as if the anaesthetist was having difficulty closing the door and turned. Dr Swire was slipping something into his pocket. There was a dead, airless atmosphere in the room that made her feel claustrophobic.

'You don't seem excited by your experience, Kate. You ought to be,' he said.

'I find it spooky.'

'You're quick enough to see a front-page scoop in a girl who may have been buried alive, but not in the first human being to have proof of survival of death?'

She thought at first he was being humorous. Then she saw the malice in his face. Her throat tightened.

'I'd like to do some tests with you.'

'Tests?'

'See if we can take this experience further.'

'Repeat it?'

'Yes. In a more controlled situation.' He was rubbing his hands together. 'Think what an amazing journalistic scoop it would be for you!'

'No, thanks.'

'Why not?'

She looked away from his eyes, up at the bland styrofoam ceiling tiles. Dora Runcorn's words swirled through her mind. She saw the image of Howie. Heard the warnings. Her earlier courage was beginning to desert her. She shivered. 'Because it's dabbling, I guess, in something one shouldn't dabble in.'

'Didn't you read the Bible when you were a child? Don't you remember St Paul's letter? "When I was a child, I spake as a child, I understood as a child, I thought as a child: but when I became an adult, I put away childish things. For now we see through a glass darkly; but then face to face."'

'I remember it,' Kate said.

'God meant that on the earth plane we are only children fumbling through darkness. We can only see the light when we die. I've always felt that God's an arrogant bastard. I don't see why people shouldn't see a bit more now. Why do we always have to live in a twilight world, like half-blind creatures of the deep?' His knuckles were whitening and his anger frightened Kate. 'You are saying, "God's given me this power, but I mustn't use it." I say, why not? What's He afraid of? What's He got to hide that He doesn't want us to see?'

'Even if I was convinced myself, I don't think anyone would believe it if I did write a piece.'

His small, round mouth puckered. 'Oh yes, they would. I can prove it, you see, Kate.' He pointed at the wire mesh. 'I don't imagine you've ever seen one of these before.' He pulled a latch and swung the end section open. It was like a miniature operating theatre, with a padded steel table, an anaesthetics machine with a drip stand, gas and oxygen cylinders, a ventilator and a battery of wires and gauges. Instead of an overhead lamp, the insulated wire mesh lay about three feet above the table, stretching the entire width of the ceiling.

'It's my version of a Faraday Cage,' he said proudly.

She felt a beat of discomfort. 'What does that mean?'

'We're missing one piece of absolute proof with your experience, Kate. The one possible explanation we cannot rule out is telepathy. I knew the triangular marking was on top of the lamp, obviously, as I was the one who drew it. It is just possible that in your altered state of consciousness on the operating table, you tuned into my brainwaves and got your image of the triangle that way.'

'What does this Faraday Cage do?'

'It puts an electronic shield around the subject. If telepathy does exist it has to be a form of electronically based radio signal, powered by the brain. It would not get through the electronic shield.'

'Which would prove what?'

'If someone inside there with no brain activity was able to see things going on outside the cage, we would know conclusively that a human being's consciousness was capable of existing separately to the body.'

Kate was disturbed, as much by the anaesthetist's expression as from what he was saying. 'And you believe that would prove life after death?'

'We have to find out, Kate. We must. We *must*.' He walked across the room, opened a drawer and removed a small package wrapped in white paper. 'We *must* find out.'

'Why? Mankind has got by so far without knowing.'

'Not very well.' He removed a vial from the wrapping and held it up to the light. 'The rules have changed. Religion used to make the rules, now science makes them. Science has ruled if someone is brain dead, they are dead. But you know that isn't true, don't you?'

'Do I?'

'Of course. Your own experience. Let's say you really did float above your body, and that you went down the tunnel and returned. When you woke up you were back in your body. Weren't you?'

'I suppose.'

'What floated out of your body and went down the tunnel? Your soul? Your consciousness?'

She tried to think back, but the memory frightened her. The aloneness frightened her. She said nothing, unsure what to reply.

'It came back because it got sent back – you got sent back – by your brother Howie?'

'I – I suppose.'

'And you woke up and you were in the recovery room?'

'Yes.'

'If you had not woken and your EEG was still flat, what do you think would have happened?'

'I don't know.'

'You might have been in limbo. Floating above your body, neither alive nor dead.'

'That sounds rather far-fetched.'

He removed another package from the drawer and ripped it open. It contained a syringe. Kate watched him, fascinated.

'Not at all. Some people say the soul is attached to the body via a silver cord. I have no evidence of that, but I think the body may be like a battery. We cannot be inside a body with a flat EEG because consciousness cannot exist in a dead brain, so we float above our bodies. We can go to the frontier of the next world, but not into it. We cannot go over whilst our bodies are still alive.'

'Why not?'

'Because God wants to keep His little secrets. If you die, fine, you move to the next world, but as long as there is any life in a body, any chance of resuscitation, you get sent back. We all get the same message. *You have to go back!*' He grinned, and stuck the needle in through the top of the vial. 'So what we have to do is fool God. Create a state of death so convincing He believes it.'

'Fool God?'

He drew the fluid out of the vial, filling the syringe. 'Yes.'

'How?' She decided he was completely mad.

He held the syringe in the air and squeezed the plunger. Fluid dribbled from the needle. 'With this.'

'What is it?'

'It doesn't have a market name. It's a combination of a ganglion-blocking agent, chlorpromazine, and a long-acting phenobarbitone that was developed for the treatment of epilepsy by a Swiss pharmaceutical company, but it was too long-acting. It put people into long-term comas, shut them right down. Gave them almost identical symptoms to hypothermia – loss of blood pressure, heart rate slowed to one beat every thirty seconds and sometimes even substantially less.' He turned to her. 'I thought I'd given Sally Donaldson too much, but it seems I hadn't.'

Kate backed away. Globules of cold oily fear slid through her one at a time as she tried to read his face, to work out what he was doing.

*Something about wire he's trying to tell me. Do you deal with electrical things?*

And then she realised. Realised what the message from Dora Runcorn, the medium, had meant.

*I think you need to be very careful with wire. I think he's saying that you mustn't touch any wire.*

Wire.

Swire.

It had been staring her in the face. She felt a weight crush down through her. It was followed by a silent fury at her blindness.

'I'm very disappointed in you, Kate. I thought I'd really got lucky.

That I had a newspaper reporter who had the chance to make her name and fortune by proving with the full sanction of a respected anaesthetist that there really is life after death. And instead I'm being sneered at.'

'I'm not sneering at you,' Kate said.

He took a step towards her. Another drip fell from the end of the needle. 'Aren't you? You're just a smart bitch, aren't you? Get the story, to hell with the consequences. Doesn't matter about proving whether God exists, or whether there's life after death if you can get a few column inches with a quick, cheap rubbishing.'

'What were you doing to Sally Donaldson? Experimenting on a pregnant woman?'

'Experiments are important for mankind, Kate.'

'Didn't Hitler think that too?'

'Sneering, Kate, sneering.'

'Where's the nail you took from my apartment? And the film from my camera?'

'How's your auntie?'

'Auntie?'

'The one that's dying in the hospice.'

'You're unbelievable,' she said.

'I'll tell you what's unbelievable, little girl. I've waited twenty years for a subject like you and you're not interested. That's unbelievable. Forget Sally Donaldson, she's not important. You are. Don't you realise? I thought you'd be thrilled – that anyone would be – so thrilled that no one would care about the lignocaine. Who cares about the method? What matters is that it worked! You had the experience. Can't you see?'

'How many people have you killed in twenty years, Dr Swire? Or have you lost count?' She took a sheet of notepaper out of her coat pocket and unfolded it. 'From nineteen seventy-two to seventy-six you worked as an anaesthetist in neurosurgery and intensive care at the Royal Galashiels Infirmary, Glasgow. For the five years before you were there, they had an average of four *status epilepticus* patients a year. In the four years you were there the average went up to six per year, then dropped back to four after you left. For the five years before you were there, their mortality rate in intensive care was eighteen per cent. Whilst you were there it went up to twenty-three per cent and then dropped back after you left to sixteen per cent. Do you want me to read out the figures for the other four hospitals you've been at? You'll find they're pretty much the same.'

'You're a smart girl, Kate. Done your homework. You're a bit too smart for your own good.' He took another step towards her.

She looked at the needle. 'Going to try to kill me? I don't think you'll find it quite so easy this time with your bent undertaker and your bent coroner and bent pathologist.' Her voice sounded oddly distant.

'I don't have a bent coroner or pathologist, Kate. They just don't always know where to look or what to look for. Like with you.'

She felt disoriented for a moment, as if this was a dream. Her face went hot, then very cold. The silence of the room pressed in on her ears.

'Someone's going to find out what you've given me.' Her voice echoed.

'Of course they will, Kate. I'll tell them.'

'What do you mean?' she mouthed.

'I'll tell them you came to see me because you were feeling strange and collapsed with an epileptic fit.'

'I don't have epilepsy.'

'You do according to your medical records – since your accident.'

She shook her head. 'I was cleared by the neurologist.'

'Sad thing about epilepsy, Kate, is that neurologists can never be completely sure.'

Fear coursed through her. Dora Runcorn's voice screamed in her head. Howie screamed in her head. She ran for the door; her feet were strangely leaden; she had to work to move them. She grasped the handle, turned it, pulled. It was stiff. She pulled harder. Harder. It did not move.

'You need the key, Kate,' the anaesthetist said.

She turned her head. It turned slowly, as if her neck would not coordinate too well with her brain. He put his hand into his pocket and lifted it out. 'Why don't you come and get it?' He held the needle up a few more inches. 'You can have it if you want. But you won't get very far.'

She was panting, short hard breaths.

'Remember when you were awake in the operation, Kate? You could feel pain but your muscles were paralysed and you could not move? The drug I used is called vecuronium.'

She said nothing.

'It's similar to the curare Indians use on arrows in the Amazon jungle for paralysing their prey. And their enemies. Unfortunately, it's not effective if taken orally, so I've given you something called midazolam in your coffee. It's not as quick as intravenous because it has to work its way through the stomach lining. But you needn't worry, Kate, I'm not operating on you, so there won't be any pain. Oh, and you needn't worry about it being found in your system in the post mortem. I'll have you on the ventilator for a few days in intensive care until it's metabolised out. You'll have to be on a ventilator, you see, because you are going to go to sleep in a few minutes and your lungs will stop working and you won't be able to breathe.'

Tears rolled down her cheeks and she bit her lip. Crazy. He was crazy. There had to be a way out. She lurched past him for the other door. She had to force her legs to work, had to push each step, like wading them through water.

She grabbed the door handle, pulled it open, stumbled into a long room that was lit only by the glow from the screens of bright green oscilloscopes that stretched out in rows away from her. She saw the blips tracing their lines, sharp spikes, soft spikes, flat, steady lines.

Smelled the animal smell she'd noticed when she arrived. Strong. Almost unbearably strong. She ran in, down between the screens, between the motionless dark shapes that lay beneath them.

The eyes of some of them watched her, glinted in the dark as brightly as the screens.

She froze. More eyes appearing out of the green haze. The heads moving even though the bodies could not. Cats. Thirty or more of them, each beneath an oscilloscope, each with the top of its skull missing and electrodes attached to its raw brain.

She screamed.

Screamed again as she hit the far wall and pummelled against hard, damp brick.

In the doorway, Dr Swire stood with his syringe in his hand, motionless, waiting. She felt her legs buckling, fought back. Fought the tiredness that was sucking out her energy, was trying to close her eyes.

Christ, keep going.

Then she realised what she had to do.

She walked towards him, zigzagging, past the blips and the eyes like gemstones and the glistening brains. She bounced off the doorpost, looked at him, opened her mouth, then crumpled into a heap.

She lay still, her heart racing, deafening her. Felt his hands beneath her. He grunted. Her shoulders were jerked sharply up. She made an incoherent mumble, felt herself being dragged across the carpet tiles, heard the clatter of the wire mesh door opening.

He was panting, unfit. She tried to move her arm a fraction. It seemed to react slowly. Her eyelids felt heavy and she panicked that they would stay shut, would not open again. Her head thumped against something hard. The anaesthetist grunted again. Some of the feeling in her limbs was going.

She was lying prostrate now. She felt her coat sleeve and pullover sleeve being pushed up. Then the tap on her left wrist. More sharp taps. Felt her hand being raised. Could smell his stale breath.

Please, God, give me the strength.

Now.

She tried to part her eyelids. They would not move. She forced, forced again. They opened. She saw the startled look in his own eyes, hurled her leaden fingers up into them, ramming them hard in, twisting her body, sank her teeth into his wrist, saw the glistening needle inches from her eye. Fluid squirted from it. She grabbed it, rammed it in, deep into his stomach, pressing the plunger as he clawed blindly and fell forwards on to her, carried on pressing and gouging as he flailed at her, screamed at her.

'You bitch. You –'

# *Chapter Forty-Three*

*Sunday, 4 November*

Harvey Swire watched in horror as his body slid away beneath him, as he rose up through the mesh of the cage. Like being in an old-fashioned elevator, he thought.

He saw the reporter's fingers gouging his eyes, his hands flailing, slowing, moving desperately towards the syringe she held in his stomach, but they froze before they reached it.

He saw himself fall back against the wire mesh, slump down, head angled back, eyes open, staring up, and he wondered if he could actually see himself up here above his body in that final moment.

Then helpless fury seethed through him. Switch the power on, you stupid bitch. At least do that. Switch the cage on! He watched the reporter easing herself down from the table, the hypodermic syringe still in her clenched hand. He looked down again at his body, at his eyes that were glazing, sightless now for sure, his hair dishevelled, the points of his shirt collar sticking up, blood trickling down his cheek.

As the reporter's feet touched the ground she fell forwards, smacking her face into the mesh, hurting herself.

Good.

She clawed at the mesh to keep her balance; to keep on her feet. Just a little longer, he thought. Stay until the midazolam's taken full effect and then you'll be sorry, bitch. Just a few more minutes and you'll go to sleep. Your lungs will stop working. You'll stop breathing.

He smiled.

She lurched towards the door, then stopped, swaying, and tottered back towards his body, zigzagging across the floor, put her hand in his jacket pocket and took out the key ring.

Clever bitch.

Her legs buckled suddenly and her eyes closed; she fell sideways against the mesh, her head lolling. She stayed there some moments, then she shook, as if she had woken with a start, looked warily at his body and backed away towards the door.

He smiled again. She was still afraid of him. Afraid he was going to come after her.

She tried one key in the lock then another; the third one turned. She put both hands on the handle, heaving herself up with it. The door swung inwards and she stumbled, tripped over backwards and lay on the floor twitching, like a dying insect, he thought.

Her head rolled from side to side, her fingers slid over the carpet. Her eyes closed. She opened them and blinked, then rolled over, almost in slow motion, groped for the syringe, held on to the door handle and hauled herself back to her feet. She walked slowly and unsteadily through the doorway, touching the frame with her hands like a blind person, and into the office. She tried to pick up the telephone receiver, but her hand knocked it off the rest. She lunged after it and sent the telephone skidding off the desk to the floor, breaking its casing.

She put the phone back on the desk, crooked the receiver under her neck and moved her fingers towards the dial. The receiver slipped out and hit the desk with a loud bang. She dialled, pausing between each digit, nine, nine, nine, picked up the receiver again.

You have to wait for the switchboard to give you a line, bitch.

She held the receiver to her ear, dialled again, swayed, her eyes closing, then fell, the phone falling with her, the wire ripping out of the wall.

He saw tears rolling down her cheeks as she lay, hair tousled over her face, mouthing a silent plea for help. Then she took her weight on her elbows, got up on to her knees and crawled towards the door. She opened it, pulling herself to her feet again, and staggered out into the corridor. She lurched between the walls, bumping from side to side, then fell again at the bottom of the stone steps.

Good luck, bitch.

She began climbing them, got halfway, when her grip on the rail went and she slipped back, her face smacking against each step in turn, and crumpled in a heap at the bottom, juddering. She raised her right hand, still holding the keys and syringe, although he could see the needle had broken off. Her hand dropped limply back down. She lifted it up again, supporting it with her left hand, put the needle and keys on a step above her, gripped the rail with her fingers and slowly climbed, achieving one step at a time, pausing for breath, moving the syringe and keys up each time. She finally hauled herself over the top and through the door into the laboratory where she lay still, panting.

Then she inched forwards, got up on to one knee and crashed into the leg of a worktable. A bottle of red dye tumbled to the floor, shattering, spraying her with shards of glass. Her face slumped into the pool of dye. It reminded him of a picture he had loved as a child in *Paris Match* of a gangster lying dead at a table, blood pouring from his temple into a wine glass.

She got back to her knees, knocked another table and reeled. She reached the door, fumbled with the keys, got it open, and crawled out.

The rain and wind seemed to revive her a little. She climbed to her feet, stumbled across the compound towards the fence, then fell just short of the gate, and lay motionless again, her head sideways in a puddle.

Finished now, bitch.

Her hand twitched; clenched and relaxed. Fighting. Fighting. Water trickled into her mouth and she jerked, spluttering. She pushed her fingers through the mesh and began hauling herself up, strand by strand, tried the keys, dropped them, picked them up and tried again. The gate swung open. She swung with it. The needle dropped from her hand and rolled into a bed of nettles, but she barely noticed. She crawled across the car park, moving more slowly all the time, past the bulldozer and the Portakabins.

She reached a flanged door, pushed it with her head, crawling on her hands and knees through the heavy rubber flap on to a steeply ramped floor. A long, deserted, dingily lit corridor stretched out ahead. Steam coiled in the distance; there was a faint droning resonance from a machine. She stopped moving, the fingers of one hand clawing at a grimy lino tile, no longer strong enough to grip. Red dye or blood, or both, mingled with rain water, fell to the floor in small droplets.

Harvey Swire smiled.

There was a creak. The bang of a door. Two figures appeared down the far end. Nurses in their cloaks chatting, just come off duty.

Go away.

As they got nearer they broke into a run.

Leave her alone, bitches.

They knelt down beside Kate. 'Is she drunk?' one said.

'No, I can't smell drink. She's probably a junkie and has overdosed on something.'

'What a state, poor thing; she must have had a fall.'

Harvey Swire watched Kate look up and shake her head desperately. She mouthed silent words at them.

'What have you taken?'

Kate grunted. 'Mmmm – '

'Can you tell us what you have taken?' the nurse asked. 'A drug?' She turned to her colleague. 'Get a doctor, quickly.'

Kate's lips barely moved.

Leave the bitch alone.

'Mid – ' Kate said.

'Mid?' one nurse echoed.

Leave her alone.

'Midaz – midaz.'

Leave her alone.

'Midaz?'

'azo – midazolam.'

Leave – her . . . Then Harvey Swire was hurtling back across the compound to the lab, back to his body. The way he had done all those years before. It was all right. He was going to get the bitch. Get her before she could talk.

He was above his body now, watching it lying in the wire mesh cage, his glazed eyes staring up at him. Get her. Finish the bitch off.

Something tugged at him.

No.

Something sucking him upwards.

Let me get her.

His body was becoming smaller beneath him. He was being pulled away and did not want to go. No! he screamed. Let me get her! But no words came out. Darkness closed around him. The heat was going. It was getting cold. He felt alone, helpless. Afraid. Walls of a tunnel encircled him, sucked him like a fly down a drain and he was hurtling, spinning through a vortex of blackness.

The spinning slowed. He relaxed. He knew where he was, where he was going. He had been here before. There would be a light in a minute. A brilliant white light. It would get warm.

But it stayed dark.

The movement stopped.

He sensed people around him in the darkness, watching him. He became panicky, called out, 'Hallo?' His voice sounded small, like a frightened child.

Then he heard his mother. But there was no welcome in her voice. No kindness.

'Harvey, you have to go back.'

'Mummy!' he screamed.

'You have to go back.' Her voice was scolding. Furious.

'Mummy!'

'Back!'

'Noooo!'

Then silence. He was alone. Completely alone.

# Chapter Forty-Four

*Wednesday, 7 November*

Kate was wheeled out of the intensive care unit on Tuesday evening. She was breathing unaided and the endotracheal tube had been removed, but she was too dopey to recognise her surroundings as she was pushed out of the elevator and back into Leggett 1, to the room next to the one she had vacated only two days ago.

Patrick appeared in front of her as a blurred shape, and her badly cut lips formed a faint smile. Then she slept through the night. When she woke in the morning she stared hazily around the bare cream walls of the room, confused. She looked at the small television on its hinged arm, the cabinet, a vase of flowers.

She sat up.

She had been discharged, she was certain. Patrick had taken her home; unless that had been a dream. Then she noticed her bandaged hands and smashed nails, and anxiety corkscrewed through her. She tried to think back but it was as though a steel wall had come down in her mind. Something disturbing was on the far side of it, but she could not get there.

The curtains were open. Through the window she could see a hook suspended from the yellow jib of a crane. Beyond it, clouds crashed like surf through a metallic blue sky. Her thoughts crashed against the steel wall.

Dr Swire.

Dr Swire moving towards her. His face coming closer. Closer.

The door opened and she gripped the bedclothes, ready to scream if it was Dr Swire. But it was only a nurse, the tall, sour, fair-haired nurse she had seen several times during the previous week. 'Awake now? Want some breakfast?'

'Yes, thank you,' she said, although she did not feel hungry. The nurse left before she could say anything else. The anaesthetist's face came back, larger, closer. There was a knock on the door.

'Come in,' she said weakly.

A tall man entered, wearing an unbuttoned white coat, and slowly and purposefully closed the door behind him. He was in his late forties, with greying black hair that was brushed straight back and thinning, a serious face with neat, tidy features spoilt by bushy eyebrows, and a voice that was clipped, old-fashioned, establishment. 'I'm Dr Baynes, the senior registrar here. How are you feeling?' He ran troubled eyes over her.

'Confused.'

He had a slight twitch in the corner of his mouth. 'Yes, well, we're confused too. I thought perhaps you could enlighten us on what happened.'

Through the window Kate saw the hook moving slowly down from the jib of the crane. There had been a gap. Surely? She had gone home, and now she was back.

'Perhaps I can jog your memory for you. You were found in a drugged state in one of the hospital corridors late on Sunday night holding a bunch of keys you had clearly stolen. And there had been some sort of struggle in the hospital's research laboratories. Earlier, you had been seen with Dr Swire outside the operating theatres.'

Kate thought hard, closed her eyes for a moment. Dr Swire. Walking. Corridors. Unlocking gates. She saw Dr Swire's face. Fluid dribbling from a needle. She opened her eyes again, afraid. 'I don't know what happened,' she said. 'I'm trying to remember.'

It was coming back more clearly now, and she was not sure whether she could trust Dr Baynes. Or anyone here.

'What has Dr Swire said?' she asked.

The corners of his mouth twitched. 'Dr Swire is dead, I'm afraid.'

Kate's ears seemed to implode. A numbness spread through her body; she could sense only her pulse tugging at the wrist of her right hand. 'Dead?' There was a vibration in her throat but she did not hear the sound of the word. The doctor mouthed something back at her. Her ears popped. 'Dead?' she said again.

'So perhaps you'd like to tell me what happened?'

There was another knock on the door and Patrick came in. Kate's confidence flooded back. She wanted to leap out of bed and hug him. 'Hi,' she said.

He looked at the doctor then at her. 'Shall I wait outside for a moment?'

'If you wouldn't mind,' Dr Baynes said.

'Patrick,' she said loudly.

He glanced at her inquisitively.

'Don't go far – please.'

'I'll wait right outside.' He backed out and closed the door.

Kate turned her bandaged hands over, examining both sides. 'Dr Swire tried to kill me,' she said, feeling more courageous now.

'What? Don't be ridiculous. You're delirious still from your overdose.'

'He tried to kill me.'

'You're Catherine Hemingway, aren't you? You work for the *Evening News*?'

'Yes.'

'You're the reporter who created the exhumation nonsense. That must have really upset Dr Swire. It upset us all. You're a seriously deranged young woman. And a thief.'

'I don't believe what I'm hearing,' Kate said.

'You won't believe a lot more by the time this hospital's finished with you. Dr Swire's dead, thanks to you. He had a heart attack on Sunday night. He's been suffering from a chronic heart condition that he'd been keeping from everyone. Sally Donaldson was one of his patients. He was a dedicated man and he took your article personally. He felt it was his reputation on the line. You caused him an immense amount of unnecessary anguish and stress.'

It was coming back more clearly every moment. 'You're very mistaken.'

He pushed his hands into the pocket of his white coat. 'I'm not mistaken. This hospital's had just about enough of you. Your article's damaged our reputation. We had to spend time and money pumping a massive overdose of midazolam out of you and saving your life. You need psychiatric help, if you want my view. You are clearly unstable.'

Dr Swire grinning. The needle coming closer, inches from Kate's eye. 'How did – how did Dr Swire die?'

The door opened and the nurse brought in the breakfast tray. Kate could not see Patrick through the open doorway.

'If it's of any interest,' the doctor said, 'he had a hereditary condition called hypertrophic cardiomyopathy.'

'All right if I put this down, doctor?' the nurse asked.

'Yes.'

She set the tray down and swung the table across the bed.

'It's a horrible thing to have,' the doctor said, his tone softening a fraction. 'If you're born with the gene you have an extremely high chance of dying before forty. Dr Swire's mother had it and died at thirty-eight. His uncle had it and died at thirty-four. Very few sufferers live beyond forty-five. Dr Swire was forty-three. Apparently he'd been having treatment for the symptoms for the past two years; he could have died any day.'

'Is that why he was so interested in death?' Kate said.

'He never told anyone here about his condition. He was seeing a cardiac consultant in private.'

'Dr Swire was a very dedicated man,' the nurse said, and walked out.

'You can see how upset the staff are,' Dr Baynes said.

'Was his heart condition the reason why he was so interested in death?' Kate asked.

'Was he?'

'You must have known he was.'

Keeping his hands inside his coat pockets, he pushed them together. 'Dr Swire was interested in a great many things. He was an enormously gifted man.'

'I'd like to call the police,' she said.

His twitch worsened, and he blinked several times. 'Catherine, Dr Swire is dead. There really doesn't seem much point in involving the police. This sort of publicity doesn't do us or our patients any good. Obviously we would like to know what happened.' He took one of his hands out of his pocket and massaged his Adam's apple. 'But we'd be prepared to leave it at that.'

'What about Sally Donaldson? Wouldn't you like to know what happened to her?'

'If there's anything on Sally Donaldson that you want to say, I suggest you say it to the coroner.' He was becoming increasingly uncomfortable.

'You haven't a clue, have you, about Dr Swire? Except you know damned well I didn't take an overdose.'

'Well – perhaps you can tell us what did happen. We'd like to know very much.'

'No, I don't think you would. I don't think you'd like to know what happened at all. I don't think you'd like to know the truth about Dr Swire.'

He turned his head towards the door. 'Look – I. You have someone waiting. Shall I pop back in a little while?'

'Fine.'

As he went out, he held the door open. Patrick came in, rushed straight over to the bed and kissed her on the cheek. 'Bit less dopey than last night.'

'Thanks.'

'How do you feel?'

'I'm OK.'

'God, what on earth has happened? I haven't been able to get any sense out of anyone – except that you've taken a drug overdose. Why? What the hell's happened?'

'My coat,' she said. 'Where's my coat?'

'Coat?'

'My blue cashmere coat. I was wearing it.'

Patrick opened a cupboard door. Kate's coat was hanging inside, crumpled and ripped in several places.

'Could you bring it to me, please?'

He hitched it off the wire hanger and laid it on the bed. She put her hand in the pocket and felt relief as her fingers touched the hard casing of the recorder. She pulled out the microphone jack and removed the recorder. The tape was in place. It had reached the end and stopped. She fumbled with the controls and pressed the rewind. They listened to the squeaking shuffle as the spools rotated.

Then Kate pressed the start button and turned up the volume. There was a hiss, some scratching sounds, then Dr Swire's voice, muffled and with a faint echo.

'Perrier OK?'

Then her own voice. 'Thank you.'

'Milk? Sugar?'

'Black, please.'

The sound of an object being put down, crockery clinking, then Dr Swire's voice again. 'So you wanted to have a talk.'

'Yes. I want to know what was going on in the operating theatre.'

It was all there, all came back as she listened. They both sat in silence as it played through, the voices clear, Kate's panting, crashing, as she struggled to get away, the rattling of the keys, breaking glass, the wind and rain, the clattering of the wire mesh gate, footsteps, the voices of the nurses who found her, then abrupt silence as the tape ran out.

'I took the syringe,' Kate said. 'I remember taking it. I must have dropped it somewhere. We'd be able to find it – it would have some of the drug in it and would prove – '

Patrick sat on the edge of the bed and touched her cheek lightly with his knuckles. 'Brave girl. You don't need it. You've got all the evidence on the tape. You've got everything you need to prove you were right. They'll be able to tell what he had in him at the post mortem. Christ, what a bastard.'

'I killed him.' She swallowed. 'That's really horrible.'

'You didn't have much choice.'

The phone rang, startling them both. Kate picked up the receiver.

'Hallo, is that Catherine Hemingway?'

'Yes.' Kate tried to place the voice and couldn't for a moment.

'Still in hospital are you, dear? I wasn't sure, so I thought I'd best try you there first.'

It was Dora Runcorn.

'I have another message for you, dear. It's from your brother Howie. He says you'll know what it means. He tells me someone's knocking on wood. Does that mean anything?'

'No,' Kate said.

'I expect it will, dear.'

'Is that all?'

'Yes, dear. Just that. You give me a call when you come out and we'll have our chat.'

'Sure.' Kate thanked her and hung up.

'Who was that?' Patrick asked.

She said nothing for a moment, thinking. Feeling uncomfortable. The woman's words rattled around inside her head like a ball bearing through the gates of a maze. Knocking. Knocking. It was not possible.

Absolutely not.

'It's OK,' she said. 'Nothing.'

'I can't believe that bastard tried to kill you. When did you come back here?'

'Sunday evening after you left,' she said, distracted.

Knocking.

'You promised to wait until Monday. I was going to come with you.'

The tall, sour nurse opened the door. 'Finished with your tray?'

'Has there been a post mortem on Dr Swire?' Kate asked her.

'No, there hasn't, so far as I know.'

'Why not?'

'I don't think it was considered necessary. He'd been receiving weekly treatment from a cardiologist. It was perfectly clear what he died of.'

'Where's his body?' Kate asked.

'He's being cremated this morning. A lot of the staff have gone to the service.'

'This morning? Where?'

'At the Stamford crematorium.'

'Do you know what time?'

'At ten o'clock. You're a bit late to send flowers,' she said acidly, and carried the untouched tray out.

'Christ. What time is it now?'

'Twenty-five to eleven,' Patrick said.

'They don't always burn the body right after the service, do they?' Kate said.

'No. Someone told me they usually do them together in batches.'

'They won't believe me if I phone. They'll think I'm some kind of a nutter. I could play them the tape, they'd have to believe that. Is your car here?'

'Yes, but – '

'Can you bring it round to the front?' She swung her legs out of bed. 'I have to stop them cremating him.' She stood up unsteadily and he grabbed her.

'Why?'

'Don't you see? That stuff Dr Swire was going to inject into me – you heard on the tape. He said it was the same mixture he had injected into Sally Donaldson, right?'

He nodded.

'That stuff, whatever it was – barbiturate and something else – fooled everyone into thinking Sally Donaldson was dead, and she wasn't. He said that, right?'

'Yes.'

'That's what I injected into him. They're assuming he's had a heart attack because of his heart trouble. What if they're wrong?'

The Alfa Romeo crawled up a long straight hill, stuck behind a lorry. Patrick accelerated, eased the nose of the car out, braked and tucked it in again. A lorry thundered past in the opposite direction. Then another.

It was ten past eleven.

He eased out again, overtook and accelerated up the hill. They were passing a low brick wall on their right. Ahead of them a black Daimler limousine was nosing out of an imposing gateway.

'That's it.'

Patrick indicated and braked. He let the Daimler out, then drove in along the sweeping drive into the large, almost empty car park in front of the modern brick building of the crematorium. A couple of people in dark coats were looking at flowers laid out down the side wall.

Patrick stopped outside the front steps, then ran around to help Kate out of the car. He took her arm as they walked up the steps into the porch. On their right was a door, with a small plaque beside it marked 'General Manager'. Patrick knocked. There was no answer.

Kate opened the heavy oak doors and peered into the chapel. It was empty, silent. She walked down the aisle, her boots clicking on the floor, towards the empty catafalque that stood between the heavy blue velvet curtains. Patrick followed her. Past the catafalque was a door with a heavy brass handle.

She turned it, and as she opened the door she heard a clatter of activity and felt a blast of heat. She stepped forwards on to a concrete floor. There was a roar of flames. Immediately ahead were three coffins on trolleys. To the left was a wall of steel plates with several closed metal doors. One was open and two men in boiler suits were lifting a coffin into a brick-lined furnace behind it. Jets of flames were burning fiercely down both sides.

They pushed the coffin until it was clear of the entrance, then one pressed a green button on the wall and the metal door began to slide down. It locked shut with a loud clunk and the roar became muted.

The two men noticed them. One, burly with fair hair and streaks of grease on his cheek, walked across, frowning at them. 'Can I help you?'

Kate stared at the three coffins on the trolleys. 'Has Dr Swire been cremated yet?'

'Dr Harvey Swire?' He picked up a sheet of paper in his large, grubby hands and looked at it, then pointed at the furnace. 'That's him. Gone in now, this second.'

Kate turned and ran towards the metal door. She reached it, then turned. 'Can you stop it? Is there any way you can stop it?'

The man shook his head. 'Sorry, no, not possible.' He smiled at her gently. 'You shouldn't really be here, you know. Go back to the chapel. It's nicer in there.'

'Come on,' Patrick said.

He put his arm around her and led her away. She bit her lip and they walked slowly across the room. As they got to the door three loud, sharp raps rang out from inside the furnace.

She spun round, her eyes riveted to the metal door, her chest thudding.

There was a long silence; just the roar of the gas and the hiss of the flames.

'The wood,' the man in the boiler suit said. 'Does that sometimes. Splitting from the heat.'

All Orion/Phoenix titles are available at your local bookshop or from the following address:

Mail Order Department
Littlehampton Book Services
FREEPOST BR535
Worthing, West Sussex, BN13 3BR
*telephone* 01903 828503, *facsimile* 01903 828802
*e-mail* MailOrders@lbsltd.co.uk
(Please ensure that you include full postal address details)

Payment can be made either by credit/debit card (Visa, Mastercard, Access and Switch accepted) or by sending a £ Sterling cheque or postal order made payable to *Littlehampton Book Services*.
DO NOT SEND CASH OR CURRENCY

**Please add the following to cover postage and packing**

*UK and BFPO:*
£1.50 for the first book, and 50p for each additional book to a maximum of £3.50

*Overseas and Eire:*
£2.50 for the first book plus £1.00 for the second book and 50p for each additional book ordered

BLOCK CAPITALS PLEASE

*name of cardholder* ..............................

*address of cardholder* ..............................

..............................

..............................

..............................

*postcode* ..............................

*delivery address*
*(if different from cardholder)*

..............................

..............................

..............................

..............................

*postcode* ..............................

☐ I enclose my remittance for £..............................

☐ please debit my Mastercard/Visa/Access/Switch (delete as appropriate)

card number ☐☐☐☐☐☐☐☐☐☐☐☐☐☐☐☐

expiry date ☐☐☐☐ Switch issue no. ☐☐

signature ..............................

*prices and availability are subject to change without notice*